the edge of over there

SHAWN SMUCKER

Revell

a division of Baker Publishing Group
Grand Rapids, Michigan

© 2018 by Shawn Smucker

Published by Revell
a division of Baker Publishing Group
PO Box 6287, Grand Rapids, MI 49516-6287
www.revellbooks.com

Printed in the United States of America

Library of Congress Cataloging-in-Publication Data
Names: Smucker, Shawn, author.
Title: The edge of over there / Shawn Smucker.
Description: Grand Rapids, MI : Revell, a division of Baker Publishing
    Group, [2018]
Identifiers: LCCN 2017061366 | ISBN 9780800728502 (hardcover : acid-
    free paper)
Subjects: LCSH: Quests (Expeditions)—Fiction. | Teenage girls—Fiction. |
    GSAFD: Christian fiction.
Classification: LCC PS3619.M83 E34 2018 | DDC 813/.6—dc23
LC record available at https://lccn.loc.gov/2017061366

18 19 20 21 22 23 24   7 6 5 4 3 2 1

To Mom and Dad.
Thank you for all the books.

MARIE LAVEAU—Marie Laveau is a prominent person in American folklore, yet her history lies in shadow. Rumor has it she was born in the French Quarter of New Orleans in 1794, her father a white planter, her mother a black woman. Her death was announced in the New Orleans newspapers on June 16, 1881, which is of great interest considering she continued to be spotted in the town long after her supposed death. She was laid to rest in the Saint Louis Cemetery in New Orleans.[1]

THE LEGEND OF THE SEVEN GATES—According to legend, there are seven gates through which souls can travel to the afterlife. Each continent has its own gate: Africa's gate lies under the paw of the sphinx; Asia's gate is near the Temple Mount; Europe's gate lies at the Père Lachaise Paris Cemetery; South America's gate is hidden beneath the *Christ the Redeemer* statue; Antarctica's gate sits at the South Pole; Australia's gate is in the vicinity of the Rookwood Cemetery; and North America's gate is situated at Saint Louis Cemetery No. 1, inside the grave of Marie Laveau.

THE TREE OF LIFE—There is a famous oak tree in Audubon Park in New Orleans that has received the nickname "The Tree of Life." It is a rather famous oak, having been registered with the Live Oak Society and officially named the Etienne de Boré oak. The tree's circumference is just under thirty-five feet and was number 13 on Dr. Edwin Lewis Stephens's list of forty-three original inductee trees into the Live Oak Society. A tree this size could possibly be five hundred years of age or older.[2]

Prologue

ABRA COULD ALMOST FEEL THE RAIN, even though it was only a dream. She was surrounded by leaves and branches. The drops clattered down through them, all around her. That's when she realized she was up in a tree, up in its highest branches, and immediately she was afraid. She clung to the branch she was on, a branch much too thin to hold her. It broke, and she fell. She grabbed for anything she could hold on to, finding another thin branch. She dangled there, looking down between her feet at the ground far below.

She watched a huge wolf-like creature pick up a small girl in its jaws and toss her aside. She watched as a boy grabbed on to a small sword, cried out in pain before swinging it again and again. She watched as the sword found its mark and the huge animal listed to the side like a boat preparing to sink. When the creature fell, the boy collapsed.

She twisted and turned where she hung from the branch, wondering if the girl was okay. Wondering where she was. That's when she saw a streak of light, and a man, or something in the shape of a man, knelt beside the girl. He put his hands on her head and closed his eyes, and Abra knew, in the way that you can know something in a dream, that the man was bringing the girl back to life. Or calling her back from wherever it was her soul was heading.

Suddenly she could hear through the girl's ears. She was still dangling there in the air; she was still feeling the soft patter of rain on her head and bare arms, the drops tickling her face; she could still feel the thin branch slipping ever so slowly from her grasp. But for some reason her hearing was now the girl's hearing, and she heard the man whisper.

"Abra, this is very important. I have a few things I need to tell you . . ."

But as the Abra hanging from the tree realized the girl on the ground was her, and as she thought she was going to hear something very important, her fingers slipped from the branch.

I should have hit the ground by now, she thought. She looked down. The ground was rushing at her, and she caught her breath.

Abra woke in the hospital bed and took a long breath, trying to calm herself. There is a kind of silence only experienced in hospitals in the middle of the night. It is never a complete silence—there is always the beeping of empty IV bags, the humming of air conditioners, the rolling of wheels over waxed tiles. But in between all of those noises is a kind of medicated silence, a waiting to see what will come next. At night, a hospital holds its breath.

A nurse crept in and out of Abra's room, and she pretended to be asleep, but her heart pounded and her eyes twitched under their closed lids.

It was just a dream, she told herself. *Just a dream.*

But something had brought her out of her sleep, she was sure of it—some sound. Someone who needed her. She heard it again: a whimper, or a quiet gasp. Was it coming through the ceiling? Was it slinking through the air ducts?

Was it Sam?

The nurse walked out into the hall, and the door latched behind her. Abra's eyes flicked open. She looked around, but that's also when the pain returned, a deep ache from the center of her abdomen, a pain that radiated out to her ribs, her pelvis, her neck, her legs. Her foot throbbed. She bit her lip to keep from crying out and wrapped her right arm gingerly around her stomach, trying to hold every painful thing in place. Her pain medication was wearing off.

The space where her father had been sitting, the small armchair in the corner of the room, was empty. There was still the impression of him in the cushion. Maybe he had gone looking for her mother. Maybe he had gone on yet another search for a decent cup of coffee. In any case, he was gone, and Abra was alone.

She lifted her legs and turned until she sat on the edge of the bed. She listened, and again she thought she heard it. The sound came from far away, but it drew her, even through her pain. She glanced longingly at her pillow. Maybe she should stretch out on the bed again, go back to sleep.

But what if Sam needs me?

She carefully placed her feet on the cold tiles and leaned forward, sliding off the bed. Oh, the pain! With each fragile step, the traction strips on the bottom of her hospital socks made a barely audible peeling sound on the floor, like a Band-Aid pulling away. She was attached at the back of her hand to an IV that in turn was attached to two bags holding clear liquid, both hanging from a sort of coatrack on wheels. She pulled it along beside her as she walked, and the wheels squeaked a rhythm. It was the middle of the night, and her hospital room was dark.

The door that led from her room to the main hallway was a heavy wooden door with a metal push bar on the inside. She leaned slowly against the bar, gritting her teeth at the loud sound the bolt made when it opened, but no one seemed to have heard. She peeked through the crack in the door toward the nurse's station. The on-duty nurses were occupied. She didn't see anyone, so she crept into the hallway and snuck toward the elevator.

The doors opened. She slipped inside. The doors closed. She pressed number 4.

Inside the elevator, she lifted her hands to her face, feeling the tug of the IV. Her skin still smelled of smoke from the fire she and Sam had barely escaped. She grimaced at the strong odor, wondering what it would take to wash away the memory of what had happened only that morning. Could it be not even an entire day had passed?

The Amarok.

Mr. Tennin, falling.

Mr. Jinn's leering words.

She shivered and pulled the garment closer around her body, realizing even it smelled of smoke. She had to see Sam. She had to make sure he was okay. She had to talk with him about what had happened, if only to assure herself it hadn't been a dream. For a moment, she thought the elevator doors would open to the psychiatric ward of some faraway hospital—maybe everything had been a series of hallucinations, and now they were trying to treat her as she teetered on the edge of insanity.

The pain again. It raced through her body, and with it memories she could not have made up. She recalled being shaken in the mouth of the Amarok, feeling like a rag doll. For one brief instant, she recalled the breaking of her own bones, and she almost cried out right there in the elevator, the pain escaping from her in tiny, wordless whimpers. But there was another memory hidden, a memory of healing she could only find traces of. Was it just a dream, or had Mr. Tennin brought her back from some deep place?

She shivered again. The elevator doors opened, and she stepped out, fully prepared to be questioned by a nurse, reprimanded, and sent back to her room. But it was another empty floor. It was late at night, but it still seemed like there should have been patients walking around. Why was it so quiet? Where were all the nurses and doctors?

She didn't know exactly which room Sam was in—only that he had been placed on the fourth floor because of the burns on his hands. She looked down at her own hands, smelling them again. The smoke. The weight of the blade as she had lifted it. The way it had picked up speed as it had flown toward Mr. Jinn. How was it possible? How could she have even thrown the sword that far?

The shiver went through her body again, and it felt like shock setting in. She stopped, wishing the wheels of her cart weren't so loud. She lifted the clear bags off of where they hung and carried them, one in each hand, and left the cart behind. The bags were heavy and slippery and warm. Now she could move without making a sound.

She went from room to room, carefully peeking inside each one, hoping to find Sam. She wasn't sure what she would say if she found him. What was there to say? Confirmation, that's what she thought she was looking for. Friendship too. The old friendship. For the first time since they emerged from the burning forest, she thought of Sam's mother. She felt tears gathering.

Abra looked in the next room and retreated quickly, putting her back against the wall. Sam was in the room. But there was someone else. A nurse, maybe. Or a doctor.

She looked again, trying to stay out of sight. The woman standing there was dressed like an employee of the hospital. Except for her shoes. Most of the nurses wore white tennis shoes, and this woman had on shiny black heels. And her hair wasn't up in a bun or a ponytail but instead fell down around her shoulders. She was asking Sam questions, but Abra couldn't hear the words. Sam was sitting up, his back off the bed.

He shook his head. He said something. He shook his head again.

Abra gasped and looked closer. Was that Sam's mom? It couldn't be. Unless . . . Had the Tree of Life somehow brought her back? From behind, even from the side, the woman looked exactly like Lucy Chambers. But Sam slid backward, farther up his bed and away from the woman. He looked terrified. Abra knew in that instant it was most definitely not Sam's mom.

Abra was about to go in and interrupt whatever was going on, but something terrible kept her at bay. The woman carried a darkness about her, not tangible, but it gave Abra the shivers. She looked up and down the hall, suddenly hoping for a nurse to appear. Where was everyone? Where was someone who could intervene?

She watched as the woman walked around to the head of Sam's bed and bent down, her face close to his. Abra knew for sure this was no nurse, and just as she was about to go in or shout for help, the woman straightened up. She turned to walk toward the door.

Toward Abra.

Abra shuffled as quickly as her painful body would allow, slipping behind the open door to Sam's room. There was just enough space for her there if she straightened her shoulders, if she pressed herself against the cold wall. Pain radiated out again from her center, and she bit her bottom lip so hard it bled. A tear ran down her cheek. She knew she could not let this woman see her. Somehow, she knew this.

Through the wide crack in the open door, Abra saw the woman stop and stand in the doorway. She looked up and down the hall, apparently trying to decide which way to go. She was about to walk away when she stopped again, suddenly tense, looking this way and that. Then the woman did something strange, something Abra wouldn't have believed if she hadn't seen it.

The woman tilted her nose into the air, closed her eyes, and sniffed. Like a dog that has caught the scent of its prey.

Abra held her breath. The woman stepped away from the doorway, and Abra couldn't see her anymore. Which way had she gone? Was she about to swing the door away from the wall and reveal Abra?

But she walked in the other direction, away from Abra. As she left, Abra could hear her humming a tune, something she didn't recognize, a few simple notes that for some reason filled Abra with dread and fear and a kind of darkness she couldn't understand or explain.

And then the woman was gone.

Abra crept out from behind the door and peeked into the room. Sam was asleep. That seemed fast. But she knew if she was in a bed right now, she'd fall asleep in three seconds flat. She considered going over, waking him, asking him all the questions she wanted to ask, but her pain had begun radiating without end, and it was exhausting. Besides, he looked so peaceful lying there. She knew he needed the rest. They both did. There was always tomorrow.

Another thought entered Abra's brain, one that eclipsed her concerns for Sam, her worries for herself, even the physical pain. The sword! The sword was still in her room! What if the woman had gone looking for it?

She hobbled as quickly as she could down the hallway, still holding the two IV bags with their clear liquid. She put them back on the cart and kept going. The pain was searing through her with each step, but all she could think about now was the sword tucked in her bag of possessions, the sword that somehow everyone had overlooked. She was beginning to realize it could hide itself when it wanted to—it could blend in, become like a seam in her jeans or a shadow in the corner. But if the woman was looking for it, would she see it?

The floor came alive just as Abra slipped into the elevator. Nurses walked the halls again, a patient wandered to the water fountain, a doctor stood in the corner staring at charts. Abra found it odd—it was like someone had flipped a switch, waking the hospital up again from some kind of unnatural sleep.

That woman did it, she thought. *Somehow that woman made everything stop.*

She pushed the number 2 in the elevator and willed it to move quickly.

"C'mon, c'mon, c'mon," Abra whispered. *Ding.* The elevator stopped at level 3. The doors opened. Abra tried to look confident, like she was on the way to somewhere she was supposed to be.

A nurse came in and gave her a strange look. "It's late, honey," she said in a kind voice. "You shouldn't be wandering around at this hour."

Abra nodded, tried to smile, but what she saw next made her eyes open wide. She could feel an old fear jolting through her in pulsing waves.

Behind the nurse, also entering the elevator, was the strange woman from Sam's room. She stared hard at Abra, her eyes narrowing down to slits. Then she smiled, a slight, subtle smile filled with satisfaction. She crossed her arms. She glanced at the lit-up number 2 on the elevator panel.

Ding.

The nurse walked out.

Abra followed her.

The strange woman followed Abra.

Abra limped down the hall, looking over her shoulder. The woman wandered behind her, staying a fair ways back.

The pain! It shot through Abra like knives. She would get to her bed and hit the red button to call a nurse. They would save her from whatever this woman wanted.

Abra turned to go into her room, but the strange woman grabbed her shoulder.

"Excuse me," she said in a quiet, hissing voice.

Abra didn't turn to look at her. The woman's hands were ice-cold, a new kind of pain.

"I think you have something I'm looking for."

Abra didn't move. She wanted to cry out, to call for help. The pain from her injuries was so intense that a blackness encroached on the corners of her eyesight. She was about to pass out. The room began to spin.

"Abra!" a familiar voice called.

It was her father. He gently lifted her up off the ground and carried her to her bed, wheeling her IV rack alongside. He laid her down softly, plumped her pillows, and pulled the covers up over her.

"Where have you been?" he asked, worry in his voice. "You're in no state to be wandering around."

She looked up at him through tired eyes. "Dad," she whispered, "where did you go? Did you see the doctor, the woman?" But she didn't have the strength to say or do anything else. Immediately she passed into a deep sleep where she dreamed again of hanging from a tree and seeing Mr. Tennin lean in to say something, something crucial, only to have the end of the dream interrupt him.

The next day, when she woke up, her breakfast tray was there. Her father was sleeping beside her bed in a plush chair with hard wooden armrests. She sat up, already feeling much better, though her injuries ached. She reached for the small plastic cup of orange juice. That's when she saw the handwritten note.

Get better. I'll see you soon.

It was signed only with two curling letters of the alphabet.

KN

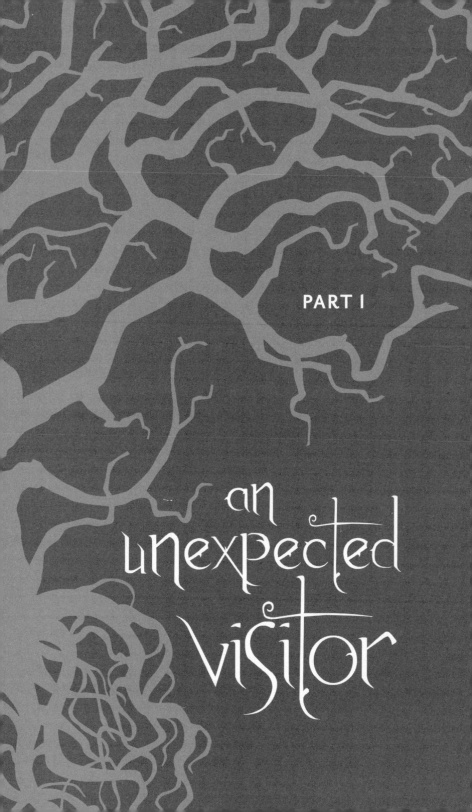

PART I

an unexpected visitor

O think of the home over there,

By the side of the river of light,

Where the saints, all immortal and fair,

Are robed in their garments of light.

Over there, over there,

O think of the home over there,

Over there, over there,

O think of the home over there.

FROM DEWITT C. HUNTINGTON'S
HYMN "OVER THERE"

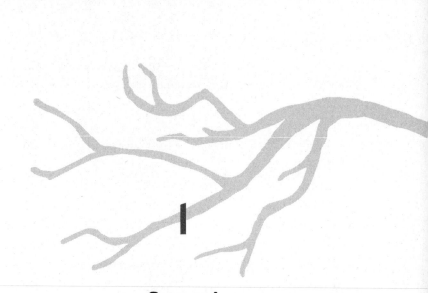

I

Samuel

A MAN FOLLOWS ME down the sidewalk. He is bald and his eyes are circled with wrinkles, and the wrinkles are like ripples moving outward from the place where two stones fell into dark water. His cheeks are dragged down by time and heavy memories. Skin dangles under his chin. But among the wrinkles are tattoos of small, five-pointed stars that scatter up in a mist toward his temples. His stretched, see-through earlobes gape with large gauges. Piercings dot his eyebrows and lips. More piercings than I've seen before, more than I thought possible on one face.

It's not his wrinkles or the tattoos or the piercings that make me the most nervous. It's his eyes, eyes that have the look of the ocean my mother crossed in my dreams. They have a never-ending feel to them that's hard to describe, something I would not have recognized had I not crossed paths with Mr. Tennin and Mr. Jinn so long ago. This man following me is one of them. I can tell you that much. I can tell by his eyes.

Can you kill someone like Mr. Jinn and go unpunished? Probably not.

I've spent the last few months looking through Abra's journal, thinking back over the day the angels fell, and I have to wonder if we have truly gotten away with it. Did Abra and I eliminate Mr. Jinn without any consequences? I seem to remember being scared when I was a kid, frightened that we would pay for what we had done. But as the years went by, the feeling faded. I stopped being afraid. I started to wonder if it had all actually happened, or if the memory I had of two angels fighting over a Tree was only part of a dream, or a dream within a dream. Children are so good at pretending. Maybe Abra and I had made it all up.

But things changed. Abra is gone, dead, leaving me her journal and the sword. Why did she leave it to me, when I still can't even hold it? Did she want me to hide it? Use it? More than anyone on the planet, I'm aware of its significance, but what am I supposed to do with it? Having it in the house feels like hiding a state secret.

All of this is flying through my mind at lightning speed because this bald man with the star tattoos is following me through Deen, toward Mr. Pelle's Antiques.

Back to where it all started.

I glance down the alley that is still there between Pelle's and the pizza place. I stare at the baseball field off in the distance. It's not used for baseball anymore. Baseball has been abandoned, at least here in Deen, and the field drowns in brown weeds and overgrown, leafless trees. Saplings are entwined in the chain-link fence that used to be a backstop. When a strong wind blows, the winter branches clatter and scrape against the metal.

I'm not sure which is worse: land that's been swallowed up by "progress," or land that's been forgotten. We want things to stay the same, but the roads between "now" and "back then" are always changing, and by the time you manage to return home, if you can ever find your winding way, you realize it was never actually yours, not forever. These homes of ours, these fields, the things that make up the landscape of our childhood, they are only ever ours for such a short time, and they owe us nothing.

I look down the sidewalk. The man is still there, pacing, stopping, looking up at me occasionally. The piercings around his eyes glitter in the cold light. I take a deep breath, and when he turns away for a moment, I limp and sort of stumble into the narrow alley. My cane catches on the gravel and slips on the frozen dirt. I panic. I move quickly, or as quickly as I can. I look over my shoulder, expecting him to be right there, running toward me. I get to the side door of Pelle's Antiques, the same one I ran through so many years ago while trying to get out of the rain.

Trying to escape the lightning.

I'm sure it's locked, but I pull on the handle anyway.

It opens.

I've only just said that nothing stays the same, but when I walk through the doorway into the warehouse area of Pelle's Antiques, I realize I'm wrong. This place has not changed, not one bit. It even smells the same. There are old mirrors and dressers and bed frames without mattresses. There are lamps without bulbs and wardrobes begging to be hid in. And through it all, through the furniture and the shadows and the shapes, there is a narrow path, the same narrow path. I'm sure there are doors to all kinds of places right there in the warehouse area of Pelle's Antiques. I'm sure you could find a door to anywhere in the universe, if you knew which hutch to look behind, which empty window to open and crawl through.

I go down that path between all things, through the shadows and gaping holes and dust. I feel like I'm walking on a tightrope between worlds and that the slightest misstep could send me plummeting into somewhere else.

"Mr. Chambers," a voice says quietly, and even though my eyes are still adjusting to the dark, I know it's the man. The man with the stars around his eyes and the invisible mission on his shoulders. The shadows seem to creep away from us, back into the corners of the room, and I'm left staring at his unique face. I become lost in it, the way a child becomes lost staring up into the night sky.

"Samuel Chambers," he says, and I nod, even though he's not asking a question. He knows who I am. That much I can tell.

"Can we talk?" he asks.

I don't know what else to say, so I nod again, waiting for fire to fall from above and eliminate me as retribution for the long-ago death of Mr. Jinn. I wait for him to snuff me out. But he does not. Instead, he sighs, moves to put his hand on my shoulder, and then seems to think better of it.

"Good," he says. "I didn't want to scare you off."

He moves toward the door that leads outside, the door I just came through. I walk slowly behind him, and as we get out onto the sidewalk, I lean more heavily on my cane than I have for some time.

"Where can we go?" he asks.

I look up and down the street. There is no good place to talk privately in this town, no quiet spot, and if I take him to the diner or the coffee shop or the pizza parlor, if I go into those places with this man who looks the way he looks, the entire town will be wagging their collective tongues about it. Jerry, the man who takes care of my farm, will come looking for me, wondering if everything is okay. He'll ask if I need money—that's the first thing he asks when something out of the ordinary happens, as if money is the answer to every unasked question, every strange occurrence.

"I live ten minutes away," I say in a tired voice. "We could go there."

"Yes, but I'll need a ride, if that's okay. I don't have a car."

"Of course you don't," I say. "How'd you get here?"

He looks at me and raises his pierced eyebrows, smiling.

"Of course you did," I mutter. "You didn't tell me your name."

"Call me Mr. Henry," he says.

"When people tell me to call them something," I say in a low voice, clearing my throat, "it makes me wonder if it's their real name."

He smiles again. The collection of wrinkles and tattoos and piercings makes it difficult for me to tell if it's a friendly smile or a leering one. The air feels suddenly icy, the way it feels before the snow falls.

We walk back to my cold car and get in. We drive north, leaving Deen behind us. I can see the car's exhaust clouding up, and everything is silent under the gray sky.

There is beauty in a barren winter day, the way the sky drifts lower and the cut cornstalks stand in their dry rows like beard stubble on a very old, very kind face. The mountains, covered in their leafless trees, are somewhere between brown, gray, and deep violet, or maybe all of those at once, and there are streaks of ice lining the shadowy places like diamond veins.

The wind kicks up and batters the car. There is the smell of new snow in the air.

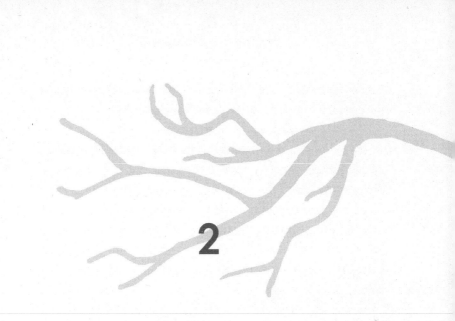

2

I PARK IN THE FARMHOUSE LANE and sit there without moving. Thirty seconds pass. A minute.

"Are you okay?" Mr. Henry asks. We didn't say a word during the entire drive. I had the feeling that he was waiting for me to ask him questions, but I wasn't in the mood. Besides, he's the one who wanted to talk. He can start whenever he's good and ready.

"I'm fine," I say, suddenly regretting my decision to bring him here to my home. I wonder if it would offend him if I turn the car back on, drive into town, and ask him to get out.

"Are we going to go in?" he asks.

"Wait."

The last thing I need is Jerry seeing me go into the house with this character. I look around for him or his son, but it's the time of day when they are usually back at their own farm. They spend less time here in the winter. The fruit trees are old, cold twigs—it's impossible to believe fruit will grow from them again in the spring, when life returns to everything. The garden is only the remains of dead plants, the husks of things not harvested.

Can those of us facing the winter of our lives somehow gather the courage to believe spring will come again?

"Okay," I say with a sigh. "Let's go."

We get out, and the sound of the two car doors slamming in quick succession sends pigeons flying out from under the eaves of the barn. They dart and swoop for the woods across the street, up into the cold gray forest of the eastern mountains. The slamming doors sound foreign under the blanket of winter. I shuffle through the brittle grass, in the direction of the house, and he moves to steady me by holding my elbow but pulls away when I glare at him.

We get inside where it's warm, and I go into the kitchen to make coffee because I have a feeling this is going to be a long conversation.

"What do you want?" I ask him, breaking the silence.

He sits down in a chair in the dining room. He is a large man. It seems unusual to me that a man who looks so old could still be so solid. When he talks I notice a distant clicking and realize it comes from a piercing in his tongue, a metal stud, tapping like Morse code against his teeth.

"I wanted to talk to you about Abra."

"No, I mean what do you want in your coffee? Sugar? Cream?"

"Oh yes. I'm sorry. I drink it black." He pauses. "But that *is* why I'm here. I need to talk to you about Abra."

I feel a growing sense of alarm. I'm suddenly on high alert. I know why this man is here. I know what he has come for.

The sword.

"Abra? What about her?" I ask, avoiding his eyes, trying to sound light, trying to sound innocent. "I didn't speak with Abra for many years, you know. Many years. We grew apart."

I pour two cups of coffee, my nerves on edge. The glass spout of the coffeepot chatters against each of our porcelain mugs like the teeth of a cold man. Steam rises, swirling, and the smell calms my nerves.

"Yours is here on the counter," I say as I make my way to the table, holding my own scalding mug.

I had forgotten the very particular feeling that comes when sitting across the table from someone like him, someone who is what he is, but when he returns to the table and settles in, it comes rushing back: the sense that you are not sitting across from a person as much as you are sitting across from an era, an epoch. Looking at this man was like looking at the Grand Canyon and seeing all those lines in the rock, all those different ages of the earth.

"Did you know anything about what she did after the summer your mother died?" he asks.

"How do you know about my mother?" I ask.

"Everyone knows about your mother," he says with a hint of impatience. I clench my jaw at this strange reference to my mother. I wonder who he means by "everyone." I want to ask him about my mother, but I don't. I don't know why. Maybe he's good at steering a conversation, or maybe I want to say as little as possible. Or maybe I'm afraid that I'll find out something about her, something strange, something disappointing.

"Your mother," he says before shaking his head, changing course. "What do you know about what Abra did after your mother's passing?"

"She was my best friend. I gave her some things. Our friendship died. No, it didn't die—it wasn't that dramatic. We grew apart."

"You could have helped her, you know," he says, sipping his coffee, glancing at me over the rim of his cup.

I shake my head and look down. "No," I murmur into my own coffee. "I was never strong enough."

"Come now. That's not true?" he says, his voice turning the words into a question.

I look at him. "Apparently you know the story. I don't have to tell you about it."

"Our weaknesses are poised to become our greatest strengths. If we are patient and if we believe. The switch will often happen when we most need it to. Weakness"—he pauses, tilting his head from one side to the other—"to strength."

"I don't think that switch ever happened in me."

"Maybe you haven't needed it yet," he says. "What did you give her?"

"That summer? I gave her the box. With everything."

He nods. He knows about the box. Of course he does. Mr. Tennin had it—they probably all wanted it after what happened at the Tree.

"Recently. Did you give her anything recently? Or did she give you anything?"

I stare into the black depths of my drink, and it feels like I'm still staring into this man's eyes. His eyes are everywhere.

I picture the box I put into her coffin. The atlas. The notes. I put those items in there because I thought everything was over. I thought Abra's death meant the end of all this. But then her husband gave me the sword and the journal. Why?

"I can't help you. I don't know you."

I say these things in a voice that I hope will communicate that it's time for him to leave. I am too old for this. I have nothing to do with whatever real or imagined saga is going on around me, behind the curtain.

That phrase sticks in my mind: *behind the curtain*. That's how

Abra and I used to talk about the strange things that happened, as if normal life was on one side of a veil, and the other things— the Tree, Mr. Tennin, Mr. Jinn, the Amarok—were behind it. If we looked hard enough in those days, we could see the rustling. But not now. I have not seen it for many, many years.

"I appreciate your . . . discretion. But there is something Abra had that we need." He waits, then speaks again in a careful, insinuating tone. "I think you might have it. Here."

My heart pounds. I have no way of knowing which side this man is on. I have no way of knowing if he is a Mr. Tennin or a Mr. Jinn. I look in his eyes, desperately searching for something. Kindness, maybe.

"There's nothing here for you," I say, nerves stealing my breath.

He nods. His dangling earlobes sway. He reaches up and strokes his eyebrow with its seven small piercings all in a line. The space between them is the space between stars, which means that he and I, across the table from each other, must be light-years apart. How long do his words take to reach me? How many worlds have fallen in the time it takes me to refill his coffee?

"Do you have time for a story, Mr. Chambers?" he asks.

"I have as much time as I have," I say, shrugging. "Look at me. I have no friends. I have no family. I have very little money. Time is all I have."

He smiles a sad smile. "You have less time than you think. This is a long story."

I take a drink of coffee.

"It's about Abra," he says.

I nod, and the sadness rises again, this time without the apprehension.

"Let me put it this way," he says. "It's primarily about Abra, but there are others involved. It took me time to gather all these

31

stories together. Decades. There were large gaps. Recently I had to reopen doors that were meant never to be opened again. I spoke with people who were there when these events took place, and with others like me. I sat in the shadows for years, looking for answers, always looking. Always seeing, rarely comprehending. I went very close to the Edge."

His voice fades. The wind kicks against the door. The windows rattle. Sleet falls for a minute or two, tapping against the glass, but it turns to snow, a swirling cloud of thick, hypnotic flakes.

"Do you know about her trip to New Orleans?" he asks.

"Only the basics," I say. "She mentioned it in her journal, but it was only a few paragraphs. Something terrible happened there, something she didn't want to write about. She was different after that. Her journal went from descriptive and flowery to matter-of-fact."

Mr. Henry sighs and nods. "How about Egypt?" he asks. "Jerusalem? Paris? Rio? The South Pole? Sydney?"

I am stunned but try not to let it show. I had no idea.

"Those are only the major journeys she took. There were smaller trips. Side trips, you might say. New Orleans was . . . unexpected. For all of us. And we only knew about the Tree growing there after Tennin fell. By then Abra held the sword. The shadows were rising everywhere. People like me were turning. No one could be trusted. Two Trees at once! Who could have ever imagined? Jinn's replacement was . . . ruthless. Her name was Koli Naal. She wanted it all," he says, shaking his head. "She wanted every last thing. Not only the Tree. Not only everything and everyone here."

The name shoots through me like the memory of an intense pain. Koli Naal. I have never spoken that name to anyone.

He pauses, staring hard at me to see if I understand what he's saying. "You've heard that name before," he says, and it sounds like he feels sorry for me.

I nod.

"She wanted every last thing," he repeats. "Those who came before her, the Mr. Jinns of the world, wanted only all of this." He raises his arms and they take in the walls of the house, the ends of the earth. "They wanted all of you—all of humanity and all of this earth. But Koli Naal wanted even more than that. She wanted everything."

When it's obvious I'm not catching on, he says something in a whisper, something I can barely hear. He whispers it as if it's blasphemy.

"She wanted Over There too."

"Over There?" I ask.

We stare at each other there in my little farmhouse, frost on the windows, the snow sliding along the hard ground. We stare at each other over mugs of coffee that are slowly cooling. We stare at each other over eternities and galaxies, cities and friendships, swords and shadows.

He shrugs as if it will all make perfect sense to me at some point. "There was no one else who could go inside and do what needed to be done. Only Abra. Those were dark times."

"They must have been," I say in an even voice, "if you had to turn to a young girl to rescue you."

When he speaks again, there is something tender there, something that begs me for understanding. Or forgiveness. I wonder if he can be trusted after all. Perhaps.

"She was the only one who could go," he insists. "I would have gone. I hope you understand that. But it had to be her."

I wait, and the steam from our mugs rises between us like spirits.

"The story starts four years before the Tree appeared here in Deen. Four years before the two of you killed Jinn and the Amarok and Mr. Tennin fell. Four years before your mother died."

"I didn't actually kill Jinn, you know," I say in a quiet voice. "Abra took care of that."

It feels like a cowardly thing to say, as if I'm trying to pawn all the dirt of that summer onto Abra, trying to save my own skin in case this man has come for revenge. But I have a feeling that he knows far more about those events than I do, even though I was there and he was not.

He keeps talking as if he didn't hear me. I stare past him out the window. The snow is really coming down now. It looks like a blizzard is on the way.

"This is the story I gathered—what people told me, what I found. Some things I have had to guess at."

He pauses, nodding his head as if satisfied with the work that went into the story he is about to tell. He leans back in his chair.

"As best as I can tell, this is what happened the day Ruby vanished from the world."

ruby's disappearance

"Only a fool is not afraid."

MADELEINE L'ENGLE,
A WRINKLE IN TIME

3

ON THE VERY SAME DAY his sister disappeared, and only a few hours before he walked alone through the streets of New Orleans all the way to Saint Louis Cemetery No. 1, Leo Jardine hid in the closet, trying to breathe slow and quiet. He calmed himself by counting the long, straight wires in his pocket, a lock-picking set that was a gift from a great-uncle he could barely remember. He traced the wires with his finger, some jagged, some straight, and he knew them all by touch.

This one straight as an arrow for locks that could be popped open.

This one with teeth for reaching and twisting.

This one with a hook on the end, like the answer to a question.

His father and the doctor were upstairs in his sister's room. The doctor—her last name started with an N, but he had never heard it clearly or seen it written down—reminded him of the slender, straight pick in his lock-picking set. She was firm and direct, no-nonsense. She came and went quickly, and always walked the shortest distance from here to there. She did not look to one side or the other.

Leo leaned against the wall in the closet down the hall from the dining room, where the two always sat after his sister's check-ups, and he waited for them to come down.

Leo's father Amos owned a house with many doors. There was the weighty front door that opened out onto a wide front porch shaded by ancient, leaning sycamore trees, their bark shedding in strips like sunburned skin. That same front door was flanked by two windows, each clouded by thick, heavy drapes, solemn as guardian angels. When the drapes were drawn, not a speck of light could get in.

Then there was the side door, the door everyone used, the one clinging to its hinges. It moved without a sound. It was a friendly door, one that even strangers felt comfortable knocking on or pushing open a few inches before calling inside.

There was the back door, the one that led from the kitchen into a yard thick with overgrown azaleas planted in straight lines. Rising around them were tall cedar trees that fought their way among each other, higher, reaching for the sun. Their lower branches were dead and snapped off—only the highest branches still flaunted green needles, so far from the ground, too afraid to let go.

Inside the house there were even more doors, some of which Leo had never been through. His father's office door, for example—he was absolutely, positively, never-in-a-million years to go through that door. He could only imagine the consequences. He heard strange things on the other side, muffled conversations and sliding filing cabinet drawers that clicked closed. There was the latching of padlocks and the soft spinning of a safe's dial. *Tick tick tick tick tick tick tick.*

There was the attic door, the one that led up up up into darkness and dust. His father had never made any rules about that door, but he didn't have to. Leo was terrified of that uppermost level, scared of what might be there.

Perhaps the most peculiar door was the small trapdoor in the floor of the guest room closet, a door he had never had reason to lift. He noticed the small round handle the first time he explored the house, and he had pushed at the loose boards of the flat door, but it seemed harmless enough, and rather plain and boring. Curiosity about what was under it came at strange times, like the middle of the night, or when he was staying at his mother's house. But when he was in his father's house, when it would have made sense to open it, the thought never occurred to him.

There were also bedroom doors and pantry doors, heavy sliding doors and soundless French doors. Most importantly, there was a closet door in the hallway just inside the front door. It was a deep closet that ran the length of the stairwell, the kind where the ceiling got lower and lower the further in you went, all the way down to nothing.

The air where he hid smelled old and musty, and the wood floor was smooth and hesitant beneath him, ready to give him away. He stood up straight and leaned against the wall again. He left the closet door barely open because he was ten years old and still a little bit scared of the dark, a little bit worried about what crept around in the deep spaces he could not see. He had this fear that if he closed the door, he wouldn't be able to open it again.

Recently he had begun to doubt the stories he always believed to be true—stories about knights and dragons, angels and demons, secret worlds and invisible people. Even at ten years old, he knew belief was slipping away from him. He could feel it going, like honey through a crack in the jar. But in that closet, he could believe those things might be true. Was it the darkness? The stillness? The feeling that there were live things all around him, things he could not see?

He peeked through the door, and a slanted line of golden light ran diagonally down his face and over his eye.

His father's house was a tired one, and it leaned and creaked when you walked through it. It was the kind of house that would talk to you if you were the only one there, the kind of house that sighed when it thought about all the people it had known. Many things had taken place in that house, nearly unimaginable things, some so small that they'd make no difference to you—nothing more than a sigh that marked the change of a friendship or a glance that sparked the flames of love. That house was like a kind old man: a little crazy, a little angry, but mostly quiet and reflective. And waiting. Always waiting.

Leo felt his father and the doctor approach before he heard them, their footsteps shifting down the long flight of stairs from the third floor to the second floor to the main level. His father's steps were loose and uneven. He walked without any semblance of a rhythm. He was the opposite of clinical, the definition of superstitious. When he walked anywhere, he hurried, his limbs flailing.

Behind his father's footsteps came the unremarkable steps of the doctor. Firm. Calculated. Their beat was so constant that a conductor could have directed an entire symphony under their guidance. She seemed to pause as she walked past the closet where Leo was hiding, a rest in the stanza. Leo froze in place. He thought he heard the doctor sniffing as if catching his scent, but immediately after that he thought, *What a silly thing to think. People don't sniff for things the same way animals do.*

Did they?

The two moved past the closet, along the short hall, and sat down at the dining room table. Leo held his breath so he could hear them.

"I'm sorry, Amos," the doctor said, and her voice soaked into the walls of the house, ran quietly along the high oak baseboards. It seemed muffled and distant.

"What do you mean, you're sorry?" Leo's father asked, his voice sounding weary. Scratchy. Leo couldn't see him, but he could tell by the sound that his father held his hand over his own mouth while he spoke, as if trying to hold in the questions that would lead to the diagnosis he didn't want to hear.

The doctor sighed. "I'm sorry," she said again, "because your daughter is not getting better. She is, in fact, declining. Fading. There is very little that I can do."

She said the last sentence quickly, as if trying to rid her mouth of the words. The sound of them soaked into the walls. Leo wondered where those words went. He wondered if you could find them again. He wondered if you scratched deep enough into the plaster, would you find all the words the walls had ever heard? He suddenly thought of the trapdoor in the bottom of the guest room closet. He imagined opening it, pulling all of its weight up by the small round ring, and being overcome by a wave of trapped words, emerging in an overwhelming stream like a burst of bats from a cave.

"Fine. I'll take her somewhere else. Someone else can help her. Not everyone is as incompetent as you."

"There is very little that anyone else could do," the doctor said. She didn't sound angry at Amos's slight. Her words came out like her footsteps, measured and matter-of-fact. She was not threatened by his anger or grief. Her response waved off both of them like pesky flies.

Silence settled in the house again, more imposing than a

shout. Leo tried very hard not to make a sound. His father was touchy these days, as Ruby's health declined. She was only five years old, but her breathing sounded like the wheezing of an old woman. Her skin was pale, nearly transparent, and she slept all the time. She threw up whatever she ate.

"If you'd like," the doctor said, "I could meet with you and your wife together, review the girl's condition, explain our options?"

Leo's father laughed. "No, no, that won't do," he said, then paused as if trying to decide how much to say. "Her mother is away. She left last week. It's all happened very quickly. It wouldn't do to worry her."

Leo pictured his mother waiting to board a plane somewhere in some other city. He pictured her in her professional clothes, carrying her professional bag. She, too, walked straight, had goals, knew the most direct path to achieve them. But he could also imagine her chewing her fingernails, wondering if her children were okay, finding a clock and staring at it as the second hand went around and around. He had seen her do that before. He had wondered what was in her mind as she watched the moments pass.

Leo knew his mother loved him fiercely. He could not have told you how he knew this, but he knew it. On the other hand, his father's love for him had somehow faded, and he knew this too, in some intangible way. When Ruby became sick, her illness had become his father's obsession, so that nothing could exist alongside it. When his father sat with his sister, Leo could say anything he wanted but his father would only nod and blink, his gaze never leaving Ruby. Sometimes, when Leo came in the house, he would find his father staring at a crack in the wall or a doorknob or a streak of light between shadows. Leo's existence had faded from his father's awareness. There was only Ruby and her sickness, and like a spot that burns into your vision if you stare at the sun too long, Amos couldn't see past it.

"Amos," the doctor said again, as if saying the name would change things, be a key in a lock that opened the door to a better time. Her voice had gone quieter, calmer. "Amos. What are you going to do?"

It seemed a strange question. Leo heard the inexplicable sound of his father weeping. He nearly walked out of the closet in order to see it. Unbelievable. He had thought his father incapable of tears. When he leaned forward to try to see what was going on, the floorboards creaked beneath his feet. He held his breath and stopped blinking, as if even the movement of his eyelids would give him away. The two stopped talking, and for a moment Leo was sure he had been found out.

"Is it a curse?" Leo heard his father mumble. "Is it something I've done? Did I bring this on the girl?"

"I don't think—" the doctor began, but Leo's father interrupted.

"Is it this house? Is this house under some kind of an ancient spell? If I burn it down, will she recover?" His voice became louder and more urgent with each far-fetched grasp at a cure. "You know this city, Doctor. You know what people are capable of here. There is a darkness."

The doctor didn't reply.

"What if we ran? Took off. Could we leave all of this behind us?" Amos asked.

And when he said "all of this," Leo knew he meant everything: the sickness, the city, Leo's mother.

Leo.

His father would leave everything, including him.

Leo peered through the crack in the door again, and he could barely see the doctor, her pale white skin, the way her hands were folded on the table, fingers laced together, one finger tapping, tapping, tapping. The dining room had a low chandelier, and it shone like a spotlight on him.

"If you want to leave—I mean *really* leave," the doctor said, "I might know someone who could help you do that."

Amos laughed again, and the sound scared Leo. He reached into his pocket and again felt the ten pieces of wire, roughly the length of his little finger, each attached to a key ring. Each wire was a different thickness, each bent in different ways. The lock-picking set could get him to the other side of almost any door. Feeling the cold metal, the pointed ends, the familiar bending here and there—all of it comforted him.

"My wife would find us, Doctor. No matter where we went. No matter how far. Trust me—you don't know her like I do. I could never rest because she would find us, and then what? I'd end up in prison for kidnapping, or worse."

"I can assure you that she would never find you. And there is hope in this other place, hope for your daughter."

Amos went from laughing to sounding angry.

"What do you mean? Hope? What's that? I thought you said there was nothing you could do. I thought you said there was no hope."

"I didn't tell you because this place," the doctor said slowly, "is at the Edge of Over There. If you go, you can't come back. Not ever."

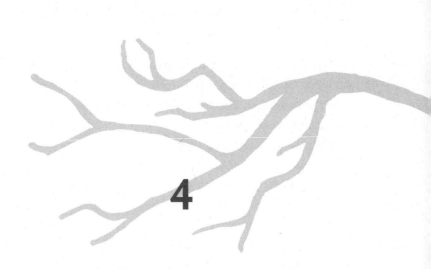

4

"WHERE IS IT?" Amos asked, his voice suddenly hungry. "How far?"

The doctor leaned in closer. She sounded like a temptress, as if this was what she had wanted all along.

"The distance isn't important. You have to stop thinking about things the way you have before. Everything there is different. The distance, that means nothing. There is no place like it. What's important is that you realize your daughter can find healing there. But if you go, you can never come back."

"What do you mean? Is it outside the country? I don't have a passport."

The doctor lifted her hands and rubbed her temples, then repeated herself. "It's Over There, Amos. You will, both you and your daughter, be gone. Forever. There is no coming back. Imagine a door that locks behind you, and there is no key to open it again."

"What do I need to do?" Amos asked without hesitating. "I would do anything to keep her alive, to get her away from here. Did you know her mother has threatened to take both children away from me? A custody battle over a dying little girl—that's all my future holds right now."

His voice caught. He choked out the next sentence.

"I need to get out of here."

"Why did she leave them with you now?"

Amos spat. "Bah! She had no choice. It was all very last minute, very important. She was desperate to find someone to watch them. But this will be the last time they stay with me. You don't know her. I'm telling you. You don't."

The doctor sighed and stood up. She walked to each of the three dining room windows and pulled the heavy blinds closed. Her skin went from pale to gray in the shadows. She paced back and forth a few times in the fresh darkness before sitting back down and leaning toward Amos.

"There's a woman," she began.

"Yes?" Amos urged her.

"There's a woman," she said again. "Her name is Marie Laveau."

The doctor waited a moment, as if to see if the name meant anything to Amos. It clearly did not, so she went on.

"She has a key."

She stopped, as if reconsidering.

"If I tell you this, there is no going back. You cannot change your mind. Once you know, either you leave or everything will be much, much worse for you."

"I want to go," Amos said in a firm voice.

"Give me something to write with."

"Of course, of course," Amos stuttered, and Leo heard his chair grate against the wood floor. It banged the wall. Amos walked past the closet door, his shadow dark and cold. Leo stiffened. He wouldn't mind if his father vanished, but he couldn't imagine life without Ruby.

His parents' divorce, his sister's sickness—these things had been planted in his life, seeds of a terrible sadness, and the sadness had grown until it filled him to bursting. Ruby's presence was the last good thing. He thought he loved her only because she was his sister, or because she was the little girl who followed him around with great devotion, but really he loved her because she was the thing that kept his belief alive. Her presence in his life was like that of a fairy, and it made him wonder if maybe, just maybe, all of those unbelievable things were somehow true.

He heard his father rummaging through a drawer in his desk down the hall. Then he came back quickly. He left a wake of scents behind him: stale cigarettes and Stetson cologne and sweat. It was a warm summer day, and the heavy stillness sifted in through the walls of the house.

The doctor took the pen and paper from Amos and scribbled a few short notes on it.

"This is her name. This is where you can find her," she said, pointing at each line on the paper one at a time. "And this is what you need to say, word for word."

The doctor stared at Amos while he read over the information.

"'I need to leave,'" Amos read in a firm voice. "'Can I use the—'"

"Stop!" the doctor shouted, looking around, angry for the first time. "Stop! Don't say it out loud. Not now. Don't be so foolish! Go here," she said, and stabbed at the line on the piece of paper, "and ask for her"—she stabbed the paper again—"and say that. But not before. Not out loud. Not now."

Amos cleared his throat. The room was silent again, but only for a moment.

"When can I go?"

"You need to go soon. Now. I can't have someone with this kind of knowledge wandering around the city. It puts not only you at risk. There are others who would suffer if this became common knowledge."

"But I have to pack. I have to . . ."

"You can't take anything with you, not Over There. Nothing except the clothes on your back. Everything is there already. I don't have time to explain it. You don't have time."

"Wait a second! You never said—"

"And I wouldn't show your daughter to Marie, not at first. I don't know that she has ever allowed a child to go. But if she refuses, tell her I sent you, and explain the child's condition. That might sway her. She was a mother once. Remember that."

She said it as if she was trying to reassure herself that it would work.

"She had a daughter."

Silence. The clock on the mantel chimed six. *Ding. Ding. Ding. Ding. Ding. Ding.*

"Tonight," the doctor said, standing. She pushed her chair in under the table. "You must go tonight or your situation will become much worse, now that you know this. Having this information is not the key to a long life in New Orleans."

The two of them stood there for a moment staring at each other, neither one saying a word. Finally, the doctor spoke again.

"Do you have it all memorized?" she asked Amos.

"Yes. Yes, I do."

The doctor pulled a book of matches from her pocket and struck one of them. It made a sizzling sound that lit up the dark dining room. She set the paper on fire. The smoke rose like a black promise, twisting and dancing. Leo could smell it from where he stood in the closet, the smell of burning things, the smell of endings.

"There is one more thing," the doctor said. Leo had not thought her words could become more abrupt, more serious, but they did. Each syllable fell like iron.

"You must take this with you."

She reached under the table and lifted something with two hands, a small plant the size of a volleyball. It looked like some type of orchid. The stem was a bright lime green, almost neon, and there were three blossoms drooping from the main stem, white as the moon. When she placed it on the table, the pot it was in grated heavily against the wood, as if it was made of stone.

Amos was mesmerized. "What is that?" he asked in a whisper so that Leo could barely hear him. "What . . . is . . . that?"

The doctor laughed, and it was a strange sound. Happy, yes, but with other things mixed in, greedy things, things that crawl out from under your bed in the middle of the night.

"This is the key to your daughter's healing."

Amos reached out tentatively.

"Wait," the doctor said.

Amos's hand stopped, then drifted back to his side.

"I have more instructions. You cannot let anyone know you have this, not here, and not on the other side of the door. No one."

Amos nodded.

"Take this plant in the bowl to the tallest building you can find, the one in the middle of the city. Light a fire close to it. Here are some matches to take with you. There is plenty of wood in the building."

Amos nodded again, his face filled with longing.

"Finally, and this is very important, you will need to prick

49

Ruby's finger and place a drop of her blood at the root of the plant."

Amos looked disgusted. He shook his head as if almost waking from a dream. "What?"

"Listen to what I'm saying, Amos. This is her healing. The leaves on this plant, when it grows into a tree, will heal her. It will grow quickly once you light the fire and feed the tree. You must plant it in the tall building. You must guard it. The time to eat from it will come later, but in the meantime, the leaves, Amos! The leaves! Do you hear what I'm saying? Do. Not. Eat. The. Fruit. Wait until I send someone. But the leaves will heal Ruby."

Amos's shoulders drooped. "I don't know if I can remember it all."

For a moment, the doctor drew in a breath and looked ready to erupt with anger or frustration, but then she exhaled quietly. She stood up and walked around the table, her footsteps suddenly silent. She placed her pale, white hands on Amos's shoulders, and the two of them stood there for a long time. The image made Leo uncomfortable, this strange woman with her hands on his father's shoulders. The two of them stared at the small plant.

She lifted her hands and, for a brief moment, held tightly to Amos's head, but her hands dropped quickly, and Leo wondered if he had even seen it happen.

"You will remember everything," she said quietly.

She walked back to her side of the table, lifted the bowl with the plant, and placed it inside a black bag. She wiped her hands together, as if discarding small parts of something undesirable. She sighed, and everything she had said went up in a kind of drifting haze. Leo blinked, held his eyes together tightly, and opened them again.

What had just happened? He could barely remember.

"Tonight," the doctor said again. "Be gone tonight. You have no choice now."

She walked down the hallway in long, forceful steps, opened the front door (the door that no one ever used), and slammed it hard behind her. It made a sound like distant thunder.

5

LEO SAT DOWN INSIDE THE CLOSET, trying not to make a sound. Where could his father possibly go that was unfindable? What kind of person knew of a place like that? He felt his way through the lock picks, touching one, then another, as if the answer was there, hidden among the short wires. All the answers to all the questions.

A shadow moved over the crack in the door and hovered there like a cloud covering the sun. A large hand reached inside and opened the door a few inches.

"Leo." Amos said his son's name in one long sigh. There were entire conversations in that one word, explanations and admonitions and sadness. He said it three more times for good measure, as if he didn't know what else to say. "Leo, Leo, Leo."

The air in the house went completely still. Leo felt like the closet had been illuminated by a spotlight. He was caught, and he squinted in the glare.

"How long have you been in there?" Amos asked, but Leo didn't say a word.

"Too long, I suppose," Amos continued. It was almost like

he was having a conversation with an imaginary friend—he wasn't waiting for answers. It was a one-sided discussion, and no response was necessary.

Amos looked off in the distance, as if the closet extended for miles. "Of course, you'll need to stay in here tonight. I'm sorry, Son. Sleeping in a closet won't be pleasant, but your mother will come first thing in the morning, as she always does. She never could leave well enough alone. I'll leave the back door unlocked, and she'll come in, you know how she does, shouting at me already over some such thing, this or that. Not taking off her shoes. Never taking off her shoes, bringing in the dirt."

For a moment, Leo thought his father might be having second thoughts. His voice had taken on the tone of someone who was waking up after talking in their sleep and realizing that everything they had said before was irrelevant nonsense. But that didn't last long.

"But I won't be here, and neither will Ruby," he said.

"No." Leo found his voice. "You can't take her. You can't. She's my sister."

"If I don't, she'll die. Is that what you want?"

The two stayed there for what felt like a very long time, staring into each other's eyes, both of them contemplating the one thing that meant the most in the world to each of them: Ruby. A little five-year-old girl, the center of their universe.

"But if you take her and you never come back, it's like she's dead anyway," Leo whispered. "At least to me."

"But she won't be dead, not really, and that's what matters," Amos said, and it sounded like he was convincing himself now. "I don't have a choice. Your mother will come in the morning and she'll hear you. All you have to do is call out and she'll open the door, she'll let you out, and you'll have each other. But this is Ruby's only chance. There is no other way."

Amos pushed the door closed slowly, as if something in him wanted his son to fight back, to push against the weight of his choices. But there was no shoving match, no test of strength, and the golden sliver of light winked out. Leo heard a loud click in the darkness, and he knew that his father had locked the door.

Leo's father had been kind only to lock the door and not to give him a thrashing. It's one of the ways Leo knew his father was leaving for real. That unexpected kindness.

For the next hour, he heard his father running around the house, opening drawers and slamming doors and looking, looking, looking. Leo wondered what was taking him so long. He had heard the doctor say he wasn't allowed to take anything with him. What could his father be doing? He felt the lock picks in his pocket and knew it wouldn't take him long to get out, but he had to do it after his father left, because if he did it before, his father would put him back in the closet and prop something against the door to keep him from escaping again. Or worse.

So, Leo waited.

The house went quiet, and Leo guessed that his father must be up on the third floor, getting Ruby ready. She was small for her age, and frail, and Leo worried that she wouldn't survive the trip his father was about to take her on. He willed her to live. He pressed his forehead against the door and muttered a prayer, a serious prayer, one more full of earnest asking than any other prayer he had ever said. The door was cold on his forehead. He wondered if you had to close your eyes when praying in the dark.

Even after he prayed, it remained quiet, as if no one had been listening. Maybe the house heard his prayer. Maybe the house had been listening. Or maybe Someone else heard, Someone beyond the house, beyond the darkness. Beyond everything. Someone Over There.

The words of the doctor echoed in his mind. The Edge of Over There. What could it mean? Where could it be?

Leo heard his father come down the stairs again, his steps slow, and Leo knew he must be carrying Ruby. He waited until the side door closed before working one of the short lengths of wire into the hole. It was an old door with one of those skeleton-key holes, nearly large enough to see through. Leo knew how those locks worked. He could feel it adjusting at the end of the wire, ticking this way, slipping that way. For a moment he was inside the lock, testing edges, sensing the riddle, the question. Finally, a click, an answer, and the door drifted open.

He sprinted down the hall and into the outside world. It was dusk, and the fresh air felt wonderful. Everything out there was alive, especially after his time in the dark closet. Hope lived there, in that time of day before the birds began their evening song.

He knew there was no point in trying to call his mother—she would still be traveling, not getting home until at least the middle of the night and maybe not until morning. Besides, he had no phone number where he could reach her. He glanced back and forth down the street, and among the handful of cars and people he saw his father walking along the sidewalk.

Amos carried little Ruby against his chest, her head on his shoulder. They weren't close, but Leo thought she was still sleeping. Amos walked fast but not fast enough to garner any undue attention. He even waved slightly at the people they passed. He looked like any father at the end of a long day, carrying his small, exhausted child home for an early bedtime.

In one of his hands he also carried the black bag, and Leo remembered, as if from a dream, that in that bag was the plant, the strange-looking plant with its too-green stem and small leaves and drooping white flowers. The bag was taut. The stone bowl was heavy inside it.

Leo followed. He felt calm now that he was free of the closet, now that he could keep his father in his sights. He would follow them for as long as he had to. He would follow them and follow them and when they finally stopped he would see where they stopped and he would call his mother in the morning and she would come and rescue Ruby and his father would go to prison and it would be only him and his mother and Ruby again. It made him sad to think about his father going to prison; it made him sad to think about not seeing him. But he was afraid of him now, and he would never go into that house again, not while his father and that doctor were on the loose, stealing people and talking about places you could never return from.

They walked until Leo heard the distant sound of cars on the freeway. It made him nervous, that sound of fast movement, that sound of people rushing away. He suddenly had a feeling that his father was carrying everything that mattered to him in the world. Every good thing. It made Leo pick up his feet a little faster. He didn't care anymore if his father saw him. He had to stop him from going any further. He looked around for a weapon, and he wondered if he had the capability of attacking his father if it meant saving Ruby. He didn't think so. He wasn't sure.

Leo grew closer. One hundred yards, fifty yards. The streets grew broader and more spaced out. The light faded in the west and streetlights began winking on. Mosquitoes rose up out of the damp ground, and the shadows of the trees lining the streets melded together into one unending blackness. The lights of New Orleans burned like stars, hiding among the treetops.

Leo followed his father along a tall, faded wall, a mixture of brick and concrete. He knew where they were—he had ridden his bike by there a few times. It was a quiet part of town, one deep with superstition and mystery. A few of Leo's classmates lived close by, and he knew what was on the other side of the tall wall. That knowledge made him shiver.

His father turned abruptly to the right, vanishing. Leo sprinted up to where he had turned and stared through a barely opened gate. There it was, stretching out in front of him.

Saint Louis Cemetery No. 1.

6

LEO HELD THE GATE as he walked through, making sure it didn't close behind him, because any ten-year-old boy knows the last thing you want when entering a cemetery is for the gate to close behind you. It's terribly bad luck, and who wants to spend the night sleeping on the ground when there are bodies hidden all around you? Who knows what time the groundskeeper might arrive in the morning?

Besides, it would be scary enough if you got locked into a normal graveyard, and this was no normal graveyard.

This was Saint Louis Cemetery No. 1.

Saint Louis Cemetery No. 1 was an aboveground cemetery—all the graves, instead of being below the earth, were crypts built like miniature houses. Some were plain, rectangular boxes while others had peaked roofs and elaborate doors. Some were behind tall iron gates while others were right there where you could touch them, lined up one after another, so close you could barely walk between them. Most were white, but some were crumbling brick or smooth stucco painted a bright color, like peach or pink or lime green. The rows between the crypts were long and straight.

Leo had lost sight of his father, so he headed into the cemetery, staying close to the wall, ducking behind the larger crypts, hiding in their shadows. Night had arrived. There were no lights in the cemetery, but light from the street and neighboring houses crept in over the tall wall, casting angular shadows in different directions.

Leo realized that even though he normally felt like he was losing his belief, at night his belief was still very much intact. The shadows seemed to be living things, and while he was scared, he was also excited because his belief was right there where he could see it. Perhaps this was why so many people like to watch scary movies—it reminds them of what it feels like to believe in something they cannot see.

The moon was up, high over the city. He held the lock picks tight in his pocket so they wouldn't bump against each other while he walked. There was a dim flickering of light up ahead, close to an intersection of two of the main walkways. He leaned in against a tall crypt. It was the color of moonlight and massive, probably ten feet long. Small tufts of grass grew out of the cracks on its roof. He peered around the front. People had left small glass vases of flowers, and notes. There was rotting fruit there. The crypt was covered in handwriting.

His father came walking down the opposite aisle, and Leo flattened himself in the shadow along the grave, holding his breath. His father still carried Ruby like a baby in front of him, and he looked exhausted from lugging her so far. Her breathing was hoarse and labored, and one of her arms hung limp at her side like a pendulum in a clock that no longer works. The bag hung heavy from one of Amos's hands.

"Excuse me?" Amos said as he turned in between two of the crypts, and at first Leo thought his father was talking to him. He tensed up, preparing to run or to fight. He wondered how fast he could move while carrying his sister. But then his father kept talking, and he realized there was someone else.

"Are you Marie?"

"I am," a woman replied, and in those two words her voice was magical, soft as silk. It moved like melted chocolate. There was something deep and ancient about it, like starlight falling through a forest of one-hundred-year-old trees. Leo could barely resist the overwhelming urge to get closer to her, to see her.

"I need to leave," Amos said, and Leo thought he could hear tears in his father's voice. But there was also something mechanical there, and Leo realized his father must be repeating the lines the doctor had given him. "Can I use the key?"

"I heard you were coming," she said slowly. "That's why I waited, but the night came first. I thought perhaps you had changed your mind."

"No, no," he said, and his voice held a lining of fear, the thinnest thread. "I'm going. I'm ready to go."

Leo peeked around the corner of the crypt. His father's back faced him. On the other side of his father was a tiny fire, almost comical in its smallness, yet producing a surprising amount of light.

But Leo wasn't looking for his father or even his sister anymore. He was trying to see where the beautiful voice came from. At first, he saw nothing but shadows, nothing but flickering light against the chalky white of surrounding graves that rose high into the night sky. Higher than he remembered. It was like he had shrunk down to the size of a mouse.

Marie stepped forward, into the orange light from the fire.

She was a large woman, made taller by a scarf wrapped around her head. It rose in an unruly white bunch and had red stripes running through it, some thick, some thin, like a cobweb that's been brushed aside. Her ponderous but elegant body was draped in a patterned red robe, light and silky. It rustled in the breeze, or maybe it was the small fire that made it move? Beneath everything she wore black clothes that blended in with the shadows around her, so at times her body looked like nothing more than a red robe floating in the movement of the flames.

But her face! Oh, her face! She was beautiful. Her skin was the color of caramel toffee. Small bits of jet-black hair snuck out from under her headscarf and curled in wiry wisps near her round, brown eyes. Her nose and mouth were soft and full.

Marie sighed, and Leo felt the breathlessness that comes when a boy first recognizes beauty in a woman. He felt bashful and curious and couldn't stop staring.

"You cannot take the little one, and you cannot take the bag," she said with regret in her voice. She talked to Amos the same way most adults talk to children who say they want to go to the moon. "It's no place for a little one. Perhaps someday, but not yet."

Amos shook his head, slowly at first and then vigorously. "She's very, very ill, and this is what I need to make her better. She won't survive much longer. I have to take her. The doctor said . . ."

Amos fumbled in his pocket as best he could while holding his daughter. He pulled out a thick mound of bills, holding them tight in his fist. A few of them drifted to the ground.

"I brought double," he said, his whining voice rising higher until he was nearly shouting in desperation. "I brought double! I can pay for both of us!"

Marie stretched out her hand, but Leo couldn't tell if she was reaching out to touch Ruby or to take the money or to reject both. Before she did anything, she pulled back.

"Who told you to find me?"

"It was the doctor. My friend." Amos's words came in a panicked rush, as if he was afraid to say too little, terrified to say too much. "Her name is . . ."

Marie interrupted him suddenly, loudly. "Stop! Do not say that name here. She is a friend to no one, and if she is helping you, the only thing she is truly doing is helping herself. She helped me once, long ago. Helped." Each time she said the word "helped," it came out like a curse word.

The two stood there, the tiny fire between them. Finally she said quietly, sighing, "I cannot allow you to take the little one. You can go if you'd like, but alone. I will take the child wherever you'd like me to take her. I will leave her wherever you ask me to leave her."

She stared at Amos, and in her eyes there was a strange sort of power. She looked at Ruby as if she already owned her, as if she was her child for the taking. But there was kindness there too, mixed in with it all, and Leo didn't know what to think of this strange woman named Marie.

"There's no point in me going in there without her," Amos said in a slow voice, emphasizing each word. "She's dying. Her only hope is . . . Over There. I can't leave her."

"Very well," Marie said, stepping forward, lifting her robe, and stretching one of her bare feet above the fire as if to snuff it out.

"Wait!" Amos shouted, and the whole earth stopped, or seemed to. "Wait. Weren't you ever a mother? Didn't you ever hold your own child?"

Marie stared at him.

"Didn't you ever wait with them while they were sick? God forbid you ever had to watch them die!"

Marie didn't move.

"I have nothing to wait for," Amos said, and his voice was quieter now. "She will be gone soon. So really, you are only letting me go in because—look at her!—she will not be alive much longer."

Leo heard a car drive by on the street outside the tall wall. He could see a few dim stars in the night sky—most were drowned out by the city's glow. Another car drove by, its headlights moving the shadows, forcing them to drift one way, then the other, like ocean waves. After the car moved into the distance, the shadows seemed more eager, stronger, and they reached for the flames.

"Enough!" Marie shouted, and Amos jumped back a step. Leo felt his heart thud inside his chest. A desire to shout out, to reveal himself, nearly overcame him. She seemed to even have power over the shadows, and for a moment Leo thought that's what she had shouted at.

"You must listen very closely," Marie said while throwing a few small sticks onto the dying fire. She spoke faster, the words blurring together like watercolors. Her accent became stronger, and her *t*'s sounded like a snare drum. "The Passageway has become . . . treacherous in recent years. Your doctor friend has been sending more and more people in through this gate. But you will find all you need for you and for your little one."

"Where are we going?" Amos asked with urgency. "Where are you taking us?"

Marie sighed, started talking a few times, but each attempt trailed off. Leo could tell she was having trouble knowing where to begin.

"I am not taking you anywhere," she said. "I am simply unlocking the door and pointing you in the right direction, pointing you to the Edge."

She stopped and stared at Amos, her eyes challenging him to run away. When he did not, she poked the fire and sparks flew upward.

She withdrew a large key and walked to the crypt Leo was hiding behind. The key was white as a bone, the size of her forearm. She held it by the head. The shoulders of the key were harsh squares. The shaft was long and straight, and there were teeth at the very end, five or six of them, like the skyline of a shadow city. Leo pulled back around the corner, out of sight, and listened. There was a deep scraping, like distant thunder crackling along the horizon, and where Leo leaned against the house-shaped tomb, it felt as though an earthquake shook it.

There was a loud creaking, the sound of rock crashing onto rock, and Leo was certain that a neighboring crypt must have fallen over. Then he heard again—no, he *felt*—the grating sound of the key, deep and harsh, somewhere in the bowels of the earth, where earthquakes wait to shift and lava bides its time and history goes to live.

"Be careful," Marie said. "Take care of the child."

What had happened? Leo felt suddenly awake, as if a skin of numbness had fallen off of him. He took a deep breath, and it was like a first breath. He could smell the summer, the approaching rain, the city. Life swirled around him, even in Saint Louis Cemetery No. 1.

Why had he waited there so long beside the crypt? Why hadn't he raced in and grabbed his sister or told the woman she was right not to let his father take her in? Why hadn't he fought for her?

Why had he done nothing but stand by and watch?

He glanced around the corner once more, and at that moment the fire went out in a rain of sparks like falling stars. Darkness roared in to fill up the space between the aboveground graves.

No one was there.

7

LEO RAN A FEW ROWS in one direction, his feet slipping on the cement. He sprinted back again. He went out to the main walkway and looked one way, then the other. Marie was gone. There was no sign of her or Ruby or his father. No flowing red dress, no white headscarf, no father carrying a daughter with his arms weighed down by a heavy black bag holding a bowl, a plant. He felt lost, like someone overboard: the boat comes in and out of view as the waves rise and fall, but with each glimpse the craft is farther and farther away.

Leo dashed back to the dark side of the crypt and looked for any signs of a door, any handles or knobs or latches. The smell of smoke drifted around him, and the embers were dying, dimming. He ran his hands up and down the rough white stone, and he felt it. At first it was only a crack, a gash in the rock the width of a pen, but as he explored it more he realized it had square edges. It was no natural crack. It was there for a reason.

Leo plucked the lock-picking wires from his pocket, dropping them in his haste, and they made a clinking sound when they hit the concrete. He grabbed for them, chose the thickest one, and went to work. Even though it was dark he closed his eyes, focusing on the point of the pick, feeling what it felt. It scratched inside the hole, snagged on various surfaces, but there was nothing that would budge, nothing that even considered giving way. He pressed it along the inside.

Snap. The pick broke.

He chose another piece of wire from the ring. He tried to calm himself, tried to see with the lock pick the way he always did, but there was nothing.

Snap. He broke another.

Snap.

Snap.

Snap.

He was down to his last hope. His last answer. He held it up and looked at it in the light—it was a hairpin bent into the shape of a lightning bolt. It made a dark scar against the sky, a rip in the fabric. He had found this particular piece of wire in a church parking lot where he searched for fool's gold.

For a moment, he thought about Ruby. For a moment, he wondered if perhaps he should let her go with his father. Maybe she would find healing there, wherever they were going. Maybe the doctor was right. Who was he to keep her from that?

But none of it felt right. None of it. Not the sneaking or the stealing away or the secrecy. Certainly not the door in the side of a grave. No, his sister belonged here, with him.

Leo put the small lock pick in, but he realized that the keyhole was far too deep for his short piece of wire. Still, he probed the sides of the hole again, scraping with the pick for any notches, any edges. In every lock he had ever picked there was space and emptiness, but there was also a crucial encounter, when he picked up on the location of the mechanism. After that always came the slightest pressure followed by a reluctant giving in, a release.

Snap.

His last pick had broken.

He pounded his palms against the rock. He pushed. He shouted Ruby's name. He fell to his knees, leaning his back against the stone.

"Ruby!" he shouted one last time, putting his face in his hands and weeping. How could his father do this?

Every good thing was gone. The shadows that lined Saint Louis Cemetery No. 1 gathered around him like pools of black water, bottomless, insatiable.

Time did not exist there in those middle-of-the-night hours, and whether that was a product of Leo's imagination or something Marie had left him with, no one will ever know. But if he'd worn a watch he might have seen the second hand stop for what would normally have been minutes, hours. Perhaps he even would have seen it tick backward, reaching to some ancient beginning. And he would have seen the minute hand dance forward, unfettered by any normal kind of passing. This is what grief will do, and loss. Time stumbles under the weight of deep sadness.

Leo sat there, the stone hard against his backbone, until the eastern sky began to lighten. Eventually he stood, the numbness upon him again. He stared at the tomb he had slept against, the tomb with the square keyhole in it. He saw a small plaque.

This Greek revival tomb is the reputed burial place of Marie Laveau.

He stared at it for a long time.

Marie.

He turned and walked to the gate of Saint Louis Cemetery No. 1. It was still open, so he squeezed sideways through the gap. He didn't care anymore if anyone saw him. He could see a man in a house across the street making coffee in his kitchen. Leo wondered what the man would think if he looked out and saw him. Would he think Leo was a boy, or a ghost?

Leo walked back the way he had come, staring at the cracks in the sidewalks, noticing for the first time how their crooked winding was the same shape as the lock picks he had snapped. The dim stars faded and the streetlights blinked out and the morning had nearly arrived in full when he turned down the sidewalk to his father's house. He walked up to the front door and walked inside. He did not lock the door behind him.

Up three flights of stairs to the top floor of the house, to Ruby's room. There, he fell asleep in her bed and dreamed of her. The two of them ran and ran, always through a never-ending city, always through alleys and side streets and the dark, dank basements of abandoned warehouses. But no matter where they went, there was always the sound of footsteps trailing behind or tapping lightly on the floor above them. When he and Ruby finally left their pursuers behind, they came out into the light, only to find Marie standing there, a stern look on her beautiful face.

He woke to the sound of his mother coming into the house.

"Amos!" she shouted in a hesitant voice, not wanting to come inside without an invitation, or at least an acknowledgment. The two of them had created very separate lives, and there was no longer that familiar freedom of simply walking into the other's house without knocking first.

"Amos!" she shouted again, and Leo did not have the heart to go to her, not yet. He could tell she was very worried. His father never left the house unlocked, and he never went anywhere early in the morning. He was a late-night kind of guy, one who rubbed his eyes and complained about the brightness of 9:00 a.m. while tightening the shades.

"Leo!" his mother shouted, and this time her voice had an edge of panic. "Is anyone here?"

He tried to shout back to her, but at his first attempt his voice came out in the sound of a sob.

Ruby, he wondered, *where have you gone?*

He took another breath, cleared his throat, and tried again. His throat ached from crying.

"Mom!"

He heard her footsteps dancing up the stairs. They were light, barely touching each step. She pushed open the door, and there was worry on her face. When she saw him, the worry fled, but only for a moment, because she saw the look on his face and the empty space in Ruby's bed.

"Ruby?" she asked. That was all, one word. Oh, the power of individual words, the power of individual names!

Leo shook his head. "She's gone," he said, putting his face in his hands.

Outside the window, he could hear the birds singing.

His mother sat down on the floor beside him. It was as if she had been expecting this all along, and now that it had happened, some kind of unnatural calm (or shock) had settled on her, stifling her. It seemed to take all of her effort simply to speak.

"Gone?" she asked.

"He took her," Leo whispered.

"Where?" she asked. "Leo, where did he take her?"

Leo looked up in his mother's face. "I don't know," he said. "I don't know."

"What do you mean, you don't know?"

Leo shrugged, an almost indifferent motion, but a solitary tear made a shiny path down his cheek.

"I don't know," he said again. "He locked me in the closet. I got out. I tried to follow them."

All the weariness from the night before came over him and he closed his eyes. His mother was here now. She would take care of everything. She would know how to find Ruby. She would be able to bring her back. He opened his eyes and looked up at her. She seemed to be rising up out of deep water, coming back to life.

"He didn't take the car," she said, her voice picking up speed. "Did he call a cab?"

Leo shook his head and said the same three sentences again. "He locked me in the closet. I got out. I tried to follow them."

It was the only thing he would ever tell her about that evening. It was the only thing he would later tell the police when they questioned him. It was his attempt to block out everything else he had seen, everything else that he did not understand.

Leo couldn't bring himself to tell anyone anything more. Besides, what had he seen? Nothing, really. A strange woman hovering over a dying fire. His father holding his sister, their backs to him. Where they went from there, well, he hadn't actually seen anything. He'd only heard the deep echo of a boulder crashing against another boulder, the primal turning of an ancient key. He'd seen nothing.

He didn't think his mother would believe him if he told her

what he thought had happened, that his father had carried his sister through a doorway into a crypt opened by a beautiful black woman named Marie, probably the same Marie whose name was on that very grave. No one would believe him. He barely believed himself.

"He won't be far," his mother said, jumping back to her feet and moving for the door.

"Mom, he left hours ago. Last night. A long time ago."

She stopped, so easily deflated, and grabbed on to the door frame. She leaned against it as if trying to hold up the house, a structure that threatened to fall in on itself.

"Leo," she said again, this time not looking for an answer, simply looking for someone who would listen to her ask the question again. "Where did he take her?"

8

THE CHILD DRIFTED close to death.

The air felt suddenly cooler as her father carried her into a deep darkness, away from the small fire. He stood there for a moment. Pitch-black. Not a sight, not a sound. It was the darkness that lives inside holes or endless caves. She heard and felt a grating sort of crash, like a landslide but without the gradual beginning and ending. The sound was abrupt and final. She tried to lift her hand to her face. She almost had to touch her eyes to prove to herself that they were open. The darkness was a tangible object that could be touched and tasted. She breathed in the darkness like air, and it left a coating on her tongue. The darkness transformed into a Person that whispered things to her in a language she didn't understand.

Darkness filled the space the same way water does, or smoke.

The child wondered if she had gone blind. Her father began to walk. She swayed back and forth in his uneven rhythm and peeked in the direction they were going. A pinpoint of light existed far in the distance, like a single star in a vast sky. She laid her head against her father's chest and drifted off.

Time passed. Days? Weeks? There was constant movement and a long, straight road, the only road. It was dirt, interrupted occasionally by the breaking through of a large rock, and besides those breakthroughs the road was packed firm and flat and level, as if a hundred million people had traveled that way before her, made the dirt hard as concrete. There were glimpses of small, abandoned houses with spaces for windows or doors but nothing in them, like faces with eyes and mouths wide open. When she opened her own eyes at dusk or at dawn, when the light wasn't so bright, she could see a city far in the distance, rising above the trees in the direction the road was taking them.

The sky was always some shade of red.

It was during this journey that her father started talking to himself, a whispering kind of mumble clear enough that some-times she thought he was waiting for her to reply. The sound of his voice made her feel more alone, not less, and she wished he would stop. She knew she was dying. At five years old, she wouldn't have been able to tell you that (she didn't know the words for it), but she felt a gradual erosion, a slow passing away of something deep inside her, something crucial.

The beautiful part of the sadness was that she did not know enough to be afraid of death. Her mind was not haunted with visions of angels and demons; there were no images of golden streets or bottomless pits of fire; there was no judgment or fear or uncertainty. To her, at that young age, death meant relief, hope for an easy breath, a dissipating fever, and she did not resist its coming.

But her father did. He resisted her death with every ounce of his being so that even when she gave up, his will kept her going.

"No, no, no," he whispered. "Now's not the time. We're almost Over There, almost Over There. She'll be okay. And then . . . and then . . . you'll see."

He panted the words as if they were breath itself, and the black bag he carried banged against her leg. He argued with someone who wasn't there. She didn't know where they were going, and as they walked farther and farther along the road, she realized her father didn't know either.

"The tall building in the middle of the city," he mumbled. "Put it there. 'You will find all you need'—that's what the doctor said. 'You will find all you need.'"

He spat at the ground, anger increasing his pace. They walked always until the red light in the sky grew dark, and her father would carry her a short distance into the woods and rest her back against a tree. He piled up dead leaves and the soft boughs of evergreens and laid her in the mound it made. The smell of earth and leaves and rich soil hugged her as her father laid fresh greens over the top of her.

"To keep her warm," he muttered. "To keep her warm. And if she doesn't move we'll make it. If she lies still and rests, everything will be okay."

He disappeared into the woods, leaving behind a complete stillness that sometimes made the child wonder if she had died or if it was all a dream and she would wake up in her bed on the third floor of her father's house in New Orleans, warm rays of sunlight falling through the window, birds singing out on the ledge, her mother walking into the room, picking her up, taking her home. Her brother. Yes, her brother. Wonderful Leo. The bright, happy boy who listened to her.

Ever since they went through the door the world felt empty. There was no other way of saying it. They didn't cross paths with anyone else. They never even saw animals or insects. The sky was the same red quality all the time, the only difference being that it would brighten and fade as day came and went. Now a fiery red like orange embers, now a dull red like a sunset, now a crimson red, the color of the stripes in the woman's headscarf. The woman she had seen over her father's shoulder as they walked into the darkness.

Her father returned carrying two handfuls of wild berries. They were the shape of blueberries but tart, and they filled her up like a loaf of bread. She only ever ate two or three before falling asleep, but as she drifted off she could hear the voice of her father droning on and on.

"To the city. We have to make it to the city. Doesn't make sense. We're surrounded by trees now—here would be the place to plant it. But not here. Not now. In the city. Has to be. Wherever that is."

One night she woke up. They had not gone as far from the road that night. She heard a whooshing sound that reminded her of the cars driving past her father's house in New Orleans. The sound started from far away, a gentle shushing, and it grew closer, closer, and finally it raced past. Once, she thought she saw something that went with the sound, perhaps what was making the sound, and it was a movement, a glimmer of light and dark.

She woke up another time during the day to find that her father had grown weary and lain down in the middle of the road. She was facedown on top of him. The bag stood beside them, slightly open, and she could see the bright green, the brilliant white. Her father slept, his mouth wide open, and she took in the stillness around her. She tried to move off of him, to stand up, but when she adjusted her weight, he stirred, so she decided not to try to get up. She waited there, lying on top of her sleeping father, watching the small breeze move the leaves on the trees. She could hear his heart beating.

There was no one around, no other person. She thought they might be the last two people. Or the first two.

"The tallest building," her father muttered in his sleep. "The center of the city."

Her conscious moments became fewer and farther between. When they had first entered, she felt better, as if the air there was helping her recover her strength. But it was a short-lived recovery. Soon she was wheezing again, feverish and weak.

She opened her eyes to find they had arrived in the city. It was a large city, one that could hold far more people than she was seeing. Ten-story buildings rose around them. Thirty-story buildings gathered themselves and dashed upward. They passed warehouses and train stations and large universities, all empty. They walked through back alleyways and climbed to the top of apartment buildings so that her father could look out over the city. So few people. A handful. Or that is how it appeared.

But she soon realized there were people everywhere if you knew where to look. In the panes of glass, for instance, when the light wasn't glaring off, there were faces watching them. And at the top edge of every flat-topped building, she could see people peeking down at them. She saw them at the back of every alley, standing straight in the shadows.

It was sometime in the afternoon, and the light was beginning to fade. The shadows grew long, stretching out in front of them, running away. That's when they saw one old woman sitting in a rocking chair on the front porch of an old row home, leaning forward and back, forward and back. The chair whined when she came forward. The porch had iron rails, and the house was mostly made up of tan bricks with dark brown trim. It stretched up a full three floors.

The child's father stopped for a moment. When he spoke, his voice was tired and filled with snagging edges.

"I'm looking for the center," he said. "I'm trying to get to the center."

The woman laughed, the sound of a dozen crows cawing against the winter breeze.

"Aren't we all?" she managed to gasp out before laughing again. "Aren't we all!"

"Can you tell me which way to go?" he asked.

She nodded. "Keep going. Just keep walking." She spat on the porch in disgust. "But get off the street before dark."

"What happens after dark?" her father asked.

The old woman's face changed. She started to speak, then shook her head.

"What happens?" he asked again.

She laughed, but this time it was a dry, humorless laugh. She stood gingerly and walked to the door.

"Trust me," she muttered over her shoulder. "It's getting dark. The Frenzies come out at night. Get out of the streets."

She walked into her house.

"Frenzies?" her father called out. "What are Frenzies?"

The door slammed on them, but his question was answered moments later, with what first sounded like rushing water, a lot of it. The child listened hard. Her father held his breath. They stood there in the middle of an empty street, in the middle of a quiet yet somehow full city, listening. The rushing clarified as it grew closer, splitting into individual sounds that she soon realized were people shouting. Wood splintering. Glass shattering.

"Oh my," her father said, walking as fast as he could, a movement that turned into a kind of trot. The girl's head banged against his shoulder, and the heavy bag bumped their legs as he scooted along, faster and faster. He stumbled but didn't fall. She heard a terrible scream come from all the sound, and terror rendered her suddenly very awake.

"Can you run?" her father whimpered, and she realized he was talking to her.

"I . . . I don't know," she replied, her voice scratchy from not using it.

Behind them, the screaming and breaking turned onto their street. Her father spun into an alley and put her on her own two feet. Her knees wobbled.

"Come," he said. "Hurry."

They ran together farther into the dark alley, her father dragging her and the bag. They climbed over old boxes and beams. There were boards with nails sticking out and small piles of brick and stone. Broken glass was hidden in the dark. The alley dead-ended, but there was a black door in the side of one of the tall buildings that flanked the alley.

"Hey!" a voice called from the street and down the alley. "Who's that?"

The girl knew they were talking about her father. About her.

"Come, Ruby. Hurry."

Her father pushed open the door and they stumbled into the darkness. He blindly searched for a light, sweeping his hands in large arcs around the wall, and there was a switch that turned on a single, naked bulb hanging down from the ceiling by its cord. The room was full of junk. Her father managed to wedge the door in place with boards, then piled more and more things in front of it.

Pounding. Fists on the metal. An iron bar breaking through the narrow strip of glass in the door, and crazed eyes and fists trying to come in, but the door would not budge, and the opening was too small.

More banging. Her father grabbed her and the bag, scooped them both up, and ran farther into the building, following hallways and stairways, always up, always away.

So that was a Frenzy, she thought as she passed out.

When she came to, she was on the roof of a building. The sky faded as she sat there. It was the highest building yet, and her father wandered around the edge of it, staring off into the distance, mumbling to himself before finally coming and sitting beside her. He seemed nearly as weak as she felt. She thought he must be exhausted—he had carried her all that way, and they lived only on the berries he had found in the woods or strange scraps they found in the alleys.

There were no suburbs—she was close enough to the edge that she could look out over the city in the direction they had come from. The forest grew right up to the edge of the buildings. There were no other streets outside the city apart from the dirt road they had walked in on, and that was a thin, straight sliver through the woods, like a thread pulled tight. She thought she saw something moving along the road, and she sat up straighter. She was sure of it. A cloud of dust rose far in the distance, growing ever closer.

Her father saw it too. She saw it reflected in his eyes.

But before they could see what caused the cloud, they heard the most terrible noise: screaming and moaning and shouting, all coming from that cloud. She realized these were the glimmering shadows and light she had seen a few nights before. They were in one long, streaming group, like runners in a race, and when they arrived at the city they didn't stop—they kept on going. The whooshing sound was loud and flooded past the base of the building on which she stood with her father. She thought the building might collapse under the force of their passing. The whole red sky trembled.

"There!" he gasped. "Yes. Yes. I see it now! I see it."

He picked her up, snatched up the black bag, and ran-stumbled to the stairwell. Her body jarred against his, as if they were wrestling. He repeated the same words to himself, a spell or a mantra, and his voice echoed through the stairwell, lulling her to sleep.

"The tall building. The tall building. The tall building."

9

RUBY WOKE UP ALONE, in a strange place, and two things drew her attention. First of all, she felt a pain in the tip of her right ring finger. When she looked at it, she saw a tiny red dot, like the hole a splinter leaves behind. But there was also something else: the most glorious smell.

"Daddy?" she whispered. "Daddy?"

Dim red light filtered through constellations of dust specks. She was in a large, dark building. The walls looked to be made of brick. The ceilings and floors were bare wood planks. The entire floor she was on was empty—she could see from one end to the other, deep into the shadows. Except in the middle. There was something solid in the middle of the room.

She felt energized. She stood up and walked. She took a deep breath—even in all that dust, her breathing was clean and clear. In the middle of the room, her bare feet came down on broken, brittle leaves and they crunched under her as she walked. It was strange to her, these leaves inside the building, and soon she realized that was where the smell was coming from—the leaves. Ruby took another deep breath and found her energy came from the leaves. She felt health moving through her veins.

She got down on her hands and knees and stuck her nose right against the floor, against the precious dust of crumbled leaves, and took a deep breath. Instead of clogging her nose, it somehow expanded her airways. She felt like she could run a hundred miles. She felt like she could fly if she tried.

Ruby stood and walked closer to the thing in the middle of the room. It was round, so thick that she would have had to hold hands with three or four friends in order to reach all the way around it, and it stretched from the floor to the ceiling. It looked like the outside of a powdered piece of chocolate, brown and dusty and warm. She touched it. The surface was leathery and gave way like a very firm sponge.

It was the trunk of a massive tree, one that had grown up through the floor, but the ceiling had not been able to stop it. She peered through the ceiling where the boards had split and cracked to make room, and she could see the tree had already grown through two or three more floors. She wanted to see how far up it went, so she ran to the edge of the room and found a stairwell.

The next level was empty too except for the tree growing up through it, and at each level the trunk grew smaller. She went up two floors before seeing branches split off from the main trunk. She ran over to one and felt the silky leaves. She plucked one off and it broke in her hands, fragile and tender. A substance like aloe oozed out, and the smell filled her with a heady kind of joy, a feeling that nothing would go wrong ever again. She licked it, and it satisfied her hunger immediately. She knew she was cured in the way a child who wakes up one morning after an extended period of sickness somehow knows they have turned the corner.

She sat down with her back against the tree, and she slipped into the deepest sleep she had ever experienced. A dream came and it felt thick and slow, the way dreams sometimes will. In her dream, a breeze blew through the building, rustling the leaves. That's when she saw the fruit—it had been invisible to her at first because it was the same color as the leaves, but it moved differently in the wind. Now that she saw it, she realized it was everywhere in various shapes and sizes.

"Who are you?" a voice asked from one of the shadowy corners of the building.

"I'm Ruby," she said in her little girl voice, and in the midst of that empty floor and in the midst of that massive tree, her voice sounded far away and tiny. Lost.

"Ruby," the voice said, tasting the word. "Ruby. That's a beautiful name. You can call me B."

A woman came out of the shadows. A beautiful, small woman with reddish-brown hair and soft features. She looked so kind and caring. Without thinking twice about it, Ruby ran to her around the tree, dust clouding up at each step. She threw herself into the arms of the woman.

"I don't know where my dad is," she said, tears choking her voice, and in her dream this was suddenly very concerning, the absence of her father. "I don't know where he is."

"Oh, it's okay," B said, holding her close, stroking her forehead. "It's okay."

Ruby looked up into her face, a round tear falling from each of her eyes. "I like you," she said.

"I like you too," the woman said. "Are you feeling better? You were very sick."

Ruby nodded. "I feel good."

"Of course you do. Better than good."

B looked around, holding Ruby at arm's length while bending down and talking to her at her height.

"It's the tree," she whispered. "Isn't it wonderful?"

Ruby nodded. A thought came to her then, from some far-away place, that this might not be a dream. In the uncertainty, she felt like she might float away, cease to exist. She joined her hands in front of her, needing to hold on to something.

But there was still the tree. Being reminded of it made her reach up for another leaf, which she broke off. The tree was so full of sap that when she pulled the leaf away from its stem, a long string of it drooped along. Ruby licked the sap off of her fingers, feeling more alive, more energized by the second. She broke the leaf in half and licked the sap again, and before she knew what she was doing, she had stuck the entire leaf in her mouth and was munching on it like a salad. It had a green taste to it, but it was also sweet. She closed her eyes and savored each chew.

"It's wonderful," Ruby repeated.

"Have you tried the fruit yet?" the woman asked, reaching up and plucking a piece from one of the lower branches.

Ruby shook her head. No, she hadn't.

The woman held the fruit in between them and, separated from the tree, it took on a new appearance. While hanging in the tree it had looked shiny and solid, but up close Ruby realized she could see inside of it. She saw strange things swirling around inside the fruit, visions of things that had happened to her. She saw her bedroom in her father's house! She saw the backyard of azaleas, her brother Leo chasing her down the rows!

"Leo," she said quietly. In what dream had she had a brother? In what world?

"Did you know the fruit of this tree grows in twelve different seasons?" the woman asked her. "When one of the types begins to drop, another type begins to grow. They don't all grow at once, but they do overlap—that's why you see three or four different kinds of fruit in this one tree."

The woman shook her head in awe, and Ruby could tell that she found the tree fascinating.

"Have you ever eaten your dreams?" the woman asked, lifting the fruit to her mouth and taking a large bite. Juice dripped down onto her chin, and she closed her eyes, seemingly overwhelmed with delight at the taste of the fruit.

Ruby reached for a piece that hung heavy on a branch close to her head. She plucked it off and looked at it, looked inside it. She saw visions of her mother and her brother and a lady standing with her father in Saint Louis Cemetery No. 1. Her small, five-year-old hand held that large piece of fruit, and it smelled wonderful. She had never wanted to do anything more than eat that fruit.

Ruby stopped, staring at the fruit. The woman's voice was so clear, so present. It couldn't be a dream.

Could it?

Ruby felt something strange well up inside of her, another new feeling: it was the sense that she wanted to do something she should not do. But that wasn't new—she had often felt that. The new sensation was her awareness of it, and her deep desire to disobey for the sake of disobedience. She wanted to be sneaky. She stared at the woman for encouragement.

The woman nodded, her eyes beckoning Ruby to take a bite. "Go ahead," she said. "There's nothing to be afraid of."

As if to illustrate this, the woman reached for another piece of fruit and plucked it from the tree. The sap hung in a draping string from the tree to the stem of the fruit. But this time, when the beautiful woman lifted the piece of fruit to her lips, Ruby noticed something about her that made her drop her own piece to the dusty floor.

The woman's teeth, they didn't look like normal teeth. They were pointed instead of flat, like the teeth of a shark, and her mouth opened farther than it should. This time she didn't take a bite of the fruit—she closed her eyes and put the entire thing in her mouth, devoured it, the way a snake consumes an animal that at first appears much too big for it.

Ruby took a few steps back.

The woman opened her eyes, and they were deep pools. She looked at Ruby, and when she saw the child's reaction to how she had eaten the fruit, her voice swelled with alarm.

"Oh, child, I'm so sorry," she said, lifting her arm and using her sleeve to clean the light green sap from the corners of her mouth. She seemed embarrassed, as though Ruby had caught her doing something improper, like talking with her mouth full or picking her nose.

"I'm sorry," she said again. "Did I frighten you?"

Ruby nodded, taking another step back. This was not a dream. This was real, and it was a nightmare.

"There's nothing to be afraid of. Go ahead, take a piece."

For a moment Ruby didn't move. On the one side, there was the absence of her father and the presence of what appeared to be a kind, caring woman. Yet there was something about this woman that felt horrid—her sharp teeth and the way she ate with such greed. But Ruby liked how the leaf had made her feel. She liked feeling healthy. She enjoyed it. She imagined the fruit would be like that, perhaps even more so.

Ruby looked down at the piece of fruit she had dropped on the floor. It was dusty, so she picked it up and rubbed it off, but already it had grown too soft, and as she rubbed it the skin pulled back and the fruit fell apart in her hands. Within moments the inside of it had blackened and she dropped it back down to the floor. Ruby watched as it decayed before her eyes, turning to dust. All that dust. She became aware of something she hadn't heard before: a soft thudding sound. It wasn't happening very often, which is perhaps why had she hadn't noticed it, but there, in the silence of indecision, she heard it off to her right. She looked and watched as another piece of fruit fell and turned to dust in less than a minute.

"You can't keep it, you know," the woman whispered. "It won't last. Otherwise we could take it from here by the truckload and give it to everyone outside. Everyone could feel this way! But it won't keep. We've tried everything. And they destroy the tree every time it grows out there. Now go on. Eat."

Ruby nodded, reached above her, and plucked another piece. She took a deep breath. What was it inside of her that held back? She raised the fruit and opened her mouth, pushing through the uncertainty.

"Ruby!" a different voice shouted. "No!"

It was the voice of her father.

PART 3

the
curtain

Sometimes it seemed to him that his life was delicate as a dandelion. One little puff from any direction, and it was blown to bits.

KATHERINE PATERSON,
BRIDGE TO TERABITHIA

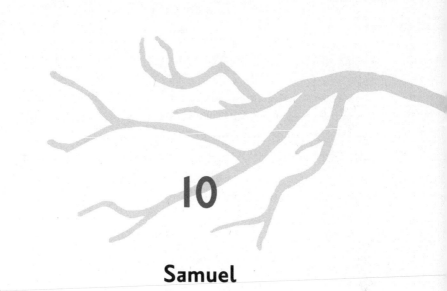

10

Samuel

I FEEL LIKE I'VE BARELY BREATHED since Mr. Henry started the story. When he finally pauses, I wonder if he's had me in some kind of a spell. Maybe he kept me transfixed so he could go upstairs and steal the sword. I look at the window and it's nearly dark out, one of those snowy winter nights when you're glad to be inside. The dusk is a purplish-gray and the snow howls against the house, a beast checking for any way inside. My coffee is cold.

"You're probably wondering what happened to that little girl," Mr. Henry says with a serious look on his face.

"Actually, I was wondering what happened to the story you were going to tell me about Abra," I say, staring at him for a moment before standing and taking our empty mugs into the kitchen for a refill. Despite my sarcasm, I have to admit that he has drawn me in. I pour myself another cup and steady my breath. I have to push the fear back down. I pour him another cup.

I stay for an extra minute in the kitchen, wondering if I should slip out the back door and make a run for it. So to speak. Could Mr. Henry be gaining my friendship only to let me down at the end? Fear is a physical thing and it rises inside of me, pushing upward from my gut and into my throat, threatening to choke me, threatening to take away my breath.

"Fear is a funny thing," he says, his voice coming to me from where he sits at the table. For a moment I think he's talking to himself. "It can make you freeze up, or it can make you run faster."

I wonder if he can read my mind. It feels like, in all of this, he is appraising me. I know he's one of them. But is he a Mr. Jinn or a Mr. Tennin? Is he shadow or light?

"When it came to fear, I was always a runner," I say loudly, still in the kitchen.

I take a deep breath. I walk back to him with the two steaming mugs. I sit down and stare at Mr. Henry.

"So, the city where the man took his child. That is Over There?"

Mr. Henry shakes his head harshly while taking a sip of too-hot coffee. "No, no. Absolutely not. The city is only the Edge of Over There, although many who find their way there don't realize it."

"I don't understand. I'm not going to pretend I do."

He smiles. "You will, when the story is over. You'll understand more than you ever have."

"How did Abra get involved with this?" I ask.

"Well, as I said, Ruby and her father walked through the grave of Marie Laveau four years before the Tree appeared here in Deen, four years before you fought the Amarok. Four years before you killed Jinn."

"It wasn't really me," I said.

He frowned. "Then, after all that, another four years passed. By then, you and Abra were sixteen."

"By then, the little girl, Ruby, must have been . . ."

"Yes, eight long years had passed since Amos had taken her and the Tree through the grave. She was thirteen years old."

"And Leo . . . "

"Eighteen years old. He never stopped trying to find a way into the grave of Marie Laveau. But he had nearly lost hope."

I stare out the window into the snow. I wish I could be more critical of Ruby's father. I wish I could despise Amos for running away with his child. But I can't. I would have done the same with my mother all those long years ago, if I'd been given the choice. I would have taken her through whatever door I needed to, if her healing lay on the other side.

"Hope." Mr. Henry says the word quietly, as if even the sound of it is fragile. "Hope can last a long time, longer than we expect or imagine. Even after you think it's gone, the smallest of things can bring it back."

"They lived in the city all that time?" I ask. "At the Edge of Over There? For eight years?"

"For eight long years, yes, they did. And much happened during that time. But first, Abra's story."

I nod. The wind has begun to howl.

II

ABRA COULD ALMOST FEEL THE RAIN, even though it was only the dream again. She was surrounded by the same old leaves and branches, details she recognized easily now that she had been having the dream off and on for nearly four years. The drops clattered down through them, all around her. She was up in the tree again, up in its highest branches, and despite her familiarity with this particular dream, she was still afraid. She clung to the branch she was on, a branch much too thin to hold her. It broke, and she fell. She grabbed for anything she could hold on to, eventually finding another branch much too thin to hold her for long. It was the same branch she always grabbed. She dangled there, looking down at the ground far below.

She watched a huge wolf-like creature pick up the small girl in its jaws and toss her aside. She watched as the boy grabbed on to a small sword, cried out in pain before swinging it again and again at the wolf. She watched as the sword found its mark and the huge creature listed to the side like a boat preparing to sink. When the creature fell, the boy fell.

She twisted and turned where she hung from the branch,

wondering if the girl was okay. Wondering if she could do something differently this time, but it was always the same. That's when the streak of light came, and a man, or something in the shape of a man, knelt beside the girl. He put his hands on her head and closed his eyes, and Abra knew that the man was bringing the girl back to life.

She could hear through the girl's ears again. She was still dangling there in the air; she was still feeling the soft patter of rain on her head and bare arms; she could still feel the thin branch slipping ever so slowly from her grasp. But there it was: her hearing was the girl's, and she heard the man begin to whisper.

"Abra, this is very important. I have a few things I need to tell you . . ."

But again, she fell.

I should have hit the ground by now, she thought. And just as she remembered this thought always came to her in this dream, she looked down, and there was the ground coming up at her, and she took a sharp breath.

She woke up.

She was not hanging from a tree. There was no rain falling on her head. There was no Amarok, no boy, no man speaking into her ear. It was only her, alone in her bed while the dim, early morning light crept up over the eastern horizon. She could tell it would be another cold winter day. She tried to enjoy the warmth under her covers, but the images wouldn't go away.

The man in her dream had been Mr. Tennin.

He had saved her life.

What had he been trying to tell her?

She had dreamed the dream on an almost monthly basis for

the last four years, ever since that first night in the hospital on the day the angels fell. It didn't surprise her. Nothing surprised her anymore.

This didn't mean everything was the same as it had always been.

Before the Amarok and the Tree of Life, everything about the valley had felt predictable. She went to school. She worked around the farm. There was baseball and fireflies and bike riding all summer. There was the church at the end of Sam's lane. There were the mountains rising up on either side, solid and unmoving.

But since the Tree, everything felt tenuous, as if the slightest movement could change everything. It was like holding a soap bubble in the palm of her hand. The reality she saw felt thin and breakable, a film of ice covering a deep, still pool. Her eyes had been opened to another layer of reality, and she spent those weeks and months looking for signs of the other world, waiting for it to break through.

Four years is a long time. A northern red oak, for example, grows more than two feet per year. That's eight feet of living bark and twigs and leaves shooting for the sky. A red maple grows three to five feet per year—that's twenty feet in four years. A weeping willow can stand at the edge of a pond, its wispy tendrils flowing, and grow up to thirty-two feet in four years.

A child. A child can become a young adult in four years. A friendship can grow faster than trees or vanish altogether in that time. The world is always changing all around us, molecules shifting from this to that, so that in four years, what is recognizable? What could possibly remain the same under the erosion of so much flowing time?

On one particular day, after those four long years had passed, Abra found herself lying on her bed after school, the heavy sword beside her, pressing down the blankets. You would barely recognize her if you saw her lying there on her stomach, legs crossed and propped up behind her. Her hair was longer and straighter. Her form had somehow become less awkward, the way a foal grows into its stride. She rolled over and her blue eyes stared at the ceiling. She thought about the dream that wouldn't go away. She thought, for the first time in a long time, about Sam. She thought about all that had happened that summer. And she was filled with a familiar, aching disappointment.

Of all the things she remembered about that day when the angels fell, the thing she recalled with the most detail was the final sentence Mr. Jinn had said, smirking.

"And you," he said, staring deep into her eyes, looking for something. "You have only just begun."

He had seemed to utter those words like a curse, but they filled her like a promise. She reached over and gripped the sword beside her on the bed, and it fit her hand like the right puzzle piece.

When everything happened, she had felt suddenly crucial. She had a feeling that she was something more (and oh how silly it seems for her to even think these words), that she was Mr. Tennin's replacement, given the responsibility to destroy the Tree of Life whenever and wherever it appeared.

Replacing an angel.

Abra Miller.

The idea had filled her with purpose, but it seemed ridiculous four years later, in the light of day. She was still only a teenager, after all, and how could she take over a task of such massive importance?

She wandered over to the window, staring aimlessly in the direction of the eastern mountain range.

That's when she saw the woman.

It was a fair distance from her window to the road, but even from there something intrigued her about the woman. First of all, Abra couldn't remember the last person who had walked up Kincade Road. She lived a long way from town, and unless you were going to her house or Sam's house, there was no other reason to go out that road.

She looked closer. The woman wore a tan jacket over a light blue dress. She had brown hair, and it rustled in the cold breeze. But that wasn't what got Abra's attention.

"Mrs. Chambers?" she whispered to herself, because the woman she saw on the other side of the road looked exactly like Sam's mom. His mom, who had died when lightning struck the oak tree all those years ago.

She dropped everything and ran out of the house without even putting on her coat. She sprinted down the lane—it was the kind of run where she nearly outran herself, where every stride felt like it might lead to a fall. Her feet pounded all the way to the stone road, and the cold swept down, stinging her eyes and her ears and her nose. It was so cold.

She stopped, panting the icy air into her aching lungs. She looked both ways, peering into the woods that stood dark against the drab grays and tans of winter. There hadn't been any snow recently, but the air smelled crisp and the clouds were low and flat with no blue sky to be seen.

Who was that woman? Where had she gone?

She remembered, as if out of nowhere, the woman she had seen in Sam's room in the hospital that first night. She shivered again as memories of her came rushing back. Abra had forgotten the terror on Sam's face as he pushed away from her. She had forgotten the way the woman had sniffed as if seeking out her prey. She had forgotten the ice-cold touch of the woman's hand on her shoulder.

And for the first time in a long time, she remembered the initials signed at the bottom of the note on her hospital tray.

KN.

For the next four months, from winter into spring, Abra felt a renewed sense of purpose, and she spent every spare minute studying the atlas and reading the notes written in Mr. Tennin's handwriting. She took long, slow walks, looking for the lady who looked like Sam's mother. Her parents worried about her, gave her more chores to keep her outside, but she did them quickly and retreated to her room. Even when spring arrived, Abra's favorite season of the year, she came home from school and walked straight past the new blooms peeking up through the wet ground. Daffodils and tulips held nothing for her. Her sixteenth birthday came and went.

She was distracted at school. Teachers taught and she continued to get decent grades, but her mind went round and round. She desperately wanted to know her role with the sword or how she would find the next Tree of Life. The responsibility of her mission became heavier, and she turned increasingly inward, became more and more obsessed with the atlas and the notes. She thought of all that was at stake.

The Tree might be growing, and there was no one but her to stop it.

One week after high school let out for the summer, Abra pushed her blonde hair behind her ears and stood by one of her bedroom windows, staring out across the yard and beyond Kincade Road. If anyone had pulled up to the house at that moment, they would have seen her standing there, perfectly framed by the window, looking like an apparition mourning a long-ago life.

She didn't remember how she had ended up with the atlas and the notes and the sword, but Sam hadn't seemed interested in reclaiming them. She was frustrated and close to giving up. The forest was green and there was no sign of the fire. She marveled at how things can change, how the old empty spaces can be filled in.

That's when she saw the woman again, standing at the edge of the woods on the other side of the road.

A chill moved up and down Abra's back. She dropped everything and ran.

12

ABRA RACED DOWNSTAIRS. Should she call Sam? How could this woman be Sam's mother? Had someone miraculously saved a piece of fruit from the Tree of Life and brought her back? Had Sam done it?

She stopped in her tracks as that last thought sank in. Had Sam actually done it? Had he found another Tree of Life? In that moment, she realized why their friendship had crumbled so quickly after the incident of the Amarok. She couldn't trust him.

Her friendship with Sam had gone the way many friendships go after surviving something dramatic. For the first few months, there had been a surge of closeness. They spent every afternoon together scanning the book for new clues, things they may have missed. They took turns keeping the box with the atlas and Tennin's notes. She followed Sam to the dead Tree almost every afternoon, and they sat there in the remaining heat of summer, into the autumn. The charred forest watched them, welcomed them.

But as winter came and months passed, a year eased behind them, and then another, and a kind of coldness drifted in. It was the chill of shared doubt. Could it all have really happened? Could they actually have had a chance to bring Sam's mom back? And if so, why hadn't they seized the opportunity? The reasons they had done the things they had done became foggy. They stopped talking to each other in school, which is the easiest place for a friendship to fade because there are always plenty of other people around. You can convince yourself you're not avoiding someone—you're simply talking to other people. But she stopped riding her bike to his farm, and he stopped asking where she had been, and soon whatever they had between them drifted away, out of reach.

She couldn't go tell him now. He wouldn't believe her. Besides, she had deep, lingering doubts as well, because even though the woman looked exactly like Sam's mom, there was that other woman, the woman from the hospital. KN. Could this be her?

Abra was certain that once she got out into the yard, the woman wouldn't be there anymore, simply a product of her imagination or her intense recent focus on finding the next place where the Tree of Life would grow. But when she ran through the front door and onto the porch, the woman was still there, facing the house. The breeze pressed the dress against her body, something that made her seem even more real, more tangible. For a moment Abra hesitated, unsure of where this overwhelming sense of fear had come from, but she ran on, slowing to a walk as she approached the end of the lane.

Closer now. The woman still resembled Sam's mother, but there was also something about the way she stood there that didn't look like Sam's mother in the least. There was something powerful and sinister about her, as if she was in complete control of everything. The sun. The wind. The grass. Everything. She held her hands behind her back and stood up straight, rigid, like a tower. She glanced at Abra as she approached, and her face shifted into an expression that at first looked like a smirk but slid seamlessly into something more sympathetic.

It was the woman from the hospital. It was KN.

They stood there across the street from each other, and anyone driving up Kincade Road could have easily mistaken them for mother and daughter. They had fair features, round, button noses, and large eyes. Both had pink lips and rosy cheeks.

But if that same passerby would have waited and watched and looked closer, they also would have been struck by the opposite nature of the two, the same way something in a mirror can be the same image but reversed.

If you could look at the essence of Good in a mirror, would you see Good reversed, or would you see the essence of Evil?

The woman turned away from Abra and walked slowly north on Kincade Road, in the direction of Sam's house. Abra skittered across the street and followed, maintaining a safe distance. She wished she would have brought the sword. The woman bent over and plucked a white wildflower. Abra stopped. The woman started walking again, walking north, and Abra followed.

"So, you're the famous Abra," the woman said in a singsong voice. Her hair blew back behind her, though the wind didn't seem strong enough to cause that. Her dress, too, lifted slightly around her, giving her the appearance of floating instead of walking. She was the center of an invisible storm. "It's lovely to see you. Again."

Abra didn't reply.

"You don't have to say anything," the woman said. "It's okay. I know . . . I know."

"Who are you?" Abra asked, fighting an incredibly strong

urge to run back to her house, to run in any direction but the way this woman was walking, to run away.

"My name," the woman replied, then paused. "Yes, I do have a name. It's Koli. Koli Naal."

She laughed an absentminded laugh and plucked a white petal from the flower. She dropped it over her shoulder as she continued walking away. Abra watched the petal as it fell, spinning, disappearing into the tall grass.

"I have been away for so long," the woman said. "I have been very busy."

"How do you know who I am?" Abra asked, gathering her courage. She had found her way to the other side of the curtain—of that she was sure. This was not normal life in Deen. This had something to do with the Tree.

"You? The famous Abra? Abra the Amarok slayer? Abra, the one who brought Jinn low? Who doesn't know about Abra!"

Abra's fear was instantly accompanied by something else: pride. She hadn't disappeared off the radar! People knew what had happened—important people, people on the other side of the curtain—and she had a role to play. Not only that, but she was famous. Of course, she hadn't actually slain the Amarok; Sam had done that. And while she had thrown the sword at Mr. Jinn, some mysterious force had given it momentum. She never could have thrown it that far on her own.

Yet there seemed no reason to mention these things.

"Yes," Koli said. "I know you."

Her voice had lost its singsong quality. There was nothing light about it—it was all weight and gravity. Ominous. Koli stopped walking and knelt down, still facing away from Abra. She picked the flower petals from the flower faster, letting them fall, shredded. She plucked at the longer strands of grass. What made Abra shudder was that Koli didn't pick at things absent-mindedly, the way a child will pull out grass by the roots in entire fistfuls. No, Koli pulled at the grass and decimated the flower in a way that said she knew what she was doing. She was snapping life in half, and she would gladly continue doing so until there wasn't another piece of grass left on the planet. Not a single flower still holding its petals.

"Why are you here?" Abra asked quietly.

Koli smiled, and for a moment Abra wondered if she had misread this woman. Her smile went from mocking and de-meaning to something that at first appeared genuinely kind, sincerely happy. Koli tilted her head to the side, took a deep breath, and sighed, all in a way that communicated a sort of resignation, as if Abra had bested her already, so easily. Her body looked soft and welcoming, like that of a long-lost aunt, someone who would explain everything to her.

"There has been a problem," Koli said. When she spoke with that newly found kind voice, her beauty was almost overwhelming.

"What problem?" Abra managed to stutter.

"There is a door, a door that should never have been locked. But it has been locked. People are trapped on the other side, good people. A man by the name of Amos, for example, and his daughter Ruby. They have been there for many years. I need your help to unlock the door."

Abra sensed the lies in what Koli was saying—not the spe-cifics of the lies, but the sense of lies twisted up in truth, like strands of hair baked into bread.

"Where is it?" Abra asked.

"New Orleans," Koli whispered.

"Why do you need my help?"

"There was someone else who was helping us, someone else

who had a key to this door. But she is gone now, took the key with her. We can no longer get in, and the people in there can no longer get out. We need your help because you have the only other key."

"But I don't," Abra began, but an image of the sword flashed into her mind. Somehow, she knew that's what Koli was talking about. The sword was also a key?

"Yes, you know, don't you," Koli said. "You do have the key, though you didn't know it. That's the way with all the most important kinds of keys—we have them without even realizing it."

The resemblance flickered again in front of Abra's eyes, that strange similarity between Koli and Sam's mother. She remembered the night Mrs. Chambers had died, the storms that had come through. The lightning. She remembered Mr. Tennin's words.

Death is a gift.

A question floated up into Abra's mind, a question about why Koli looked so much like Sam's mom. She didn't think it was by accident. Had she somehow tried to look like her to draw Abra in? Was that even possible—could these things, these beings, change the way they looked? There was something odd going on, and it made Abra's insides twist and turn.

Abra looked up at Koli and wanted to tell her she wouldn't do it, she wouldn't unlock whatever door it was that Koli wanted unlocked. She wanted to tell her, but she couldn't speak. She couldn't open her mouth. Abra stood there and shook her head back and forth, and even though the words wouldn't come, she felt defiant and strong.

Koli approached Abra, one slow step after another. She had a puffed-up look as if she had taken in a deep breath and held it, her mouth open but no breath moving. Abra took a step back. Koli walked up to her and examined her face. She smiled, and her teeth . . . Maybe Abra simply hadn't noticed before, or maybe they changed in that moment, but suddenly her teeth were pointed, like miniature shark teeth, and her tongue had turned black.

"Unlock the door!" Koli screamed.

Abra jumped back and tripped over her own two feet. She raised her hands to protect herself—from what? A woman? A demon? She sat there in the grass, cringing, waiting, but the day had gone completely still. The breeze blew Abra's hair back, and she heard birds singing in the woods that lined the river. She looked up.

Koli was gone.

Abra walked back to the house. The sun was warmer, nearly hot, and the almost-knee-high cornstalks rustled, whispered in a million voices. They reminded her of warnings, of that little feeling you get when something isn't quite right. They also reminded her of the summer she had run with Sam through the field between his house and Mr. Jinn's, chasing the vultures.

The house was quiet when she returned. Her mom had gone out and her dad was working in the barn, and she felt both thankful for an empty house and scared that Koli would return. She couldn't get that image of Koli's teeth out of her mind, or the way she had screamed at her.

"Unlock the door!"

The words echoed in Abra's mind. Koli had sounded angry, but she had also sounded frustrated, as if she realized she couldn't force or trick Abra to do this one thing. Abra wondered why it was so important to her that she unlock the door and free the man and his daughter. It didn't seem like Koli would be particularly concerned about anyone's well-being unless it somehow served her own purpose, whatever that was.

Koli hadn't told her much. Abra didn't know exactly where this entrance was, or how to use the sword to unlock it. And would they be waiting right inside the door, like a lost puppy finally home, or would she have to go inside and bring them out? Or was she simply supposed to unlock the door, or the gate, or whatever it was, and leave it open?

Too many questions. The light inside the house was quiet and still, although the windows were open and a breeze rustled the curtains. Abra walked up the stairs slowly, thinking about all that the woman had told her. She didn't trust Koli. She believed the facts of what she had told her, and she was beautiful, but she was also terrifying and evil and definitely, definitely lying about something.

Abra went into her room. The atlas was in the middle of the floor, open. Had her mother found it? Had someone been in her room? She walked closer and got down on her knees. She leaned forward and stared at the page. It was a map of the southern half of Louisiana. The city of New Orleans had an old, worn number written beside it. #27. So it must have been one of the earlier sites of a Tree of Life. But something new was written right beside the #27.

It was another number, #69, circled and written in red. The Tree in Deen, the one she had killed four summers ago, was #68. Where had this new number come from? She glanced around, moved quickly to the door, and looked down the hall. Had someone been in there?

Had Koli Naal been in her room?

She was sure that number hadn't been there before, which

meant there was a new Tree of Life, and based on the map it was somewhere in or close to New Orleans.

Was someone already trying to possess it, or, even worse, had someone already eaten from it? How would she find it?

She saw an obvious connection between that strange woman wanting her to go to New Orleans and the Tree, but she had a lot of questions. There was only one place she knew to go for answers. The fair would be back in Deen, starting in four weeks. She had to find the three old women.

13

"DON'T STAY TOO LONG," her mother said in a pleading voice, biting her lip. She looked as though she might change her mind. "Don't wander around dark places on your own. Please?"

Abra nodded and forced a smile. "I won't be late, Mom. I promise."

"Okay," her mom said. She looked in the side-view mirror of the car and pulled away, into the slow-moving fair traffic gliding up and down Kincade Road.

Abra stared at a large puddle outside the fair entrance, and lights from the rides reflected in it like multicolored stars. She looked farther into the water and touched the surface with the toe of her shoe, and ripples sprinkled the light. She could almost believe that if she jumped into that tiny, shimmering pool, she'd be jumping into nothingness, the void between galaxies. The puddle was a portal to somewhere different, somewhere important.

She imagined floating through the curtain that separated normal, everyday life in Deen from what couldn't be easily seen. It had been four weeks since Koli Naal had told her she had to unlock the door, four weeks since she had seen the number written beside New Orleans in the atlas, open and in the center of her bedroom floor. And nothing at all interesting had happened since. How badly she wanted to know what she was supposed to do! How badly she wanted to see something miraculous, something extraordinary.

She couldn't get New Orleans out of her head. She had an uncle there, her mom's only brother, but he was much older than her mom and Abra had never met him. Every so often they received a handwritten letter from him, a New Orleans address scrawled in the return section of the envelope. Even his writing looked ancient, with its large, sloping loops and meticulous dottings and crossings. Abra would stare at the letter the whole way up the drive, wondering what this strange man had to say. It seemed odd that she could be connected to someone so intimately yet not even know what he looked like. But whenever she handed the letter to her mom, her mom would sigh, slit the envelope open quickly, skim the contents, and stuff the letter into her pocket.

She remembered the name on the envelope: Mr. M. L. Henry.

A few nights after the new number appeared in the atlas, Abra had nearly packed a bag and hitchhiked to New Orleans. She thought she might be able to stay with her uncle while she searched for the Tree. If she could find him. But reality settled in quickly—she knew she wouldn't get far. Her parents would find out about it, and they would track her down.

New Orleans! The distance between her and that city was mind-boggling, especially to someone who had never traveled more than fifty miles from her own small town. She knew the valley better than anyone—blindfold her, lead her into a field, spin her around, and uncover her eyes, and she'd know exactly where she was. But drive for an hour in any direction and it would all be new. New Orleans? The Tree might as well be growing on the moon.

She stood there staring into the puddle for a long time, thinking, and the fair music grew more and more distant in her mind. A group of kids pushed past her, one of them stepping in the puddle, splashing water on her jeans. No one fell into that sky of stars. There was no sudden passage to another universe. She sighed and followed the group of kids to the Deen fair entrance, her one wet toe leaving a strange track on the sidewalk.

Is this all there is? she wondered. *Is the world really only made up of what I can see?*

A girl at the back of the pack looked over her shoulder. "Abra?" she asked. "Is that you?"

Abra saw a girl about her age with reddish-brown hair pulled back into two braids. Her eyes were dark brown, and they immediately reminded Abra of the pools she had been looking in, both because of their depth and the way they reflected the lights from the fair. She didn't recognize her, which was strange, because in a town like Deen you usually recognized people. You certainly didn't know everyone, but most faces were familiar, especially someone your own age in a town where everyone went to the same school.

"Hey," Abra said hesitantly. "Do I . . . Do we know each other?"

"It's me, Beatrice!" the girl said, running to her and linking arms with her.

Abra fought the urge to pull away. "Hi, uh, Beatrice," she said, still searching the girl's face for something she recognized. It struck her as extremely odd how familiar this girl was pretending to be, when she couldn't remember ever seeing her before in her life.

"Stop that! You always call me B," the girl said in a bashful voice. "Everyone else does too. I'm going into the fair. You too?"

Abra nodded, still not sure what to say or do.

"Your friends are going inside," Abra warned the girl, motioning toward the group that had left her behind, hoping B would run off and leave her. But the longer Abra looked at her, the more she thought, yes, there might be something familiar about the girl, something in her eyes, and it was this something that kept Abra from telling the girl to get lost.

B waved at the group of kids dismissively. "That's okay. They don't like any of the good rides anyway."

The two girls walked through the admissions gate. They wandered the animal exhibits, and Abra secretly hoped B would leave her alone, go find her friends. The girl continued to give her an uneasy feeling, and Abra wanted to head down into the dark part of the fairgrounds. She was retracing the steps she had walked with Sam four summers before.

But as the two girls walked together, Abra found herself softening toward B. They both laughed at the chickens with the strange combs and reached in through iron bars to pet the calves' hard heads and down-soft sides. Slowly, gradually, something shifted in Abra. She began to hope B wouldn't leave her. She'd had no one to talk to for a long time, not like this, and the spring had stretched on long and lonely. After her exchange with Koli Naal, she had wanted more than anything to run to Sam's place and tell him what was going on. But she still didn't trust him. She didn't know if he would try to find the Tree for himself. The space between them felt impossible.

Before the two girls got too far into the fair, they were talking quickly like long-lost friends. Abra felt herself giving in to B's easygoing manner, even though she asked a lot of questions.

Abra was a loner, and B's loud, friendly personality fascinated her. She'd pepper Abra with surface-level questions like, "How old is your brother?" or "How long have you lived at the farm?" or "Do you have any pets?" Then she'd ask Abra something deep, something that made Abra feel strange, as if B had been watching her closely for a very long time.

"How are things between you and Sam?"

"What ever happened to your neighbor to the north of Sam's house after the fire?"

"Do you think they'll rebuild the church?"

The easy questions, well, she answered those simply enough. B didn't ask too many of the intrusive questions in a row, but when she did ask them, they stuck out like an unexpected splinter on an otherwise smooth table. But now Abra was looking for reasons to like B, and she reminded herself that Deen was a small town, the kind of place where everyone knew everyone else's business. That explained why B knew so much about her— everyone else did too.

It was unlike Abra to take to Beatrice as quickly as she did. She went from wondering who this girl was to laughing hysterically with her on the carousel and shouting down at strangers from the top of the Ferris wheel. If she had been her normal self, she would have had the awareness to question what was happening.

But she wasn't herself, not in those days between meeting Koli Naal and what came next. She was distracted by thoughts of New Orleans and the possibility of another Tree. She was disoriented, searching for signs of the hidden, the rustling curtain, and it was easy for someone to take her by the arm and lead her where they wanted her to go.

The two girls came off the Ferris wheel. Abra's face was flushed from the summer night and the excitement of ride after ride.

B was going on and on about the town where she had grown up—turns out she hadn't grown up in Deen but in a town on the other side of the mountain. She had story after story, each one funnier or more entertaining or more solemn than the one before it. When B told stories, Abra felt herself getting caught up in them, swirling in something like a make-believe world. It was a relief not having to worry about the Tree or New Orleans or Koli Naal. It was a pleasant kind of distraction.

Then, there stood Sam.

He seemed suddenly older, a stranger. He stood there with his friends, his hands in his pockets. The boys were being rowdy, pushing and shouting the way young men sometimes do in order to get attention or prove themselves. But Sam stood at the fringe, and Abra couldn't help but think he didn't belong in that group. She knew he was more thoughtful than that. After all they had experienced together, it seemed as though they had both skipped through that stage of life, going straight from childhood to adulthood.

"Hey, Abra," he said when he caught her eye.

"Hi, Sam," she said.

Beatrice launched herself in between them. "Hi, I'm B," she said in a chipper voice. "I've seen you around."

She laughed when she finished a sentence. It was like her way of saying she was finished talking, at least for a moment.

"Hi," Sam said to Beatrice, but he didn't look at her. He was still looking at Abra. "How's it going?" he asked.

Abra was suddenly filled with a great sense of sadness at the loss of a good friend. She wished it all away—the sword, the Tree, everything that had happened. She wished they could have gone on being friends, exploring the valley, watching the river. She thought about childhood and how it passes too quickly, how it's one of those things you can't look directly at or it will flee. She wondered where those four years had gone and if she could get them back.

"It's going okay," Abra said, shrugging. "How's your dad?"

"Dad? He's good. Things are good."

"Good," Abra said.

The three of them stood there for a little longer than what felt appropriate. An awkwardness settled between them.

"Anything new?" Sam asked. It was an innocent question, two words people ask each other every single day. But to Abra they felt different. Maybe it was in Sam's voice, the way it made the question sound important, or maybe it was in his eyes, the way they suddenly stared intently, or maybe it was the way his body tensed up. Abra knew he wasn't asking about life in general—he wanted to know if she had found anything new in the atlas, if she had seen anything strange, and she knew this the way best friends know things about each other.

He hadn't forgotten.

She paused. She would have told him about Koli Naal and about the red #69 written beside New Orleans, a new number signifying the new Tree. She wanted to. She wanted to bring him back into it all with her. She was willing to forgive him his obsession with the Tree, his previous insistence on using it to bring back his mother. She would have told him. But as she opened her mouth to speak, she sensed Beatrice right there beside her, eyes staring, mouth suddenly and strangely quiet.

B hadn't stopped talking all night, but now she was all ears.

"Nah," Abra said, shrugging, trying to look indifferent. "Nothing new."

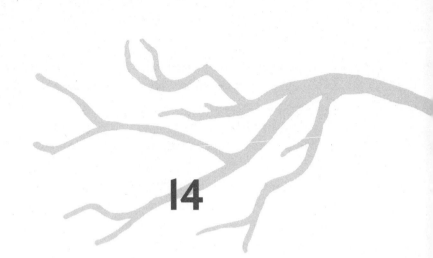

14

ABRA COULD ALMOST FEEL THE RAIN, and she knew she was in that dream again, the way you can know it's a dream but still feel like there's no way out. But she didn't feel trapped—she felt relieved to be back. There was something unfinished, something she needed to revisit. She was surrounded by the same leaves and branches, the same sound of drops pattering down through it all. She was up in the same tree, hanging by one of its highest branches, but there was something different this time.

She wasn't afraid.

Her heart raced and her muscles tensed, but the heavy drag of fear wasn't there. She clung to the branch she was on, a branch that was still much too thin to hold her, and she felt herself beginning to fall down through the tree, but still there was no fear. She grabbed for anything she could hold on to, confident this time without a seed of panic. There she was, dangling, looking down at the ground far below.

She watched as the same small girl was picked up in the jaws of the same huge, wolf-like creature and tossed aside. She watched as the boy grabbed on to the small sword, cried out in pain, and swung it again and again at the wolf. She watched, waiting for the moment when the sword found its mark and the huge creature listed to the side, drifting, plummeting. Then it was down, and the boy fell.

She twisted and turned where she hung from the branch, and for some reason this time she didn't worry about the girl. This time, in the dream, she knew she would be okay. The streak of light came exactly when she expected it, and the man, or something in the shape of a man, knelt beside the girl. He put his hands on her head and closed his eyes, and brought the girl back to life.

And like every other time, she heard the man begin to whisper.

"Abra, this is very important. I have a few things I need to tell you."

But this time she didn't fall. This time he kept talking, and she heard what he said. She heard again what Mr. Tennin had told her almost exactly four years ago, words she had somehow grown over or forgotten.

"You will have to be very strong. I don't understand why this responsibility is passing to you, but it is. And who knows? Maybe children are the only ones brave and true enough to save the world."

He smiled a sad smile, looked over his shoulder, and then looked back at her, serious and determined.

"The sword is also a key, or perhaps you already know that by now. There are seven gates. Lock the gates with the sword. But don't only lock them—seal them. You'll know how when you get there. The atlas will show you where to go."

He paused, and when he spoke again he sounded sad and confused.

"There is another Tree. I know that now. They are trying to plant the Tree on the other side of one of the gates. This one in Deen was only a diversion. The other one is already growing. Two at once. You will have to destroy it." His voice trailed off. A sonic boom reverberated and the fire roared across the river.

"It's all up to you now," Mr. Tennin said as he stood up, then shot into the sky like a rocket.

Abra woke up as if rising out of cool water on a warm day. There was no falling this time. Her eyes opened and she stared at the ceiling, wondering where Mr. Tennin had gone. Had he died? Could angels die? Or, as he had said, had he simply passed on?

Was there a difference?

Reality returned to her slowly like an old memory. It was an early morning in July. The sun hadn't yet risen, and the setting moon cast a pale light that would soon fade as the east turned a navy blue that grew into purple, red, and finally orange. The sun would drift into the morning sky. She stared out into that pale darkness. Stillness settled over everything on her farm at that time of day. The trees were heavy with dew, motionless. The barns held sleeping animals. The cornstalks, nearly approaching waist height, stood very still, listening.

The fair had been a dead end. Abra hadn't wanted to go exploring with Beatrice constantly looking over her shoulder, chatting and smiling and waiting. Because no matter what Beatrice had said, no matter how she had acted, Abra had been overwhelmed with the sense that she was searching for something.

Abra looked down the lane and across the road, and she wasn't surprised to see Koli standing there, facing away this time, facing the river. She was the only thing that wasn't still—her hair and dress billowed out to the south as the north wind swept out of the narrow place where the east and west mountains collided. Koli stood there clasping her hands behind her back.

Abra crept downstairs without even changing out of her night-gown, opened the front door quietly, and guided it back until it rested against the frame. She danced lightly over the wet grass. This time she took the short sword. The cold metal somehow felt alive to Abra, as if it was a thinking, living, breathing being. She looked at it in her hands while she walked, examined its dullness. From a distance, someone would have thought she was carrying a piece of gray plastic or an ashy branch already burned. But it felt full of life, and she wondered why she hadn't named it yet.

Already the light gathered. The moon, directly to her left, was sinking down below the mountains. The air felt like warm water with streaks of coolness in it, the way the surface of a swimming hole can be warm while arms of cold reach up from the depths. The curtain felt light to Abra that morning—whatever it was that divided Deen from the Tree of Life seemed especially thin, almost transparent. She kept looking around, expecting to see anything. Nothing would have surprised her.

But nothing out of the ordinary showed itself. Nothing except Koli Naal, facing the river.

Abra continued down the driveway, the stones digging into the soles of her feet. She wasn't afraid. After the dream and Mr. Tennin's words, Koli was nothing more than a distraction off to the side, something only marginally important. Abra knew now what the sword would do for her. She knew her mission, and this time she carried it. She would go to New Orleans and destroy the Tree. Somehow, she would do it. Abra felt powerful, invincible.

The moonlight faded and the morning paused, neither night nor day. The woods across the street had their own sounds: crickets and cicadas and the rustling of young leaves learning to dance for the first time. And always the river, always the river, that distant roar of time and life. Rivers run, always the same, always different. Out of the blue Abra remembered something she had read during all of her research into the Tree of Life.

A river flowed from the land of Eden, watering the garden and then dividing into four branches.

A river flowed.

Koli started walking away again, walking north on Kincade Road, and Abra followed her. They were like two stars, gravity pushing and pulling, spinning through the endless universe. Koli seemed somehow less than she had been the previous time, as if some crucial part of her had been spent on another venture.

They arrived at the parking lot, the place the church used to stand, and Koli walked around its ruins with light steps. She seemed to draw a power from those remains, as if desolation and abandonment filled her up. Abra stood on the edge and watched. Waited.

"Will you help the man and his child? Will you unlock the gate?" Koli asked absentmindedly without turning to face Abra.

"I'm going to New Orleans, if that's what you mean," Abra said. She felt annoyed with this . . . thing. Whatever Koli was. And not knowing made Abra even more annoyed.

"That's not what I mean, and you know it," Koli said slowly, her voice somewhere between a hiss and a whisper. She turned and looked at Abra, and she had that horrid face again, the one that had terrified Abra before.

"You can't scare me," Abra said, clutching the sword.

Koli glanced at the sword. "What, this?" She pointed at her own face, which suddenly reverted to that of a beautiful woman, with smooth teeth and gentle, pink tongue. "Oh, Abra, that's nothing. That's simply a preview, a glimpse, a foretaste. You have no idea."

"I do know. I know who you are and I know what you're trying to do," Abra said. "I stopped Mr. Jinn and I can stop you."

"You did not stop Jinn. He grew . . . tired, careless," Koli said in a sympathetic voice. "And who can blame him? Tree after Tree after Tree. Tennin always waiting, always sitting there with that smirk on his face, sword buried up to its hilt in the soft bark. No, Jinn was a tiny, dying flame. Snuffing him out required so little."

Her eyes were like fire.

"I will not be so easily extinguished," she said.

Abra took a deep breath. "Why don't you take the sword from me? Unlock it yourself?"

Koli seemed to grow angry at that, and she paced the ruins faster, waving her arms as she spoke. "Take the sword? I won't disgrace myself by touching it."

It burns you too, Abra thought.

"Why did you think I would help you?" she asked. "Why would I go all the way to New Orleans and unlock a gate without knowing what will come out?"

"Help me? Child, it's much bigger than that. You don't see what's coming. I don't have to scare you into helping me. Once you see what is happening, you'll gladly help. You'll see why our side is the right side."

"No," Abra said.

Koli shrugged. "Go to New Orleans, child." When she said "child" it was in a pitying, whiny voice reserved for parents talking to the youngest of children. "Go to New Orleans. Unlock the gate that leads to Over There, and leave it unlocked. Leave the door open. That is why you have the sword. Use it."

"No," Abra said again. Every word took an incredible effort. It felt like there was a spell clamping her mouth shut.

"When you get there," Koli said, "you'll find that our missions are not so far apart."

Abra shook her head—no, she would not. The silence between them was alive, as loud a silence as you will ever experience. Abra gripped the sword, held it with two hands out in front of her, and her white nightgown blew around her in the breeze. For a moment she felt otherworldly, a child warrior from a long-ago legend. But some of her hair drifted into her face, and she pushed it back with a shaking hand, and she was simply Abra again, a sixteen-year-old trembling with fear and adrenaline.

"Save the man and his child. Unlock the door," Koli said in a firm but quiet voice. "Let those who are trapped go free. Or, perhaps, do it for more selfish reasons, knowing that if you do not, your family is mine. Your clumsy bore of a father . . . your mindless mother . . . your lamb of a baby brother. Jinn didn't have such . . . negotiating tools when dealing with your friend. Sam had already lost nearly everything. But you?"

Koli Naal leaned her head to the side, and her voice was quiet and compassionate.

"You are different. You do not know loss, so you fear it."

"If you do anything to my family . . ."

"What, child? What will you do?"

⁓

The walk home felt long, and Abra wanted to go back to bed. Her feet hurt from walking barefoot on the stone road and through the weeds around the church. She had been thrust back into the middle of this fight, but it didn't feel like the wonderful adventure she remembered from before. No, it felt hard and dangerous and already hopeless, and she wondered if her first adventure had seemed that way too when she was in the middle of it. She wondered if all adventures are wonderful to talk about and reflect on but actually contain more pain and sorrow than we remember or are willing to recall.

She walked through the front door, and there was her mom in the kitchen with her back facing her. Her wonderful mother, whom she was suddenly desperate not to lose. She wouldn't let Koli do anything to her family. She would protect them. She would never sleep. She would pace the house at all hours, watch all the doors, sit beneath all the windows to make sure Koli could never come in.

"I'm sorry," Abra said in an attempt to head off her mother's protests about going out in her nightgown. She held the sword behind her. "I wanted to go for a walk this morning..."

Her mother turned around and stared blankly at her. "Child, you can wear whatever you want, but it would help me if you called before you came over for breakfast. Good thing for you I made extra this morning."

Child? Her mother never called her that.

"Are you okay?" Abra asked.

Her mother didn't look at her this time. She kept washing a few dishes in the sink.

"Now that you mention it, I do worry what your parents will think about you scurrying over here so often. Doesn't your own mother want you around for breakfast some mornings?"

"My own mother?" Abra asked, confused.

Her mom looked over her shoulder a moment. "What's that

124

look on your face, child? Don't get me wrong, I like when you visit. It's nice having a young one around. But I worry, that's all, about what your parents will think."

Abra walked slowly to the kitchen counter. Her mother didn't look at her.

"Who am I?" Abra asked in a quiet voice.

Her mother looked at her and smiled a strange smile. "Who are you, child?"

"Yes, who am I?"

Her mother stopped washing the dishes and put a wet, sudsy hand on Abra's shoulder. She started to laugh. She laughed and laughed, one of those good, hard laughs that leave your sides hurting and your belly sore. She stopped laughing and sighed.

"Child, if you don't know who you are, why don't you hurry back to your house and ask your brother Sam?"

A tidal wave of emotions washed over Abra: panic, grief, confusion. But when the wave receded, all it left behind was anger. Koli had done this. Koli had caused her mom to forget who she was. She knew it.

"Now, if you're finished asking silly questions, you'll say hello to your friend."

"Who?"

"Your friend," Abra's mother said, and she motioned with her chin in the direction of the dining room. "She walked in before you did."

Abra turned around. It was the girl she had met at the fair.

"Beatrice?" Abra said.

"It's just B, remember?" she said with a laugh. Her eyes were deep pools, and they sparkled.

15

BEATRICE ACTED as if she was some great friend from the past, but there was nothing there—it was all pretend: the knowing glances, the nodding, the eagerness. And now she showed up at the exact moment that Abra's mom forgot who she was? Abra's mind spun. She wasn't scared. She was methodically working the puzzle in front of her, trying this piece here, that piece there. And at the root of it all was Beatrice. She knew that now. Beatrice and Koli Naal.

"We should go outside," Abra said to Beatrice as they stood there in the house, her mother still washing dishes, humming to herself. Abra knew a confrontation with Beatrice was coming, and she thought it would be best to be outdoors, away from her mother and her baby brother, wherever he was. But Beatrice wouldn't let her control the situation.

"Let's go upstairs first," Beatrice said with that same plastic smile on her face. "I've never seen your room!"

Abra's mind raced, and she glanced at her mom to see if she'd react to Beatrice asking about her room, but if she heard it, she didn't seem alarmed by the fact. Abra still had the sword, and she held it behind her back. It felt alive again, the sword, and there was a tingling sensation in her hand. She pictured her room, the atlas on the floor, a few of the notes spread out around it, and she didn't want to take Beatrice up there.

"Let's go outside, B," Abra insisted. "I'll show you around."

"Young lady," her mother said in a motherly voice, "you are absolutely not going anywhere until you change your clothes and put away that stick you're carrying behind your back. I see it, so stop pretending it's not there. Remember the extra set of clothes your mother sent for you to keep here? You go straight upstairs and change immediately. Your mother would kill me if she knew I was letting you wander around in your nightgown."

Abra's mother gave her one of those looks that said, *See? You can't get anything past me.*

"Okay," Abra said hesitantly, starting up the stairs, her face hot with anger, her mind racing. Her world was falling apart, and all because of Koli Naal, all because of the sword and the Tree and everything else. For the first time, she felt defeated. Part of her wanted out. Part of her wished someone would draw the curtain between the normal world and this new one, and she wanted to forget about it. Someone else could kill the Tree. Someone else could protect people from living forever. She wanted to be a regular girl again.

But that was just part of her. And it wasn't the part that won out—she was too angry, too determined to defeat Koli Naal. This was just the beginning, she knew that, and she was ready to fight.

About halfway up the stairs she heard Beatrice.

"Thank you, Mrs. Miller, I'll just go up and see how Abra's coming along," she said in a polite voice. Abra heard her coming up the stairs.

"Please wait outside while I change," Abra called over her shoulder before running into her bedroom, slamming the door, and leaning against it. This Beatrice was very persistent, whoever she really was. Whatever she was. Abra felt like Beatrice was inside her head, or at least trying to get there. Abra recognized this was a strange thing to think and tried to push the thought away. But even in doing that she encountered Beatrice in there somewhere, or trying to get in. She was like a rat outside a house in the middle of winter, sniffing around the basement windows, climbing up the downspouts, investigating every nook and cranny, every crack and ledge. That was Beatrice, and Abra found herself mentally running around, making sure all the doors were locked, all the holes stuffed closed.

Abra stood in her room for a few seconds, catching her breath. She dashed to her dresser and pulled out some clothes. She dressed automatically, her mind elsewhere, thinking about her mom, her dad, her little brother.

She could see Beatrice's shadow moving back and forth, slowly, along the crack under the door. It gave her the feeling that it was no longer Beatrice out there, but someone entirely different. This didn't make sense, not at all, and she pushed the thought to the back of her mind as she pulled on her jeans, socks, and sneakers.

"Almost ready!" Abra said. Beatrice didn't say anything back to her.

Abra pulled a T-shirt over her head, then moved quickly to clean up the atlas and the papers. She put the sword on the floor for a moment, but before picking up the articles she stopped and stared at the open atlas. The second Tree, the one Tennin had told her about in the dream, was in New Orleans. How was she supposed to get there? She wondered about her uncle who lived there, and how long it would take her to walk a thousand miles, or however far it was. She wondered if the Trees normally appeared in such rapid succession, only a few years apart. If she interpreted the atlas and the articles correctly, it seemed like there were usually decades, sometimes centuries, between the appearances of the Tree.

"Ouch!" someone shouted.

Abra turned and there stood Beatrice, holding her palm, the sword at her feet. Abra stared at the open door, wondering how she had managed to come in so quietly.

"That thing burned me!" she squealed.

"Shh, shh," Abra said, racing over and closing the door before her mother heard them and came up to investigate. "You can't touch that. What are you doing in here? I asked you to wait outside."

"I got bored," Beatrice said quietly, tears pooling in her eyes. "And why do you have a sword? In your room?"

Abra shrugged. "It's a long story. Are you okay?"

Beatrice nodded, still staring at the sword.

"Come here. Let me see your hand."

Abra held Beatrice's hand and glanced quickly at her face. Beatrice's palm was red, and for a moment Abra was back in the forest at the end of the Road to Nowhere, the fire raging around them, Sam's hands badly burned. Abra had a clear vision of time, how it moves constantly, not linear but swirling like a tornado, picking up things from here and there, past and future, and mixing them together until you can't tell yesterday from tomorrow.

This is what it feels like to lose your mind, Abra thought. She felt displaced, unhinged, floating outside of hours and minutes and seconds. Outside of years. She was, for that moment, a No

One. She was certain her father wouldn't recognize her either. She didn't have a home. She didn't belong anywhere.

"Go to the bathroom at the end of the hall," Abra said absently, her voice coming out robotically. "Run some cold water over it for a minute or two. If it still hurts, I'll get some salve from downstairs."

Beatrice left the room like a chastised puppy. She clutched her hand as if it might fall off. If Beatrice and Koli Naal were in this together, or somehow one and the same, what was she supposed to do?

Abra stood there quietly until she heard the water turn on, the small rushing sound, and she found it strange, the different sounds water can make: the rushing of the river, the tapping of the rain on her window, the stillness of the puddle from the fair the other night, the one that looked like an escape hatch into a faraway galaxy with constellations the shape of a Ferris wheel. And now there was the soothing cold water running from a faucet.

She picked up the sword and turned back to the atlas. That's when the sword began to get heavier. Abra stared at it in her hand, and because she didn't understand what was happening, at first it felt like a betrayal. Like the turning away of a once-close friend. It grew heavier and heavier until she had to rest the point of it against the floor, but the point dug into the carpet farther, farther, and it became so heavy that she had to lay it down. Her fingers nearly became trapped under it because the increase in weight happened so quickly. Soon it was pressing deep into the floor and she panicked, because what if it continued? What if it became so heavy that it broke through into the living room below her?

The journal was right there at the point of the sword, still opened to New Orleans with its two numbers. The sword crept forward, quivering like a divining rod, the point growing closer to the dot on the map that signified the city. Abra tried to pick it up again, but she couldn't—she could only hold on to it, and still it moved toward the atlas. She had a sense that something huge was about to happen, and something in her didn't want it to happen. That's the part of her that pulled on the sword, pulled in vain as it crept those few inches, pointing at New Orleans.

Two things happened at once. Beatrice came running into the room, still holding her hand, shouting as if trying to stop whatever was happening. She grabbed Abra's shoulder and Abra tried to push her away, but Beatrice held on tight. Her strong grip was no child's grip. Her fingers were icy, digging into Abra's flesh, threatening to shatter her collarbone.

At the same time, the very point of the sword touched the dot of New Orleans in the atlas.

A flash of light.

The sound of Beatrice screaming.

Abra felt a tremor through her body, like a shudder when you swallow a piece of slimy food you didn't want to eat.

Everything went still.

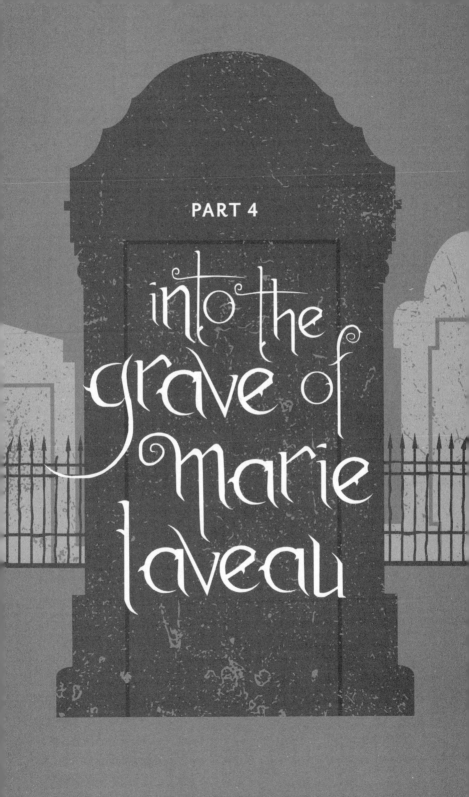

PART 4

into the
grave of
marie
laveau

"Perhaps," said the man, "you would like to be lost with us. I have found it much more agreeable to be lost in the company of others."

KATE DICAMILLO, *THE MIRACULOUS JOURNEY OF EDWARD TULANE*

16

LEO WALKED AWAY from the hospital where his mother had been kept for the last eight years. She had tried so hard to find Ruby. The search, the hopelessness of it, had caused her to lose her way, and she had sunk deep into herself. One day, when the search hit yet another dead end, she passed out from exhaustion and despair. When she regained consciousness in the hospital, she was unresponsive. He visited her every day after school and lived with a distant relative on the other side of the city, a kind, older woman who walked in a hunched-over way and spoke in a whisper.

The leads had all gone cold. His mother hadn't spoken a word in years.

As Leo left the hospital and crawled into his car, he almost turned around to go back to his mother again. It was a feeling he had every time he left, a sense that he was missing something. Instead he sat in the driver's seat and glanced through the papers the doctors had given him. Charts and recommendations and new prescriptions, new plans, new diagnoses. All of them signed with the initials of his mother's main doctor.

KN.

It was one of those perfect summer days that felt more like early fall. Leo rolled his windows down as he drove, and the air swept through the car. There was a coolness there, relief from week after week of heat and humidity. The trees' leaves rustled in a refreshing breeze. Spanish moss waved from the branches like drapes in an open window.

His car wandered in the same meandering way as his mind, and before he knew it, he was driving up the street of his father's old house. He hadn't gone that way in a long time. When he approached it, he pulled off and stopped along the sidewalk. He parked there and thought about the ten-year-old boy he had been, the one who had drifted home from the cemetery on that early morning, the one with the lost look on his face and the gaping hole inside of him.

No one had bought the house after his father and sister disappeared. For a long time—years—it had sat there with a small "For Sale" sign in the front yard, but soon even that was gone, and as far as Leo knew the house had never sold. His mother, before she had vanished inside of herself, had complained about foreclosures and short sales, but Leo had been young and she didn't involve him in the conversations that took place. He wondered who owned it. He wondered if anyone had been inside recently.

He wondered if the door was locked.

It was a small thought at first, the tiniest of suggestions. But it stuck the way a seashell will catch hold in the sand, and as the waves wash away everything around it, the seashell remains. Another wave, another layer of sand pulled back, and more of the shell shows through. It was a small thought, but the longer he sat there, the more prominent it became.

Leo did something he had never done in all those years of

stopping to look at his father's old house: he turned off the car. That alone felt strange enough, because it implied that he wasn't only passing through. He was stopping. And you only stop when you have something else to do, so he climbed out of the car, looked up and down the sidewalk, glanced over his shoulder to see if anyone was around, and finally approached the house, feeling skittish.

He walked up to the front door first. The large windows still stood on either side, guarding the house. He smiled when he remembered how afraid of those windows he had always been. He knocked and listened. He knocked again, and the sound of it was empty and distant, like knocking on the doorway to another universe. He reached for the knob and turned it, but it was locked, something that didn't surprise him at all. No one had ever used that door anyway, even when people lived there—why would it be unlocked now? He looked up at the porch ceiling and remembered how he and Ruby used to come out on the front porch. She had often rested out there. Watching over her had been a full-time job, something he had sometimes resented.

Why do I always have to watch her? he'd wondered.

How he wished he could watch her again.

Leo looked around one more time before making his way to the side door of the house. The fact that no one emerged to tell him to mind his own business, stop snooping around, had him feeling more and more brave. The bushes separating the short driveway from the neighbor's house were wild and expanding beyond their boundaries. The driveway had nearly vanished, and he had to walk sideways in some places to fit between the branches, the weeds, and the side of the house.

The screen door had fallen off completely at some point and lay on the narrow walkway. The inside door still had loose hinges and a slightly rotten door frame. If someone had ever tried to sell this house, they certainly hadn't given it a very good effort. He looked around one more time, grabbed on to the doorknob, and tried to turn it.

It was locked.

He reached into his pocket and pulled out something that looked like a pocketknife, but if you looked closer you'd realize that instead of blades it held a series of lock picks. It was a lock-picking set, much more sophisticated than the one he had when he was ten years old. He had never lost his obsession with locks, his deep desire to open all the doors. He extended one of the picks from the set and tried to fit it into the lock, but it was too wide. He tried another, and it slipped inside. He felt around for a moment, closing his eyes, envisioning the edges, the tumblers of the lock, the teeth of the pick probing and fitting. He tried the knob again.

The door opened. He walked inside.

To say that Leo's old house was completely still would be like saying the bottom of the sea is dark. It unnerved him when he entered. That stillness was the primary reason he didn't close the side door behind him. If you've ever been in an empty house, you might understand a little bit about stillness, but even an empty house that's currently being lived in has small signs of life. The ticking of a clock. The small gust of air moving when the air conditioner turns on. The occasional hum of the refrigerator. The smell of being.

Not Leo's old house. It was beyond still. There were no vital signs. The clocks' batteries had all died years ago, so they simply sat there staring down at him, their hands frozen at random times. The air ducts and vents were covered in dust. The appliances were lifeless, their displays blank. He wandered through the first floor, smelling only humidity and dust and the musty odor of disuse.

He went all the way up to the third floor and peeked into Ruby's room, but he didn't have the heart to stay there very long. Her bed was still there, the furniture all in its place, a time capsule from eight years before, another life. He reached up and touched the door frame, still remembering how his mother had leaned against it when he told her that Ruby was gone.

Leo, where did he take her?

I don't know.

He had thought over that question and answer a million times since, his mother asking, him answering. Her question genuine. His answer clouded in dishonesty. He did know where his father had taken her, but no one would have believed him, so he had kept it all to himself. The woman, Marie, standing by the small fire. The sound of rock moving against rock. The darkness that followed.

He walked down the stairs, his footsteps loud and out of place. As he turned the corner at the bottom and walked past the closet, he remembered the trapdoor in the guest room closet. It was the first time he'd thought of that door for years, and he walked slowly through the house, attracted to it the way a small sliver of metal trembles on its way to the magnet. The side door was still open, and as he walked past it, shadows drifted down with the summer leaves that fell, spinning from the sycamore trees.

The guest room door was locked, which seemed strange. He didn't remember that his father had kept that room locked. He pulled out his lock-picking set and made short work of the flimsy indoor lock. The door popped open as if it had been held there by a spring and only needed someone to nudge it. The door whined as it opened, and he walked straight to the closet door.

That door also whined, but when it stopped he could still hear something. Strange sounds coming from . . . where? Far away? Nearby? He held his breath and listened, and he realized the sounds grew closer, louder. He ran to the window and opened it to see if the sounds were coming from outside. The summer breeze blew in, warmer now, and he looked into the backyard, the space that had turned into a jungle. The azaleas were still there with their spots of color, but they had grown untrimmed and were sparse and thin the way uncared-for things will sometimes deteriorate. A snake slid through the undergrowth, its belly hissing on the leaves. Tiny lizards flicked here and there, running from their own shadows. A squirrel danced two or three steps, stopped, lifted something to its face with its two tiny hands. The whole backyard was alive and moving—everything there went on precisely as if nothing had ever happened in that house, as if that house wasn't even there.

But the sound—Leo could still hear a sound coming from somewhere.

He turned back to face the room and looked down the hallway, the way he had come, but the noise was not coming from the main part of the house. He listened to the walls—that's where the noise seemed to be coming from. Somewhere deep, somewhere close to where he had always imagined the words had gone, where all the words lay hidden. He walked back over to the trapdoor, and that's when he knew it.

The sounds were coming from the other side of that door.

He got down on his hands and knees and listened. It was a

slow, steady pounding sound. A *tap*, *tap*, *tap*. But also voices? Yes, he thought he heard voices too.

Suddenly, pounding on the trapdoor. He jumped back.

"Help!" a voice shouted. "Is anyone there? Let us out!"

Leo sat there for a moment, stunned. He thought he must be dreaming. He stared at the door, waiting to see what would happen.

"Please! Is anyone there? Help!"

"Who are you?" Leo blurted out, still staring at the trapdoor, still on his hands and knees on the floor of the guest room.

The banging stopped. The person stopped shouting.

"Who are you?" the voice asked in return, a little hesitant, a little timid.

"What are you doing in my house?" Leo asked, and it felt a little bit like a lie, that question, but also like the truth.

Silence again.

"Please let us in. I can explain."

"Well, I have a gun," Leo said. "So you'd better not try anything."

He didn't have a gun. He didn't have anything of the sort.

"Please don't shoot us," a different voice said, followed quickly by a loud shushing noise.

Leo leaned forward and tried to lift the metal ring that would open the trapdoor, but it was too heavy. He stood up and grabbed on to it with two hands, lifted with all of his might. It still didn't budge. That's when he saw the lock, a tiny round thing that had been painted over. He scraped away some of the paint and pulled the lock picks from his pocket again. He chose the thinnest one and worked the inside of the lock.

"What are you doing? Please open the door!"

"Be patient!" Leo shouted. "It's locked."

"Do you have the key?"

"No," he said.

"We'll be stuck here forever!" the second voice whined, followed again by the shushing sound.

"One second," Leo shouted back, biting his lip as he tried to pick the lock. Something budged, the lock turned. He put the set back in his pocket and grabbed on to the ring and pulled. The door came open easily, like peeling the skin off a banana.

"Thank you," the first person said, climbing up out of the hole. The second person came close behind and collapsed onto the floor.

Leo looked down the hole. It was round, maybe three feet across, and went down through nothing more than rocks and brown earth. A wooden ladder came up one side, a few of its rickety rungs broken or missing. No matter how hard Leo peered down into the hole, he couldn't see the bottom.

He looked at the two people who had come up through the trapdoor, and he was completely surprised: two teenage girls. The second one who had come up looked terrified. She sat on the floor, her back against the wall under the open window, and she looked around like a bird in a cage.

The first one, on the other hand, was already standing, and she held a short dagger in her hand. She looked strong and determined and pushed her long blonde hair out of her eyes. Leo thought she was probably a few years younger than him, but she was very pretty.

"Who are you?" Leo stammered, his eyes not leaving the blonde-haired girl.

"Who are you?" hissed the terrified girl still sitting on the floor.

"I'm Leo," he said, still staring at the blonde girl.

She leaned the blade against the wall and took a deep breath, as if she had crossed an immeasurable distance. She looked out the window, then back at Leo.

"Is this New Orleans?" she asked, and there was something bashful in her voice, something that didn't match the assertive way she carried herself.

He nodded. "Yeah, of course it is. So, who are you?" he asked again. "And how'd you get into my house?"

The girl smiled, and there was confidence there, the face of a person who embraced adventure. Her bashfulness fled, and Leo liked her even more. There was a strength about her: she seemed determined, and kind, and unwavering.

"I'm Abra," she said. "I need you to help me find a tree."

17

ABRA'S MIND COULDN'T COMPREHEND exactly what had happened. There had been the flash of light, the heavy sensation of Beatrice dragging her down, her ice-cold hands holding tight. Out of nowhere the ladder's rungs had appeared in her hands as if they had always been there. She started climbing. She heard Beatrice below her, felt her movements tremble through the wooden ladder. She had banged her head on what she thought was a ceiling. It turned out to be a floor, a floor that opened. Now she was standing there, staring at the young man.

"What are you doing here? How'd you get in there?" Leo asked.

Abra didn't want to sit around answering questions, and what did she have to tell him? She didn't know how she had gotten in there, not really, and she was on the path of something big. She had to be close. In her mind, she was thinking this would take a few hours. Maybe she could even find the Tree, destroy it, and be home in time for supper. She tried not to think about the fact that her mother didn't know who she was. She'd deal with that later.

"Like I said, I'm Abra."

She looked over her shoulder at Beatrice. Abra was becoming less and less sure about what to do with her.

"That's B," she said.

"Where did you come from? How did you get in there?" Leo kept asking.

Abra sighed, glanced out the window, then looked back at Leo. "I'll tell you more later. But we're looking for a tree."

"A tree?" Leo asked, staring at her.

She blushed and nodded. "Yeah, a tree. Something... fantastic. Something old."

"This is New Orleans," Leo said. "Everything's fantastic. Everything's old."

"Something huge," Abra insisted. "It's a tree... like... I don't know."

Abra paced around the room in frustration, thinking hard. She wished she had the atlas. She wondered if the dot had been in someplace specific—north of the city? Right in the middle? She tried to picture it, but all she saw was the red dot with the number beside it.

"There's only one special tree I know about," Leo said quietly. "My mom used to take me and my sister there on the weekends. We'd pack sandwiches and something fun to do. It was in Audubon Park. It was called the Tree of Life."

Abra's head snapped up out of her discouragement. "Are you kidding me?" she practically shouted.

He nodded.

"Can you take me there?"

Leo drove them ten or fifteen minutes from his father's house to Audubon Park. Maybe it took longer—Abra lost track. Neither he nor Abra nor Beatrice said much during the trip.

In fact, Abra had spent most of the drive stealing glances

at Beatrice. If, as Abra suspected, Beatrice had been at least partially responsible for her mother forgetting about her, she couldn't figure out why. And if Beatrice was somehow working with or for Koli Naal, it made Abra shiver to have her so close while she searched for the Tree. But she didn't know what else to do. Until Beatrice confirmed Abra's worries, Abra decided to let her come along for the ride. But she knew she had to keep a close eye on her.

"There it is," Leo said, pointing across a green expanse of grass at a gnarled old tree.

Abra ran to the tree, and Leo and Beatrice followed. It had a massive trunk, and its lower branches were each the size of large trees themselves, sticking straight out, so long and heavy that Abra couldn't understand how they didn't snap off. She stood in the shadows of the tree, and they were deeper than normal shadows, and darker. She didn't see any fruit, but she pulled out the sword anyway and tried to plunge it into the tree.

It didn't go in. The point barely stuck into the wood.

"Hey!" Leo hissed. "You can't do that! The park rangers will be all over us! That's a protected tree. What is wrong with you?"

Abra glanced over at Beatrice to see if she, too, thought Abra's actions were strange, but Beatrice wasn't looking at her. She was looking at the sword, and there was a strange hunger in her eyes. The sun went behind a cloud and the day dimmed. Abra slid the blade back inside her waistband, where it nearly vanished.

Abra looked back at the bark of the tree and ran her hands along it. The bark was old, but not the same old that the Tree of Life had been in the woods close to her house. That Tree had felt like something edible. This tree felt . . . normal.

"This isn't it," she said, disappointment in her voice. "This isn't the Tree of Life."

"I don't know what you mean," Leo said. "This is definitely the Tree of Life. Everybody calls it that. Look—read the plaque."

Abra stared at the small plaque mounted beside the trunk. He was right. That's what the tree was called.

The three of them sat down in the shade.

"I don't know why you helped us," Abra said suddenly, glancing up at Leo. "But thanks. I'm going to have to think about this a little more. This isn't the right tree. If you need to go, you can go."

A voice like rumbling stones startled them.

"You're right, girl," a man said. "You're right. The Tree you're looking for? It won't be so easy to find. Certainly not in your backyard. Not like the last one."

Abra turned around and saw one of the strangest-looking people she had ever seen.

"I knew it," he said, his eyes wide with the happiness of being right. He chuckled. "I knew you'd come here. You're a smart one." He pointed at her with a long finger and laughed to himself again. "'This is where we'll find her,' I said. That's what I told them. 'This is where we'll find her, at the tree.'"

"Who?" Abra asked. "Who'd you tell that to? And who are you?"

"Don't worry about a thing, Abra. We'll get you pointed in the right direction."

"Who are you?" she asked the man again, emphasizing each word as if talking to someone who didn't completely understand the language, and this time he smiled with a sort of kindness that she recognized. It was a sad, melancholy affection, and her heart jumped inside of her.

"Mr. Tennin?" she whispered.

The melancholy part of his kindness swelled until it was only sadness. Feelings can do that. Anger can swell up until you realize it has transformed into a fierce kind of love. Happiness can slowly inflate so that tears fall from your eyes. This transformation of emotions is one of the most amazing things in the universe, like exploding stars or a baby being born.

"No, I'm sorry, Abra," he said, and his voice trembled so that he had to clear his throat to continue. "I'm so sorry. I wish! I wish Mr. Tennin was here. But he is . . . gone now. Long gone, across the water."

"How do you know this guy?" Leo asked, but Abra held up her hand, telling him to wait.

"Where?" she asked the man. "Where did Tennin go?"

The man stared at her for a moment. "My name is Mr. Henry, and we need to talk," he said. "Somewhere in private. Come."

He turned and walked away, and for the first time Abra realized he was an old man. He walked in that hesitant fashion of someone who is expecting to be tripped up. While motionless he stood up straight, but when he walked he bent forward, slightly hunched. The shaved head and piercings hid his age, or tried to.

The three followed him into a shadowy grove of trees. He leaned against a trunk and crossed his arms, and he was suddenly young again.

"Go ahead, sit down, sit down. First, tell me who you all are. I was only expecting one of you."

Leo and Beatrice looked at each other.

"You can call me B," Beatrice said, and for once her smile failed to rise. She looked like a fairy whose wings had been clipped. The man stared at her, squinting. She shuddered. He took a deep breath.

"I think I know who you are," he said to Beatrice in a voice that wasn't very kind. "And furthermore, I forbid you to speak in our presence."

Beatrice glared wide-eyed at Mr. Henry but made no move to contradict him. Abra stared hard at her, but B wouldn't make eye contact. Abra took a few steps away from her. Mr. Henry's comments confirmed her concerns all along, that B was not who she said she was. It made Abra feel nervous and angry and even more certain than before that Beatrice had something to do with her mother not recognizing her.

Mr. Henry turned, looked at Leo, and raised his ring-laden eyebrows. "You?"

"I'm Leo. Leo Jardine."

The man straightened up. "Leo Jardine?"

Leo nodded. "Yeah."

"Your father, was he Amos Jardine?"

Leo nodded again, looking confused.

"And you had a sister, Ruby Jardine?"

"How do you know all this stuff? And how did you know Abra's name? Who are you, anyway?"

The man took a deep breath and held it for what seemed an uncomfortably long period of time. When he finally exhaled, the air came bursting out through puffed-up cheeks, and Abra felt herself exhale with relief.

"Who am I, who am I . . ." he muttered to himself, rubbing his chin with his hand and then rubbing his eyes as if he was very tired.

Abra spoke quietly in the silence. "I know *what* you are," she said. "But I don't know *who*."

He smiled. "Yes, yes, you do," he said. "And I know what you are here to do, though you do not yet know. At least not precisely. Do we ever know exactly what it is we are to do until we do it? I doubt it."

He took another deep breath. He was like a bellows pumping air into some invisible fire. Some of the piercings on his face made a tinkling sound as they bumped against each other during his next boisterous exhale.

"In any case," he said, as if he had finally made an important decision, "as I said, you can call me Mr. Henry."

"And *what* are you?" Leo asked.

Abra glanced quickly at him. There was something disrespectful about his tone, something sarcastic, as if he was talking to a child.

But Mr. Henry paid him no mind. He only laughed. "You have words for it, but if I used those words then it would mislead you down well-worn paths that, unfortunately for you, go in the wrong direction. Those words, the words you have for what I am, are not quite right. I am light and darkness, I am power and weakness, I am vast and I am barely anything at all. There are no single words in your language that will suffice, so I will not tease you by using them."

He laughed again, and his laugh pushed back the shadows. Abra liked it when he laughed. The sound was like its own person, the kind of person you always feel comfortable around, the kind of person who helps you forget the things you need to forget, at least for a time.

"Words," he said, shaking his head. "Words should only be used as a last resort, a final attempt to communicate when all else has failed. They are unsteady ground. Words are nothing more than manipulated air."

He laughed another joyous laugh. Even Leo smiled this time.

"Then why are you using so many of them?" Leo asked sarcastically.

"Because words are all you humans have," Mr. Henry said,

suddenly scowling, and his scowl was as fierce as his laugh was joyful. "Words are the only anchors you recognize. Words are also why you're so . . . unsteady. Don't you ever want to flow with the movement of the river? Lift up your anchor, man!"

Abra had a quiet confidence in Mr. Henry. How did she know he was good? She couldn't have put it into words, but if she could have, she would have said that all the angels she'd ever met had at times been happy, and all of them had at times been nice (or seemed so), and all of them had at times been powerful, but only the good ones had ever been truly kind. She was beginning to think that the only distinguishing factor between good and evil, the only thing good possessed that could not be effectively copied by evil, was kindness.

Perhaps Mr. Henry knew where the Tree was and she could simply cut it in half. Or maybe he knew where to look, and they would find it soon enough.

"I'm here now," she said. "Will you tell me what to do next?"

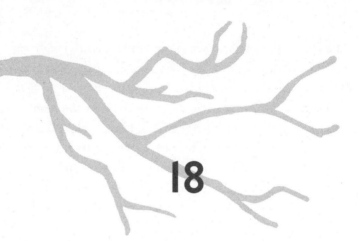

18

It was nearly lunchtime, and the crowd in the park had grown. Abra watched children run through the grass. Her eyes followed the drifting movement of Frisbees floating through the air. Some people had spread out blankets for picnics. The sunlight grew weary from cutting through the humidity, and it faded as large, white clouds flattened out. It looked like a storm was building far to the south.

"Do you know the darkness in the angel who tried to possess the Tree of Life from the beginning?" Mr. Henry barked. "Of course you don't. How would you know that? You've been alive for such a short period of time! A blink. Not even a blink. You've been alive for the first half of the first half of the thought of a blink."

Abra, Beatrice, and Leo stared at the man. He stopped talking and glared at them, as if they were the cause of his going on and on, as if their constant need for explanations was causing him to use too many of those despised things called words. When he started talking again, he shouted, and they all jumped.

"It is a darkness you cannot imagine! The angel you know

as Jinn was consumed by it. How you managed to bring him down . . ." His voice faded to a mumble. "We're still wondering."

He stared this time at Abra, his eyes burning with questions and perhaps even a hint of suspicion. He continued in a whisper.

"Do you know how many Beings of Light have pursued and destroyed the Tree of Life in all of its appearances from one end of the earth to the other? Since the beginning of time? Do you know?" His voice cracked at the end with emotion.

The three listening to the story shook their heads slowly, back and forth.

This time the man did not speak right away. He grew more emotional, and tears filled his eyes as he held up his index finger. He nodded resolutely.

"One. One. The one you know as Tennin was the only one tasked to destroy the Tree. Until now. He was there in the beginning, when everything was sung into place. He was there in the beginning, when the first ones came to be. He was there in the beginning, when the dark angel wished to possess the Tree of Life and give its fruit to humans."

Mr. Henry reached out with one hand and grasped at an invisible piece of fruit, his face covered in anguish.

"The Tree of Life?" Leo asked. Abra was surprised at how matter-of-fact the question was. He didn't seem surprised by this new knowledge at all.

"Are you talking about the Tree of Life?" Leo asked again.

Abra and Mr. Henry exchanged a glance. When they looked back at Leo, they both seemed to be deep in consideration about how much they should tell him.

"Because if you're talking about the Tree of Life," he continued, "if you're talking about a Tree that would let people live forever, then why would you ever want to destroy it?"

Abra recognized Sam in Leo's face, the sincerity, the longing for deep, aching wrongs to be made right.

"Leo," she said in a quiet voice, "these bodies can't live forever. Why would you want to live here on this earth forever? What if you were seriously injured but could not die? What if all of those you loved passed away and you were left here alone? What if your body grew old and frail until you couldn't move or talk or see or hear?"

"Anything is better than death," Beatrice interrupted in her singsong, know-it-all voice. "It's a black nothing that waits for you. Darkness and shadows and a long sleep, nothing more."

"Silence," Mr. Henry hissed, and Beatrice shrunk back.

In the past Abra would have grown indignant at what Beatrice said, argued in a mean voice against such talk, but the truth had softened her, as it does to all who encounter it. Knowing the truth, really knowing it, deflects the sharpest blows of cynicism or anger or bitterness.

"Death is not a curse," Abra whispered, looking at Beatrice with compassion. "It's a gift."

Beatrice's face curled up in disgust. "That's no kind of gift at all."

"You will not speak again in my presence," Mr. Henry said to Beatrice, and that was that. Abra thought there was something about those words that felt binding, as if he could actually control her speech. Beatrice's power, if she had any, was manipulative and mischievous. Mr. Henry's was deep, foundational, and solid.

Abra looked from Beatrice back to Mr. Henry. "Is it okay for us to talk about this now?" she whispered, looking sideways at Beatrice. Beatrice refused to make eye contact, staring straight ahead now as if she couldn't hear a thing being said.

Mr. Henry shrugged. "If she is who I think she is, she knows all of this already. If she isn't, then it does no harm."

"Okay. How did it happen?" she asked. "And why? If Mr. Tennin was the one, why did he fail at the Tree in Deen? Why did I end up with the sword? I don't understand it, not any of it. Why me?"

Mr. Henry softened. He reached out a hand and put it on Abra's shoulder. "I don't understand either. But I'm not sure that he failed. Let me also tell you this. This unexpected Tree of Life growing at the Edge of Over There, well, it is impossible for an Angel of Light to go there. We are not permitted. Angels of darkness, on the other hand, may do what they please."

He stared at Beatrice again. It seemed to Abra that he was constantly probing, constantly trying to make a final conclusion. But something seemed to stop him from fully understanding. Maybe B was more powerful than she thought.

"So, you mean . . ." Abra began.

"Yes," he said. "Mr. Tennin would not have been able to go there to destroy the Tree. Perhaps this is why it has appeared there, or perhaps it was only chance and a matter of time before it happened. Maybe this is why Mr. Tennin fell, so that he could pass on his duty to someone able to enter. Someone like you. Whatever the case, Mr. Tennin would not have been able to take the sword to the Edge of Over There to kill the Tree."

Abra stared at him. "But I can go there? To the Edge of Over There?" she asked.

He nodded. His eyes smiled and the piercings in his face seemed like a constellation of stars leading the way. "Maybe Tennin knew there was a Tree of Life at the Edge of Over There. Impossible to say for sure. It was there even before the Tree in your valley came to be. He certainly knew he could not go there.

And then he meets you, and he makes sure you end up with that"—he points to the sword—"and he gives you instructions that lead you here."

"I thought only one Tree can exist at a time," Abra said.

"We can't explain that," Mr. Henry said. "We're still . . . searching for answers. Maybe the one in Deen was only a diversion. Maybe the one at the Edge of Over There can exist because it is outside of the world. Which poses its own problems. The main one being, there are seven gates that souls can go through to leave the world, and as of right now, we don't know much about who has the keys."

"I dreamed about Mr. Tennin," Abra said in a still voice like undisturbed water.

Mr. Henry looked at her and his pierced eyebrows raised. "Yes?"

"Yes."

"What happened?"

She hesitated. "He told me about the seven gates that need to be locked. And he told me to destroy the Tree, the one that was growing at the same time as our Tree, the one here in New Orleans."

"So, he did know," Mr. Henry said.

He went into deep thought for what felt like a long time. Children ran past them. Parents called the children back. The entirety of life rushed from here to there, all around, but Abra was nearly oblivious to it, staring at Mr. Henry, waiting to see what he would say.

Finally, he spoke.

"You are only the second to hold that sword since the very beginning of time, and you are nothing more than a blink, but maybe you are here for just such a time."

Abra took a deep breath. "I'm the third to hold it," she said quietly. "My friend Sam used it to kill the Amarok."

"So he did," Mr. Henry said, nodding with respect.

"How do I get to the Edge of Over There?" she asked.

Mr. Henry looked over at Leo. "Do you mind driving us?"

Sitting in the back seat with Beatrice felt like being in a cage with a sleeping tiger. Abra felt a shift taking place. Before, when Beatrice still thought she might have convinced Abra she was nothing more than a schoolgirl, she had played the part well, coming across as weak and flighty and friendly. She had over-played a fake fear when they first arrived, but Abra had been too excited to notice. Yet now that Beatrice knew her mask had been taken off, she came across as sullen bordering on angry. Abra wasn't exactly afraid of her, especially not with Mr. Henry in the front seat of the car, but Beatrice's slow and steady trans-formation was disconcerting.

"Turn right here," Mr. Henry said, giving directions to Leo as they drove.

"Why won't you tell me where we're going?"

"Left. Turn left," Mr. Henry said. "Because if I told you where we're going, you would go the way that you know to go. But I have a way I want to go, and that's the right way."

"What is the Edge of Over There?" Abra asked. She didn't want to look at Beatrice, so she stared at the back of Mr. Henry's head as he shouted out instructions to Leo. Even with the win-dows rolled down, Abra was sweating. Rivulets ran down the back of Mr. Henry's shiny, bald head. Tiny drops like tears.

"The Edge of Over There. Hmm. Yes. Well, Over There is the

great by-and-by. The far shore. It is the place everyone goes after they die. You have other words for it, but they are all insufficient."

"You mean heaven and hell?" Leo said.

Mr. Henry practically growled at him. "Ha! First of all, you have no possible way of coming close to accurately imagining the beauty and terror contained in those two words. Second of all . . . oh, never mind. Never mind. I'm not going into that right now."

"But if that's Over There, what's the Edge of Over There?" Abra interrupted.

"Yes, well, as I've said far too many times before, there are seven Passageways that lead from here to Over There. Seven. The Passageways are the ways souls travel after the body has died—souls pass through the gate whether it is locked or not."

He paused.

"But here in New Orleans, someone unlocked the gate and allowed the living to enter. The living can only go so far. They can enter the gate, and they can approach Over There, but they cannot cross the Great Water unless they are dead."

Abra stared at Leo as he looked over at Mr. Henry with wonder in his eyes, but he didn't say anything.

"Of course, there have been a handful of exceptions to that. There are always exceptions! The problem—turn right here, boy!—is that these Passageways were never intended for the living. These Passageways are . . . elsewhere. It's difficult to explain. But as living people entered this particular Passageway, it expanded. It grew into an entire city, a city that runs right up against the Great Water, a barrier that only souls can cross."

Mr. Henry sighed.

"Now they have the Tree of Life, and this poses some serious problems. One, they could create a never-ending city of people who would never die. And why is this a problem?"

He waited, but no one answered.

"Because it is a place that will eventually be full of only pain and sadness. There will be no reprieve for anyone there if they eat from the Tree, because even though they would eventually grow old, they would never die. Of course—left here, left!—if there was no Tree there, we could always lock the gate and let them die normal or not-so-normal deaths, at which point they would cross the Great Water into eternity. But if we lock the gate now, and they all become immortals, what will become of them? And what if someone lets them out, back into this world, and they bring their immortality with them?"

He turned and stared at Beatrice in the back seat.

"No. That cannot happen. That must not happen. It's all a frightful mess. So, you must go and kill the Tree, and we can all hope together that no one has eaten from it yet. After you destroy the Tree, you can come back out, and we can use the sword to lock the gate."

Mr. Henry said this as if he was asking her to check the mail and take out the garbage, as if going to the Edge of Over There and destroying the Tree were daily occurrences, things he did most days before lunchtime.

"They will live out their lives there, those who remain, and as the population returns to zero, the Passageway will diminish and return to what it has always been—a thoroughfare for the souls of men to escape this world. Right! Turn right!"

"And this sword is a key?" Abra asked.

Mr. Henry nodded. "How did you know?"

"Mr. Tennin told me that too. In the dream. But there was also someone else. Someone . . . I don't know, someone who tried to convince me to unlock the gate and leave it open, not in order to kill the Tree, but for other reasons."

Mr. Henry turned in his seat again, this time so he could see Abra. "Who was it?"

"Koli Naal."

He nodded. "That's what I thought." He turned back around. "Did she say anything else?"

"I don't know," Abra said. "I guess she said a lot of things. I don't remember."

"She is Mr. Jinn's replacement. Or successor. Or overthrower. Probably all of those in some way. Koli Naal was waiting in the wings for a long time, much longer than four years. "

They stopped talking and the wind blew through the car.

"Some believe she orchestrated his downfall—they fight not only us but one another as well. She will do everything she can to deliver the Tree to humanity. She will do everything she can to rob them of death."

"The gift of death?" Leo muttered skeptically, but only Abra heard him.

"Stop!" Mr. Henry shouted, and as soon as Leo had applied the brakes, Mr. Henry jumped out of the car and walked through a gate that led through a stone wall.

"Where are we?" Abra asked Leo.

He turned and looked at her. "This is Saint Louis Cemetery No. 1."

The northern sky held small patches of candy blue, but directly above them it was slate gray, and low. The southern sky held a swirl of gathering darkness under which a heavy mist of approaching rain fell. An occasional flash of lightning jolted the earth. Abra looked uneasily over her shoulder at the storm as they followed Mr. Henry through the entrance of Saint Louis Cemetery No. 1.

They wound their way among the stones. Mr. Henry was hunched over, and Abra wondered how old he was, but he also reminded her of a bloodhound on the scent, leading with his nose. He seemed eager to get where he was going, as if he had been waiting a long time for something that was now very close at hand.

Beatrice jogged every so often to keep up with everyone else, and Abra stared at her. She continued to shift into something different. The giggling girl had been replaced by a very serious child—no, *child* wasn't even the proper word. Abra felt she was looking at an adult in a child's body.

Mr. Henry grunted in reply to some voice or suggestion Abra hadn't heard, and he kept walking. He stopped in front of an aboveground grave, a crypt the shape of a miniature house.

"This is it," Mr. Henry said, and the four of them stood there for a moment, staring. Large raindrops began falling from the sky, intermittent, without any sort of rhythm. They made heavy sounds against the pavement and the surrounding crypts, as if someone was tapping, tapping, tapping.

"This is the last place I saw my father and my sister," Leo said in a flat voice, walking up to the crypt and running his fingers down along one of the thin cracks in the cement. It was the shape of a long, country road or a lightning bolt.

The other three stared at him, waiting for more, but when he didn't keep talking Abra wasn't surprised. Cemeteries are the one place on earth where people can stop talking whenever they want and no one will press them for more. Which makes sense, since cemeteries hold so much unfinished business. You can visit a cemetery with a friend and stand by a grave for an hour and not say a word. Words mean less in cemeteries than they do anywhere else in the universe. Cemeteries devour words.

Mr. Henry walked up to the grave beside Leo and put both hands on it. "Have you heard of Marie Laveau?" he asked no one in particular.

"I have," Leo said quietly.

Mr. Henry looked at Leo. "You have?"

Leo nodded.

"And do you know when she died?" Mr. Henry asked.

"She did not die," Leo said, looking over at him.

"She didn't die?" Abra asked.

"That's the legend." Mr. Henry shrugged, and it seemed he knew more than he was saying.

"It's not a legend," Leo said, cutting him short. "I saw her. Eight years ago I saw her standing right here in this spot."

Mr. Henry stared at Leo for a moment, then looked at Abra. "Marie Laveau ate from the Tree of Life. She snatched a piece of fruit and took a bite before Mr. Tennin could kill it."

"So she will live forever?" Abra asked.

Mr. Henry nodded. "She will. Whether or not she still wants to is another matter entirely."

"She had a key," Leo said. "She had a key that opened a door."

"How did she get a key?" Abra asked.

Mr. Henry shrugged again. "We don't know. We don't know everything. She has many connections, both solid and spirit. She has ways of getting things—she was always very good at that. But it would seem that after working with Koli Naal for some time, Marie has now vanished and Koli cannot get back in. Or let her henchmen in."

"Which is why she came to me," Abra said in a flat voice.

Mr. Henry nodded.

"Don't we need the key to open the door?" Leo asked.

"Yes," Mr. Henry said, pointing at Abra. "But we already have one. The key Marie had was a poor copy. We have the original."

Abra pulled the sword out and it was ice blue along the edges, the same color the northern sky had been before the clouds completely obscured it.

"What do I do?" she asked.

"Put it in the keyhole."

She walked over to the side of the grave and stood there for a moment. She stared at the weathered cement, the small cracks, the graffiti on the walls. She saw the smallest of notches, a rectangle-shaped hole. Abra lifted the sword and slid it into the stone—surprisingly, it slid in the entire way.

"Now turn it," Mr. Henry said, and there was a light shining in his eyes. The lightning glinted off the diamonds and silver of the piercings on his face. The stud in his tongue tapped lightly against his teeth, and the rain fell harder.

Abra grasped the small hilt with two hands and turned it. There was a grating sound.

"Go ahead," Mr. Henry said in a gentle voice.

Abra was surprised at how easily the gate swung open. She was surprised at how the darkness inside repelled the light so that it looked like a black curtain hanging over the opening. The darkness shimmered against the approaching storm like something solid, like something alive.

19

ABRA STARED INTO THE LIVING DARKNESS, and fear moved through her like a tremor. "Mr. Henry," she whispered, "I don't think I can do it."

"You need to be brave," he said in a kind voice. "We need you."

Abra reached her hand out toward the crypt and put it in the darkness of the doorway. The shadow seemed to ripple like water.

"I don't think I can do it," she said again.

"Abra," Mr. Henry began, but then he glanced at Leo and Beatrice. Abra thought he seemed torn, as if he had important things to tell her that he didn't want the others overhearing, but he also didn't want to leave them by the open door on their own.

"Come away with me for a moment, Abra," Mr. Henry said, walking a short distance away. Abra followed behind him.

The rain came down harder and soon they were wet through. Abra looked over her shoulder and saw Beatrice and Leo still standing beside the crypt, water dripping from their faces, their hair matted down against their heads. They did not follow Abra and Mr. Henry. They stood there quietly, almost motionless, watching the two walk away. Mr. Henry, on the other hand, looked otherworldly, shrouded by the rain, and Abra felt tiny beside him.

"You know, being bald is a nice, simple way to live, but when it rains, all that water runs right down into your eyes." He smiled. Abra felt a kindness coming from him she had rarely experienced in her life. A fondness. He wiped his face with both palms, trying to clear the water.

"Choice is a funny thing, young lady. Choice. Every day we have it. Every day we make it. This way or that, that way or this. The small choices we make today and the next day and the next day, combined all together in a long, crooked path, can lead us here, or they can lead us there, and the difference between here and there can be a great distance after so many choices. But most choices seem small at the time. Inconsequential."

He stopped and let the water run down over his face. When he spoke again, rain sprayed out from his mouth in small droplets, and he blinked in that awkward way that someone blinks when it's raining hard in their eyes.

"I cannot make this choice for you," he said, squinting. "If you go in, you may never come out. Or you may come out so changed that you will not recognize yourself. I do not know what the Passageway will do to you or what you will find at the Edge of Over There. If you kill the Tree, the whole place might collapse in on itself. Of course, if you don't come back out of the Passageway, perhaps it's grace that Koli Naal made your mother forget you. In my experience, there is grace to be found in everything, even in what first appears to be pure pain."

Abra nodded but didn't say anything. She felt the weight of the moment, the weight of the decision, but if she was honest with herself, she didn't feel that she had much of a choice. There are things that should be done, and there are things that must be done. Abra felt she must go through that curtain of darkness. She didn't know what would happen after that.

"I know," Abra said. "I know. But what should I do about the people who live in there? Should I just leave them inside? That seems rather horrible, getting locked in a place like that forever. I don't know if I could do that to anyone."

"Choice is a funny thing," Mr. Henry said again. "Every person in there has made their choice. If they have not yet eaten from the Tree, they will eventually die like anyone else, here or there. If they have eaten from the Tree, they must not be allowed to come back here. You can see the kind of trouble that immortals like Marie Laveau bring about here on earth."

"But what will happen to the people who have eternal life and are trapped inside?"

Mr. Henry looked up at the sky and closed his eyes as the rain pummeled his cheeks and his forehead. When he looked at her, it was as if his face had been washed by the water.

"I don't know. None of us knows what will happen at the end of time to those who live forever. But they should not, must not, come back here, through the gate. That, I know."

Abra nodded. "And Leo's father? His sister?"

Mr. Henry bit his lip, and for the first time since Abra had met him he appeared unsure, uncertain. She saw the kindness in his eyes again, the kindness of Mr. Tennin, and she was surprised that Mr. Henry had scared her when she first saw him in the park with all of his piercings and tattoos. She realized that his harsh exterior only served to hide a kindhearted man. She wondered how many times that was the case.

"If they have not yet eaten from the Tree, it seems like that will be your choice to make," he said. "But your primary purpose—remember this! Your primary purpose is to go in and destroy the Tree, come back out, and seal the gate. I will wait here while you're inside, because I have to. I will guard the door and make sure no one comes in or goes out."

The rain lessened, and the two stood there for a few more minutes before turning and walking back to Marie Laveau's grave. The rain stopped suddenly, and steam rose up off the pavement in foggy clouds of vapor. Throughout the whole city, a heavy mist was rising, creating a cloud that drifted over the streets and the buildings, thick as soup. The sunlight glared down through the white so that you could barely see.

Abra and Mr. Henry walked back to the grave of Marie Laveau through the mist. They were wet, and something about their conversation had exhausted them. But Abra also felt eager— eager to get on with the task, eager to see what waited for her on the other side of the curtain of darkness. There was something inside of her that came alive when she thought about taking the sword into the darkness, finding the Tree of Life, and getting rid of it. It felt like something she had been created to do.

When Abra and Mr. Henry arrived back at the open door to the grave, Abra's mouth fell open and Mr. Henry sighed.

Beatrice and Leo were gone.

⁓

"Mr. Henry," Abra said quietly. "They've gone in."

"Yes, young lady. They have."

"What are we going to do?" she asked him.

"What are you going to do?"

Abra paused for a moment. "I have to find the Tree. I have to come back out and lock the gate."

Mr. Henry nodded, and his head looked heavy on his shoulders, the way it swayed slowly forward and back.

"Young lady, who do you think Beatrice is?"

"What do you mean?"

"Had you ever seen her before this summer?"

Abra shook her head.

"Yet she claimed to go to your small school."

Abra stared into the curtain of darkness that shrouded the opening in the grave. "She arrived at the same time as Koli Naal," she said. "She was there when my mother stopped knowing who I was. She just so happened to be there when the sword brought me to New Orleans."

Mr. Henry nodded.

"I should have done something sooner. I should have ditched her earlier." Abra paused. "I should have gotten rid of her earlier."

"Now, now," Mr. Henry said. "That's not you speaking, is it? There are so few, if any, we are responsible for 'getting rid of.' That's the last thing you should be thinking or worrying about."

"What should I do?" she asked.

"She does complicate things," he admitted, rubbing his eyes with his palms as if he were weary, weary to the bone. "I'm guessing she belongs to Koli Naal. I'm guessing she's been back and forth through the gate and into the Passageway, at first with the help of Marie Laveau, and then, when Marie stopped helping them, they came looking for you. I'm guessing that Koli won't risk going inside herself for fear of being locked in forever, so she uses Beatrice to do her work."

He looked at Abra, and even in that moment, he laughed.

"That's a lot of guesses," he said. "But I'm a good guesser. They must have been desperate if they came looking for you and your sword—it might have been able to get them through the gate, but it is also the very thing that can kill the Tree. It appears we have something in common with Koli Naal."

Abra was surprised. "What?"

"We both need to get inside."

"I thought you couldn't go inside. I thought angels couldn't go in."

"Beings of Light, young lady. Beings of Light cannot, will not, should not—any of those and all of them at the same time. Cannot, will not, should not. Koli Naal and her kind, on the other hand . . . I suppose that might be seen as a benefit of their kind. They go where and when they please."

He rubbed his eyes again.

"I'm tired, Abra."

"You're tired? You're an angel. How can you get tired?"

"You know I don't like that word. You have a lot of questions, don't you?"

She waited.

"Beatrice will be Beatrice," he concluded. "She will do what's in the best interest of her master. I would be wary if you see her again—she will not play the part of your school friend any longer."

Abra took one step toward the doorway.

"Wait, young lady. Wait."

Mr. Henry motioned toward the sword. Abra reached up and grabbed on to it, pulled it smoothly from the lock. It shone silver and white in the mist. But even the mist was fading. The world was returning from the shadows, taking shape all around them as if emerging on the first day. First the crypts came into view, followed by the wall, and finally the trees beyond it.

"Hurry," Mr. Henry said, staring at the sword. "I will push the gate nearly closed behind you, but I cannot lock it without the sword, and you will need to take that with you. I will wait here for a hundred days or a hundred years—however long it takes you to do what you must. I will sit here with my back against the door, but it will remain unlocked until you return. You should be able to see the light around the edges. When you return, walk to the light. I will be waiting."

She nodded solemnly at Mr. Henry and slid the sword into the side of her jeans. But then she thought better of that and took it back out. She held it in front of her, both of her hands clutching the small hilt. She had many thoughts as she walked into the darkness. She thought first of her mother—she wondered if going in was made easier by the fact that her mother no longer knew her. It was some comfort to think that if she didn't return, her mother would not be saddened by her absence.

Abra also thought about Sam and, not for the last time, wished he was there with her.

She thought about the Amarok and took comfort in knowing it had been the last of its kind, but she wondered what other creatures Koli Naal might have set loose in the Passageway. She thought about Beatrice, wondering what she was up to. And that's when she had her first important revelation—if Beatrice was involved, then surely she would know where the Tree was! It was the only lead Abra had, and she made up her mind. She had to follow Beatrice.

She looked over her shoulder after she was a few steps inside and caught a vision of Mr. Henry, a tiny sliver of his face still visible through the crack in the door. Behind him was light and the dissipating fog and the emerging city, and beyond that the whole wide world.

"I'm afraid," she said in a small voice, small as a lone firefly in an endless field.

"I know," he said. "But fear always comes with a door, a door that leads straight through."

Abra tried to smile at him and took a deep breath, the sword trembling in her hands. She nodded at him and he nodded at her, and as she turned to walk farther into the darkness, he slowly pushed the stone door closed so that all she could see was a thin sliver of light around the outside of it.

She hoped she would see it again soon.

through doors we should not open

There is a river we must cross over.

When Life's sun goes to sleep in the west.

There'll be a Light for me at the crossing

Guiding me to that home of sweet rest.

FROM C. M. HENDERSON'S HYMN
"LIGHT AT THE RIVER"

20

LEO STOOD THERE WATCHING Abra and Mr. Henry walk away through the downpour. He barely noticed the rain—the last thing he was thinking about was the rain. It took everything in him not to scream at them as they walked away.

Don't you realize my sister is in there! How can you be so calm! What are we waiting for?

But he didn't scream anything. He stood there. And he waited.

Beside him stood Beatrice. She had been silent at the park. She had been silent in the car on the drive over. She even remained silent while they stood there in the rain. He had nearly forgotten about her. He hadn't taken much notice of her at all since she had emerged from the trapdoor, whining and complaining. But she moved, there in the rain, and he looked over at her.

Beatrice walked through the doorway.

Just like that, without a word, without an explanation, without so much as a sound or a look his way, she took ten steps and vanished into the darkness. He almost missed it because he had been staring at Mr. Henry and Abra, and Beatrice didn't make a sound when she moved. The only thing he really saw was the back of her blending in with the shadows inside of Marie Laveau's grave.

"Beatrice!" he said, but she didn't stop. He walked over to the opening and stared inside—it was like staring into a vat of black oil. He couldn't see a thing. His mind started to wander.

Leo's sadness about losing his sister hadn't lessened through the years, but it had changed, somehow lost its sharp edges. The sadness that remained seemed fuller, more permanent. Standing there in the very spot where he had last seen her eight years before, the door now open in front of him, was a powerful experience. He scoured the area for any signs of Marie, but there were no ashes on the ground, no signs of a miniature fire, no reminders of that night. He wondered what had become of his father and his sister. Were they still in there? Had they been waiting all those years for someone to unlock the gate so they could come back out? Were they even alive?

Before he knew it, he was surrounded in darkness.

He had gone in.

He kept walking forward even though he couldn't see anything. The ground beneath his feet seemed temporary in that blackness, as if he might start floating away. The darkness suffocated him at first, and he had to breathe deliberately. Sometimes he thought maybe he *was* floating. But in those moments of uncertainty he would look back at the doorway, framed in light. The door was still there, smaller as he walked farther in, but still there.

When distance threatened to make the door invisible behind him, he noticed a shifting in the darkness ahead. It became less oily, less solid. It shifted into a gray sort of murkiness, and he felt stones and dirt crunching under his feet, and he walked farther and realized the darkness to each side of him was no longer a void but the shadows of a thick forest. When he looked behind him, all he saw was the dirt road as far as he could see. He wondered, if he walked back that way, would he reenter the darkness, or was that door lost to him forever?

He kept going forward until something flew out of the woods and grabbed him from behind. All he felt were tight arms around his neck, and he fell to the ground. He couldn't breathe, and darkness closed in around the edges of his vision. The last thing he saw was the expressionless face of Beatrice, looking down as she choked the life out of him.

He gasped for one long breath, gulping in air. When he came to, he didn't know if it was moments or hours later. He looked up through branches and realized he was on the side of the road. His neck hurt, and each breath felt like someone was pushing sandpaper down his throat, but he kept trying, and he kept breathing, and each inhale hurt less and less. Finally, he sat up.

How was he still alive?

The day seemed brighter, or perhaps his eyes had grown accustomed to the level of light. He wondered what had happened to Beatrice, where she had gone, why she had attacked him like that. He was perplexed at how such a small girl had been able to bring him down. He looked around quickly at the thought of her, hoping she wasn't there.

He was alone in the woods.

It is difficult to describe what being truly alone felt like for Leo, a young man who had grown up on the outskirts of a city, a young man who drove a loud car and had loud friends and lived the life of an eighteen-year-old. Perhaps for some that sense of being alone would have driven them insane. To be in what appeared an endless forest on the edge of a long road to nowhere would have been too much space, too much emptiness. For others, this being alone would have led them to activity. They would have churned down the road for as long and as far as their legs would take them, ready to rid themselves of that empty feeling.

But for Leo, being alone felt like freedom.

The everyday troubles that a young man has to deal with, especially a young man who has lost a sibling and one of his parents (and was in the process of losing the other), were gone in an instant. The only thing in front of him was the possibility of finally finding out what had happened to his sister, and that filled him with anticipation. He stood up, and he would have continued down the road feeling that way, except for the fact that he heard someone coming. He ducked into the trees and waited, and the footsteps came at a slow pace.

Leo saw her—it was Abra, and she walked in the middle of the road as if she was nothing more than a country girl wandering along a dirt road on a cool summer day.

"Abra," he hissed. "Hey, Abra!"

She peered into the trees. "Leo? Is that you?"

Abra ran to the side of the road. He was surprised at how happy he was to see her.

"Leo! I'm so glad I found you. You have to go back. Get out of here! That door won't be unlocked for long, and once it's locked again, you might never get out!"

"I'm not going anywhere," he said quietly. "I'm here to find my sister."

Abra shook her head. She pushed her hair out of her eyes,

and it was this seriousness of hers that he found so fascinating. She was only a teenager, but she carried the concern of an old monk looking out over the world from a high place.

"I can't wait around for you to find her. There are more important things—" She stopped short.

"More important?" he asked.

"I didn't mean it like that. I have to find the Tree, and then I have to lock the gate," she said, sighing. "When I leave, I have to lock and seal the door. I can't wait for anyone. If we get separated, you'll be here. For the rest of your life. Please. Go back."

She looked so desperate and so kind and so thoughtful for someone her age that he could hear the wisdom in what she said. Her blonde hair perfectly framed her face. He stared at her, seeing her for the first time—or maybe she had changed, entering the darkness. Maybe he had changed too. But then he shook his head.

"I can't leave until I at least find out what happened to my sister. I have to know."

Abra looked at him and there was a deep regret in her eyes, as if she could see the ending, and the ending she could see wasn't good. He wanted to ask her what she saw, what she knew, but he didn't.

"Have you seen Beatrice?" Abra asked, and he was glad to see that she wasn't going to try to convince him to leave anymore.

"Did more than see her," Leo said, reaching up and tenderly rubbing his neck. "She tried to kill me." He told her what had happened, how he had woken up in the trees. They both stood there in silence for a while, thinking about Beatrice.

"I think if I can find her, I'll find the Tree," Abra said.

Leo nodded. "I might as well stick with you," he said. "I guess

Beatrice could lead us to my sister. But watch out. She has a strong grip."

Abra sighed. "All right. Let's go."

The two of them followed the flat dirt road farther in.

"Maybe we should take a rest," Leo suggested. The sky had been a dull, rusty red all day but was beginning to fade to darkness. He hadn't been able to see the sun, and there weren't any stars. Abra stopped in the middle of the road and peered ahead. Leo stared at the long, straight stretch.

"Maybe," Abra said before walking over to the side of the road and sitting down with her back against a tree.

Leo followed her. "Maybe we should go a little farther into the woods, to take cover," he said, standing there beside her.

She took a deep breath. "Yeah, sure," she said.

They walked twenty paces into the woods and sat down, both of them resting their backs against the same huge tree trunk.

"How long do you think this forest has been here?" Leo asked, looking up into the motionless leaves.

Abra didn't say anything right away, and he wondered if she had fallen asleep. The same lightness fell over him once again, the same freedom. He took a deep breath and was amazed at how incredible the air smelled, as if it was unused, fresh, unlike the stale air back home that had been breathed in by people and machines and exhaled over and over again for thousands of years. There, off the edge of the road, only the trees breathed, and the sky.

"Not long and forever," Abra said. "That's how long this forest has been here. Can't you feel it? Something about it is new, and something else is old. Very old."

Leo thought she was right.

"Are you worried you might not find your sister?" she asked him.

"A little," he said. "It's been eight years. A lot can happen in eight years."

"Yeah," Abra said. "Actually, it doesn't even take that long."

Abra's breathing became soft and rhythmic, and Leo thought she must be asleep. He felt suddenly energized and regretted his suggestion to stop, so he stood up and walked over to the road, glancing over his shoulder to see if he had woken her up. In all of that great stillness, every one of his steps sounded to him like an explosion of twigs and leaves, but Abra slept on.

He waited there by the road, and something inside of him wanted to go stand in the middle of it, and something else inside of him warned him that it wouldn't be a good idea. He wasn't sure where those feelings came from or what caused them, but their combined effect left him standing there on the edge of the road, hiding behind a tree with a trunk that split off into five main sections close to the ground. He didn't know why he felt like hiding, but he pressed himself up against the tree and waited. For what, he didn't know.

He felt ready for the journey, ready to discover answers to eight-year-old questions. What he was not ready for was witnessing those who used the road—those for whom the Passageway had been created.

Long before Marie Laveau had begun letting people through the gate in her grave, the Passageway had been in use, as Mr. Henry had explained to them. This was what gave the place its ancient feel. This was what rubbed the dirt road so smooth that it looked paved.

Leo heard them before he saw them.

At first it was only one. This thing—this spirit as some might call it, this soul as others might refer to it—whisked past him so fast and with such intensity that at first he wondered if he'd had a flash of light-headedness. It was a bright whiteness, that one, and when it passed him it made the sound of a scream. It made him drop to his knees.

He was terrified.

He waited for what felt like a very long time, and when he felt it might be safe to move out from behind the tree, another rushed past him. Instinctively, he ducked. He couldn't figure out how big they were, in the same way that it's hard to tell how big a water bug is while it skims over the surface of the water. The second one he saw was darker than the first, and the shriek it made was much lower, almost like a moan, the wind in the trees.

He thought he should probably go get Abra, but she was already coming slowly through the trees.

"What was that noise?" she asked. Leo held up his finger, telling her to wait.

More came down the road every few minutes, like bats from a cave. At first they emerged in singles. After that they came in twos and threes and fours. Finally, they were one long, constant stream, and the sound was overwhelming. Abra and Leo both fell to the ground, covering their ears, afraid it would never end. Even with their arms wrapped up around their heads, the sound was a physical force that pounded and tore at their bodies. Leo felt like he was in a boxing match.

Abra stood up. Leo looked up at her, wondering what she was doing. He reached up to pull her back down beside him, into safety, but she shed his hand and, still covering her ears, walked out into the street. The bright ones and the shadowy ones and all of the in-between ones roared around her like water in a stream rushing around a new rock. She spread out her arms and looked straight up into the sky, and the movement almost seemed to go through her. Leo wanted to cry out to her, beg her to come back, but he didn't, and she stayed until the lights and the shadows became a trickle, until the stragglers rushed past them.

The silence they left behind in the dim, red light filled Leo with an emptiness he had never felt before.

21

THREE DAYS PASSED before they saw the city off in the distance. Three long days of walking the hard-packed dust of the road, three long nights of hearing the souls of the dead rush past on their way to Over There. Three days is a long time when you don't know exactly where you're going and your surroundings don't change a bit. They found food, small berries growing in thickets on both sides of the road. They drank from springs that gurgled up about a half day's walk apart. Leo wondered if they had been spaced deliberately.

The food itself seemed to nourish him on a molecular level, as if it was somehow pure nutrients, the exact stuff his body needed. Not just any body, but his. The spring water tasted slightly sweet, like the sap from a maple tree before it has been reduced down to syrup. They were eating less than they had ever eaten before, but they felt healthier, more nourished.

The first house they saw was just outside the city. It was a small, one-story brick cottage with large windows and a red door. The shutters were black. The air around the house felt a little off—if the rest of the Edge of Over There seemed specifically designed for human life, the house itself felt slightly askew, like the slightest bend in an otherwise perfectly straight wire. Abra walked quietly up to one of the windows and peered inside.

"I don't think anyone lives here," she said.

Leo knocked on the door, and when no one answered, he shouted, "Anybody there?"

But no one was there, or at least no one answered. The forest swallowed his voice. When Leo tried to turn the knob, he found it was locked. He reached inside his pocket and felt the lock-picking set, the cold metal, the multiple picks. He decided to leave it in his pocket. If he had been alone, without Abra, he probably would have given it a try, but there was something embarrassing about being someone who could break into places, someone who could undo things not meant to be undone. So he shrugged, and they walked away with many backward glances. The house gave them the feeling that someone was watching them, someone they shouldn't turn their backs to.

They passed a few more houses built in the woods off the road, but they weren't paying attention to the houses anymore. The city was closer now, its buildings rising up out of the trees. But there was one building in particular that got their attention, deep in the city, one that rose so high above the others that it looked thin and exposed.

"There's something strange about that building," Leo said on the morning of the day they would reach the city. This marked their fourth day inside the grave of Marie Laveau.

"You mean besides the fact that it's so tall?" Abra asked.

"Yeah. I don't like the look of it."

They walked quietly, their feet patting a gentle rhythm against the hard dirt of the road.

"It doesn't have windows," Leo said.

"What?" Abra asked.

"The tall building. It doesn't have windows."

They kept walking, the two of them staring up, the way flowers' faces follow the sun. Abra shielded her eyes from the midday light.

"Are you sure?"

Leo nodded. "You know what else I'm sure of?"

Abra looked at him.

"That's where my father is," Leo said.

"How do you know?" she asked.

He looked at her and smiled. "I just know," he said, shrugging. "That's where he is. And if he's there, my sister's there too."

~

Arriving at that city was like arriving at no other city in the world. The woods ran right up to it—no suburbs, no gradual urbanization, no high overpasses that skirted factories and ran over no-man's-land. This city simply grew right up out of the trees. One minute they were on the dirt road that led from the gateway, and with their next step they were on the first city street, looking up at the tall buildings. It was like emerging from Central Park in New York City, a head-spinning transition from grass and green spaces to concrete and thin slivers of sky.

"Where do you think everyone is?" Leo asked. The quiet of the woods was one thing—the silence of the city under the red sky was something entirely different.

"How do you know there is anyone? Maybe it's empty. Maybe something happened," Abra said.

"Do you think the quiet has something to do with the Tree you're looking for?"

"I don't know. Maybe."

A breeze blew from the far side of the city, came rushing through the streets, and passed them by. It moved the branches and the leaves of the forest and made a loud shushing sound. Abra's hair danced in the breeze.

"Smells kind of like the ocean," Leo said.

"There's definitely water out there somewhere, the sea that Mr. Henry told us about. I wonder what it's like. I wonder how far away it is," Abra said in a wistful voice. She pointed down the street to their right, the one that ran along the forest. "What's that?"

Leo squinted. "Is that . . . ?" he began.

"Beatrice?" Abra said.

It looked like her. She was nearly out of view, blending into the shadows on the forest side of the street. She walked fast, sometimes skipping a step, then slowing again to a walk. She didn't look back.

Leo moved to cross that first street and enter the city at exactly the same time that Abra turned right and started walking the line between the city and the forest.

They both stopped in their tracks.

"Where are you going?" she asked him.

"I have to go to that building," he said. "I'm sure that's where my sister is." He stared at her, and when she didn't say anything, he asked, "Where are you going?"

"I have to find the Tree of Life. Beatrice knows where it is. I'm positive."

They stared at each other for a moment, waiting for the other person to change their mind and follow. Leo had grown used to Abra's company. He didn't want to walk alone.

"But how do you know?" he asked. "I mean, the Tree could be anywhere. It could be a trap."

"How do you know your sister is in the building?" she replied sarcastically.

Leo clenched his fists and took a deep breath. "We really should stay together," he said, trying to remain calm. "We don't know what's happened to this city. We don't know where all the people are. We don't know who's in that building. I think until we figure some of this stuff out, we should stay together."

"I agree. We should stay together. So, come on, let's go. Beatrice might lead us to your sister too!"

"Why do you have to be so stubborn! You don't know the Tree is that way. It could be anywhere!"

"And you *know* your father is in that building? How?"

Leo bit his lip and shook his head. "Listen, come with me for today, a few hours. I bet we can be at the building by the time it gets dark. If my sister isn't there, I'll come with you."

"And waste two days walking in and walking back out when your father isn't there? I'm following Beatrice."

"Okay," Leo said. "Whatever." He threw his hands up in the air and turned to walk away, trying to hide the disappointment and frustration that welled up inside of him. It reminded him of the day his father and sister had gone into Marie Laveau's crypt. He didn't think he would ever find Abra again.

"Good luck," Abra called after him. He turned to look at her, and she looked like a little girl again, small and pale against the backdrop of that immense forest. But there was still something that seemed much older. Maybe it was her eyes—they held a certain kind of sadness, as if she was about to enter a trial she had already experienced before, the kind where she knew the pain before it even started.

"Same to you," he said, but his voice came out dismissive and curt.

The streets were empty of people, but there were signs of destruction everywhere, a kind of chaos the silence did not explain. Glass windows were shattered and lying in shards on the sidewalk. Doors were bent and mutilated, hanging from hinges. Even the brick and concrete of the buildings bore huge craters, as if someone had gone along with a sledgehammer and randomly taken swings. But it wasn't only explosive destruction—there were also the marks of time. Long cracks split the sidewalks, and the glass was coated and streaked in dust. It was eerie, the emptiness paired with the destruction.

When he got to the other side of that first street, he turned to look for Abra again. She was farther away than he expected.

"If you get out before we do, give us some time. Leave the gate open," he called out. "I won't be long."

She turned and looked at him. He couldn't tell if she had heard what he said, but she raised her hand in one final wave, then continued down the street that ran along the edge of the city. She reminded Leo of a tiny balloon, floating higher and higher into the sky until you can't really see it, even though you think you can.

He turned away and walked faster. The afternoon shadows lengthened. He wanted to be at the building by nightfall.

But that didn't happen.

The farther into the city Leo went, the stranger it became. At first the only thing that seemed to change was that the forest receded behind him and the sea smell in the air grew stronger. It was unsettling, looking back over his shoulder and discovering he could no longer see the trees. He had walked nearly twenty blocks into the city, twenty blocks of high buildings and broken glass, twenty blocks of the wind howling through the alleyways. Twenty blocks and the only sound were his footsteps on dusty concrete or grinding the occasional shard of glass.

But after twenty blocks or so he realized something else was different too. At first, he didn't know what it was—he thought it was his imagination. Soon he realized the difference he felt was that, somewhere in all of those darkened office buildings and apartment complexes, someone was watching him. Or more than one someone. He didn't know why he felt that way—he still hadn't seen any real live human beings. But he knew he wasn't alone.

He kept expecting someone to call out to him from one of the glass-shattered lobbies or rooftop terraces. He glanced up the fire escapes, peered down the narrow side roads, glanced quickly over his shoulder. There was no one. As the afternoon waned and he got within ten blocks of the huge building, something changed.

Leo heard a sound.

It started off small and far away. He thought it was only the wind. As it grew louder, he thought it might be some kind of vehicle, a line of traffic or an airplane approaching from another city. By the time he realized what it was, it was too late and they had already seen him.

A huge group of people came jostling onto his street a few blocks ahead, shouting and laughing and arguing. They were his age or slightly older. And they kept coming around the corner, more and more of them. He thought there must be hundreds, maybe even a thousand, and he tried to duck into the building he was walking past, but it was one of the few with intact front glass and locked doors. He had nowhere to go.

"Hey, who's that?" one of the front-runners called out, and soon the entire throbbing mob was around him and pressing in.

"I only arrived today," he stammered.

"A newbie!" one of them shouted to the pack, and everyone cheered and some of them leered and their faces were close and loud.

"Are you here by yourself?" someone else screamed, and it unsettled Leo, the way the voices came from people he could not identify. It was like the mob was speaking, and not any one individual.

"Yeah," he said, nodding quickly. "Yeah, I'm alone."

The crowd shifted, parted, and a small, brown-haired young man walked through. He had hazel eyes and his face was covered in freckles. He wore jeans and a white T-shirt that seemed remarkably clean in that environment of broken buildings and mobs of people. He smiled, pushed his hair out of his eyes, and held out his hand.

"I'm Jeremiah," he said. "Do you have a name?"

A ripple of laughter spread through the mob.

"I'm Leo."

The two shook hands, and Leo was surprised, almost alarmed, at how quickly he was welcomed into the group. Jeremiah was also an enigma. The strength in his handshake didn't fit with his boyish looks. His fingers may have been small but they felt like wire traps. His forearms were thin, steel cables. Leo thought Jeremiah was probably about his age, maybe slightly older.

"You're welcome to join us."

Leo nodded, glancing down at the cracked sidewalk, amazed at the crowd of feet and legs and bodies in front of him. What he wanted to do was say, "No thanks, I'll keep traveling alone," but that didn't feel like an option. He decided to go along with it for now. His eyes went from the ground up to the red sky. He nodded again.

"We only have a few rules," Jeremiah said.

"Okay." Leo felt less and less comfortable, more and more like a prisoner.

"Three, mostly, although we have to add some from time to time. Don't steal anything from anyone else in the group—there's plenty to go around. That's probably the most important one. Stay with the group—that's number two. If for some reason you have to head out on your own, and I can't think of a good reason you would ever do that, let me know. Number three—if one of us fights, we all fight. We stand up for each other. Always."

Leo nodded, the second rule sticking in his mind. *Stay with the group.* How did he even become part of this group? It had all happened way too fast, but he couldn't shake the strong sense that to separate himself from the group at that point would only lead to them devouring him.

"Don't steal, stay with the group, all for one," Leo repeated in a monotone voice, now staring at Jeremiah. He hadn't come all this way to get waylaid by a punk. His sister was in the city somewhere. Abra would find the Tree and leave them all behind if he didn't hurry.

But for now, he had to bide his time.

"You got it?" Jeremiah asked.

"Yeah." Leo shifted his weight from one foot to the other. He wished they would get on with whatever it was they had been doing. He didn't like being the center of attention.

"Good."

Jeremiah smiled and turned to face the rest of the crowd. Leo doubted his initial estimate of hundreds. There were definitely at least a thousand. He wondered how this small young man had managed to become the leader of such an unruly, disorganized bunch.

192

"Welcome, Leo!"

The crowd cheered, and some of them gave him a welcoming slap on the back. A few of the girls even leaned in and hugged him. Leo went from feeling defensive to slightly, and surprisingly, emotional. They seemed really happy to have him. In that moment, when everyone was hooting and hollering and clapping, Leo felt like he could become part of something.

He had never had that before. He had to remind himself why he was there in the first place.

"We're staying here tonight," Jeremiah shouted, and the group erupted in cheers again.

Moments later Leo heard an explosion of shattering glass, and he ducked his head. But no one else looked alarmed, so he turned and saw a large portion of the group smashing the first-floor glass walls of the building behind them. The glass was destroyed in seconds. They kicked the larger shards out of the way, and the group moved into the building like a virus entering its host. They swarmed through, everyone looking for a comfortable place to sleep. Leo hung back, watching in amazement at the efficiency of their chaotic destruction. In less than a minute, the building had been taken over.

He felt a hand on his shoulder.

"Get used to it," Jeremiah said. "This city is ours."

Leo nodded and watched quietly as Jeremiah walked toward the building, surrounded by six or seven others. Leo assumed they were his inner circle. There were a few girls, a few guys. They dressed the same as everyone else but carried themselves with a certain air that separated them. They seemed to be above the fray, better than the chaos. They waited until all the glass was broken before they walked in.

"Find a spot," Jeremiah said. "The Wailers are coming."

Leo walked through the glass, and it ground under his feet, coarse and threatening. He ducked under the jagged edge of a glass wall that had not been completely cleared and brushed off the bottom of his shoes on a carpet inside. A hundred or so of the group had already settled there in the lobby, away from the broken glass, sitting in small circles, talking.

Leo found some stairs and followed them up a few floors. He wanted to find a place where he could be alone and think for a minute. He wanted to find a floor where he might be able to separate himself from the group. He opened a door and walked into a mostly dark level. There were some desks—it looked like an office building that had never been used. He found an unoccupied desk and pushed it against the wall, then crawled beneath it and stretched out, staring through the glass side of the building that stretched from the floor to the ceiling.

He felt very lonely lying there in the darkness. He listened to the sound of the Wailers, and soon they flashed past the window, white and black and every shade of gray in between, and the song they made was haunting but also a little beautiful. It reminded him of walking through the forest with Abra, of the nights they had spent together in the trees that lined the dirt road. They hadn't really said much on those few nights, but he had become used to her presence.

He wondered where she had taken refuge that night. He wondered if she had found Beatrice or her Tree.

22

ABRA TURNED ONE LAST TIME and watched Leo disappear into the city. He was older than her, but his slumped shoulders and hesitant steps made him look like a little boy, lost in the big world. She almost called out to him. Maybe he was right. Maybe they should stick together. But in the end, she didn't say anything.

She thought that would probably be the last time she'd ever see him. She knew she would lock the Passageway after she destroyed the Tree, whether or not Leo was there, and this knowledge scared her. She wondered, with alarm, if she was a heartless person.

She continued down the long, straight road with the city across the street to her left, the forest directly to her right. Sometimes the branches grew out over the sidewalk and she had to walk in the crumbling pavement. Sometimes she peered into the shadows among the trees and wondered how far that forest went, and if it had an end, or if in every direction, if one walked far enough, there would be a gradually increasing darkness. And then nothing.

Beatrice was always just barely at the far reaches of what she could see. Always moving ahead at a brisk pace. Always walking on the same side of the road as the trees, in and out of the shadows.

The city was silent. The only sound was the scraping of her shoes on the sidewalk or the occasional snapping of the twigs she stepped on. It was one of the strangest moments of her life, walking along a city of that size without hearing anything. After ten or fifteen blocks she realized something else—there were no animals. No birds swooping through the air, no squirrels dashing here and there around the trees. No ants in the sidewalks. No pigeons roosting on the buildings. Nothing.

She stared into the forest a lot because she still thought that might be where she would find the Tree of Life. She stared particularly hard when the wind blew, because she remembered how that would make it easier to see the heavy fruit hanging in the midst of the fluttering leaves. Sometimes she thought she saw something, and she stopped, peering through the vines and the shrubs and the low branches.

Abra had never been tempted by the Tree when it appeared along the Road to Nowhere north of her farm in the outskirts of Deen. She had plunged the sword into its trunk without hesitation. But she recognized something strange inside of her as she walked that long, straight street, something deep inside of her that she had not felt four years before. It could perhaps be best symbolized by the tiniest of question marks.

That was it. There were no words with the question mark, no tangible concerns or hesitations as to why she should not kill the Tree. Nothing she could put her finger on. But there it was anyway, a small seed of uncertainty. Was she thinking of Sam's mother again, her loveliness gone from the world because of death? Was she thinking of the lamb that had died, its innocence erased from the world by death?

Or was she thinking of her own mother, now not even aware that Abra was her daughter? Abra's mother had given Abra her only firsthand experience of erasure, the kind of clean slate that death can cause. She thought back over Mr. Tennin's words and wondered if they were true.

Death is a gift.

Then it happened. Beatrice was gone. Abra ran ahead, staring down each street that led into the city, peering into the trees. But somehow, at some point, she had lost Beatrice. Abra's insides dropped. She wondered for the first time if she should have stayed with Leo.

The sky began to fade and Abra saw something strange up ahead. The trees looked like they grew on the street, but as she got closer she could see that wasn't it at all. The street she was on turned sharply to the left, and the forest lined that road as well. When she made the turn, she saw that, once again, this street was a long, straight street that separated the city from the forest. So the city, at least in this part, was like the corner of a square. She continued on.

The air changed as she headed in that direction. The smell of the large body of water became stronger, more melancholy. She didn't know how she knew it was the smell of water. She had never been to a beach. But something planted that in her mind. An image of water crashing on the sand. The endless water blending with the sky at the horizon.

Abra smiled.

It grew dark faster than she had expected. Already the corner she had passed was far behind her, blocks and blocks and blocks, and still she had not seen a single person or a single animal, or heard a single sound other than those her own feet made. She walked a few paces into the woods, cleared a small space, and lay down. She fell asleep.

Abra's eyes popped open in the middle of the night and she lay there, completely still. She thought she'd been woken up by the sound of someone, or something, entering the woods from the road. Someone, or something, that was still close by. The sky was a red that was almost black, but it showed through the canopy of leaves, and the trees rustled slightly in a warm breeze. It felt like a strange dream—the red glow, the smell of the ocean, the dark outline of the city.

Was that it? Was it only a dream? Had she heard nothing more than the wind in the trees?

But no, there it was again. The snapping of a dry twig, the subtle scraping of leaves breaking under someone's foot. Abra tried to control her breathing. She lifted her head from the ground as slowly and quietly as she could, peering up and over the edge of the small hollow she had lain down in a few hours before.

Immediately in front of her face was a large tangle of tree roots. Beyond that, through the filter of the red night's dark light, she could see a few large rocks all in a row, poking up through the rich dirt. Trees grew in a line along the outcropping—one even sprouted out of a crack in the rocks. But it's what she saw in front of the rocks and the thick line of trees, only ten yards away, that made her heart beat faster.

Beatrice was leaning over, searching around on the ground. She bent her head this way and that, and the strange movement of her neck reminded Abra of a bird of prey, an eagle or a hawk, the way they study something with a sinister curiosity before tearing it to shreds. Beatrice went on staring in that curious way for another minute before standing up slowly and continuing along the line of rocks.

Abra waited a moment. Beatrice seemed taller to her now, and she wondered about the powers of Beatrice and those like her, if they could really change their size or if they had a way of presenting themselves as bigger or smaller depending on what they needed. She wondered if Beatrice was more powerful here in this world at the Edge than she was back on earth. Beatrice's face—what Abra could see of it—seemed strangely neutral the entire time. Her mouth was straight. Her eyes dim and un-blinking.

Abra pulled herself to her hands and knees, wincing at the sound of leaves rustling under her. She froze, again holding her breath. She rose to her feet and hid behind a tree, peeking around the rough bark. Beatrice continued on through the woods, along the jagged rocks, walking slowly and directly away from the city. Her black dress flowed quietly around her, smooth and rippling. Abra stared at her back. Beatrice was a tear in space, or the moving trunk of a tree.

Abra trembled and leaned against the tree, but she also knew she didn't have time to spare. As she stood there, Beatrice was disappearing into the trees, still walking away from the city. Toward what? The dark borders of this strange land? The river? The Tree?

Abra sighed, peered ahead into the darkness, and walked forward along the rocks, trailing Beatrice. The light in the sky was still a dark red, and it tinted everything. As she moved forward, she realized a narrow path ran along the outcropping of rocks. It was a worn path, not pressed all the way down to the dust, but she was able to see it and follow it, even in the dark. She slowed down, not wanting Beatrice to hear her.

Every so often she came around a corner and saw Beatrice not as far ahead, so she lessened her pace. Other times the path twisted, and when it straightened again, Abra couldn't see Beatrice, so she walked faster. Never once did Beatrice look over her shoulder. Never once did she turn to address Abra. The farther they went, the more Abra thought Beatrice might just be leading her along, farther from the city. Farther from the Tree? It might be a trap. But the slim chance that Beatrice was making for the Tree was too great a pull, and Abra continued on.

The rocks grew taller and soon became a solid wall of rock, one she couldn't see over. They held deep gashes in their flat surfaces, fracture lines that seemed to bear witness to a great and powerful collision, one of seismic proportion. Embedded every so often in or beside these deep fissures were long threads of silver, glittering lines that drew Abra's eye. She traced the silver with her finger and it left sparkling gray dust on her fingertips. She smelled the residue, and if starlight had a smell, this would have been it—fresh like spring water but with a metallic, sharp foundation. She let her hand run over the rock as she walked, and soon her entire palm was coated in it, and her fingers, and it even crept up her wrist. There was something glorious about that silver dust. Something invigorating.

The trees thinned out, the space between them filling in with plants holding red flowers that looked like poppies. She plucked one with her right hand and it shed its redness onto her, the way buttercups will leave a yellow haze on the soft curve of your chin. The darkness seeped away. The light grew ever so slightly.

Abra's mind wandered far and wide while she followed the trail. She thought of her mom, her dad, her little brother. She thought of Sam and Tennin and remembered Jinn. She thought one of them had told her the Amarok was the last of its kind, but there, in that strange wood with the long, straight rock wall that was growing into a cliff, she wouldn't have been surprised to see another. Absently, she felt for the sword, its hard edge a straight line down her leg.

Beatrice was in view again, drifting the way she did along the rocky cliff that rose high above them on the left. To the right and straight ahead the forest was thickening again, and the flowers were gone. It looked like they were approaching a dead end.

That's when Beatrice disappeared. Again.

Abra stopped, the path feeling hard under her feet. She looked behind her, and then back to the front. She felt panic rising up inside of her, wondering if it was possible that she was lost. Lost forever in this dark wood, the red sky above her.

But there was the path. There was always the path. And the line of rock. She could follow that back to the road and the city. And Leo. She took a few more hesitant steps forward, no longer touching the wall, no longer enjoying the flowers. Her left hand was silver and her right hand was red as she arrived at the place where Beatrice had vanished.

There was a narrow pathway that went into the rock, so narrow that it looked like, if she went in, at some point she might have to turn sideways to squeeze through. On both sides it was flanked by a high cliff. Abra paused. She couldn't go forward anymore—the trees grew too thick, too close together. It was either into the narrow path that went into the cliff or back the way she had come. Beatrice must have gone down the narrow path.

Abra took one last look around, shook her head in disbelief that she was doing it, and entered the narrow gorge.

At first she could walk, one foot in front of the other, and her shoulders only occasionally brushed the rock sides of the path, but the farther in she went, the tighter it got, until soon she was sliding along the crevice sideways, sometimes ducking in order to get below a piece of the wall that stuck out at head height. She drew in her stomach and scratched her way along. The silver veins had grown larger, and now her entire body was covered in a fine layer of silver dust. A feeling of claustrophobia welled up inside of her, but she pushed it down by taking a deep breath and stopping for a moment.

She gazed up at the thin crack of red light at the top of the crevice, maybe thirty feet above her. The sky. She imagined cool, fresh air pouring in, and she took another deep breath. Day had arrived, it seemed, and the red sky was bright.

A quick movement along that narrow skyline caught her attention. She watched Beatrice climb up and out of the passageway, into freedom. Abra clenched her jaw with anger and determination. She refused to be left behind, so she started looking for handholds and footholds, places in the narrow space where she could work her way up off the ground and toward the top.

The path continued to narrow, so climbing up was easier than she expected it to be. In fact, the walls were so close together that even if she fell, the worst that could happen was that she might get wedged between the cliffs. That thought wasn't entirely comforting, but soon she was at the top. She peeked up over the ledge and took in a sharp breath.

It looked like the landscape of the moon, except there was no dust—just an endless plain of granite-colored rock. She looked to the left of the narrow crevice and saw the stone plain gradually go back down to the forest, and beyond the forest, miles and miles away, the city rose through the red haze of morning. She looked in the opposite direction, away from the city, and the rock plain stretched out as far as she could see.

That's when she saw Beatrice, her form like a granite statue against the red sky.

23

THE FIRST THING ABRA NOTICED as she pulled herself out was that there wasn't a single tree in sight. The Tree of Life definitely was not here, so why had Beatrice come to this place? Had she lured Abra in the wrong direction? Should Abra run back toward the city? Or was this the moment she was supposed to face Beatrice, the same way she had stood up to Jinn?

But these questions fled from her mind as she saw what else was spread out on the stone plain.

The rock itself was uneven and generally flat, without any large outcroppings or formations. There didn't seem to be any other deep crevices like the one she had climbed up. But what she did see were giant pockmarks spread out all the way to the horizon, like the dimples on a golf ball, except they were about ten feet apart, and they were deep. And they were filled with crystal-clear water.

Abra meandered slowly among the deep pools, walking in the general direction of Beatrice. She kept her hand on the hilt of the sword—it seemed to grow heavier as she approached Beatrice. This in itself heightened her senses.

She glanced into one of the pools she was walking around. She stopped. She fell to her knees. She stared harder into the water, forgetting all about the sword, all about Beatrice, all about the red light that bathed them.

Inside the pool, she saw a scene. It was like she was watching television, only more tangible. She saw the image of her mother washing dishes. A deep sense of homesickness rose inside of Abra, and a tear formed in the corner of her eye. What was this strange magic? Her mother was there at the sink, the way she always was after dinner. She wore the same apron she always wore when working in the kitchen. Abra could see the dishes on the counter, the hot pads under the pots.

"Such a sweet, sweet image," Beatrice said, and Abra looked up, startled. Beatrice was across the pool from her, only seven or eight feet away. Abra hadn't even seen her move.

She got up off her knees. Her hand hovered close to the sword. "What is this?" she said in a low voice.

Beatrice smiled. She laughed, and it was a joyful sound that went on seemingly forever. "This place? These pools? Oh, Abra. This place is full of incredible wonders."

"This place?" Abra asked.

"Yes! This is the Edge of Over There. We had no idea what would happen if we brought living, breathing humans into the Passageway. But isn't this remarkable? An entire city grew up around them, finished houses and buildings and infrastructure no one had to build. Food and water appeared, the kind of simple food that is completely nourishing, water that fills the stomach with anything it needs. It's all rather incredible. We simply brought the people and it appeared. Something out of nothing."

Beatrice sat down at the edge of the pool Abra had been

staring into. She wore no shoes, and she lowered her feet into the pool until the water reached nearly to her knees. She sat there, swirling her feet through the clear water, disturbing the image of Abra's mother.

"Did you make my mother forget me?" Abra asked.

Beatrice pretended not to hear. "Whoever looks into these pools"—she raised her arms, beckoning toward the entire rock plain—"will find every scene on earth, having to do with their lives, waiting to be watched. Past, present, and . . ."

She paused, squinted a bit, and stared hard at Abra.

"Future."

Abra's heart raced. She looked down into the silent pool again to try to see if this one was past or present or future, and she saw herself enter the kitchen, a little girl, crying. She walked up to her mother, held up a finger. Her mother bent down with concern etched on her face, and the two of them walked out of the scene together.

"Simply beautiful," Beatrice said, sighing, swirling her foot through Abra's mother's head as she reappeared at the beginning of the sequence, once again washing dishes.

Abra started circling the area. If what Beatrice said was true, if some of these pools showed the future, she wanted to see if she could find a future scene where her mother remembered her. She wanted to be sure of what was to come.

"How can they show the future?" Abra asked. She thought if she could keep Beatrice talking, it might buy her some time, but Beatrice didn't seem to be in any rush.

"Well, that can be a little tricky," Beatrice said. "You know, they show your future based on where you are right now. But as the decisions you make shift your future, the pools change."

"I don't know what you mean," Abra said.

"Your future pools would look very different, empty even, if I killed you right now."

Abra's head jerked up and she stared at Beatrice.

"Just an example, you know, a hypothetical," Beatrice said slowly with a slight smile on her face. "Don't look so alarmed."

Abra worked her way out from Beatrice in a kind of expanding search of the deep pools, and she had to tear herself away from each one. There she was, riding her bike to Sam's house along Kincade Road. There she was, reading a book in the haymow. There she was, at the fair during who knows which year, wandering the grounds with cotton candy obscuring her face.

A baby in a bassinet.

Sitting in middle school taking a test.

Just last spring, walking out to get the mail.

But in the next pool, something strange.

First of all, it was hazier than the others, as if someone had spilled a bit of milk into a cup of water. Inside the pool, she watched as an old woman with silver hair sat in a bed, her back against the headboard, her eyes closed. The woman's breathing was labored. There was a picture on the wall behind the woman, but it was unclear in the dim light of the room where she was resting. Abra looked closer. The woman looked like she was dying. She seemed to take one final, rattling breath. Her breath stopped.

Was that her? Was that Abra?

She backed away on all fours, scrambling to try to unsee what she had seen. She even rubbed her eyes, as if that would cleanse the images from her retinas. It seemed improper, almost indecent, peering into her own future, watching her final moments. Had that been her, dying on a bed, entering her final sleep under a white quilt embroidered with red flowers?

Were those poppies on the quilt?

Had she been alone?

She moved backward so fast that she almost fell into the pool behind her. She turned and looked, and again the pool was hazy. She saw an old man walking down the streets of Deen, an older man. Deen seemed different, and she didn't recognize some of the objects. Everything she could see of the town in that small snapshot seemed to be crumbling. The man stopped. Bent over. He collapsed onto the ground. Someone ran over to help him.

Was that Sam in his old age?

"Why did you bring me here?" Abra asked, her question floating out into the air, her voice suddenly full of deep pain. She turned away from those two pools, now facing a third. She looked up. She looked around the eerie landscape.

Where was Beatrice?

But Beatrice was right behind her. She pushed Abra to her knees, then pushed her again so that her upper body dipped into one of the deep pools. And Beatrice held her there.

For a minute, Abra didn't feel like she was sinking—she felt like she was floating. Down she went, the heaviness of Beatrice's hand on the back of her head, pushing, pushing. Deeper. Deeper than she thought the clear pool of water could possibly be. Farther down than Beatrice's arm could reach. And then she stopped.

She couldn't breathe, but that didn't seem to be a problem. She didn't feel like she was running out of air. Stranger yet, she had arrived at the scene of her life portrayed in that particular pool—she was hovering above her very own kitchen. The same old linoleum covered the floor, the same old cabinets lined the walls. But everything looked newer, cleaner. She was right about at ceiling height, looking down.

There were three adults in the kitchen, and as the scene moved along she realized there were two babies crawling on the floor. She didn't recognize the babies at first, but she knew the adults. The first one, the one sitting on the floor so that one of the babies could pull itself up on her knees, was her mother. She looked younger, much younger, with fewer lines on her face. Her skin was smooth. Her hair was longer than Abra was used to seeing.

There was another adult, this one sitting in one of the chairs over by the refrigerator: Sam's mom. She, too, looked much younger, and she reached down to where the second baby was crawling, picked him up high in the air, and kissed his cheek. It brought tears to Abra's eyes, this memory of what a kind woman Sam's mom had been.

Of course, by now Abra knew exactly who the two babies were—Sam was the baby Mrs. Chambers had picked up and kissed, and Abra was the baby crawling all over her mother.

A third adult entered the room, and because of Abra's view from the ceiling, at first she wasn't exactly sure who the man was. He was dressed in a black suit with shiny black shoes. His hair was the color of deep space, and his skin was tan.

"It's important that you both hear the information I have gathered," he said in a low voice. Abra immediately knew who he was, even though he was speaking quietly.

It was Mr. Tennin.

She couldn't believe it. This was a scene from her life that took place fifteen years ago! That meant Sam's mom and her mom both knew Mr. Tennin long before the Tree appeared in Deen! Why hadn't her mother said anything? But her thinking was distracting her from their conversation—she tried to simply listen.

"There has been a vision of Samuel"—Mr. Tennin looked

down at the baby boy with a sad expression on his face—"dying in a lightning tree."

"You mean . . . " Lucy Chambers began.

"Yes," Mr. Tennin interrupted her. "Yes. The death of your son could very well coincide with the next arrival of the Tree."

"What if I take his place?" she asked, tears in her voice. "What then?"

Mr. Tennin tried to sound convincing when he spoke. "Lucy, you and I both know visions of the future are far from reliable. There are too many variables, too many . . . chances to change even those things that seem inevitable."

"But if it's true," she insisted, "can I take his place?"

"Perhaps," Mr. Tennin said, nodding slowly, staring at the floor. "Perhaps."

Abra was flabbergasted. Sam's mother had known. Sam's mother had known all along. But why was her mom there in that room, and why were the three of them talking as if they were working together?

As if they were equals?

"My contact also said the girl will have 'significant influence' in the events of the Tree. Crucial."

"How is that even possible?" Abra's mother asked in a whisper. "She's not like us."

Mr. Tennin shrugged. "Another puzzle, I'm afraid. Another unclear thing. Which, if you'll recall I've already said, is to be expected when gazing into the haze of the future. No one knows. No one on this side."

He paused.

"And, of course, they do not have . . . it . . . in their blood. You are both second generation. They are third generation. These things do not pass to the third. So maybe it was all a mistake."

Tennin stopped talking abruptly and looked up toward the ceiling with a strange expression on his face. Fear? Understanding? Abra felt like he was looking at her. But that wasn't possible.

Was it?

"Abra," he said firmly, and the two women looked at him, puzzled. Baby Abra, on the floor, smiled. "The sword. Use the sword."

Abra suddenly realized she was drowning, running out of air. She also realized Mr. Tennin was talking to her. She reached for the sword at her hip, twisted in the water, pushed it up toward Beatrice's image rippling above the water. There was a loud scream as the sword eased into something solid. Abra felt herself erupt out of the water and land hard on the rock. She lay there, dripping, holding the sword, gasping for air.

Beatrice. Where was Beatrice?

Abra looked toward the city and saw Beatrice limping among the pools, moving quickly now, hunched over. She walked and walked for quite some time, and Abra was too spent to follow. She watched as Beatrice disappeared where the gentle downward slope of the rock plain met the forest.

Abra rolled over, lying on her back. It was day, and all of the pools, even the one she had so recently emerged from, were calm, glassy reflections of the bright red sky.

24

LEO WAS NEARLY LEFT BEHIND on his first morning with the group. For a few moments after he woke up, he couldn't remember where he was or what he was doing. As he crawled out from under the desk and stared out over the shattered city, it all came back to him: the trek with Abra, meeting Jeremiah and the group, falling asleep under the desk while the Wailers raced through the night, singing their song. At that point, he realized the floor was empty of people.

Well, almost empty. Someone was staring at him from the door. It was one of Jeremiah's inner circle, a short young man with broad shoulders and a scar that ran from the corner of his left eye to the top crease of his ear.

"Are you coming?" the young man asked Leo, but it didn't come across like a question. It was more an expectation, or a quiz.

Leo mumbled an apology and hurried downstairs just in time to join the last of the group as they trickled out onto the street and walked back the way they had come the afternoon before.

He felt sore and stiff after sleeping on the floor, and he wondered if anyone had an extra toothbrush, but those things were beginning to feel like faraway dreams, things he would never see again. He didn't want to draw any unnecessary attention to himself, and he thought he should stay in the back in case there was an opportunity to get away from the group. He started to see how the larger group had its own subgroups, which in turn had their own small groups, and he tried to fit in with a band of young people walking at the back of the mob.

"You're the new guy from yesterday, right?" a girl asked him. She wore a red bandana over red hair and had a round face. He thought she was probably in her early twenties.

"Yeah. I'm Leo," he said.

"I'm Sandra. This is Kate, Rob, Justin, Mary."

The people she pointed to paused and looked over at Leo. A few smiled, a few nodded, but they each returned to their own quiet conversations.

"How long have you been here?" Leo asked her.

"Me? I'm not sure. Feels long. Maybe a year. Maybe five years. No one really keeps track of that kind of thing here."

"Do you like it?"

"I didn't have much choice. I found a lot of trouble outside. Someone told me about this place and I thought, hey, why not? Same with most of the folks here—everyone had to get away for one reason or another."

Leo hadn't thought of that before, but it made sense that the people who had escaped the world had a reason to do so. He looked at the mob a little differently after that, wondering what each person had run away from. He thought about why he was there.

"So that's the only reason you came, to get away from your life?"

Sandra shrugged. "Mostly, yeah. But there are other reasons too—rumors. About other things." Her voice trailed off.

"Like what?" he asked, his interest piqued.

She sighed. "You'll probably think it's crazy. I do too. But some folks say the fountain of youth is here somewhere. The secret to living forever." She gave a jaded kind of laugh.

Abra's Tree, Leo thought.

"Whatever," she said, as if debating herself. "To be honest? If I had a chance, I'd get out of here, head back to the real world. This place is mostly a dump."

Leo couldn't argue with that. The entire city seemed like it had been reduced to rubble.

"And you? Why are you here?" Sandra asked him.

"I'm looking for someone," Leo said.

"Huh," she said, looking at him with a strange expression on her face, as if she'd noticed something about him she hadn't before. "I've never heard that one before."

But she didn't ask any more questions. That seemed to be one of the unwritten rules—no questions. They walked in silence for a few blocks. The rest of the mob was quiet that morning, and Leo wondered if they were always so subdued when the sun first came up.

"Quiet group," he said with a chuckle.

The five people he had met looked at him quickly before glancing at each other.

"So you haven't heard?" Sandra asked him.

"Heard what?" Leo asked.

"Where we're going. That's why everyone's so quiet this morning."

"Where are we going?" Leo felt rather ignorant having to ask so many questions.

Sandra stared at him with tired eyes.

"We're going to war."

⁓

For the next hour or so they took a roundabout way south, their passage obstructed and turned this way and that by strange roadblocks, piles of furniture and rubble. Sometimes they cut through darkened buildings lit only by sunlight streaming through small windows, particles of dust orbiting through the rays. Sometimes they jogged along alleyways, moving in columns two people wide. As evening had fallen the previous night, the group had filled him with a sense of dread, almost awe, but now, in the light of day, they seemed little more than what they were: a large group of misfit young people meandering through a broken city.

Leo noticed a young man about his age who drifted back through the group. He probably caught Leo's eye because he wasn't talking to anyone else—everyone seemed to be in a small group of some sort, but this one, with his hunched shoulders and gaze shifting from side to side, traveled alone. He reached the very back of the group and was only a few feet away from Leo as the tail of the mob followed the rest around a corner.

One minute the young man was there, and then he was gone.

Chaos broke out for a second. A different group of about twenty people came running back from the front, and the entire mob stopped so abruptly that in some cases, where people hadn't been paying close attention, they lurched into the people in front of them. Leo peeked back around the corner from where they had come, and in addition to the twenty or so who had run through the mob, another ten young men and women sprinted out from the surrounding buildings. They wore black clothes and moved fast, running over the rubble and the crumbling sidewalks in a balanced, subtle way. They all had one target: the boy who had left the group.

Soon they had him, like those images you see on nature shows of lions converging on a running, wounded wildebeest. The poor boy tried to run this way and that, zigzagging among his pursuers, but soon they were on top of him. They picked him up and carried him, legs flailing, into the first floor of a neighboring high-rise. Five minutes later the group came out.

The boy did not.

The original twenty ran back up through the middle of the mob, and the group proceeded to walk forward.

"What was that about?" Leo hissed to Sandra.

She looked at him with wide eyes and held a finger in front of her lips. She looked around before edging closer to Leo, talking into his ear.

"You don't leave your Frenzy. That's what that was all about."

"What's a Frenzy?" he asked.

Sandra beckoned at the entire group. "This is."

Leo nodded.

"There are always others watching," she said. "Don't try to leave. It's impossible."

Leo nodded, but inside he felt despair creep up into his throat. He was wasting too much time! Abra would be gone soon, and he'd be left here forever! What had he gotten himself into?

Lunch was passed around: bags and bags of the berries Leo and Abra had eaten on the path to the city, and large plastic jugs of clear water. Again he was amazed at how filling the fruit was. And drinking the water somehow left him with the same satisfaction as eating food. He couldn't understand it.

The group stopped walking for a long time, and Leo looked around hopelessly for a way of escape. But while he scanned the buildings and the alleyways, he couldn't get the image out of his mind of the young man trying to escape, and the group chasing him down.

"Where does all this food come from?" he asked Sandra while they sat in their small group.

She shrugged.

"No one knows," Mary said quietly, the first thing Leo had heard her say. "It's one of the main reasons people follow Jeremiah. We don't know where to get food here in the city."

She took a large handful from her cup of berries. She gulped from the container they shared, and some of the water ran down the sides of her cheeks, trickled a long line down her neck, and made wet spots around the collar of her T-shirt.

Leo wondered where Abra was. He wondered if she had found the Tree yet. But there were no answers. It seemed to be a city made up of only questions. The red sky brightened and the breeze grew stronger, carrying the smell of some nearby sea. But no answers. There were never any answers.

In the afternoon, a rustling started at the front and made its way back, like a ripple in a pond, and they started out again. Walking, walking, walking. They destroyed every building they passed like locusts stripping leaves. It was almost as if they couldn't help it, as if something about their presence in that in-between world drove them to tear it all down.

After one especially destructive hour, Leo turned to Sandra. "The city is huge, but destruction at this rate? Seems like the whole city should be rubble by now."

"This city is a strange place," she said, and the others in their little group nodded. Sandra paused. "I'm just going to say it— you don't have to believe me. You'll see it soon enough for yourself. But a lot of times we'll come around the corner to a street I'm sure we've already destroyed, and there it is again, new as can be."

"You mean, the city regenerates?"

Sandra shrugged. "Not when we're around. Not even when we're close by—you'd have to hear that taking place, right? And sometimes we'll turn onto a street and it will still be in ruins. But I think it's when we don't go somewhere for a long time and then return. I don't know. If you last long enough, you'll see."

If you last long enough. The phrase struck Leo, reminded him of his situation.

Just before dark, the Frenzies arrived in a large open area of the city. Leo still couldn't figure out if the city had ever been populated or if it had always been an empty metropolis, somehow set down in this strange space in the universe. But when they turned into the square, Leo was shocked. Not by the tall buildings that surrounded them. He wasn't surprised at the openness of the square, which reminded him of Times Square, though he had only seen it on television. He didn't even take note of how the Frenzies split up and headed in different directions, their first sign of disarray since the night before.

No, what got Leo's attention was the fact that there were thousands of other young people waiting there, and a few of them started cheering when Jeremiah's Frenzy arrived. This caused a lot of smiling and nodding within the group, and even a few hugs between individuals of different Frenzies, as if they had been together before, not long ago.

Leo stayed close to Sandra and her group as they wandered

the area looking for a place to spend the night, and soon they were on the third floor of a darkened building. The evening seemed to come quick there in the city, and they stood inside the glass walls, looking out on the square.

"Who are you looking for?" Sandra asked him when she had finished eating. Leo wondered if he would ever tire of eating the berries they gave them. He couldn't imagine it.

Leo held up a finger, asking her to wait while he finished what he was eating. He swallowed heavily.

"My sister," he said. "Her name is Ruby. My father brought her in here many years ago."

Sandra nodded. "I heard a legend about a young girl living somewhere in the city," she said, "but I never thought it was true. That would be ridiculous, right? A little kid, here? Who would do that?"

"It's no legend," Leo said. He felt a lurch of excitement. Someone had heard of a child in the city! It had to be Ruby.

"How'd you get in here?" he asked Sandra. Around them, people settled in for the evening. There were groups of four or eight playing card games. A few pairs threw dice up against a wall. At the far end of the room, someone sitting on a chair and surrounded by a large group of people on the floor appeared to be telling a story. Someone else played quiet tunes on a mournful harmonica.

"I think everyone came through the crypt. I don't think there is another way."

"Yeah, me too," he said.

They sat there in silence for a moment, listening to the quiet voices around them.

"Do you think you'll find her?" she asked.

"I hope so," he said. "I don't know."

She paused a moment before starting again. "You know you can't get back out, right? The door is locked from the other side. We tried it once, and we nearly got lost in the darkness."

He stared at the ground, not sure what to say. He was worried about telling the truth, but he didn't want to lie to Sandra. She had proven herself trustworthy so far, and there was something about her that felt separate from the Frenzy, as if she would leave if she could. That was it: Leo thought that Sandra didn't really belong there, with those other people.

"I know someone," he said, looking around to make sure no one else was listening. "I know someone who can open the door."

Sandra looked at him, uncertain. "Really," she said in a flat, disbelieving voice.

Leo nodded. "Yeah. But she's not going to be around forever. She might already be gone. If I can't find my sister and meet this girl back at the gateway . . . she'll leave us behind."

Sandra took all of it in without saying a word. He saw something in her eyes that he didn't recognize at first, something soft and distant. He realized it was compassion. She started to say something, and he thought it was coming out of that space of kindness. He leaned in closer as the people on the floor grew louder, but he still couldn't hear. There was a surge of people moving to the windows, and Sandra and Leo were overwhelmed.

He looked around, wondering what was going on. Ever since that young man had tried to run away and instead had been quickly eliminated, Leo had been on edge. Anxious. The sudden movement of everyone around him caught him off guard and made him jump to his feet. Someone opened all the windows, and everyone on that level crowded toward the space overlooking the square. People struggled to see over each other's shoulders, trying to get a better view. Leo had already been close to the glass before the mass movement, so he had a front-row seat.

The city felt ominous in the half-light. The narrow spaces between the buildings where the red light crept through made the streets look like they had narrow strips of red laid over them, thin paths lining the solid black shadows. Every window, for as far as Leo could see, was dark.

Four large spotlights turned on, making loud thunking noises as the switches were thrown. Leo hadn't been close to artificial light in days, maybe a week, and to him those four spotlights were like four suns suddenly brought into existence. Their rays went up and up forever, into the sky. And in their midst, the center around which they all revolved, stood a figure.

He seemed small at first, lost in all of that light, and because no matter which direction you viewed him from he had light behind him, he looked like a shadow man, the outline of a man. He was a person turned into pure darkness. For at least a minute there was only silence, and Leo was sure that everyone else was doing exactly what he was doing: holding their breath.

The figure raised his hands slowly until both arms were lifted, turning him into the shape of a cross. Leo remembered a Bible story from his childhood, when his mother had occasionally taken them to church in downtown New Orleans. In the story, there was a leader watching a war, and as long as that man's arms were raised, his army continued to win. But when his arms dropped, his army began to lose.

A voice called out to the thousands in the crowd, incredibly loud considering it was not amplified with a microphone or speakers.

It was Jeremiah.

25

"WELCOME!" JEREMIAH SAID, and the applause started off small and scattered, but gathered and grew like a storm until it was crashing through the streets.

His arms came down.

And then the war was lost, Leo thought.

The applause died down.

Whispers swept along the glass in hiss-shaped silence as Jeremiah prepared to speak.

"He managed to unite the Frenzies," one voice whispered.

"He's the leader of all of us," someone else said in a hushed voice.

But one sentiment was whispered more than any other.

"Now the war begins."

"A handful of you were here when I first arrived in the city," Jeremiah said in a somber voice. "When we had nothing. We lived off the scraps we found along the edges. They hunted us, those who lived in the center of the city. They drove us into the forest time and time again. They wanted to keep everything for themselves."

He pounded the air with his hands. He struck at the injustices, each one of them, and tore them down with his own fists so that all of those watching from the surrounding buildings could barely contain their excitement. Scattered applause began again, but Jeremiah struck his way through it.

"Not this time!" he shouted. "Their actions led us to destroy the city, one block at a time, one building at a time, one brick at a time. If we couldn't have it, no one would have it. And our numbers grew, because everyone who arrived recognized the strength of our cause. Now, those who would have driven us into starvation are nothing more than an island in the midst of this great city. We have surrounded them."

A round of cheers shook the square again.

"All we want is to live peaceful lives," Jeremiah said, and his voice pulled at the emotions of everyone listening, even Leo. "All we want is to settle down and have children, create a new society. That's it. That's all we want. But they have proven that they Will. Not. Let. This. Happen."

Boos sounded out like the moaning of the Wailers.

"I know. I know! We will see peace. I promise you. But first, there must be war. There must always be war before peace, because peace is precious, and nothing precious is free. Peace does not come without a price. Peace must be fought for."

He paused, and in the distance Leo could hear the approach of the Wailers. It was like the sound of a freight train approaching from miles and miles away: first the distant throbbing, and as the train grows closer the detail of the sound emerges. Finally, as it races over your head, there is the ear-piercing scream of the whistle.

"To peace!" Jeremiah screamed, and the crowd went wild.

The Wailers began racing through the streets on their way to the water at the opposite end of the city. First one at a time.

Soon they came in small groups of two or three. At the last it was a steady stream of light and shadow, bright white and cloaked gray and the deepest blacks, all swirling and dashing around Jeremiah, who by now had raised his arms again.

Leo remembered how Abra had stood in the midst of them. Leo shook his head to clear the memory, and at that moment the spotlights winked out.

"C'mon," Sandra said to Leo and the rest of her group. The six of them ducked and squirmed through the crowd that was cheering now and plastered against the glass, hoping that the speech wasn't over. She led them into a nearby stairwell and they went up and up and up. Leo almost asked her why they were going so high, but he decided against it, instead staring at his feet as they scaled each and every step. Up. Up. Up.

Sandra pushed on a bar and opened a metal door that led out onto the roof of the building. One of Jeremiah's guards, dressed in black, stood at the edge, looking over the city, but when Sandra and her crew came out, the guard retreated back down the steps without a word. She led them over to the side of the building where the guard had been standing, and they lined up.

The sheer height took Leo's breath away, and his knees shook, so he took a few steps back. They were probably twenty floors up. The city stretched away from the forest, mile after mile, all the way to the water. Most of the city was dark with nothing but empty windows and the square outlines of buildings against a not-quite-as-dark sky. But the water, off in the distance, shimmered as the Wailers approached and swept out over it, racing over the waves like the light that chases the setting sun.

"That's incredible," Leo whispered, but Sandra pointed in the other direction.

Leo's breath was taken away again, but while the first time it had been because of his distance from the ground, this time it was because of the distance between him and the top of the tall building. He looked up and up and up, and the tall building he and Abra had seen on their walk to the city was right there, not more than five blocks away.

The buildings around the tall building were lit up, and it reminded him of his own city on a normal night. He imagined families there, although it was hard to believe that would be the case—the city didn't seem the kind of place that families could live or survive in, and Sandra had told him there weren't children. But he imagined them anyway, families around the dinner table, kids shouting and parents telling them to stop shouting, people turning on the television for the night or switching on the light and opening a book. He imagined all the most ordinary things, and they put an ache in his heart, an ache for ordinary life. An ache for home.

"Who lives there?" he asked.

"I don't know," Sandra said. "It doesn't matter. Jeremiah hates them, so tomorrow they'll be our enemies."

Leo looked at Sandra. "Why did you bring me up here?" he asked.

She shrugged.

"I thought you should see it. It's beautiful, isn't it? The city, the water." Her voice trailed off.

They stood there for a long time, staring into the quiet darkness of a city on the edge of war.

"It's a beautiful place," she said again.

Leo woke up the next morning having lost track of Sandra. He left the level he had slept on and walked down to the floor where they had watched Jeremiah's speech. He found almost everyone pressed up against the glass again, so he wandered over and nudged his way through the crowd until he could see what they were staring at.

A large table had been set up in the square where Jeremiah had stood the night before. On this morning, he was at the head of the table and there were other young leaders sitting around it, pointing at various papers strewn across the wood surface.

"Who are those guys?" Leo asked no one in particular.

A girl turned and looked at him. She had pale skin and a mouth that twitched when she spoke. She wore glasses, and one of the lenses was cracked. She seemed annoyed at the question.

"The leaders of the Frenzies," she said.

Leo nodded. "What are they doing?"

She sighed at his stupidity. "Battle plans."

Leo stared through the glass. There were easily over a hundred young people on that level alone, and when he looked closely at the surrounding buildings he could see that each building had multiple levels packed full of more young people, faces and hands plastered against the glass. They were like harmless, mindless sheep, blindly following Jeremiah to victory. Or to slaughter.

"Let's go, everyone outside!" a voice shouted, and everyone turned to go. Everyone except Leo. He remained at the glass, watching while all the leaders except for Jeremiah left the table. Jeremiah remained, appearing deep in thought, but it was impossible to tell if he was actually deep in thought or if he was posing for those still looking through the glass. He looked up at the building where Leo stood. Soon he was staring at Leo, with Leo staring back. They stood that way for a few moments.

Jeremiah put his pen down on the table and walked away. Leo turned and followed the group down the stairs.

Leo still couldn't find Sandra, and when he walked outside he saw that everyone was being herded into different lines, presumably for different responsibilities in the upcoming war. Mostly the distinction seemed to be made by size, and Leo was directed into a line of taller young men. He waited with his arms crossed, scanning the crowd for Sandra. Still no sign of her.

Each of the lines of people (and there were thousands of people now, waiting, shuffling forward slowly) led to a table, and most of the tables were covered with weapons. Leo noticed immediately that there were no guns. Pretty soon after that he noticed there were no "real" weapons. All of the weapons had been constructed out of something else. Knives had been made out of thick shards of glass tied tightly to wooden handles. Spears had been made the same way. There were slingshots and clubs and some things that looked like axes.

Leo wondered about this for a long time as he waited in line. This world, this city, seemed to have provided everything someone would need to live here. There was shelter, the berries they ate every day seemed to be way more than just berries, and most of the buildings were fully furnished, though they also seemed to have never been used before.

Yet there were no ready-made weapons. No guns or knives, no bullets or blades. It was interesting to him, and it seemed to suggest that the city would provide anything you needed, but if you wanted to destroy life or create war, you had to take the gifts it gave you and twist them into something ugly.

He arrived at the front of the line and was given two knives, both with glass blades attached to pieces of wood that looked like they had come from a wooden pallet. He held them in his hands and they were light. The glass was thick and looked intensely sharp, and when he stared at it he could see his reflection, stretched and thin, with the red sky far above him. He wondered how he had ended up there so far from his own city, his own normal life. Now he was being swept up into a war he knew nothing about, following leaders with darkness at their core. He had to find a way out.

"Attention!" a voice shouted. The person didn't have to shout because the square, though filled to the brim with young people, was mostly silent. Of course, there were small pockets who seemed almost giddy with anticipation of the coming action, but most of the people in the square stared at their weapons. The reality of war often doesn't begin to settle in until the weapon is fit into the hand.

"Return to your original Frenzy for instructions!" the same voice shouted, and Leo looked around, trying to figure out where it was coming from.

The crowd sifted in on itself as people searched for their original groups, and soon they were divided. The groups began walking, some here and some there, some in this direction and some in that, and Leo guessed that they were following some preordained plan for which group was to attack which flank and which group was to stand firm until a particular time. His group started walking down the street that traveled in the direction of the tall building. It made sense that the largest Frenzy would lead the frontal attack while some of the smaller groups looked for ways to break through.

Leo knew he had to leave. He didn't have time to get tangled up in this pointless war. It could take days to end, maybe weeks. Maybe even longer! Meanwhile, Abra would find the Tree and get out. Leo's palms grew sweaty where they clutched the wooden handles of his glass knives. Adrenaline made him feel shaky. He had to get away. He had to find Ruby.

He drifted to the back. Still no sign of Sandra or the others. He glanced up at the buildings around him and didn't see any sign of the guards dressed in black. Maybe they were in the ranks, participating in the war. He imagined that Jeremiah would need every able body fighting, not wasting anyone to guard. As the group turned a corner, he slipped into the shadows of a small storefront.

Leo dashed through the store, glancing over his shoulder. No one followed him. He went through the store into a small back room, then pushed his way through a door that led into a hallway. He ran down the hall and found a stairwell, so he went up. He figured he'd hide out for a while, let the Frenzies clear while he figured out what to do next. But when he got into the stairwell, he heard footsteps coming down, so he turned back around and took a different hallway deeper into the building. There were no lights, so he felt his way along, his fingers running over the cinder-block walls.

He came to another door and tried to open it quietly. The click made by the latch sounded loud as a gunshot to him in the midst of that silence, and he stood there, waiting, holding his breath. When he didn't hear any response, he crept into the room and the door closed behind him, again making a loud click. A line of narrow windows faced the outside world, allowing a dim red glow to settle in the room like mist.

Leo realized there were others in the room. Dressed in black, they walked silently. He turned to run, but someone was at the door.

It was Jeremiah. Who was this young man, that he could be everywhere at once, lead thousands of people without a hint of mutiny, and supply everyone with enough food and water?

Who was he?

What was he?

"Hello, Leo," he said, coming into the room. The guards formed a small circle around Leo and Jeremiah. "Where are you going?"

"This isn't my war," Leo said quietly.

"Oh, but it is," Jeremiah said, chuckling to himself. "Haven't we fed you and protected you? Haven't we led you on straight paths through the city? Haven't we given you friends? People like Sandra."

"Where's Sandra?" Leo asked.

Jeremiah smiled. "Questions, questions. But I asked you first. Where are you going?"

Leo stared at Jeremiah, and he felt like the only chance he had in that moment was to tell the truth.

"I'm looking for my sister."

"She's not here with us?"

"I haven't seen her."

"Then she must be with the enemy."

Those words sank into Leo, deep and harsh. He had considered that. If his sister and his father weren't here, with the Frenzies, they must be in the center of the city, where he'd originally thought they would be, close to the tall building.

"I don't know where she is."

"I think," Jeremiah said, now talking to the guards, "that what we have here is a spy." He stared at Leo. "I don't have time for this," he hissed. "But you might know something important."

Leo waited to hear his fate. Jeremiah paused for a moment.

"Take him somewhere safe," he said. "I have a city to win."

He turned and left the room.

26

JEREMIAH TOOK most of the guards with him, leaving only two to escort Leo "somewhere safe." Leo was relatively sure that Jeremiah wasn't concerned with his safety as much as his containment. The two guards each had a hand on one of Leo's shoulders, and they pushed him through the dark hallways at a light jog, directing him here, there. They climbed stairs and ducked through an alley.

The two were strong, and they kept their faces turned away from him as much as they could, as if they didn't want to be identified. They ran down dark corridors without hesitating, and it seemed like they could see in the dark. He tried to start a conversation with them, hoping there was something human hidden behind their robotic obedience, but they never replied.

One moment they pushed him faster, faster, and the next moment they stopped, motionless. He looked over his shoulder at one of them, and the guard lifted a finger to his lips.

"Shh."

The three of them stood in almost complete darkness in the bowels of a building. That's when Leo heard scurrying sounds, the lightest whisper of feet, of people trying not to be heard, not to be seen. He thought everyone was with Jeremiah, preparing to fight a war. The room's ceiling was low, and he couldn't see any walls.

Leo didn't know exactly what happened, but in a blink the guards were gone. The weight of their hands on his shoulders slid away. The sound of people wrestling, fighting wordlessly, was followed by the shushing sound of people being dragged over a floor, their clothes scratching at the carpet. Still, Leo didn't move. Maybe the attackers had forgotten about him. Maybe they hadn't seen him. Maybe they had seen him but didn't care.

"Come on," a familiar voice whispered, and a soft hand gripped his shoulder, pulled him farther along. He followed. They moved quickly, quietly, for a few minutes before finding a patch of light. Five figures emerged from the shadows.

Sandra and her friends. They moved like ghosts.

"Why?" Leo asked, hugging each of them fiercely.

Sandra looked around at the others. "I don't know," she admitted. She started talking again, but her voice trailed off, and she mumbled again, "I don't know."

"How did you get away?" Leo asked. "What about the other guards?"

"They have their hands full," Mary said in her gentle voice. "It turns out a lot of people don't want to fight a war."

"So, the war isn't going to happen?" Leo asked.

"It's going to happen," Sandra said. "But it's not as organized as Jeremiah wants it to be. A lot of people deserted. We're getting out of here. We think we might be country folk, maybe try living in the forest for a time."

"I have to find my sister," Leo said.

Sandra stared at him. "This city is going down," she said in a serious voice. "Once Jeremiah starts what he wants to start, nothing will get out alive. Probably not even him. They're not called Frenzies for nothing."

"I can't leave now," Leo said.

"You really think the gate is still open?"

"I don't know. I doubt it. But I have to try, right? She's my sister."

Sandra stood there quietly for what felt like a long time, but darkness has a way of magnifying time, stretching it.

"Follow me," she finally said, walking through the long room and out a door. Leo followed her as they descended. Five flights down, six flights down, seven flights down. He hadn't realized the guards had taken him up that high. Sandra kept going down.

It was pitch-black, and they made their way by holding to a handrail. Leo followed the gentle sound of Sandra's footsteps, and there was nothing but the sound of their feet and the rail slipping through his hands, that line of cold metal. It was the sound of loss, the sound of movement, the sound of losing everything. If he somehow misplaced that rail, he thought he might float away into the nothingness around him.

At the bottom, Sandra gathered them all together and struck a match. The light flared up, and everyone's faces looked orange, flickering in the shadows.

"Here is the door," Sandra said, pointing. Her match went out, and all the light in the world fled with it, but she kept talking in the dark.

"That door leads to an underground passageway. Tunnels, maybe. I'm not sure what they were for at first. But at each intersection of tunnels you'll see arrows in different colors. Follow the red arrows and they will bring you to the basement of a house in the heart of the city. You said you wanted to get to the middle, close to the tall building. I think you're crazy. I think you're going in the wrong direction. If I were you, I would go to the trees and hide until this madness passes. Or leave. Head back to the doorway."

"Why don't you come with me?" Leo asked in an excited voice. "Come with me! We'll find my sister. We'll get out of here. You can come back through the doorway with us."

When Sandra spoke, he knew she was speaking for all of them.

"We can't go back," she said. "None of us. I've thought about it, believe me. But there's nothing for us, not there."

"But . . ." Leo tried to interrupt.

"Forget it, Leo," she said. "Forget it."

Leo heard sadness in her voice, and regret, and he realized that in those few short days Sandra had become his friend.

"The red arrows will lead you to the basement of a house, very close to the tall building. If that's what you want to do, if you think that's where your sister is, follow those arrows."

"Who mapped them out? That must have taken forever," Leo said.

"Yeah. I don't know. But whoever did it was organized, and they knew the city. Blue arrows go all the way to the river. Yellow ones lead to the tall building—I wouldn't go straight there if I were you. Too many guards. Too many people." She paused. "There are green arrows too, but we're not sure about them. We never followed green to the end. Our investigation was interrupted."

"You've seen the water? You've been to the tall building?" Leo asked, surprised.

"We've been close enough to hear the water, but never climbed out onto the street. We've been under the tall building but never inside of it."

"Is the passage lit?"

"No," Sandra said, pressing a small box into his hands. "That's most of our matches. Walk with your hand against the wall. When you come to a turn or an intersection, light a match, follow the red arrow. Don't use them all the time or you'll run out. It's not far, but there are a lot of turns. A lot."

Leo could hear their breath, he could smell it as it mingled with his own, there in the darkness under the city. He wanted to say a lot of things to Sandra.

"Thank you" was all he said.

He walked over to where he thought the door had been, but it wasn't there. He felt around for the doorknob but couldn't find it. He struck a match, and light burned an image in his eyes. He reached for the door handle and looked over his shoulder.

"Good-bye, Sandra. Thank you."

They were already gone.

—

There are a lot of things to think about when you're walking almost silently through pitch-black tunnels beneath a city about to go to war. You'll find you have a lot of questions about life, about yourself, about where you're going and where you might go back to. Leo did. He wondered all of those things and more. As he walked, step-by-step, his hand sliding along the rough walls of the tunnel, he wondered about his father. He wondered about his sister. He wondered about what this city was, how it had gotten there, and what would happen once it was destroyed.

Most of all, he wondered about Abra. He wondered if she had found the Tree, if she had already left and locked the Passageway behind her. He didn't think he could live with that if it was him. He didn't think he could lock people out of the world for the rest of their lives. But he didn't know Abra, not really. He didn't know what she would do or what was at stake.

He hurried forward, one hand on the wall, the other hand waving in front of him in case something blocked his path. At first, he didn't trust the darkness and he walked slowly, but the farther he went, the faster he allowed himself to walk. The passageways seemed clear—every time he lit a match, he noticed there was nothing there except more empty passages. Most of the intersections were four-way crossings.

There was the blue arrow, and it had consistently been the one pointing to his right for quite some time. The green arrow always seemed to be pointing to the left. The red and yellow arrows both pointed straight ahead. He walked forward, one hand guarding the flame, keeping the light as long as he could. It sizzled out, and he dropped the match and kept walking forward into the darkness.

Sometimes he sloshed through shallow puddles, sometimes he even heard water trickling down the sides of the gray cement walls. When he struck a match at the intersections, he saw naked light bulbs in the ceiling, broken or burned-out long ago. Or maybe they had never worked. That was the thing about the city—you never could tell if anything was old or new.

At some intersections, all the arrows pointed down the same passage, which made him think there must be multiple ways of getting somewhere, which in turn made him wonder if they weren't set out in a grid like streets, with multiple crossings, multiple meanderings. But the red and yellow arrows ran together almost every time.

His hand swept off the wall and into midair. Another intersection. His matches were getting low. A surge of panic overwhelmed him as he thought about running out of matches and wandering this endless underground maze for the rest of his life. He imagined trying to chart it all in his mind—the grids, the paths, the darkness. Trying to find his way without light. Counting steps. Counting breaths.

He pulled out one of his last matches and struck it against the cement wall. It hissed and scratched, bringing light out of nothing, light out of emptiness, light out of death. To his left, a narrower passageway with the green arrow. To his right, also a narrower passageway with the blue arrow. In front of him a door with two large circles drawn on it: one red, one yellow.

A door.

Leo turned the doorknob. It was locked. His match went lower and lower. He held it, staring at the lock until the flame burned his fingers.

"Ouch!" he said, throwing the matchstick to the ground.

He pulled out his lock-picking set and flipped out the correct wire. He didn't even bother to light another match, simply inserted the pick and nudged it here, twitched it there, and tried the knob again. It turned, and the door eased its way open, not making a sound. He walked into a room. Dim light entered through short basement windows that lined the top of the walls.

He looked around. He thought he was in a cellar of some sort—the walls were stone with white plaster sealing the joints, the ceiling was bare crossbeams and wires and pipes, and there was a stairway at the far end. He walked over and around the contents of the basement, which were numerous and strange: aluminum pails, tools in a plastic container, a pink bicycle, three long, flat boards, a pile of nails, a pile of stones. He would have classified every single thing as junk except the contents were so well organized that it seemed someone must have cared about what was there. He got to the stairs and walked up, through another door.

He was no longer looking for the arrows. The rooms on the main level were normal rooms, although the house looked abandoned. There was a back door, locked, so he went toward the front of the house, cutting through a kitchen, a dining room, and into a front room. Everything was dusty, and his shoes left tracks as if he was walking through dirty snow or ash. He looked through the front window, out onto the street.

That's when he saw her.

Ruby.

She was much older, but he'd recognize that soft nose anywhere. Her eyes.

"Ruby," he whispered, tears forming in his eyes.

She ran up the street, and she was fast, but she was only growing into her body, and there was something clumsy about the way she moved. There is a striving in the way a young person runs at that age, as if their uncertain emotional journey is reflected in their physical movement. Her feet slid on the street as she changed direction. She pumped her arms. She kept looking over her shoulder as if she expected a tidal wave to crash around the corner at any moment. Leo waved to her through the dim glass, tapped on the window, anything to get her attention. He ran to the door, pushed it open, and shouted for her.

She glanced up at him and for a second he thought she would run past. He prepared to chase after her, but at that very moment she veered in the street and ran for the abandoned house where he stood. She came up the steps and ran past, through the doorway, without even stopping to look at him. He followed her inside and pulled the door closed behind them. Immediately everything felt still. The empty house around them was like a bubble.

"Who are you?" she asked, breathing hard.

"There isn't time," he heard himself saying, but it all seemed like it was happening in some far-off place. "Come on."

They snuck back into the dark house. She paused in the front room.

"Don't stop now," he hissed, going back farther into the house, into the darkness. The only thought in his mind was of Abra and the key. He wondered if she had already found the Tree and left them behind. He pictured walking into the darkness only to find that the darkness was all there was—no door outlined in light, no way out.

"Who are you?" she whispered, and her voice was precisely as he had always imagined it would be. The words were muffled in the empty house, like sand through a sieve. In the flash of a moment he remembered singing her to sleep or sitting beside her bed or feeling her forehead when she was sick, feeling the heat.

"There isn't time," he repeated. Tears rose in his eyes again. He pushed them back with the palms of his hands. He wanted to hug her. He wanted to hold her face. "You need to come with me."

"What are you doing here?" she asked.

"Are you Ruby Jardine?" he asked, wanting to hear her say it.

"Who are you?" she asked again, but now there was a hint of recognition on her face, as if she had seen him in a dream long ago.

"Are you Ruby Jardine?" Leo insisted.

"Yes," she said. "I'm Ruby."

They got to the back of the house.

"Ruby," he said in a quiet voice, "you're not going to believe me."

He paused.

"I'm your brother. I'm Leo."

Suddenly, pain surged from the top of his head and traveled down the core of his being. He fell to the ground, grabbing behind him to try to ward off his attacker, but another blow dropped him further. A group of hands lifted him, and a voice that he thought he recognized said, "Take him up with the other spy. Level 27. I'll come up later."

Strange sounds. The same voice said, in a suddenly gentle tone, "Ruby, Ruby, are you okay?"

The darkness he traveled through in those moments was darker than the underground passageways, a kind of darkness that swirled with loose pieces of light, and for a time he thought he might be lost forever in it, the shifting shadows and the piercing moments of pain like a match being struck. They carried him, and he bounced up and down and sometimes caught the corners of walls as they passed by. Up and up and up, stairs and stairs and into the sky, until he lost count of the floors and the men who carried him puffed hard breaths of weariness. Finally, through a door, and oh how his head hurt, and they opened a side door and went down a long hall and through another door, and they threw him inside.

Pain surged when he hit the ground and he nearly gave in to the darkness again, but he didn't, because he heard a voice. And he realized it wasn't his imagination. The voice was coming from right there in the corner, in the shadows of a windowless room.

"Leo, is that you?"

PART 6

there is a river

Soon we'll reach the silver river,

Soon our pilgrimage will cease;

Soon our happy hearts will quiver

With the melody of peace.

FROM ROBERT LOWRY'S HYMN
"SHALL WE GATHER AT THE RIVER?"

27

THERE ARE THINGS that happened to Ruby before Leo showed up, things about her and her father Amos, that are important. Not too long before Leo appeared to her in the abandoned house, claiming to be her brother and upending everything she knew about her world, she was sitting in her bedroom, her father delivering some important news.

"Very soon, Ruby," her father began, and he held his own breath with the anticipation of it all. When he couldn't hold it in any longer, he practically popped with the words. "I'm going to take you somewhere. I'm going to take you for a tour in the building."

She looked at him with questions in her eyes, to see if it was really true, and he nodded his head in a flurry of up-and-down movements, giving a crooked grin.

Ruby glanced away from him and stared out the window. The tall building behind their house blocked most of the sky, so that the shadowy light that fell down in the alley was tinted the color of rust. The narrow shards of sky she could see on either side of the building were a dark maroon. Night was falling in that city under the red sky.

The building behind her house was always growing, always getting taller. Carpenters and masons and engineers had worked on it for as long as she could remember, and every year it climbed higher, until it grew so tall that sometimes the low-lying orange clouds obscured the top of it and at night it seemed to rise right up through the blood-red sky. She wondered if they would ever finish working on it. She wondered what went on inside.

Her father stood in the doorway, staring at her. She could tell he wanted to see some kind of excitement, some sign that she was as eager to walk through the building as he was eager to show it to her.

"That night, after I give you the tour, there's going to be a meeting with all the people I know in the city who are ready to . . . make changes," he said. "We're ready to make this city into something wonderful. Something new."

"Dad," she started to say, but her voice trailed off. He took over again, going on and on about the glorious future, the new days ahead, the shining city. He started pacing from the hallway and into her room. Back into the hallway. Back into her room.

"We're not far off. But we have to maintain . . . space. The Frenzies. We have to eliminate them. After that we can build a new foundation. A new . . . " His voice faded.

He stopped walking and looked up at Ruby. "Very soon, you'll understand. Very soon. Ha! Oh, Ruby. I'm so sorry I haven't been able to tell you any of it. I'm sorry for all the secrets." He took a deep breath. "But soon you'll understand, and you'll know everything. This city will be . . . it will be . . . wonderful. Better than anything from . . . before. Better than anything."

He turned abruptly and walked into the hallway. He closed

her door carefully as if it was made of tissue paper and might tear. The latch clicked. Ruby heard him turn the key and lock her into her room. He did it every night. He said the city was unsafe. He said it was for her own good. He said it was to protect her in case the Frenzies came into the house.

This is what he told her, and she believed him, the way a child will often believe their parent even when their parent is not telling the truth.

She stared at the building again, thinking about the word she thought she'd heard her father say.

"After that we can build a new foundation. A new . . . *heaven*."

The house Ruby lived in, her father's house, was a house of many doors.

Of course, there were many windows too, but they didn't interest her—perhaps because they had large metal bars over the outside, so that even if you opened the windows as high as they could go, there was no way to get through. The bars were an inch thick and four inches apart, black as shadows. Ruby could reach her arm through them, right up to her shoulder, but no farther. The black bars were cold to the touch, even in the summer. Once a year, her father spent three or four late afternoons painting them in slow up-and-down strokes with a look on his face that made Ruby think that even though he was painting he was not thinking about painting. The paint he used was black, black, black, like spilled ink.

While the windows did not interest her, the many doors did. Her father kept most of them locked, but there were no bars over them, so there was at least some hope of passing through, if she could only have the keys. There was the large wooden front door, stained with a light cedar stain, and it creaked when it opened. The front door led into a small entranceway, and then another door like the first led into the house. There were the two large pocket doors to the left of the hall as you went in, heavy as cinder blocks. They slid smoothly over their rollers and covered the entrance to her father's study. There were the white, five-panel doors that led to three second-floor bedrooms, all empty, the doors always locked. And there were the third-floor doors, the ones that opened up to her bedroom, her father's bedroom, and the attic.

If only she had the keys.

All of those doors had antique keyholes below the doorknobs, the kind that are large enough to peek through. They were set in decorative brass plates with raised images around the edges: flowers and leaves and oblong shapes that looked like tears. Her father kept all the keys to all the doors hanging in his study on a square arrangement of hooks. Under each hook was the name of the room the key belonged to, and every single hook had a key on it.

The narrow door to the attic was down the hall from her room, and Ruby had heard from someone that the attic connected all the houses on her street. Even if she had the key, she never, never, ever would have opened that door because her father had told her that opening it would let all manner of terrible things into the world, things that would take up residence under her bed and never leave. They were awful things. Some of them were alive and could think for themselves, he said. They were growing things, and while some would remain under her bed, other things that came through the door would go out into the city: the seeds to poisonous trees or plants that could bring down entire buildings, ivy strong enough to crumble cement blocks, flowers with roots that upended sidewalks. Irresistible things. And the only way to keep them out of their world was to keep the door to the attic shut tight.

"Doors are made to keep things out," her father always said, raising his eyebrows and pointing his finger with each word.

She believed anything he told her, and the stories stuck and hardened like plaster, and no matter what she told herself, those stories remained, impossible to chip away. She didn't have the right tools for that.

These days her father was always writing, writing, writing in a stack of journals he kept on his desk. Or making frantic phone calls in his office, his voice rising until she could hear every word he said. He was very concerned about the city. He was very concerned that the Frenzies were driving it into chaos. She started hearing words that alarmed her, words like "surrounded" and "only option" and "last stand."

But sometimes he would stop working, stop making calls, and sigh, and relent to her endless pleas for attention. He would tell her about the tunnels that ran under the city, full of things that children shouldn't have to know about, and he would tell her about the back alleys in the city where all the terrifying people lived, and he would tell her about the river to the south of the city that had no far side—just an endless stretch of waves and shifting shades of blue.

She liked the stories. She liked how the scary ones made her insides quiver. But most of all she couldn't stop thinking about the river.

"If it doesn't have a far side, why is it a river and not an ocean?" she asked her father one day, and he looked surprised.

"Why, that's a good question, Ruby. I guess it's because it flows in one direction, like a river."

"Seems like it must have a far side, if it's flowing," she said.

He stared at her for a long time. "You must be right," he whispered. "You are a very smart little girl."

"I'm not a little girl anymore, Dad," she protested. "I'm thirteen!"

She asked him often about the War. She asked him over and over again about the fate of her mother and her brother.

"Do you remember much of those days?" he would say.

"No, Dad, I don't remember anything."

He always seemed relieved at her answer. "Yes, yes. You were very ill."

He told her how the War had ravaged the city soon after she was born. He told her about the last days of her mother and brother, when the War had taken them.

"Ruby, after your mother and brother were killed, we joined a group of citizens here in the city who finally drove the Frenzies back into the woods. The city was safe for most of your childhood, perhaps most of your life that you can remember. It was safe. But time passed, and more people entered the city, and for some reason most of them sided with the Frenzies. And the Frenzies joined together. This was . . . unfortunate." He clenched his jaw, licked his lips, and shook his head as if trying to gather his thoughts. "They've been advancing. We're preparing again for war, but this time we have a weapon."

Ruby loved when her father told her stories because those were the few times her father actually spoke to her, only her. He wasn't ranting on the telephone or talking in hushed tones to someone on the front porch. He was talking only to her, and she loved his stories, loved them the way she loved the taste of something sweet. She craved those stories, the deep rumbling sound of her father's voice, the way his eyes flashed in the light.

It is possible, when we have nothing else, for stories to be the food that sustains us.

⁓

There were other doors in the house too.

There was the back door, with a screen that hung on its hinges like a loose tooth and left a scratched arc in the cement slab from being opened again and again. Sometimes the back screen door swung loose on windy nights and slapped the side of the house, as if someone was knocking and knocking but no one would let them in. She was not allowed to go through the back door on her own—the heavy door inside the flapping screen—and it was always locked.

Beyond that door was a small yard surrounded by a tall wooden fence, and beyond the fence was an alley, coarse and gray, and beyond the alley a large hole in the ground where they had torn down a part of the tall building, torn it out by its roots, but that must have been a long time ago, because now they were building the rest of it up, higher and higher, floor after floor.

The hole beside the building was huge and deep, the size of a football field, and it was surrounded by a chain-link fence. Every ten feet along the fence were red signs:

NO TRESPASSING. KEEP OUT. DANGER.

There was a plain red wooden door that led into the foundation of the tall building. The door looked very old and very important, and no building that had a red door like that could be a building full of nothing. She became obsessed by the door, and she spent as much time as she could beside her bedroom window, staring at the building, staring at the door, keeping close watch on the alley, waiting for something to happen.

So, after her father left her room that night, after he told her that he was going to take her to the building very soon, she knew, she just knew, that it was something fabulously important, something life changing, something better than anything else she had ever seen. She fell asleep and dreamed of a tree, and dust, and a woman who held open her mouth and tried to make her eat the dust, so that she woke up gasping for breath, her mouth parched and dry.

She walked to her bedroom door and tried the knob, but it was still locked. She was so thirsty. She considered shouting for her dad, but he didn't like getting up in the middle of the night, so she sat down with her back to the door and fell asleep. This time she dreamed of the river and of a key longer than she was tall, a key that would open every door, if only she could lift it.

28

ON THE DAY RUBY would cross paths with her brother hiding in the abandoned house beside their own, she stared at the clock on the wall in her classroom. She got ready to leave. It was the last day of school before break, and she put all five of her books in her knapsack and tapped her foot in time to the second hand until the minute hand slid around to the twelve. Her teacher looked up at her, cleared her throat, and gave a slight nod. Ruby lifted the knapsack over her shoulder. It was tan, hung all the way down to her knees, and had been her mother's bag when Ruby was a baby, before she had died in the War. That's what her father had told her.

The school was large and vacant, and there were no other children there except Ruby.

She was the only student.

Her teacher nodded again, stood up, and walked with Ruby out of the room. Ms. Levithine had soft brown hair, pink-tinted skin, and green eyes that turned a hazel kind of brown when the red light from the sky shone through the dusty windows.

Ruby's father walked her to school in the morning, and then Ms. Levithine walked her home.

The hallways in the school were long and empty. There were many rooms, each with its own windows and chalkboards, each with its own desks and projectors. Books lined the shelves, new and unused. There were clocks in every room, perfectly synchronized, tick-tocking their way through each and every day.

Most children are thrilled after the last day of school, excited at the prospect of summer, already dreading their return the following fall. Not Ruby. She loved school, even if she was the only child there. She loved having somewhere to go every day, some excuse to get out of the quiet house. Thinking about an entire summer ahead of her, stuck in the house with her always-working father writing, writing, writing and planning, planning, planning and eventually locking her in her room at the end of every day, filled her with a sense of dread and sadness so heavy that it nearly overwhelmed her. The last place she wanted to walk to on that last day of school was her house.

"It's not safe out there. The Frenzies," her father had said to her, his voice trailing off. And when he said those words she knew he loved her, because there was genuine fear in his eyes. "It's not safe for little girls. It's not safe for you, Ruby."

Ruby walked the long halls and passed through the front door to the school. She meandered along the sidewalk, Ms. Levithine walking quietly behind her. They wandered along the city streets, and sometimes Ruby stopped and tapped her feet on the cement sidewalks as if testing the ice on a newly frozen pond, seeing if she was going to break through. Ms. Levithine would stop and wait for her to continue, never saying a word.

They got as far as Mr. Hoyt's produce stand. There were no customers there, only Mr. Hoyt standing at the back, glaring at Ruby through his deep-set eyes.

Not everyone in the city was excited about Ruby's father's plans for change.

Someone spoke, and Ruby looked around for a few moments before she realized who it was.

"I have to go," Ms. Levithine said, and her voice cracked from disuse. Ruby stared at her. Ms. Levithine had never spoken to her outside the classroom before. Not a word. After her first few years of school, Ruby had assumed Ms. Levithine didn't like her or wasn't allowed to talk to her when she wasn't teaching. She had assumed that all children, if there were more somewhere, went to school on their own and each had their very own teacher. Ruby nodded, unblinking, now wondering why she had never thought of her teacher as a real person. Ms. Levithine turned and walked back the way they had come.

Ruby watched her, the crumbling city rising on either side of her. Ms. Levithine walked comfortably, and Ruby knew, because her father had told her, that if you kept walking in that direction, eventually you'd get to the river. She had never seen the river, but she'd heard plenty about it, not from anyone who had seen it with their own two eyes, but from people who knew people who knew people who had seen it.

Then Ms. Levithine did something even more unexpected: she climbed up and over the massive roadblock put in place to keep out the Frenzies. Ruby scrambled up to the top of the pile after her and watched as Ms. Levithine continued walking away from the center of the city, away from the only place Ruby had ever known, in the direction of the river.

For a moment, Ruby wanted to follow Ms. Levithine. She so

desperately wanted to see the river. She hesitated for a moment, and her father's face came to mind, his worried face. She sighed. She couldn't do that to him. She couldn't run off, even if it meant perhaps seeing the river, the one that somehow flowed without a far bank. She turned and climbed back down the pile of rubble.

As she passed street after street, nearing home, she heard a sound that made her sick to her stomach with fear. It started far away, and initially, she didn't think about it because it was the wind and it was birds coasting through the sky that had gone brick red and it was, perhaps, people talking in their apartments high above her. But the sound was not any of those things. It was the sound of voices laughing and shouting, young voices, playful voices, mean voices. It was the sound of breaking glass and splintering wood and the occasional scream.

It was the sound of a Frenzy.

Ruby looked behind her down the street, back the way she had come. The street had filled with young people, at least fifty, roiling and boiling over and around one another, like a flash flood pushing through desert creek beds. It was a relatively small Frenzy, but that didn't matter to Ruby. She was alone.

They came along slowly, disorganized chaos, a storm of energy. Some of them threw rocks at the buildings they walked past. A few of them carried wooden boards, fighting each other, sometimes in jest and other times landing genuine blows. Some rode on each other's shoulders while others scuffled at the back of the pack.

Ruby started running. She looked over her shoulder again and again. She fell and scuffed her palms on the rough sidewalk. She got up. She ran. She heard shouts.

They'd seen her.

Ruby kept running. She turned the corner onto James Street, her small legs churning. Her house was right there.

The house to the left of hers, the house she had passed every day of the school year, was abandoned. It had a large porch, like her house did, and it had tall windows and a black front door. There were columns that held up the porch roof, and some of the glass panes on the second- and third-story windows had broken. She had asked her father about the house, why no one lived there, who owned it, but he had not looked up from his writing.

"Nothing important, Ruby dearest. Nothing important."

Ruby heard the Frenzy running up the street behind her, and the sound of their feet on the pavement filled her with terror. It was like the approach of hail or locusts or the pattering of thick drops in a storm that led the hurricane along. They shouted with glee, like animals on a hunt closing in on their prey.

"Come in here!" a voice shouted, and she saw a young man standing in the doorway of the abandoned house. "Quick!"

He had ink-black hair and a round nose. His eyes were large and dark, and his skin was only a shade darker than the white in his eyes.

"Hurry!" he said. She ran down to the sidewalk and up the short stairway. He pulled her through, into the darkness.

The boy slammed the door behind them. She glanced through the glass and saw the Frenzy racing up the street.

"Who are you?" she asked.

"Come on," he said, practically dragging her farther into the dust and the darkness.

It took a moment for her eyes to adjust to the dim light, but once they did she saw that there was another door in front of them, about four feet in. She was standing in the same small entryway that her own house had. She was fairly certain that the next door would be locked, but the young man stepped forward and the door creaked open.

There was even less light in the hallway. He raced through and she reached over for the light switch and flipped it up, but nothing happened.

The black-haired young man opened the door that led into the front room she had seen through the windows. This was a mirror room to her father's office in her own house, the first room off the hall with two large windows that looked out onto the porch and the street. The room was empty except for a dresser with three long, thin drawers in it. It was odd, that lonely piece of furniture covered in dust.

"Don't stop now," the young man hissed, and she followed the voice deeper in.

The two of them ran through a door that led deeper into the house. There were no windows in that room, although small amounts of light crept under the door, enough so that when Ruby opened her eyes she could see the rest of the room. It seemed drab and gray. She waited to see if anyone was going to come inside, but she didn't hear anything. Soon she found a little bravery and walked farther back into the house. The boy had gone ahead. She couldn't see him.

"Who are you?" she whispered. The words were muffled, like sand through a sieve.

"There isn't time," the young man replied, and his voice sounded far away, as if it was under water.

"What are you doing here?" she asked.

"Are you Ruby Jardine?"

"Who are you?" She realized she knew him, or at least she felt like she should.

"Are you Ruby Jardine?" he insisted.

"Yes," she said. "I'm Ruby."

"Ruby," the young man said in a quiet voice, "you're not going to believe me."

He paused. She felt like she knew what he was going to say even before he said it.

"I'm your brother. I'm Leo."

Shouts on the other side of the door, and it burst open. Ruby screamed. Three men jumped on the young man and dragged him outside. In his place, suddenly, unexpectedly, was Ruby's father. He knelt down and hugged her, and over his shoulder, through the door, she watched the men drag the boy through the back gate and into the alley.

29

ABRA SLEPT FOR A LONG TIME after her confrontation with Beatrice and the vision she had seen in the clear pool on the rocky plain. She lost track of how long she slept there beside the pools. When she stood up, she was still exhausted, recovering from the near drowning as well as the shock of seeing what she had seen. She stumbled between the craters of water. She refused to look. Of course, she wanted to look, but she knew why Beatrice had brought her there—she could easily spend the rest of her natural life staring into each and every pool, reliving moments until all of the pools that showed her future showed only an old woman staring in pools, reliving the past.

She wandered back into the woods, toward the city, and she slept again, a deep, dreamless sleep.

When Abra woke up the next day, she felt rested. She sat in the trees for a few minutes, gathering her thoughts. She had completely lost track of exactly how long she had been in the city. But it felt like too long—much longer than it should have been. What if Mr. Henry grew tired of waiting? What if Leo and his sister were gone already?

What if she never found the Tree?

Beatrice. Where could Beatrice have gone? In some ways, Abra felt like she was starting from scratch. She glanced through the trees, across the perimeter street, and into the city. The first thing she saw was the tall building. It rose into the sky, brick red and uneven, easily the tallest building. For a few minutes she couldn't look away. It looked perilous, unsafe, as if it might topple over at any moment. And it was hard to tell for sure from that distance, but something about it besides its tallness made it seem unsteady. It seemed too thin for its height.

For a moment she considered heading directly in, straight for the tall building. Maybe she could find Leo again? But it didn't feel like the right thing to do. She decided to continue on her original course, around the city's outskirts.

Abra came out of the woods and yawned, stretched, and started walking. That's when she heard a faraway sound, something that started out as faint as a bee's buzzing and grew louder, louder, so that within a few minutes she realized what it was. Some kind of vehicle was approaching.

She jumped into the woods just in time. Three large vehicles careened out of the city and onto the street that lined the forest. They were buses but had been reinforced with a hodgepodge of metal plates so that they looked like homemade military vehicles. They screeched as they turned, gathered speed, and roared past her in the same direction she was traveling. Within a few minutes they were gone, along with their sounds, and the day around her seemed passive and unaware, as if nothing out of the ordinary had happened.

But she had seen them. She knew she had. Three large vehicles with all metal shells and slits for windows.

She walked faster that day and looked over her shoulder a

lot. It was during that stretch of walking that she decided she couldn't trust anyone in the city, and if she saw anyone or anything, she would hide or run.

She walked all day, and in spite of her extra vigilance, she didn't see anything else. Nothing, that is, until she got to the water. She didn't see it from very far away because the city street that went along the water was ten or fifteen feet above it, but when she got within a block or two, she heard it. The breakers crashing, the lapping sound it made against the wall. She actually ran the last block, though she wasn't sure why. It felt like the water was her destination. It felt like the water would give her everything she needed.

Abra stopped with her feet right at the edge of the street and looked out over the water. It was a beautiful deep blue, like navy blue but more somber. She couldn't see a farther shore, but the water definitely flowed like a river, from her right to her left. Directly to her right, the trees still grew, going right up to the edge of the water so that it would have been hard going if you decided to walk in that direction for any distance.

Abra sat down and let her legs dangle over the wall, and she thought about death, about traveling over that huge ocean or river or whatever it was. She wondered what was on the other side. She wondered what all the Wailers were flying to Over There. Her eyes wandered down the street that now divided the city from the water. That's when she saw a man, and it looked like he had fallen into the river.

A wind came in off the ocean and drowned her voice as she shouted. She ran to the spot where she had last seen him. The fear she had felt all day about encountering someone else melted away there at the edge of the water. The river looked majestic, yes, but it also looked cold and deep. Very, very deep. And she hadn't seen any way back up the wall, so that if you fell in there would be nowhere to go but down into the invisible depths.

"Hello?" she shouted. "Are you there? Do you need help?"

She heard him before she saw him. Actually, she heard the boat. It made an uneven thunking sound as the small waves pushed it up against the wall over and over again.

Abra fell to her hands and knees and looked over the edge. Sure enough, there was a man in a boat.

"Here," he called up to her without even looking. "Take this and fasten it to that hook you're sitting on."

Abra glanced down and saw there was a hook beneath her, sticking up out of the street. The man threw a rope ladder up to her, and she found the end of it, lifted it over the small hook. Soon the ropes danced back and forth as the man climbed up out of the boat. He carried a long rope with him and also tied that to the hook, so that the hook was lost under a mass of thick knots.

He looked up at Abra and nodded. He was breathing heavily from his short climb up the rope ladder. "It's a pleasure," he said.

"I thought you were drowning!" Abra exclaimed. It came out like an accusation.

The man shrugged. "And what if I had drowned?"

"Well . . . I mean . . . it doesn't seem safe."

He stared at her for a second, as if perhaps he had mistaken her for someone else. "You're standing along the Great Water, the deep darkness that separates the living from the dead . . . and you're worried about safety?"

She sighed. It did sound silly, if you said it like that.

The man standing in front of her wore one of those plaid Irish flat caps pulled down low so that she could barely see his dark eyes. He had a lot of hair, and it came out from under the hat in curling bursts. He had a short beard too, and wore a thick sweater and tan trousers and brown boots. He looked like he was ready to go for a hike somewhere in the Irish moors.

"Who . . . What . . . Who are you?" Abra asked quietly.

"A right good question," the man said, taking off his hat and scratching his head before putting his hat back on.

"Do you mean you don't know who you are?" she asked. "Or do you mean that you can't tell me?"

"Or both?" the man asked.

"Or both," Abra said.

"Yes, I suppose it's both."

"You don't know who you are," Abra said in a disbelieving voice.

He lifted his shoulders and held them there for a moment, as if he couldn't explain his ignorance.

"What are you doing here?" Abra asked. She didn't realize how much she had missed talking to another human being until she had one standing right in front of her.

"I'm waiting," the man said.

"Waiting?"

He nodded and sat down as Abra had, his legs dangling over the wall. He looked out over the water, and this time he took his hat off for good and put it under his leg. He patted the space beside him. Abra sat down.

"What are you waiting for?" Abra asked.

"I guess I'm waiting to find out who I am, or what I'm for."

"You don't know who you are?" she asked again.

"Well, I know my name, if that's what you mean, but knowing a name doesn't mean you know who someone is."

"It's a start," Abra said.

"Well said. My name is Mallory."

"I'm Abra."

"Yes, I know."

"You know?" This man was getting more and more confusing as the minutes passed. "You know who I am but you don't know who you are?"

"Everyone knows who you are," he said, scoffing.

"You know about the Tree?" she asked.

"Yes," he said, his voice suddenly heavy. "Yes, I do."

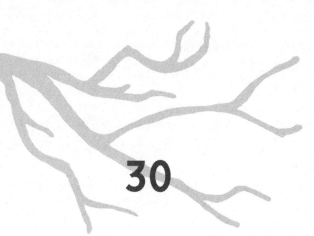

30

"Do you know where the Tree is?" Abra asked
Mallory.

"Don't you?" he asked.

She shook her head.

The two sat there, and if you had walked down the street
directly behind them, coming out of the city, you would have
thought that perhaps you were looking at a father and a daughter
fishing together. Or maybe they were throwing stones into the
water. Or maybe they were waiting for a boat to come in. Or
maybe they were saying good-bye.

"You're very strange," Abra said, glancing at the man out of
the corner of her eye to see how he would take such a charge.

He smiled without looking at her. Staring out over the sea,
he said in a quiet voice, "You haven't been into the city yet,
have you?"

"No. I'm looking for the Tree."

"Yes, yes, I know. Why wouldn't you go into the city?"

"It's a tree," she said, discouragement setting in. "Wouldn't
it be where other trees are?"

He frowned, appearing deep in thought. "Perhaps," he said. "But you don't know enough about the city. This place is young. Very young. The buildings are still standing for the most part, the streets are still level. There are other cities like this, you know, other in-between places, and they are in ruins. You can see straight through them from one end to the other, that's how far they have fallen."

"There are other cities like this?" she asked.

He nodded. "Six others. Koli Naal and those like her opened all the gates. But this is the only one with the Tree. So far."

"Koli Naal," Abra said, and the name came easily now, as the names of enemies do after you think them over and over again in your head, wearing them down with your bitterness.

"This city, it creates what is needed. Isn't that interesting? When the first live person came through the grave of Marie Laveau, there was only the one house along the road."

"We saw that house!"

"Yes. That was the first house. But as more people came through, this place grew. Now it's a city. Then I was called."

"Called?"

He shrugged. "Something like that. Me and my boat, I guess we're needed."

"For what?"

He beckoned out over the water. "For crossing."

Abra leaned forward and looked down at his tiny boat bobbing harshly in the waves. "You're going to cross all that water in that little thing?" Her voice came out part laughter at the futility, part sadness at his certain destruction. The boat was small, like a rowboat, and had two seats.

"Or sink. One or the other."

"That's what you're needed for?"

He took a deep breath, and she could tell he was getting tired of explaining.

"Every single thing in this city is here because someone needs it, either someone who is here or someone who is coming here. There are things in this city that you need that you don't even know you need, things that have been waiting here for you to come and use them. That's how this Passageway works. It was here originally because the spirits of the dead needed a way to get across the water. It provided a way for them. When living people wandered in, it kept doing that, it kept providing. Now I'm here. I don't know what I'm here for, but I'm here for something, so I'll wait right here until I figure out why I'm here."

"You really believe that?" Abra asked. "You really believe this city is like that?"

"Let me tell you a little secret, Abra." When he said her name, it sent a thrill through her. "Everything in your world is like that too. Every single thing in the world is there for someone, for their perfect use."

They sat there for a moment, listening to the water and the boat thudding against the wall. Abra kept staring off at the horizon, hoping to catch a glimpse of something, anything.

"What do I do?" she asked. "Where do I go?"

Mallory put his hand on her shoulder and gave it a squeeze. Abra didn't know if it was because she had been wandering by herself for so long or if there was actually some kind of supernatural power in his hands, but the tips of his fingers sent a jolt through her, pure energy. She became very aware of her own breathing, and her heartbeat seemed to settle into the same rhythm as the waves against the seawall.

When Mallory spoke again it was in a kind voice.

"If you don't know where to go or what to do, here is what I would recommend: go as far as you're able and do what you can. The rest will happen. I promise. The rest will always happen."

It was getting darker, and Abra would have loved to stay. She enjoyed Mallory's company. She would have liked to watch the Wailers shoot out over the water, but she felt a sudden urgency to find the Tree. Talking with Mallory set it in her bones the way cold weather puts an ache in the joints. Something was happening.

"Thank you, Mallory," she said.

He nodded and lay on his back, his legs still dangling over the edge. "Go as far as you are able," he said, and she started walking away. When she got a little farther, she heard him shout, still lying on his back, and his voice went straight up like a beacon.

"And do what you can!"

He laughed after that, and it was a joyous sound, one that Abra would carry with her until the end.

Abra walked straight into the city, down a long, wide boulevard lined with expensive-looking shops. Except, like the rest of the buildings in the city, they were empty. The darkness had nearly settled completely, and she waited to hear the approach of the Wailers, shattering the silence as they did every night. Instead, she heard a different sound.

Perhaps she had lost track of her surroundings. Perhaps she had become lost as she thought back over her conversation with Mallory. Perhaps she was tired. Perhaps her proximity to the water kept her from hearing what she had heard before from a long way off. Maybe it was all of these things, or something else entirely, but whatever the case, she didn't hear the sound of the engine and the tires crunching over broken glass until it was too late. The headlights swung around the corner and caught her full in the face. She raised her hand to shield her eyes, trying to look behind the beams.

The first vehicle was followed by two more, and she realized they were the armored buses she had seen early that morning.

"Who are you?" a voice said from the vehicle in the front, but it wasn't a normal voice—it was a voice amplified by something, and it wavered and crackled artificially in the shadows.

Abra didn't say anything. She glanced to her right and saw a shop with large display windows. The windows were cracked but not shattered, and the door hung on its hinges. Inside the building was only darkness. Her hand, the one that wasn't shielding her eyes, moved to the side of her pants and felt the hilt of the sword where it stuck out over her shirt.

"Answer the question. Who are you?"

Even in the middle of that situation, Abra smiled to herself as she remembered Mallory's words.

I guess I'm waiting to find out who I am, or what I'm for.

"I don't know," Abra replied quietly.

"Can't hear you. Speak up."

"I don't know!" Abra shouted, smiling.

The man started to say something else, but then he stopped, his voice catching the way a hand leaps backward after hitting an unseen splinter on a smooth surface. Abra heard the Wailers begin their approach from far away.

"You need to get into this vehicle right now," the man said, genuine fear in his voice.

Abra waited.

The first vehicle turned off, followed by complete silence when the other two vehicles also shut off their engines. Abra wasn't sure what they were doing, but she was getting ready to run.

"They're coming," the voice said. "You need to hurry. Get in here."

Abra still didn't move from her spot. The three vehicles shut off their lights. The sound of the Wailers grew louder, and a glow began to light up the street a few blocks away. She wasn't scared of the Wailers, but it seemed that the men in the vehicles were. Abra turned and ran through the dark doorway as the Wailers flew past, their sound like a siren in the night.

Abra felt her way through the darkness. She banged her shin on a chair and collided with a counter, then found her way around it and into a back room, almost completely dark except for occasional flashes of light as a bright white Wailer flew past outside. She pushed her way through a swinging door, opened another door, and found herself in some kind of a service hallway that must have linked up all the shops in that building with a stairwell. She wondered if it led to a parking garage or something with a roof where she could make her way back outside. She felt her way through the darkness, tripped against some stairs, and started going up.

Up, up, up she went. It took her nearly five minutes in the darkness, but she made it to the top. She couldn't find her way to the roof, so she opened a door into what might have been an apartment and walked over to a window. She peered down. The three vehicles were still there, not moving, lights off, and the Wailers swept around them and toward the water ten or fifteen blocks away.

Abra locked the door she had come through and gathered things she could feel in the darkness: a coffee table, some over-stuffed couch cushions, a thin rug. She created a small den for herself, a safe place in that foreign world, and she curled up inside of it. The air was cooler than she remembered it being. She hugged herself, curling her legs up so that she was almost in a ball. She felt safe, hidden as she was. She felt like it was a place no one would find her. She took a deep breath, pushed her hair out of her eyes, and fell fast asleep.

The tall building. The tall building. She woke up with the tall building on her mind. Why hadn't she thought of that before? If she could get there, if she could get to the top, she should be able to see the Tree. The Tree of Life that had grown in her valley had been huge, and that was in the first few hours. Imagine how big a Tree of Life would be if it had been growing for months or years!

She peeked through the window. The dim pink light of morning rested on everything like dew, and she had grown used to the silence. It was like a blanket was on the city, muffling all the sound. The trucks were gone. The road was clear. She stood up and stretched and turned on one of the faucets. Water ran out, clear and cold, and she stared at it for a little while. Was this what Mallory had been talking about? Was this the provision the city offered?

She leaned in over the sink and drank and drank and drank, and the water went down deep, filling not only her physical thirst but something deeper, something more real. Abra wiped her mouth on her shirt, then walked back out into the hallway and down the stairs and through the front door. The morning light filled her with an intense energy and hope. She wondered if Mallory was still sitting on the wall, staring out over the water.

But she didn't have much time to wonder. Before she took

ten steps down the sidewalk, men rushed at her from every direction. They pushed her down to the sidewalk and tied her hands. She felt the grit of cement on her cheek. Her breath swept away from her, and she gasped to bring it back.

"Ahhh!" one of them shouted. "Something burned me."

They were more careful after that. In a few moments she was blindfolded, and someone led her, pushed her, dragged her around the corner. She heard three large vehicles roar to life. She was lifted into one and rough hands placed her on a hard seat. She wondered why they didn't take her sword. Couldn't they feel it where it stuck out from her pants? Didn't they see the edge of the handle above her waistband?

"Let's go," a voice said, and it was the same voice from the night before.

They drove for about five minutes, and the buses heaved around corners like elephants and bounced over bumps in the road like large ships over waves.

"Everything okay in the back?" the voice asked.

"Safe and secure," a different voice said through a CB or a radio.

"10-4."

The bus stopped and Abra heard the door open. A man walked out and came right back in.

"Looks good," he said.

"Roadblock ahead," the driver said.

"Turn right on 9th Avenue," the voice replied.

"Copy."

"Frenzy, 12:00."

The bus slammed to a stop. Abra expected the vehicles behind them to crash into them, but nothing happened.

"They've seen us. They're coming this way," the driver said.

"Hold," the other voice said.

Abra ducked her head down.

"Hold," the voice said again.

"Copy," the radio replied.

Abra heard the distant sound of shouting, the far-off shattering of glass. Soon things began hitting the vehicle, heavy things, like bricks and bottles and chunks of wood.

"Straight ahead, slow and steady," the voice said.

"Copy."

The bus started forward again, and now Abra could hear hands pounding on the sides and more things smashing.

"Roadblock ahead," the driver said.

"Right again. Take Severe Drive."

The bus turned, and Abra swayed with it.

"Full speed ahead," the voice said. "Let's get out of here."

They drove and they drove fast, and Abra braced herself for a collision that never came.

"Open the gate! Open the gate!" the voice shouted into the radio.

They slowed, made a few short turns, and the bus stopped.

31

THE SOLDIERS LED her through long tunnels and up and down stairways. For most of the trip the air smelled like the earth: dark and wet and muddy. She imagined the layers and layers of things above her, the heaviness of the soil and the streets and the building on top of them all, and she felt a sour sense of panic stir in her stomach. She had to get out. She had to be in the fresh air.

Those who led her along were not silent. Her presence, that of a young woman, did not affect them. After a little while it was as if she did not exist.

"War's here," the man behind her said, and there was excitement in his voice. "They say Father Amos will make the announcement soon, and we'll win back the city."

"So they say," the man in front of her said. She could tell by the sound of his voice that he didn't turn around when he spoke to the man behind him. He kept walking forward.

"What do you mean, 'so they say'? It's going to happen, man! This whole city will be ours!"

"This whole city?" the man muttered. "They talk like that's a jewel worth grabbing. Have you been out there? Have you seen the place? It's a shambles, and we'll either be turned into slaves to rebuild it, or . . . or something else."

"Not so loud," his partner hissed. "Someone hears you, you'll be on the outside. Worse yet, thrown in the water."

Silence fell for a few moments as the men continued. The only sound was their feet scuffing over concrete.

"What do you mean by something else?" the first man asked after a spell of silence. He was the one excited for war.

At first the man in front of Abra didn't say anything. He cleared his throat, and when he spoke it was in a quieter voice, a resigned voice.

"Some say—no one you know, mind you—but some say that Beatrice has been talking about larger goals."

Abra nearly tripped at the name of Beatrice.

"C'mon, girl, watch your step," the man behind her said. "What's Beatrice saying?"

"Beatrice . . . " The man paused. "You didn't hear this from me, right?"

"Yeah, yeah."

"Rumor is, Beatrice wants to defeat the Frenzies and take this whole show over the water."

"Over the water?" the man said, his voice incredulous.

"Over the water. Over There. Take over."

The men walked in silence again. Abra could tell the man behind her was thinking through this new information.

"I don't know," he said hesitantly. "Amos seems pretty intent on cleaning this place up. Second heaven and all that."

The man in front laughed. "She's leading him along, one thing to the next. If you think that man makes any decisions

Beatrice doesn't approve of long before the idea comes into his head, then you're dumber than you look."

"Hey!"

"She runs this place." The man in front stopped, and Abra nearly ran into him. She heard him pull a ring of keys out. "She won't stop until . . ."

His voice faded away. The door opened. The man behind Abra nudged her through.

The smell changed so suddenly it was like someone had flipped a switch. Everything around her went from the odor of a musty tomb to that of springtime air and butterflies. Her growing sense of panic eased, and she felt relaxed. It was the same feeling she'd had . . .

She was overcome with a realization. She stopped walking, only to be pushed forward again.

It was the same feeling she'd had while standing under the Tree of Life at the end of the Road to Nowhere, back in Deen, four long years before.

The Tree was there somewhere. It was close. She would never forget that smell, not if she lived to be a hundred years old. She would never forget the pleasant visions it brought to mind, the gentle rocking of the soul, the sweet memories it managed to revive.

If she didn't focus, she could easily get lost in them, those memories of being a child and going on a picnic, or riding the Ferris wheel on a summer night, or running hard through a cool autumn evening, the alfalfa rustling around her knees, the fireflies lighting like a galaxy around her. Adventures with Sam and long walks into the shadowy trees that lined the mountains.

The Tree of Life! What a beautiful thing it would be, she thought, to sit under that Tree and smell its leaves, to eat its fruit, to remember everything that was good about the world, to have no worries or cares, to sleep soundly and wake more refreshed than you've ever felt before. What a beautiful thing.

But not here, not now, she reminded herself. Not here, where things are so imperfect. Not here, where death is a gift that rescues us from pain and disease and the crippling effects of age and accidents. Not here.

They led her up and up and up, stairway after stairway, until her legs were numb and her breathing hard. Finally, when she didn't think she could go up any more stairs, they veered off to the side, through a door, down a hallway.

"This is it, girl," the man in front of her said. He took off her blindfold and untied her hands.

"What are you doing?" the other man asked.

"How old are you, girl?"

"Sixteen," she said.

The man who untied her looked at the other man. "She's a kid. Relax. You're a kid, right?" he asked in a playful voice.

She nodded.

"You're harmless, right?" He laughed.

She nodded again.

"See?" he said, closing her inside the room and locking the door. Abra listened to their footsteps recede down the hallway.

"You're not even going to search her?" the man who had been walking behind her asked.

"Seriously? She's a kid."

Abra walked to a dark corner of the room and sat down. She thought of her mother, and she thought of the Tree of Life. She wondered what these people would do with it. If they ate from the Tree, would they try to go back to the other side of the grave and rule the world as immortals?

The wall behind her was brick, and the bricks were unevenly laid so that some stuck out a little farther than the others. She traced a path with her finger along the mortar, and she imagined it was her walking through the city streets, trying to find her way home.

⁓

That was a long, dark time for Abra, sitting in the shadows, communing with the darkness. She never came out of the back corner when the guards opened the door. She hid her face in the crook of her arm, the sword still tucked inside the waistband of her pants.

She was particularly deep in her thoughts when she heard the door open, and she put her face in her arm because she didn't want them to make eye contact and stay and maybe find out about the sword. She noticed again how her skin smelled like the earth, like dust. It had been so long since she'd had a bath.

Abra had a strange feeling, a sense of falling, because she realized the door had never closed. She looked up quickly and her heart started beating rapidly. She had to work very hard to control her breathing. A small person stood in the doorway.

It was Beatrice.

"I thought it was you," Beatrice said in the sweetest voice, and Abra had to remind herself that this was not a friend. This was something else entirely. "I knew it! They didn't even describe you to me—you believe me, don't you? I had a sense, I guess. I knew it."

Abra took a deep breath and put her face back in her arm.

"Oh, don't be sad," Beatrice said, still in a kind voice. "Abra. Abra! It's me. It's B."

"I know who you are," Abra whispered. "You tried to kill me. Remember?"

"Then you should be very afraid," Beatrice said in a surprised tone. "If you know what I am, you should fall to your knees and worship me so that I don't destroy you in a moment."

Abra's fists clenched, and she wanted to pull the sword out and fight Beatrice right there in the cell, but there was something inside of her that knew it wasn't time. Not yet.

Abra looked up. "I hope that when I stabbed you by the pools it didn't hurt too much," she said in an even tone. Beatrice winced and involuntarily flexed her forearm.

So that's where I got her, Abra thought.

"We are so close, Abra. So close. You need to know that once everyone eats from the Tree and I unite all the people here, the first thing we will do is march back to the other side of the grave. I will take you with me so that you can witness it all. We will take over the earth! We'll let people roam freely between there and here, and everyone will eat from the Tree. And you, the holder of the key, the one who locks and unlocks the door, will no longer be of use to us."

Abra still said nothing, and her silence seemed to agitate Beatrice. B's eyes widened, and her voice grew louder with each sentence.

"We know what you did to Jinn! We all know!"

Abra felt strength grow inside of her. Beatrice took a step back, and Abra remembered, for the first time in a while, that she had been the one to bring Jinn down. She had no reason to be afraid.

"You should be careful," Abra said.

Their eyes locked, and there was the first battle, before anything took place on the streets, before the armies marched, before the leaders met. The first battle was there in that dark room.

"You will rot here in this building," Beatrice murmured. "You will rot, and you will be the last person in this city, and no one will ever come looking for you, not even when time ends."

She spun around and slammed the door behind her.

Moments later the door burst open again, and two guards flung another figure into the room. Abra stared at the young man who was now on his hands and knees. The guards closed the door, and the sound of it echoed through the building.

"Leo," Abra asked, "is that you?"

It took a long time for them to catch up on what they had each been through. They both seemed older, like two people in middle age reflecting on a long-ago childhood. First Abra went, because Leo was still catching his breath, and his head still hurt. She told him of the pools and the man by the water and her experiences with Beatrice. Leo spoke after that, rubbing his head gingerly, talking about the Frenzies and his sister.

His sister.

They were there in the darkness for a time they could not measure. They tried to figure out how long they had been separated, but even those days were difficult to define, impossible to count. It went on and on like this, until one day the building began to vibrate with an immeasurable number of people—they could hear them, sense them. The crowd settled, the building throbbed, and Amos's voice echoed out over a loudspeaker. There were no speakers on floor 27, but they could still hear him, his voice coming from some faraway place.

They heard his plans.

They realized the building was the Tree.

And it seemed like there was nothing they could do.

PART 7

the tip
of the
blade

"If you were to be lost in the river, Jonas, your memories would not be lost with you. Memories are forever."

LOIS LOWRY, *THE GIVER*

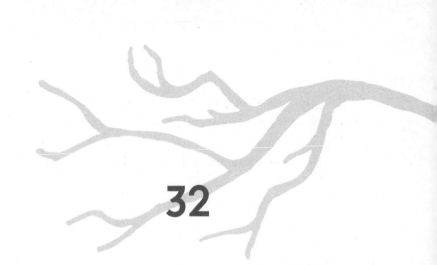

32

Ruby stared through her bedroom window, the window that faced the tall building, and in the dim glow of the alley lights she monitored the red door. Her mind could only focus on one thing.

There was a young man in that building and he had said he was her brother. She believed him, though she didn't know why, maybe because of the way the words had come out of him, sincere and intense. But if her brother was alive, where was her mother? Ruby wondered if the young man knew.

She had heard her father tell the others where to take the young man. But if he was her brother, why had her father had him dragged out of the house? Surely he would have recognized him! If that young man was her brother, wouldn't her father have fallen to his knees in thankfulness?

She remembered her father's words.

"Take him up with the other spy. Level 27. I'll come up later."

Someone wasn't telling her the truth, and no matter how hard she tried to convince herself otherwise, she kept circling around to the strong sense that her father was the liar.

—

Then came the night her father said he would take her to the important meeting in the tall building. He said it would be the next day, which meant there were only twenty-four more hours and all the secrets would be gone, or at least that's how he had made it sound. Did the secrets involve her mother? Her brother? Did the young man know the secrets, and had he come to tell her the truth?

The air was cold in the house, and she pulled a blanket off her bed and wrapped herself in it. She walked to her bedroom door and opened it. Her father hadn't come up to say good night yet, so it was still unlocked. She walked down the stairs slowly, trying not to trip on the train the blanket created. The steps creaked under her weight, but for some reason her father didn't hear her walk into his study.

Ruby stared over his shoulder. He was reading letters, a bunch of them, and they were spread out all over the desk. Each one was written in different handwriting, different ink color. She wondered where they had all come from.

"What's that?" she asked.

She didn't expect a real answer. He rarely gave her real answers when she asked serious questions. But her father surprised her.

"These are letters from other leaders in the city who want to see things change. They want to see an end to the Frenzies. They are pledging their loyalty, Ruby. We are finally ready."

She didn't make eye contact with him, only stared at the rows and rows of letters. "Ready for what?" she asked.

"Ready for war," he whispered.

The word "war" sent a shiver through her, and it felt like that shiver put a crack in her heart—a crack into which darkness and fear and uncertainty all started to leak. She shuddered.

"Is this how it was when Mother and Leo . . . died?" she asked.

Her father nodded and cleared his throat uncomfortably, and Ruby knew by that sound that he didn't want to talk about it. She didn't like the feeling of being lied to, though she still tried very hard to find the best in her father. She reasoned to herself that if he was lying to her, he was doing so for a good reason.

"So, I can still come along to the meeting?" Ruby asked.

Her father nodded.

"Is it safe?" she asked.

"That's a good question, Ruby. A very good question. This city is never completely safe, which is why these meetings are so important. Our defenses are still standing. We are going to make it safe. We are. The entire city. And that is only the beginning. The beginning! After that . . . But first we have to secure the city. I will do anything . . . *anything* . . . to make this city safe for you. For your future."

She looked up at him and felt a surge of affection. Competing with it was the urge to run out the front door and never come back. Everything he said to her was now filtered through her suspicion that he had lied to her about the most important things in her life.

"Come with me," he said, leading Ruby across his study. He gave her a sad smile and walked over to his board of keys. He scanned them quickly, reached out and took one off its hook, then came back over to Ruby and messed up her hair playfully. He held out the key.

"This is the key to your room," he said in a serious voice. "I think you're old enough to have that now."

She took it from him, and the coldness of the key bit into her hands as if he had pulled it from a freezer. She looked at its jagged teeth, pressed her fingers against the sharpness. It was a heavy key for its size. She wondered what it was made of.

Ruby looked up at her father to thank him, but he had already returned to his desk, his face glowing in the light of the lamp, eyes scanning the letters in front of him. She slipped the key into her pocket and backed slowly out of the room.

That night, Ruby lay quietly in her bed, staring at the ceiling. Her third-floor bedroom was large, almost large enough to be its own living space. The windows were tall, and in the summer she left them open a sliver so she could hear the city. At night, there wasn't much going on—people stayed inside to avoid the Frenzies and the "riffraff." That's the name her father used for the inhabitants who didn't live in one house, who roamed the city freely.

And there were a lot of those people out at night, a lot of riffraff, although they stayed in the shadows and the alleyways, always more comfortable in the darkness. Her father seemed to know a lot about what went on in the city, considering he stayed inside most days. She wondered what he wrote in his notebooks. She often heard him talking seriously with someone, and she wondered who was on the telephone when the heavy sliding doors were closed.

She got up and walked to the window. She wondered what the young man was doing. He had looked older than her, but he was still young, much younger than her father or her teacher or anyone who lived in their neighborhood. Besides occasional glimpses of the Frenzies, she hadn't seen another young person for a very, very long time. Her father said all the little children in the city went to their own school, and they all had to stay inside in order to be safe. He said the young people had all joined the Frenzies.

Ruby pulled the curtain back a few inches and looked down at the red door at the base of the tall building. She saw the outline of a man standing in the alley along the fence. He was nothing more than a shadow. Two more people came around the corner and looked down the alley before jogging back the way they had come.

She heard her father coming up the stairs, so she hopped into bed.

He peeked his head in through her door. "Good night, Ruby."

"Good night."

"I'm going to close the door, okay?"

She nodded quickly, almost nervously.

"But tonight, your door stays unlocked unless you lock it. Are you okay with that?"

She nodded again, this time one bob of her head.

He smiled, pulled back into the hallway, and closed her door.

Ruby sat in her bed. Her father's manner toward her had been changing recently. He was letting go of her, or pulling away, she couldn't tell which. Things were shifting. She appreciated her newfound freedom, but there was a dark edge to her father's recent treatment of her. It left her feeling empty, anxious, like she was being freed from a cage but into something that was somehow even worse.

Something else was going on. Something big. She was sure of it.

She waited and waited and counted to a hundred at least four times before creeping to her door. She realized for the first time, as she stood there with her hand on her bedroom doorknob, that her father had ingrained her with a deep fear of opening doors. She hadn't identified it before that night, but every time she reached for a doorknob and began turning, she had this moment where fear surged up through her throat, threatening to choke her. Every time she turned the knob on the bathroom door at school or walked through the front door of the house.

There she stood, hand on the doorknob, recognizing it for the first time.

That she turned the knob and looked into the hallway was a feat of great bravery. Her father's door was closed and locked. He always locked his door at night, as if preparing for an invasion that never happened, or hadn't happened yet. She thought about what he always said to her when he locked her in every night.

"For protection," he would tell her as the door closed.

There was no light coming out from under his door. Ruby's mind immediately went to the back door, the one that was always locked, the one that led into the alley that spilled down to the red door at the base of the tall building. She wondered if the red door was locked.

She stared at the attic door at the end of the hall and thought of all the stories her father had told her of the terrible, awful things that would come rushing through the door if she opened it: the unspeakable horrors, the indescribable beings, the forces that would tear the city up by its roots. She wondered if that young man was one of those forces. It certainly felt like it.

"I'm your brother. I'm Leo."

Those words had leveled her world, and now she was rebuilding it from scratch. She felt like someone searching the rubble of a bombed-out city, desperately seeking something that looked

familiar, something recognizable. But she found nothing. Her
father was new to her, a man who now seemed to have never told
her a true thing in all her life. Ruby didn't recognize the past
she had created for herself because it wasn't true. Her brother
wasn't dead. What about her mother?

"I'm your brother. I'm Leo."

Ruby walked to the steps, holding her breath the entire way,
walking carefully as if land mines had been placed randomly
under the floorboards. She walked down to the second level,
down to the first level, aware now of all the doors that were
locked, all the doors that needed keys. She felt an overwhelming
compulsion to run into her father's office without taking any
precautions, grab all the keys, and unlock all the doors. How
wonderful that would feel, to run through the house with all
the doors unlocked and open! How invigorating!

The darkness was heavy as another car drove by, its headlights glowing behind the cracks in the curtains and the spaces
in between the blinds and the window frames. It passed. She
stood in front of her father's office, the heavy sliding doors all
that separated her from the keys, the keys, the keys. She waited,
always expecting her father to wake, unlock his door, and come
downstairs. But it was the middle of the night. He was sleeping.
All was quiet.

Ruby pushed against one of the sliding doors and it moved
easily. Her father kept the rollers oiled so that the door moved
without a sound, almost by magic. She moved faster now that
she was inside, straight across the office. She struggled to read
the small labels under each key, but soon she found the one she
was looking for.

Back door.

She snatched it from the hook, reached into a pocket in her

pajamas, and took out her bedroom key. They looked identical, at least from a distance. When she examined them closely she could tell that the teeth were different, only slightly, and the circle of iron at the top of her bedroom key was more oval shaped than the circular ring at the top of the back door key. She stared at her key. She hated to give it up, but her father was sure to notice if there was an extra empty space on the board. She hung her bedroom key in the place of the back-door key, then left the room.

It was time to leave the house. It was time to see what was behind the red door in the tall building.

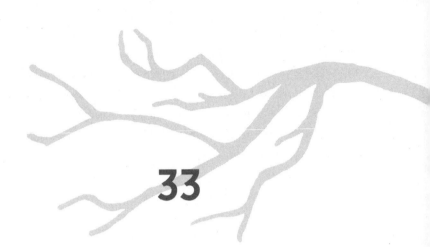

33

WALKING THE LONG DISTANCE to the back door in her house was a creaky affair. She took a step and waited. Took a step and waited. Another step. Another held breath. She found it hard to believe that her father slept through all of the noise she was making, but every time she stopped, she heard nothing.

It was in this slow, deliberate way that she made her way to the back door. She held the key tightly in her hand, squeezing it so hard that it left an indent in her fingers. She wasn't quite sure what her father would do if he caught her with the key to get out of the house. For years, she didn't even consider opening that door, so great was the fear he had instilled in her. If she opened it, what would happen? What terrors, if any, would she let inside? What would her father do to her?

She thought about her father as she walked slowly, step by step. He was a firm man. He kept to all the rules as if his life depended on keeping them. He never broke the law, at least not that Ruby was aware of, and when he spoke of those who did, he wrinkled his nose at their weakness. The crowds of young people who cruised the city were his special enemies. To Ruby's father, the Frenzies represented everything that was wrong with the city. They were the sole cause of its downward spiral.

As she came within an arm's width of the back door, she heard a Frenzy coming down the street. She wondered how they kept getting in. She wondered why her father's roadblocks were no longer keeping them out.

This particular group was smashing glass windows as they went, and the sound of glass hitting the sidewalks made a rich, tinkling sound in the night. There was an underlying soundtrack of shouting punctuated by an occasional scream. Ruby couldn't tell if the screaming came from within the crowd or from the people in the houses they were destroying. She held her breath and listened.

What she heard next made her take one step back. It was the sound of something knocking against the outside of the back door. She took another step back. The doorknob turned, but the door did not open because it was locked. Ruby turned and ran back to the front of the house in time to see her father come flying down the stairs.

"Dad!" Ruby shouted, not sure what to say, but she soon realized she wasn't in trouble.

Her father gasped when he saw her. He ran over and held her close.

"Thank God you're safe," he whispered, and there was a frantic sound in his voice, a kind of desperation she had never seen in her father before. It scared her—it made her feel like an object to be possessed.

He pulled his head back and stared into her face. "Are you okay?"

She nodded, not sure what to say.

"I heard the crowd outside," he said. "I worried that if you had your key, you might have tried to go out . . ." His voice trailed off. They both stayed there listening to the riot outside, the crashing of glass and the splintering of wood. The loud sound made by heavy things smashing against cars and signs. It felt strange to Ruby, leaning so close to her father, him on his knees. His face changed, as if he had decided something.

"Where are those defenses?" he mumbled to himself. He seemed to be listening intently for something that never came.

"Come," he finally said, straightening up but not letting go of her hand. He led her to the front door. The sounds outside grew louder. Ruby could hear the individual voices. James Street suddenly felt like a place where evil lived. She realized the key to the back door was still in her hand, all hard edges and cold metal.

Her father ran to the front door and looked through the peephole.

"It's a smaller group," he said with relief in his voice. He muttered to himself, "They must have found another breach. I thought the war was starting. Thank God."

He pulled a few latches, lowered a few pins, and pulled a large, heavy, metal door across their normal front door. It rumbled into place and clicked loudly once it covered the entire front door. There were three bolts that went into the floor, three that went into the left side of the frame, and three into the ceiling. Her father sighed.

Ruby stared at the metal door. She had never seen it before, never knew her house could do that. With every new thing she learned, with every lie exposed, she felt more and more confused about which way was up. Everything she depended on seemed to be untrue.

They ran from the door and into her father's office, where he went straight to his desk. He sat down and pulled out a few of the drawers, the banging of which was drowned out by the sound coming from the street. Now Ruby could hear individual voices shouting to one another, individual laughter the same shade as a hyena's.

"Watch this, Jimmy!" a voice clamored, followed by the sound of a brick slamming the iron bars on one of their windows, breaking the glass in the process. Ruby heard laughter as another rock shattered through a neighboring window. The glass tinkled to the floor like the sound of magic. Feet pounded onto the porch, her own porch, and faces leered through the bars.

"Well looky, looky!" one of the young women shouted, squealing with delight when she saw Ruby's father in the room. Soon three more young people joined her, staring through the bars. Soon ten more. They crowded around, trying to get a glimpse inside.

A voice shouted with authority. Only one word.

"Move!"

The sea of faces parted, and a different young woman peered through the darkness. She made eye contact with Ruby, and her eyes widened slightly.

"Who's the fastest person here?" she whispered without looking away from Ruby.

"Danny," someone replied. The crowd shuffled in their silence, and a young man was pushed to the front.

"Danny?" the young woman said.

"Yeah."

"Go tell Jeremiah."

~

"We don't have much time," Ruby's father said, grabbing her by the arm and racing to the board of keys and pulling off the one for the back door. Except Ruby knew that was actually the key to her bedroom. She held the key he wanted in her pocket, tightly in her hand. But her father didn't know that, so he grabbed her and raced to the back door. They arrived to hear pounding on the door.

"They're already in the alley," her father said, and Ruby felt a tremor in his voice, the tiniest fracture of a deep foundation. Her father was frightened.

He led them back to his office yet again. Frenzy faces still peered in, watching them. Her father grabbed the key for the attic. "Hurry, hurry," he said to Ruby, running up the stairs in front of her. She could barely keep up. They went up to the second floor, then the third floor. A crashing sound, and Ruby thought the back door must have been broken down.

"Hurry, hurry," he said again, and Ruby couldn't tell if he was talking to her or to himself. He pushed the key against the keyhole, but his hands trembled and he dropped it. He bent over quickly and grabbed the key again, his shaking hands barely able to hold it. Ruby reached over and held his hand for a moment.

"Don't worry, Dad," she said. "It's okay."

She took the key from him, and he didn't protest. With a steady hand, she slid the key into the lock and turned it. They made their way up into the attic.

"Hurry, hurry," her father kept mumbling to himself. "Hurry, hurry."

They had to get on their hands and knees as they climbed through the dust. The rumors had been correct, and Ruby looked behind her and ahead of her with amazement. All of the houses in their row were connected by a crawl space. They shuffled their way into the abandoned house, the very one where the young man had told her those words, the ones that still echoed in her mind.

"I'm your brother. I'm Leo."

Her father crawled directly to the area where stairs led down, as if he had done this many times before. Ruby followed after him, picking up splinters in her hands and knees. The dust tried to make her cough but she fought the urge.

Quietly, quietly.

They crept down the steps. In their own house they had run without any thought for sound. Now they moved like ghosts, weightless, placing each foot carefully. Down, down, down they went. All the way to the basement. Ruby heard the Frenzy next door, in her very own house, smashing and searching and breaking. She wondered what they would have done to her if they had found her.

In the basement, she followed her father all the way to the opposite end, which was right up by the street, though underground. There was a door there, and they walked through, and he closed it behind them. All was dark. She could not see a thing, and she froze there, on the other side of the door. Everything was far away: the Frenzy, her own house, the lights. There was nothing, and she stood in the middle of it.

A flashlight beam popped on.

"Come," her father said. "We're almost there."

She followed him into a narrow tunnel that he almost had to turn sideways to walk through. An intersection came out of nowhere, but her father did not hesitate. He made a quick right, another quick right, then straight on for a few hundred yards.

"We made it," he said.

They walked out into an open area, huge, the size of fifty basements. There were posts supporting the ceiling, and in the middle something massive and irregularly round, like a frozen waterfall. There were no windows and no lights were on, but in the moving beam of her father's flashlight she caught sight of a door over to her right, and she knew in that moment that she was looking at the red door she had wondered about for so many years.

The red door that led into the tall building. Except now she was on the other side of it.

She was inside.

A group of men came running at them, shouting.

"It's me! It's Amos!" her father said.

The men came close. Some of them hugged her father, and some of them patted her on the head as if they had known her for years, but she did not recognize any of them.

"Is it ready?" her father asked.

"Yes, sir," one man said, his voice trembling, but Ruby couldn't figure out why.

"So, it's time," her father said quietly, perhaps to himself. "The meeting is still on for tomorrow night?"

"Thousands are coming, sir," the man said. "Everyone is ready."

"Okay," her father said, taking a deep breath. "We don't have much time."

He glanced back and forth between Ruby and the man in front of him. The other guards stared at him as if awaiting orders. Ruby couldn't believe it. This was her father? This man who other men listened to? Obeyed without thinking? Her world continued crumbling in on itself, and she felt lost in the midst of the rubble.

"I'm going to take Ruby to the top," he said, still looking at her. "I need all forces to go to James Street. There's been a breach—a small Frenzy is in my house. Get them out of here. Or smash them. Whatever. After we're finished, I'll come find you."

Walking up the stairway through the tower was one of the strangest experiences of Ruby's young life. The stairs were made of bricks, all rough and jagged edges. There was something only vaguely professional about the way things were built. The rest of the buildings in the city felt new but looked dilapidated. The tower, on the other hand, felt dilapidated but looked new. She understood that it had been built in her lifetime, but everything about it, from the uneven steps to the bare cement-block walls to the unfinished ceilings exposing beams and wires, screamed of shoddy work, or at least work done in great haste.

And there, twisting and turning among the bricks like some kind of strange tumor, were tree branches. They had been pruned and cut and, in some cases, tied so that they had become part of the walls. The branches looked like a splinter in flesh, and something in Ruby wished she could pluck the tree out. But that would have been impossible. It was everywhere.

She struggled to keep up with her father, who after ten or fifteen floors began taking steps two at a time. It seemed he had forgotten about her, quite forgotten that a young girl was following him, trying to keep up. Soon he was far ahead, and she was left to walk the stairway on her own.

This is when the true strangeness of the situation settled in: it seemed eternal. Floor after floor—eight steps up, a landing, eight more steps, the next floor with a door leading into it. Each time, they bypassed the door and continued walking up, up, up. Eight more steps up, a landing, eight more steps, and the next floor with another door. It started to feel like a dream from which she would never wake. Her legs were tired and she walked slower and slower, sometimes stopping altogether to sit down and stare.

"Ruby!" a voice called, and it was like a voice from a mountain-top. It echoed through the stairwell with a tinny, artificial sound.

"Ruby!" the voice called again, and she realized it was her father, though it sounded like someone else entirely.

"Yes?"

"Almost there now. Hurry!"

She took a deep breath and walked up, up, up to the voice, following the father she no longer knew.

Five minutes passed. Ten. Fifteen? She didn't know.

The last door opened easily, and she walked out onto the roof of the tower, the topmost level. It took her breath away, and she forgot to look for her father. She forgot to wonder about all of the things in her life that were not what she had always believed them to be. The view drew her to the edge.

34

RUBY LOOKED DOWN AT THE CITY, now tiny and far away. She didn't know how many floors up she was (sixty? eighty? a hundred?), but the height made her knees feel weak, and she took quick, small breaths. There were no handrails, no walls, nothing separating her from a long, drifting fall that would end in . . . what? A sharp impact? Followed by what, exactly? Yet she couldn't step back. Curiosity glued her feet to the edge, and she stared out over the distance.

She faced the road that led away from the city, and she had a brief memory of that tiny thread through the dark green forest, small as a strand of DNA. Was it a memory or a dream? The trees waved in a breeze she could not feel, rustling as if they were being stirred from all directions. She knew that was where the nighttime screamers came from. Those woods. Or perhaps somewhere beyond. Above the woods, the sky. It was a deep, deep red, speckled with lighter patches. It made you want to drift away, that sky. It made you want to go to sleep.

Ruby turned and walked to the other side of the building, thirty or forty paces away. She was entranced. She felt suddenly indestructible, as if all that she could see was her domain. She looked over the city, this time in the opposite direction, and again she was overcome to the point of tears. The buildings, small and powerless, were plotted out, city block after city block. The streets were a maze, and they rebounded back on each other, endless squares of concrete and macadam and metal. But she wasn't looking at the small boxes of buildings; she was looking beyond them.

Water.

A body of water larger than anything she ever could have imagined stretched out in cold, navy blue. The water looked metallic, like mercury. Red light reflected off its breakers, and even though it was the size of an ocean, spreading out to the horizon, it moved like a river, sweeping along the edge of the city. It looked powerful to her with its constant motion and its whitecaps and the way it seemed to push back even the sky at the edge of the world. It stretched as far as she could see to the left and to the right, and Ruby realized the great forest surrounded the city on three sides. The fourth side of the city was lined by water.

Something else caught her attention. The light, the red light of the sky, seemed to emanate from across the water. It almost looked like there was another city Over There, somewhere very far away, and that the light of their own sky was only the residual light from a greater city, a more wondrous sky. She peered Over There, but she could not see far enough.

Everything that Ruby saw expanded her reality. She had heard people speak about the water, heard them whisper about the woods they had walked through to get to the city, but whether or not she had believed the legends, she had certainly never seen anything outside of the ten square city blocks where she lived.

Now she was seeing everything. Everything! And everything was so much more beautiful than she could have imagined, and so much more desolate, and so much more heartbreaking. The city was so much smaller than she had imagined. And the water . . .

The water.

Her breathing slowed. She had an indescribable urge to drink it, drink it all. She had a thought that if she could drink the river, she would become even greater than her father. Weightier. Holier? More sacred at least. Perhaps that's not the exact word, but something like it. Could she be the queen of the city along the river? Could she be the ruler of the city under the red sky?

Instead, she stepped back from the edge. Something had reminded her that she was still young, and something else had reminded her that it is no fault to be young, and she should not race to leave her youth behind. Perhaps the reminder had come from a wisp of her hair as the breeze she had watched caress the trees arrived at the top of the building and dashed playfully around her. Perhaps it was the sudden desire to take off her shoes and lie barefoot on the top of the tall building, staring at the sky in search of the shapes of things. She sighed (with relief?) and turned to find her father.

She saw that it was not only herself and her father on the roof anymore. A group of men had come up through the door and were working on something at the edge of the building, not far from where she stood. It was a cylinder, at least ten feet long, with a huge lens on one side and a small eyepiece on the other.

It was a telescope, and it was aimed across the water.

Someone stood beside her father, and at first Ruby would have described her as a girl her own age, but as Ruby approached them she came to understand that while this person looked like a young girl, she was not, in fact, a young girl. She was something else entirely.

"Hello," Ruby said hesitantly.

"Ruby, I'd like you to meet someone very important," her father began. "Someone who will help us make this city exactly what it should be."

The young girl who Ruby knew was not a young girl stepped forward with something that looked like a smile but was certainly not a smile. Perhaps it was some kind of upturned-at-the-corners grimace.

"Hi," this something-else-entirely said in a voice attempting to be kind.

Ruby nodded at her but did not immediately reach out her hand to the not-quite-a-girl.

"I'm Beatrice," the something-else-entirely said in a quiet voice.

Those were some of the only words Ruby would ever hear Beatrice say. Beatrice spent most of her time crowding in close to Ruby's father, whispering in his ear.

"What is this building?" Ruby interrupted, somehow aware that her father had at some point faced the same questions and desires that she had faced standing there at the edge. The urge to drink the entire ocean. The lust to control everything within view. And she was also aware, somehow, that he had not turned away from that desire, that he had embraced it. That he was embracing it.

Beatrice stood up on her tiptoes and whispered into her father's ear. He leaned over slightly, nodding a bit.

"Yes, yes. This building," he said, turning his attention back to Ruby, "is only a symbol of what we can do here. We will rebuild this city, and it will be unlike anything you have ever seen. Anyone has seen. Every building will be this tall. Taller! Every building will reach up to the sky. Do you know why?"

Ruby shook her head. No, she didn't know why, but for some reason the thought of a city filled with buildings like this terrified her.

Beatrice whispered again.

"Soon," her father said with a whispered intensity, "we will be high enough to see over the water. Beyond death! We will be able to see beyond death!" He waved his arms and looked at his hands, his own thin hands, as if he could not believe what he was seeing, as if the vision he had presented to Ruby was a vision that still brought him awe.

Ruby looked at him, and a strange sensation rose up in her. She did not know this person. She did not know her father anymore. He was gone, and she wondered when exactly he had wandered off, or where he had drifted to. She wished she could go back to that moment when he'd left and grab his hand, keep him from going. She wondered if that was possible, if a child could keep their parent from wandering down paths that were not good for them.

"What's that?" Ruby asked, pointing at the telescope.

He sighed. "Ruby, we built this building first and foremost because we wanted to house the Tree, but as it grew, we realized we might be able to build it tall enough to see over the water. Now that we're here, we realize we need some help. Those men are almost finished building a telescope that will let us see beyond death. We will see what lies beyond the water, and then we will build Over There here. And maybe someday we will even go Over There, and it can be ours as well. Everything will be united and beautiful: the old world, this world, and Over There."

"Soon," he began again, but Beatrice tugged on his arm and

whispered into his ear, and he nodded. "We need to go, Ruby. Time is short. Everyone is arriving, and it's time to tell them everything. All of it. They've come early because we are out of time. You will have to hear it along with everyone else, and we will begin. A new world." He shook his head in disbelief at the intense beauty of his own vision.

Beatrice led him away by the hand, to the door that led down the never-ending stairwell Ruby had climbed up only a few minutes before. When Beatrice led him, their hand-holding was not romantic. Not in the least. She held his hand the way a stranger might hold the hand of a naughty child when they are trying to find the child's parents.

It made Ruby want to cry, but she followed them anyway, because she did not know what else to do.

35

TEN OF AMOS'S GUARDS joined them inside the door, crowded together uncomfortably in the narrow landing. Ruby allowed herself to drift to the back of the pack. They did not descend that many floors before Ruby immediately sensed something different about the building. It buzzed with some kind of activity. Literally buzzed. She raced down a level and caught up with her father as he and the rest of his group went through a door that led into one of the upper floors. She didn't know which floor they were on.

She heard one of the guards whisper into her father's ear, "The building is full, sir. Every floor. Completely full."

Amos nodded, trying to tame a giddy smile that threatened to take over his entire face. "Good. Good," he said, glancing at Beatrice. She moved her head up and down once, conveying her own subdued sort of approval.

Ruby followed her father, jostled by the crowd, but she couldn't take her eyes off the tree. It grew up through the floor, and its branches spread far and wide throughout the entire level. Its fruit hung down, heavy and full. The trunk had been surrounded by a thick wooden wall, but the branches, many of them at least, had been used to support the floor above. The tree had literally grown into the building, had become the building.

Images rushed through Ruby's mind, things she had always thought were simply dreams.

Leaves with sap that hung in long, loping strings.

Fruit she could see into.

A woman who devoured the fruit whole and offered her a bite.

Ruby's breathing came heavy and fast, and she tried hard to control it. She remembered that moment clearly now. She remembered she had never eaten the fruit. Her father had stopped her.

She swallowed hard and looked around, and while at first everyone's eyes had been on her father, now they all stared at the fruit, enraptured by what they saw in its translucent flesh. Ruby did too—stared at the piece right in front of her. And she saw . . . her mother . . . a beautiful house surrounded by trees . . . a boy . . . a man—her father—carrying her into a dark doorway . . . the visions went on and on, flashes of things that came so quickly she could barely see what they were before the next image oozed into being.

And now she was holding a piece of fruit with no memory of plucking it from the branch. She dropped it and looked around to see if anyone else had noticed her take it. No one had, because everyone else had done the same thing. Everyone was holding a piece of fruit. Except Beatrice—Beatrice stared at her and smiled.

"Today is a good day," her father began, and his voice was pumped through the building with some kind of sound system. He sounded archaic and scratchy. After he spoke, all the floors erupted in cheers so that it felt as if the entire building might crumble beneath their excitement. Her father apparently had the same concern, and he frantically waved for them to stop clapping.

"Yes, yes it is," he said in response to Beatrice whispering into his ear, something she would continue to do for the duration of the speech.

"You know," Amos said, "there was a day when this building was no more than three floors high. Three floors! But here we are today, with a tower stretching higher and higher every month."

More applause. The floor shook.

"For those of you who have never heard the story, let me give you a brief version. I brought my daughter here years ago, escaping that old world the way many of you escaped. The world that held nothing but death and sadness. We came to this city with nothing. No, that's not true. We had hope. We came to this city with hope. And we came with a Tree. That's when we found this building, and inside we planted this very Tree, and it was the leaves from the Tree that healed my daughter and made her well again."

All eyes were on Ruby. She blushed, not so much at the gaze of all those strangers, but at learning that so much of what her father had told her, so much of what she had been brought up to believe, was a lie. What old world was he talking about? Coming to the city with nothing? What of her mother and brother? She stared hard at the ground, wishing he would talk about something else.

"Of course, there is the fruit. More about that later. But as we settled in the house next door, and as we saw the chaos the Frenzies caused, we realized we had to keep the Tree safe. We had to keep it secret, or they would destroy it the way they destroy everything else."

His voice was sincerely angry now, and silence echoed through the building on every floor.

"Many of you came to my aid. We blocked off the streets around our neighborhood, built walls out of the rubble left behind by the Frenzies, and eventually drove out the Frenzies to the borders of the city. We thought we had done our job, but we noticed something strange. Do you remember that day?" he asked with a smile, and many of the people on that floor nodded and smiled.

"Do you remember when we realized the Tree was growing? So quickly. Before long it was through the top of the building, branches pressing against the outer walls. So we changed our focus. We fought back the Frenzies, yes, but we also continued to build the building higher and higher to hide this amazing Tree. We continually trimmed the inside branches, and we used them in higher floors to stabilize the levels. This building and this Tree are literally one being! It's an accomplishment made possible only by our most capable architects and engineers."

He motioned toward a small group of men and women standing off to the side, their hands behind their backs. Another roar of applause, and Ruby looked around. It was beginning to make sense: the way the Tree grew up through the middle of the building, the way the branches were trimmed so precisely and ended in the walls, rippling up and down through the floors like sea monsters frozen in time.

"Today, though, is a new day. It marks a new era for us. Today, thanks to this Tree, we can get rid of the Frenzies and bring peace to this entire city!"

Anticipatory applause rumbled as people waited to hear the glorious plan.

"Today, we will launch full-scale war on the Frenzies, and we will eliminate them. But. But. But." He held up his index finger, quieting the crowd. "We have nothing to fear. We waited until today because now, finally, the Tree is large enough to feed all of us at once."

He held the silence at the tip of his finger, and in that moment, he seemed all-powerful to Ruby. He held it all, right there, right at the end of his finger. Everything. When he said his next line, he said it in a whisper barely loud enough for everyone to hear.

"Because this is the Tree of Life."

The silence grew heavier, if that was even possible.

"We will all eat from this Tree today, and we will go out and fight a war we cannot lose, because we cannot die. The fruit will keep death away from us, and the leaves will heal our wounds, and all that will be left of the Frenzies will be their bodies, which we will assemble and launch into the Great Water."

Silence.

"After that," he said, "we will rebuild this city exactly as the Great City has been built over the water. We will live in peace, forever."

This brought out the loudest cheers yet. Pieces of fruit fell from the Tree in the tumult, breaking where they hit the floor. People began reaching for new pieces of fruit—the ones they had initially taken had already rotted—and devouring it, eating as if they had never eaten before, as if the more they ate the stronger their immortality would be. Amos sat back and smiled, and Beatrice whispered into his ear.

Ruby eased her way among the people who ate loudly, greedily. She did not eat—in a moment, she was in the stairwell, running down the stairs as quickly as she could.

At each level she heard people cheering and congratulating

each other. There were small floor numbers beside each door, and it seemed a never-ending journey down.

63.

58.

46.

32.

Floor after floor, and behind each door an elated crowd, newly immortal, still eating.

She was breathing heavily and her legs ached by the time she arrived at a door that led to the only level with no one cheering, no one eating. She peeked through the glass and saw a long hallway flanked by more doors. She glanced up at the number beside the door before pushing her way through, into the dimly lit passageway.

Ruby was at level 27.

36

RUBY PUSHED OPEN THE DOOR. It was cool against her small hands, and the air inside was warmer than the stairwell, and stale.

"Hello?" she called out, and at first the dark hallway swallowed up her voice, and nearly her courage with it. There were many doors, but all of the rooms behind them were empty. She was surprised there were no guards and thought they must have run upstairs with everyone else, giddy at the excitement taking over.

When she came to the last door on the right, she took a deep breath.

"Hello?" she said. No one said anything, but she thought she heard someone walk over to the door.

"Hello?" she said again. She found courage in the sound of her own voice.

"Is that you, Ruby?" the voice on the other side of the door asked. It was the voice of the young man from the abandoned house. She was sure of it. The young man who had said things that had brought her world crumbling down around her. His words still rang in her head like a bell, far off and full of hope.

"Is it true," she asked through the door, "what you said?"

"Ruby," the young man said in a trembling voice, "I'm your brother. Our mother is alive."

Her breath caught.

"I am your brother," he said. "I'm Leo."

Ruby sat down with her back against the door. She sat there for a few moments without saying anything, but those few moments were like long periods of time. Cities were born and ground to dust. Forests grew and burned down and were reborn out of the ashes.

"Are you still there?" he asked her.

"Yes," she said, her voice wandering down the empty hall. "I . . . It's so hard to believe."

"There's more," he said. "Things even more difficult to believe than that."

Ruby took a deep breath and leaned her head back. She heard, or felt, the young man inside sit down against the door too.

"Ruby," he said, "I'm your brother. I'm Leo. Please let us out?"

Ruby waited longer than she should have, longer than was good for any of them, but her thoughts were a thousand-piece puzzle. She stood up and stared at the door, and when she reached for the latch that slid back the bolt, she watched her own hand as if it belonged to someone else, as if it was moving in slow motion. The metal was cold against her fingers. It made a loud snapping sound when opened.

"This is Abra," Leo said to Ruby, and Ruby nodded as if she understood, but she didn't. "How can we get to the Tree?"

Ruby's eyes went wide as if she had finally awoken, as if she had finally decided whose side she was on.

"Follow me!"

They sprinted down the dark hallway to the door that led into the stairwell, but they stopped there, held back by a deep rumbling sound. At first Ruby thought the entire building was coming down. She held up her hand for them to wait.

People began flooding past the small window in the door, running down the stairs like people on fire. Some of them fell as they descended, and others stepped on them and pushed past, and those that fell eventually pulled themselves up by the rail and followed, always running, always shouting. They weren't shouting words that Ruby could understand, or that anyone could understand. The sounds they made were full of excitement and anger and wrath. They were heading for war.

People streamed by for minutes on end as the building emptied. The rumbling sound spread to the streets outside the building, and the brick walls shook as if huge projectiles were colliding against them. Dust fell from the ceiling.

Abra pushed past Ruby, trying to get into the stairwell, but Ruby hissed at her, "Wait!"

The three stood there, and the people stopped going by, but still Ruby held Abra's hand on the door handle. Abra stared at her, and there was urgency in her eyes, but Ruby shook her head.

No.

A different sound came down the stairwell: two people walking very slowly. Amos and Beatrice came into view. They held hands as they walked, and Beatrice seemed to be leading him. They turned in the landing in front of the small window and began going down the next flight of stairs. Leo sighed. Abra breathed out quietly through pursed lips.

The three of them pressed against the wall and held their breath. They saw Beatrice's shadow approach, widening in the crack at the bottom of the door. Abra put an index finger over her lips.

Beatrice turned and left, leading Amos down the stairs.

"I have to get to the Tree," Abra said. "Now."

"Everyone's already eaten from it," Ruby said in a quiet voice. "It's too late."

"What?" Abra said. Her face went white.

Ruby nodded. "It's true."

Abra stood there for a moment, finally shaking her head. "Okay, okay, we can't do anything about that. But we still have to kill the Tree."

"C'mon," Ruby said, pushing through the door and running up the stairs as fast as her legs would take her. Abra and Leo followed close behind.

The three of them went up one floor and burst into the room.

"There's the trunk," Ruby said, pointing to the center of the room.

Tree branches held up the ceiling, intertwining with the structure. Smaller branches drooped down, heavy with fruit. For a moment, Ruby remembered that day long ago, the day she was healed, when she nearly ate that piece of fruit.

"Don't eat it," Abra said firmly to Leo and Ruby. "Don't even touch it. Don't even look at it." They both nodded.

She marched through the dimly lit room to the trunk. "It's covered," she said over her shoulder to Ruby and Leo.

"What?" Leo said, running over to her.

She was right. Someone had built a wooden, circular wall around the trunk, and the branches came out of it in the ceiling, so there was no way of reaching it.

"Can't you get your sword through?" Leo asked.

Abra tried stabbing the boards, but the sword simply stuck into the wood.

"Either it's Beatrice's magic or the sword is only made for the

Tree," she muttered. She jumped up and stabbed a low-hanging branch. The fruit on the branch dropped instantly and shattered, and a breeze swept through the building, carried the shards away. But the rest of the Tree remained undamaged.

"I have to get to the trunk," Abra said to Ruby.

"The trunk is covered like this all the way up through the building," Ruby said, thinking about all she had seen. "Except..."

"Except?"

"Except on the roof," she said quietly, remembering how the Tree emerged, remembering the view. "The Tree grows up out of the roof."

"The trunk is exposed up there?"

Ruby nodded. "Yes."

"Okay," Abra said, running for the door. She stopped.

"What's wrong?" Leo asked.

Abra turned to them with a grave look on her face. "Leo, when I kill the Tree, this whole building is coming down."

"What?"

"The Tree. When I kill it. It dies fast, probably faster than we can run back down. I don't think we'll make it out."

Leo and Ruby stared at her, trying to figure something out.

"You two have to go. You have to run and get out of here. Leo, you have to take Ruby out. If I can get out, I'll follow you and seal the grave, but you can't wait for me. If I don't make it, you have to tell Mr. Henry what happened."

"Abra," Leo began, but she interrupted him.

"No. You have to go."

Ruby looked at Leo, and even in the midst of everything else that was going on, one thought raced to the front of her mind.

I have a brother.

"Listen," Leo said to Abra. "You can make it out. After you

kill the Tree, go all the way down to the basement. There are tunnels there with arrows. Follow the green arrows."

"The green arrows?"

"Yeah, the green ones. I don't know where it goes, but I think it goes away from the water. It's the only way we'll get out of this city alive."

Abra nodded. "You two take care of each other, okay?" she said. "Don't eat the fruit. Whatever you do. Please." She grabbed their shoulders, stared at them through desperate eyes, then disappeared up the stairwell.

"C'mon, Ruby. Let's go," Leo said.

Ruby followed Leo down, down, down, and the rumbling sounds of war from outside the building grew louder. There were screams and shouts. Orders. She flinched at the muffled sound of buildings collapsing, crashing to the ground, threatening to cave in the tunnels.

They finally reached the basement. There was a row of flashlights on the wall where the stairs went down into the tunnel, as if the tunnels were regularly used from that point. They each grabbed one and ran into the tunnels.

"Let's take turns using the flashlights," Leo said. "I don't know how far we have to go."

They found the first green arrow spray-painted on the wall of the tunnel, and they ran in that direction. The darkness in front of them fled from the flashlight, spilled in behind them, forever running away, forever chasing them. Ruby wondered where they were going. Everything she had ever known was behind her. Every question she had ever had about her life was walking right there beside her.

37

ABOVE GROUND, the war had begun. In the midst of the screams and the blood and the debris, Beatrice stood beside Amos, still holding his hand. She looked around with a smile. The ones who had eaten from the Tree would purge the Edge of Over There of those who had not. Only the immortals would remain. And then? Who knew what they could accomplish.

But then Beatrice felt a chill. A tingling sensation slipped from the base of her skull down her spine. She dropped Amos's hand, closed her eyes, and took in a deep breath through her nose.

How could she have neglected the girl?

Beatrice ran back toward the building, no longer a little girl, not even close. She was the something-else-entirely that Ruby had sensed, and she shot up through the air like a firework, realizing their weakness had been left exposed.

38

Abra's walk to the top of the building was long and quiet. The muscles in her legs ached and she breathed hard, all the time trying not to think about the quick retreat she would have to make down through all of those levels if she did end up killing the Tree. Every ten floors or so she peeked into the main area and glanced at the trunk of the Tree, hoping to find a floor where it had not been covered, but no floor had been missed. Wide boards formed walls she could not penetrate, so she continued climbing.

When Abra went through the door at the top of the tall building, the beauty of the view stopped her in her tracks, then drew her to the edge. She stood there looking over the city, up to the road she and Leo had come down, straight through the trees. She looked to the side, and she could see the long, flat plain of stone and red light glaring off the dimple-shaped pools of clear water.

She pulled herself away from the edge, and there, in the middle of the building, was the Tree.

It came up through the roof as if this was the only part of it, as if it was only a ten-foot-high tree, not a thousand-foot tree that grew up, up, up through an entire building. The part she could see looked young and immature. She pulled out her sword and walked toward it. The bark was as she had remembered it, soft and leathery, and she took a deep breath, preparing to plunge the sword into the Tree.

Her eyes snagged on one lone piece of fruit dangling in front of her. It was lime green, the color of a lollipop, with the same translucence as clear candy. She tilted her head to the side and stared at it. At first, she could see through it to the distant buildings, and beyond that the water, far off and far below. But the fruit clouded up as she stared at it, like steam on a bathroom mirror, and then she could see inside the fruit. What she saw made her tremble.

It was her mother. She was old, much older than she was at that time, and she was in a bed, her head propped up on two pillows. Her face was pale and her eyelids closed, and Abra realized she was at the end of her life. She was dying. Abra reached up and held the fruit in her fingers. And she watched.

Her mother coughed. A tear slid down Abra's cheek. She wondered if she was seeing the future. She wondered if she was seeing the present. Was her mother at home, dying, right now? She pulled the fruit from the branch, and as it pulled away the leaves recoiled and danced back and forth.

She would take the fruit home to her mother. Her mother would never die. Her mother would . . .

"No," she muttered to herself, staring at the fruit in her hand. "No."

It started to brown, and she dropped it onto the roof, where it shattered like a Christmas ornament. A breeze blew and it was gone. She found herself stumbling along, following the dust as it flew to the other side of the building. The vision of her mother dying had distracted and disoriented her.

That's when she saw the large telescope propped up on two massive tripods. The men must have finished building it before the speech, and there it stood, waiting for Amos to gaze through it after the war was fought, after the Frenzies were destroyed and the city was his. She stared at it, and the weight of the decision pulled down on her shoulders.

Should she look?

She glanced over her shoulder at the door to the roof.

One glance wouldn't hurt.

She bent down and peered into the eyepiece. She couldn't look for long, because it was like looking directly at the sun. She fell away from the telescope and sat on the roof.

Abra wept. She had seen a faraway, terrifying darkness, yes, but that darkness had been pushed to the farthest fringe by a place of such beauty that it made her chest hurt. It was the ache a child feels when she wants to go to the moon, when she first comprehends the distance between herself and the faraway stars. It was the overwhelming joy of Christmas morning and first love and the unexpected warmth of a spring breeze, rolled into one. She felt all of that in the instant she looked through the telescope, and at the end she was left with a deep and impenetrable sadness that she could not be there now.

A desire to be there, in the beautiful place, had pulsed so strong that now she felt weak, limp.

"Oh, you shouldn't have done that," Beatrice said from the other side of the building. Abra looked over her shoulder. Beatrice stood there, and she was glowing with shadows, if that was possible.

"Beatrice," Abra said in a heavy voice, "I have to kill the Tree. You know that."

"First, let me show you something," Beatrice said.

"I've already looked."

"No, no, not that. Come here. Come close."

Abra crossed the building, her sword ready.

"Tell me what you see," Beatrice said.

Abra looked out on the city. The Frenzies had started fires in all the streets around them, so that the flames licked at the buildings and the shadows danced like old ghosts. The entire city, as far as she could see, glowed orange, and in the distance a portion of the forest had already caught. There were the sounds of war: the loud, booming crashes of destruction, and the howling of people who have allowed themselves to be turned into animals.

"This is hell," Abra whispered. "The fires, the screams, the people who cannot die but have to go on living in this."

"No," Beatrice said spitefully. "This is not hell. This is people living forever. Forever! They will never have to die!"

Abra stood there, and the red of the sky deepened as night approached.

"With your key," Beatrice said, pointing at the sword, "we could open all the gates. We could create new worlds where people would never have to die. What would be so wrong with that?"

Abra didn't move. She felt like she couldn't. Sadness was a weight on her shoulders. It all felt like too much. What could she, a teenage girl, do in the face of all this evil? How could she possibly make a difference?

But her head was shaking almost of its own accord. She felt her hand tighten around the sword's handle. Her jaw clenched.

Beatrice made a quick motion to push Abra over the edge, but Abra ducked and jumped backward. Beatrice was on top of her, and she was too strong, but Abra rolled and rolled and stabbed with the sword and somehow they were both on their feet again, facing off. Lightning or something like it crackled from Beatrice.

There was no way in the world anyone would have mistaken Beatrice for a little girl in that moment. Her clothes were in tatters, and they flapped around her in the breeze like the unwound strips of cloth from a mummy. Her skin was translucent like the fruit on the Tree, and she wasn't quite standing on the roof of the building but rather hovered a few inches above it, slowly approaching.

"What did you see through the telescope?" she asked Abra.

Abra tried to hold the sword steady. "You know what I saw."

Beatrice shrugged. "Soon you will be there," she said in the voice of an adult simplifying a complex concept for a young child.

Abra shook her head and held the sword tighter. Beatrice rushed at her, and Abra could not tell if she was flying or running. She whispered to the sword because suddenly she felt like the two of them were in this together, and the words helped her to gather confidence. She felt intimately connected to it.

Abra swung the sword once as Beatrice knocked her over. Abra landed on her back, and the wind was knocked out of her. She pulled herself up onto her hands and knees and waited. She felt certain that in the amount of time it had taken for her to get to her knees, Beatrice would be standing over her, gloating, ready to kill her. But nothing happened.

Abra heard a whimpering from the edge of the building. She turned around. Beatrice lay on her side, moaning. Abra's sword had caught her, and this time it had gone deep. Abra stood on shaky legs and walked over to where Beatrice lay. She looked down at her, and again she was overcome with sadness. Those figures, the Tennins and the Jinns and the Koli Naals and the Beatrices—they were so incredibly made that even the evil ones emanated a fierce kind of beauty. The sadness Abra felt was at how far some of them had managed to fall.

"Go ahead," Beatrice wheezed.

Abra lifted the sword and put the tip of the blade against Beatrice's throat. The skin in that spot was pale and vulnerable. Abra stared hard and thought that by any account, she should do it. She should end Beatrice. But she knew she couldn't the moment she felt Beatrice's life pulsing at the end of the sword.

She pulled it away. "Go," she said.

"I can't."

"Go!"

When Beatrice didn't move, Abra shrugged and walked over to the Tree. She pushed her sword into it. It was like pushing a dull knife into softened butter, and the trunk immediately went from velvety brown to a lifeless gray-white. The pale color spread out and down. The fruit fell, heavy, and the leaves drifted to the roof and withered, and everything was swept away by a strong breeze. The entire building trembled as if an earthquake had rocked the foundation.

Abra turned and ran to the door. She looked over her shoulder once.

Beatrice was gone.

Abra ran down through the building, level beyond level, stair after stair, usually two or three at a time. As the Tree withered and died—and it happened slower than the Tree in Abra's valley, perhaps because it was older and more established, or perhaps simply because of its size—it shrunk away from the walls and the ceilings that it supported. The entire building was structured around the Tree, and these subtle shifts were enough to begin bringing it down.

But fortunately for Abra, it didn't happen all at once. An outer wall collapsed on the 78th floor as Abra ran to the 77th floor, and a portion of that side of the building fell outward, into the streets. The Frenzies cheered, thinking they had done something in their fight against Amos. At one point the stairwell partially collapsed, and Abra fell straight down ten feet. She didn't have time to check herself for injuries—she scrambled to her feet and kept running.

Above her she could hear the building falling, bricks crumbling. A cloud of dust chased her down the steps, threatened to overtake her and choke her and steal away her vision. But she held tight to the rail and ran, all the way to the basement.

She saw a line of flashlights, and she grabbed one, turned it on, and when it didn't come on she shook it. The beam flickered on. She put her sword away and took two flashlights with her into the darkness of the tunnels, following the green arrows. She kept hearing things in the tunnel behind her, and she spun around and pointed the yellowing light into the darkness. She expected to see Beatrice.

Nothing.

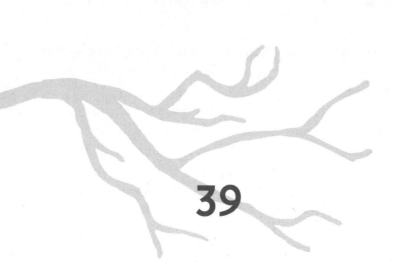

39

LEO AND RUBY JOGGED side by side for as long as they could, Leo trying to hold the flashlight steady. The tunnel in front of them stretched on without any markings apart from the occasional spray-painted green arrow on the cement walls. They kept up a good pace for as long as they could, but eventually they both tired out and had to alternate between jogging and walking.

Every so often, Leo turned the flashlight to see if anyone was coming up behind him. It was always a quick glance, and Ruby didn't ask who or what he was looking for. They went on silently in this way for a long, long time, the only sound that of their feet scuffing against the cement floor, and their breathing, heavy when they ran, slowing and relieved when they walked.

Leo stole glances at her, taking in how much she had grown since he had seen her last. She was nearly a young woman. She was strong—he could see that in her eyes and the way she held her chin. She wasn't the kind who gave up easily.

When he looked away, peering into the never-ending tunnel

that stretched ahead of them, he shook his head, still barely believing it was her.

"So," Ruby said, breaking the silence during a walking spell. "Can you tell me anything about our mom?" She looked at him out of the corner of her eye.

Leo cleared his throat to speak, stopped, tried to start again. "Mom isn't doing well," he said.

"What do you mean?"

"Ever since Dad ran off with you, she's had . . . a rough time."

"But now that I'm back?" Ruby asked.

"We'll see," Leo said, but there wasn't much hope in his voice. "Ruby, she doesn't speak. She hasn't said a single word for seven or eight years now. She stares out the window. There's nothing. Nothing there."

Leo felt an old familiar bitterness fighting to rise to the surface, always accompanied by the question of why he hadn't been good enough for his mom. Why he hadn't been enough. Sure, they'd lost so much when they lost Ruby, but they'd still had each other. But that hadn't been enough. He hadn't been enough.

"I can't wait to see her," Ruby said hesitantly.

Leo tried to be positive. "It'll be good," he said, looking at her and smiling. "It will be good for both of you."

"Look," Ruby said, pointing at the walls. They were no longer smooth concrete—they were made up of cement blocks. For some reason this felt like a good thing, like they were making progress. Of course, they had no idea if this tunnel went anywhere, if it had ever been finished. They could be walking toward a dead end. Then what? But the change encouraged them both.

"Want to jog again for a little?" Leo asked. Ruby nodded.

The sounds of the warring city had died out a long time ago.

It was easy to forget all that they had escaped, but Leo found himself thinking about Sandra and her small band of friends.

"Our father isn't all bad," Ruby said quietly. Leo pursed his lips but didn't say anything.

They walked a little farther.

"What was it like, where we grew up?" she asked.

A small smile touched Leo's mouth. "Before Mom and Dad split up, it was nice. We lived close to the water. Dad always wanted a boat. That's all he ever talked about! But he was never able to afford one. Sometimes he'd take both of us out to the end of the dock, and the three of us would sit there and watch the boats go by. He knew all the names, the lengths, the kind of motors they had. Everything."

Leo's voice trailed off in the tunnel.

"Sometimes, if we stayed out there for a long time, Mom would bring food out, and then it would be all of us. But when Mom was there, Dad never talked about the boats. He just watched them, and he'd smile or shake his head in amazement when he saw a nice one. But the water! When the sun set, Ruby? It was amazing."

They came to a section of the tunnel where the walls were stone, individually placed by some master craftsman. Leo ran his fingers over the stones. Some of them were wet from underground springs. His flashlight flickered and went out. Ruby turned hers on and handed it to him. Not long after that, the walls became dirt walls, the tunnel nothing more than a hole bored through the earth. The ceiling was lower in this section, and Leo had to bend over in order to keep his head from hitting the ceiling.

Hours and hours after they had entered the tunnel, it widened out, and the two of them came to a stairway and walked up into a small house. The same small house where Leo and Abra had peered into the windows so long ago. How long? Leo had no idea.

"Where are we?" Ruby asked.

"I don't understand," Leo said. "When Abra and I came into the city, it took us at least two or three days to walk from the house to the city. But you and I, we're here after what, a day?" He paused, muttering to himself. "Something's changing about this place. Something isn't right."

They walked out and continued along the dirt road toward the darkness, where he hoped they'd find an open door in the crypt, the door that opened up in New Orleans.

Ruby started asking something but stopped herself.

"What?" Leo asked.

"What's it like out there? Where we're from?"

Leo chuckled. "Very different from this, that's for sure."

"Like what?" She smiled.

"Well, for one, the sky is blue, not red."

"What?" she asked, disbelief in her voice. "Blue? Like the blue in people's eyes?"

"Kind of," he said, nodding.

"Wow," she said. "What else?"

"Hmmm. Well, it smells different."

"It smells different?"

"Yeah. I think everything here smells newer. Back where we live, it's old. Really old."

He could tell she was having a hard time imagining what he meant.

"The water tastes a lot better here," he said, laughing. She laughed too, and he loved the sound of it, the sound of her happiness, the sound of being carefree.

"So, why are we leaving?" she asked playfully. "The water is better here, it doesn't smell as bad, and the sky is a beautiful red instead of a strange, icy blue." He could tell she was kidding, but there was also a tiny, subtle trace of seriousness there. He realized for the first time that it would be hard for her to leave.

"Good question," he said, looking at her, feeling an overwhelming compassion and love for her like he hadn't felt before. He realized she was leaving everything she had ever known. "Mother is there, for one. You might be able to bring her back. Two? This place is falling apart, the war is awful, and the Tree complicates things. Apparently. That's what Abra says."

Ruby looked over at Leo. The sky was a dark red, nearly black. The flashlight died.

"Who is Abra?" she asked.

He shrugged. "Honestly? I don't know. But I hope she's okay." He looked over his shoulder and stopped walking.

"What?" Ruby asked.

"Is that her?" Leo asked, staring harder into the darkness behind them. A figure approached slowly, limping up the road.

"Abra?" Leo called into the darkness. But the person, ever closer, laughed, gasped in pain, laughed again.

"No, no, no," she said, and they both knew immediately that it was not Abra. It was Beatrice. She stopped about twenty feet away from them, bent over, coughing. She clutched her side just below her ribs. When she stood up, she wiped her mouth and coughed again.

"I am most certainly not Abra," she said, still managing a smile.

"Leave us alone," Leo said, trying to keep his voice steady. "We're leaving. You can have whatever you want in this world. We don't care. We just want out."

"This world?" Beatrice asked, her voice rising. "This world? You're oh so generous, aren't you? I can have whatever I want in this world?"

She stared, and she stopped smiling. Her eyes were gaping black holes and her face transformed to something hideous, something like a human face but also something completely different. Something hollow.

"There is nothing left in this world. As more and more people die in the war, this world will shrink back down to nothing. Once the gate is locked, those who ate from the Tree will be stuck here, perhaps for eternity. Koli Naal's plan has failed, thanks to Abra. Thanks to you. There is no hope in this world, not for the dead, and certainly not for the living."

She gathered herself.

"And there is no hope for you."

She shot into the air like a bullet. One moment she was standing in front of them, the next she was rising into the red darkness. When she fell back toward them, her path was white-hot.

Her movement screamed through the Edge of Over There. She moved like a falling star. Leo saw what was coming. He shoved Ruby to the side at the same moment Beatrice slammed into him. It was like being hit by a freight train. The force of her impact knocked Ruby unconscious and bent all the trees outward.

The road was silent again. Beatrice stood up and moaned. It had taken nearly every ounce of power left in her to do that. She limped away from where Leo and Ruby lay, then she fell to her knees, breathing deeply. She tried to gather her strength.

She crawled toward the door, back into the darkness.

40

ABRA STUMBLED AHEAD, trying to run, but it felt like she had been on the move for hours, and her legs refused to keep a fast pace. The tunnel went ahead, always in a straight line, and after the first ten or fifteen minutes, there were no more intersections with other tunnels. It was a lonely line. At some point the walls went from smooth cement to cement block to rock, and eventually they were nothing more than packed dirt. The floor went through the same transformation. The smell changed as she went—at first it smelled like the city, but the farther she traveled, the more it smelled like rich earth.

Her flashlight flickered off. She turned on the second one. An hour later that one flickered, then turned off. She banged it against the wall and twisted the top and it came back on, barely shining. She tried to walk faster, tried not to think about the possibility of being stuck in a tunnel without any light. Behind her she heard a loud rumbling as if the earth had split in two. The silence that followed felt like a missing tooth.

It is usually when we are going to give up that the difficulty changes, and such was the case with Abra. The tunnel felt never-ending, and she had nearly convinced herself to turn around and take her chances leaving the city above ground when things changed: she stumbled into a wide section of the tunnel. Dim light illuminated a stairway, and she went up into the red light.

She didn't realize where she was, and she crept through an empty room to a set of windows. The red light streamed through, and broken glass crunched under her feet. She ran outside.

It was the house outside the city, the house she and Leo had stopped and looked into. She was shocked at how far she had traveled in such a short time. The tunnel had led her all the way out of the city. The sky was red, fading to night, and the air was full of smoke. She looked in the direction of the city and saw flames, smoke, and the black outline of buildings as they fell.

She turned and jogged away from it toward the darkness, toward the doorway that would finally take her out of the grave of Marie Laveau. She hoped she'd find Leo and Ruby before she had to seal the Passageway closed. Now that she knew them, now that she had been with them, she didn't know how she could leave them behind. When she thought about Leo something warmed inside of her, some small flame that was not one of destruction but one of friendship.

Abra kept going, kept pushing, and the longer she went, the darker it became. The city glowed behind her, giving off a sense that night would never come, not until the fire died. Something about the woods pressed tighter against her, as if the entire Passageway was shrinking. It made her feel claustrophobic. Her breathing was tight and heavy.

Soon it was dark. The souls would be making their way through the Passageway at any moment, screaming with speed. Abra saw a hunched form on the path ahead. She slowed, peered into the distance, but kept moving forward. When she saw who it was, she ran.

"Ruby!" Abra said, gasping for breath.

Leo was on the ground beside her, stretched out, his eyes closed. His breath came slow, with large spaces in between. His shirt was torn and covered in blood.

"Ruby?" Abra asked, and there were many questions in that one word, but she already knew the answers, or at least the only answers that mattered.

"It was Beatrice," Ruby said through her tears. Her hands were covered in blood too, from where she had tried to stop up Leo's injuries.

Abra fell to her knees beside Leo and touched his face. "Leo," she whispered. "Are you still here?"

His eyelids parted, tiny slits of shining light, and he nodded. "You have to get out," he said, and each word was a deep root pulled from the earth. "You have to leave me."

Abra shook her head, but she knew he was right—they did have to keep moving. It wouldn't be long before people tried to flee the city.

"We can't leave you, Leo!" Ruby insisted. "You'll be okay! You have to come with us."

Abra reached over and held Ruby's hand.

"I remember now," Ruby whispered. "I remember the third-floor bedroom and the light streaming in. I remember the sound of the birds under the eaves. I remember how you took me out back, even when I wasn't feeling well, and pulled me around in the little red wagon, showing me the flowers. I remember how you'd point up at the tallest tree and we'd dream of climbing it, seeing the entire city."

She paused for a moment, tears dripping from her nose.

"I remember it all, Leo. I remember how much I loved you. Please don't go."

Everything grew dim. Even the fire that was the city died down, like an old-fashioned oil lamp when the wick is drawn down into the oil. The same thing happened to Leo—he withdrew into himself, and the light inside him went out.

The Wailers started streaming past Abra and Ruby where they knelt beside Leo. Their sound was loud, but it didn't seem as harsh as it had before—it felt more like the whistling the wind makes when it races along a rocky shore. The two girls sat there and let the bodies of light stream around them. Ruby's forehead was close to Leo's chest when Abra saw it begin to happen.

"Ruby," she whispered, and Ruby sat up straight.

It looked as though someone had spread white talcum powder all over the top of Leo—his face, his chest, his legs—so that even the red of the blood was covered over by this almost glowing white. It reminded Abra of the veins of silver she had seen in the cliff on her way to the rocky plain. That dust, that very dust, began to float around him the way dust sometimes floats through beams of light as it falls between tree branches or down through barns full of fresh hay. The white dust hovered there for a moment, and the only thing that stirred it was the passing of the souls as they whistled by.

"It's him, Ruby," Abra said. "It's the real Leo."

And she was right. More right than she had ever been. Because that was Leo—the very essence of him. It wasn't only that he was leaving his body behind, because there was even an element of his body there in that white dust, and it was his perfect body, a body full of cells that could never mutate or be affected by diseases, cells that could never break down. His mind was there too in its perfect form, swirling full of thoughts and memories and feelings. But all of these things were so intermingled that you never could have separated them, never could have labeled them, never could have dissected them. It wasn't the kind of thing you could take apart and later, piece by piece, put back together. No, it was a beautiful intermingling of everything that was essentially Leo.

Then he was gone. That white cloud of Leo shot off like a comet, racing along with the other souls, whistling with joy. If Abra and Ruby could have kept up with him, they would have raced through the smoke and the fire of the city. They would have seen him shoot out over the water like a star, rising, crossing an uncrossable distance, to the white cliffs and the soft green hills that waited on the other side.

Abra and Ruby walked in complete and utter darkness for hours. Have you ever had a conversation with someone in the dark when it is only the words and nothing else? The words become sounds that take on their own being—they float around looking for anything to latch on to. The voices are everything. You notice every fluctuation, every point of emphasis, every sigh. Every swallow.

"Did you know they were building a telescope to see over the water? To see beyond death?" Ruby asked, and Abra knew that she was combing her mind for something to talk about that would help her forget about the death of Leo, her only brother, the one she had barely known.

"Yes," Abra whispered.

They pulled themselves through the darkness. Abra's arm was around Ruby's shoulders, and she held her close. Ruby pressed in close to her and trembled like a baby bird.

"I looked into the telescope," Abra said, regret heavy in her voice. They were words she had to say, because it was not something she could carry on her own.

"You did?" Ruby asked, and by the way her shoulders turned, Abra could tell she was looking up at her in the darkness, searching for her face.

"Before I killed the Tree. Before I came back down. It was only a second, only a glance," Abra said, and it sounded like she was trying to convince herself that it was okay, that she had not looked into the eyepiece long enough to be changed.

"What did you see?" Ruby whispered.

Abra waited. In the darkness, she could remember it perfectly.

"There was a cliff that rose up out of the water. White waves crashed against it. The cliff was high, very high, and at the top of the cliff was the greenest grass you've ever seen, stretching on in rolling hills. Beyond that, there was a city, and all the buildings were shining white."

Abra's voice caught as a sob tried to escape.

"What else?" Ruby whispered in a small voice.

"Far off beyond everything was a terrible darkness, but it was a darkness that had no power. It was an emptiness I could not bear to look at. But that was far, far beyond the city, and it seemed almost invisible compared to the beauty of the cliff and the green and the white."

"What was the white city like?" Ruby asked. "Could you see anyone there?"

Abra shook her head. "I can't . . . I can't talk about it."

"Are you glad you looked?" Ruby asked.

Abra shook her head again. "No."

"Why not?"

Abra looked down at her and gave a sad smile. "Because I'm

sure that for the rest of my life it's the only place I will ever want to be."

For a moment, Abra imagined the years stretching out ahead of her, the distance of a life she would have to live before she could go to that city. She remembered the vision she had seen in the clear water of the old woman sitting quietly in her bed, passing away. She wondered again if that had really been her in her old age, and if that was a vision that would come to pass or one that would change. She pulled Ruby close in the darkness, and Ruby reached up and kissed her on the cheek.

"Thank you," Abra said, and they kept walking.

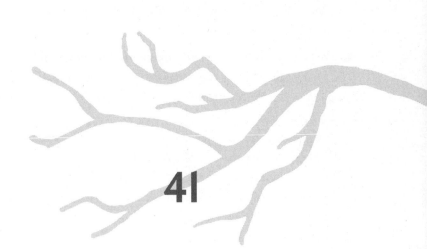

41

THE FIRST THING ABRA NOTICED when she pushed through the door was how bright and ordinary the world was after walking through that deep darkness under that red sky. She held one hand up and shielded her eyes. Ruby held onto her other hand, and when the girl saw what they had walked into, a whole new world with its different sights and smells, its blue sky and puffy white clouds, she clutched Abra's hand even tighter.

There was the sound of traffic on the other side of the wall that surrounded Saint Louis Cemetery No. 1. There was the smell of summer, the heavy air. There were the trees waving in a gentle breeze.

Abra and Ruby both sat down and leaned back against the door that did not look like a door in the side of Marie Laveau's tomb. Abra kept hoping she'd feel Leo pushing against the door, calling her name, asking to be let through, but she knew he was gone. She had seen him rise, a movement of light flashing to the sea.

The air smelled of exhaust and heat. The ground was warm, and the sun was at its peak. Everything felt numb compared to the city on the other side of the Passageway. Everything felt like it was standing still. But there was no sense of waiting as there had been in the other city, no sense of in between. Everything was here and now.

Abra glanced around once her eyes had adjusted to the light. That's when she saw the feet of Mr. Henry.

He was lying on the ground on the other side of the tomb, and only his feet were visible. Abra crawled to him and shook his foot. Ruby was right behind her.

"Mr. Henry? Mr. Henry!"

She saw there was blood on his legs, and when she came around the entire way to his side of the tombstone, she froze. His eyes were closed, all those piercings and tattoos completely still. His mouth was partially open, and a dried line of blood came from his nose. Was he dead?

"Mr. Henry?" Abra said again, crawling up beside him and holding on to his hand.

"You made it," he whispered, opening his eyes.

"You're okay!" Abra said.

"I guess being okay is a relative assessment," Mr. Henry said, groaning and sitting up. He stared at Abra, and she felt like he might be looking inside of her. When he did that—when he looked at her, really looked—she had the sense that he immediately understood all she had gone through. If not the details, the essence.

"Those were long days," he said.

"We got caught up," Abra said. "The Tree was . . . hard to find. Beatrice was worse than we thought."

He nodded. "Leo?"

Abra shook her head in short, jerky motions, and tears slid down her cheeks. Ruby started to cry.

Mr. Henry frowned. "We walk through these doors," he said. "We walk through doorways that should never have been opened. And then? It is all up in the air, a handful of dust tossed to the wind, and no one knows where the specks will fall."

"No one?" Abra asked in a whisper.

Mr. Henry smiled at her and shook his head as if remembering something important. "Of course. Someone knows."

Abra wanted to believe that. She wanted to believe it with all her heart.

"Those were long days," he said again.

Abra sighed but didn't say anything.

"I sat by this gravestone right here, in this very spot, for days. Day and night, day and night. It rained one night, and it was a cold rain for the summer, like tiny frozen stars falling from the sky. I waited and waited, and as the days passed I lost hope."

He laughed, and there was disbelief in the sound.

"Me. Even me! I lost hope."

He looked at Abra with a confused expression, then he gazed off in the distance as if he saw himself approaching and had no idea who it was.

"I didn't think I'd see you again. Losing hope is like losing your breath. It's hard to get it back on your own."

He looked at Ruby and tilted his head to the side. "Child," he said. That was it. Just the one word. *Child.* Then he continued.

"I waited, even without hope, and somehow the hope came back. I wondered if I should go in and find you. I wondered what would become of me if I did. Out of nowhere, Beatrice shot through that door like some terrible thing on fire, knocked me right over. We fought then, and she was weak, but she was also desperate. It was a strange dance of fire and bright light, and I'd imagine the neighbors all around here saw it, and what they saw will feed superstition for generations."

Mr. Henry chuckled to himself. He held the back of his hand up to his nose, wiped the blood, then looked at his hand.

"What happened to Beatrice?" Abra asked.

"She fell," Mr. Henry said, and there was no joy in his voice. He pointed a wiry finger at the wall, and Abra saw a depression in the ground similar to the one Mr. Tennin had left after falling.

"What about Koli Naal?" Abra asked.

Mr. Henry shook his head in disgust. "Do you know she sat up on that wall and watched the whole thing happen? She watched us tangle and break stones. Just sat there like a stone herself, and when she saw Beatrice fall, when she saw all was lost, she left. Shoooo! Right up into the sky. Gone."

Ruby was crying again. Mr. Henry seemed so agitated he couldn't catch his breath. Abra sat between them, and she felt responsible for everything.

"First things first," Mr. Henry continued, as if he hadn't said anything yet, as if he wasn't sure he would make it and wanted to be certain to tell her the most important bits before he died. "Use the sword to lock and seal the door."

"What do I do?" Abra asked.

"Push it closed. Lock it with the sword. Run the point of it all along the crack of the door, from the bottom up to the top, along the top, and down the side again."

"That's it?" Abra asked.

"That's it."

Abra stood to go and seal the door.

Mr. Henry tried to stand but couldn't, so he leaned against the stone and spoke to them from around the corner.

Abra looked at Mr. Henry and he nodded, so she held up

the sword, thrust it into the keyhole, and turned the blade in the door. There was a deep movement, as if the earth's stomach growled. She pulled the sword out and ran the point of it along the crack that outlined the door. It made a scratching sound and left a bright point of light for an instant where it sealed the rock like a welder's torch.

All this time Ruby watched quietly, not saying a word. Abra felt her eyes on her. Ruby's life as she had known it was over. She would never go back to the house on James Street in the Edge of Over There. She would never see her father again, at least not on this side of the water. Maybe never.

The door to the afterlife at the grave of Marie Laveau was sealed. No living person would ever pass that way again.

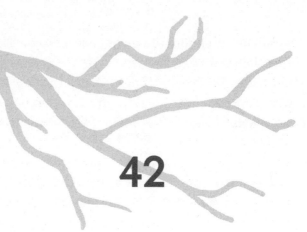

42

BACK INSIDE THE PASSAGEWAY, in the red darkness of that first night, Sandra had made her way out of the city. She and her friends had tried to avoid the war, but it was everywhere, and she alone had survived. She tried to flee along the dirt road, wondering if Leo had been telling the truth, wondering if the door had indeed been left open. But as she made her way, she felt a deep rumbling like an earthquake, and she knew immediately that it was too late. Somehow, she knew within herself that it was the sound of the door closing. She had heard that sound once before, when she had first come through the darkness. There would be no leaving, not that way.

Sandra felt older, as if the collapse of the Passageway was aging her. She turned, giving up on the gate, and headed back toward the city. The dirt path that led there already seemed narrower than it had been. The trees were closer and more brittle. The orange-red sky was lower—morning had arrived. The entire Passageway was contracting, becoming less, becoming only that which the dwindling population of people left in it needed.

Maybe the path had shortened because of so much death

in the Passageway during Amos's war that very day, or maybe there was some other reason, but whatever the case, Sandra made it to the city by that first evening. She kept walking, expecting to grow tired, but the tiredness never arrived. So she kept walking through the night, around the edge of the city. A fire raged so that even the night sky was orange, and she heard terrible screams and shouts and even something that sounded like celebrating, but she kept to the shadows. The only people she did see were running away in terror, fleeing into the forest, and they barely gave her a passing glance.

She kept walking, all day long.

By the time the light in the sky was beginning to dim, she'd arrived at the water, and she stood there at that strange confluence of water and forest and city. In the evening light, the city seemed less foreboding. Smoke still rose, but it rose into a pink-orange sky, and the shouts and screams had ended, as if peace had been found, or everyone had died. In the city's center, every so often she could see down a long street to what looked like a massive tree growing in the middle of the city, taller than any building. It was black against the morning sky, and bare, and it made her shiver with cold or dread or something related to those things. What she didn't realize was that the Tree, in its dying gasp, had shed itself of the building, and was now the tallest thing in that fading city.

She wasn't sure where to go. She had seen the Wailers, she had seen the path they followed every night, and she knew the only other place to go was over the water or through it, but how? She sat down with her feet dangling over the edge of the street, the waves crashing against the city's wall beneath her, and she watched the sky dim. Everything seemed to come from across the water—the wind, the waves, even the light. It was as if that place over the water was the sun, and she was in the far reaches of the solar system, the light and heat barely able to reach her.

When she didn't know what else to do, she stood up and walked quietly along the water, the burning city to her left. She didn't walk far before she saw a man sitting on the edge of the street, facing the river as she had not too long before. She stopped. He looked over at her.

"Hello," he said, his feet swinging, and that's when she saw the boat.

"Hi there," Sandra said, walking slower, closer.

"How are you?"

She nodded. "I'm okay. No, actually, that's not true at all. All my friends have died."

The two of them remained there, silent, thinking on her words.

"Who are you?" she asked.

"Everyone asks that," he said, shaking his head, clearly marveling at the sameness of humanity. "Everyone."

"Is that your boat?" she asked.

"Yes, it is."

"What's it for?"

"Crossing over."

"Kinda small for that, don't you think?" she asked.

"It does the job."

"Did you . . . come over the water?"

At first he nodded, but uncertainty clouded his face. He squinted as if he wasn't so sure. "I think so."

"I thought only the dead can pass over the water," she said.

"Well, there have been exceptions," he said. "Some have left the earth without their bodies dying. Very few. Enoch. Elijah. A few others. But very few."

She stood beside him, looking down at the boat. "Why, that boat has water in the bottom!"

"Yes, that's right, it does."

Sandra sat down beside him, there at the side of the street, and leaned forward hesitantly. She didn't want to fall in.

"I'm lonely," she said. "There's nothing left for me here in this city, and I can't leave through the gate. It's been locked."

He looked at her.

"I . . . would like to cross," she said.

"Well, that is an unusual problem," he said.

She laughed. "Yes, I suppose it is, seeing as I'm not dead."

He chuckled. "That is usually the way of it. What's your name?"

"Sandra," she said shyly, holding out her hand, and they shook. "What's your name?"

"Me? Oh, that's not important."

They sat there quietly for a long time.

"Do you think this boat could get us there?" she asked.

"I know it will take us where we need to go."

When the two of them climbed down the rope ladder, one at a time, it strained under their weight and swayed back and forth like a snake dancing above a clay pot. When the two of them boarded the small rowboat, it dropped nearly a foot and water spilled in over one edge.

"Whoa!" Sandra said, hands clenched like vises on the sides of the shaking boat.

The man took the one oar he had and started rowing, first this side, then that, and the boat shifted side to side as he rowed. The water was suddenly perfectly calm, a sheet of glass, and the ripples they made spread out in every direction, stirring the water like angels' wings. It was almost completely dark now, and the red-black of the sky shimmered on the water.

The boat began to sink ever so slightly as they moved forward. For every twenty feet they traveled, it sank a half inch. More water gathered in the bottom. Soon the liquid skin of the water was even with the sides of the boat.

"We'll never make it," Sandra said in a resigned tone. "We're sinking."

"It always seems that way, doesn't it?" he said with a smile. He handed her a small wooden cup. It was plain, without any decoration. "You can use this if you want."

She scooped the water out of the boat a cup at a time. There was nothing frantic in her movements, and it was enough to keep them level with the water. The water remained calm. It was like sailing on a mirror.

"If you get thirsty," the man said, motioning toward the cup.

Sandra looked at it, filled it once again, but instead of dumping it outside the boat, this time she drank it.

It was like consuming light.

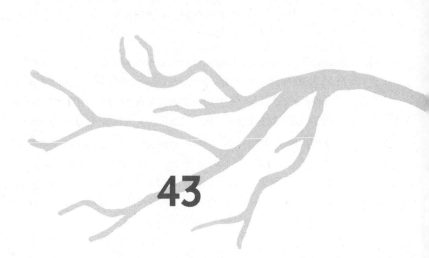

43

ABRA STOOD BESIDE THE TRAPDOOR in Leo's old house and looked at Mr. Henry and Ruby. Mr. Henry nodded his bald head encouragingly, and his large earlobes swayed forward and back, forward and back, like pendulums.

"Ruby will be fine," Mr. Henry said. "I'll watch over her until her mother comes back. She won't be gone long now that Koli Naal has moved on. They can start a new life together."

Abra nodded, and for some reason, a reason she could not identify, she did not want to leave. It was a beautiful city, but more than that, it felt like it existed at the center of the things on the other side of the curtain. Her own town, Deen, felt so far removed from the other side, with breaks that happened only occasionally. The other side was clouded when she was in Deen. But here, in New Orleans, there was no curtain. Things like Mr. Henry and Beatrice walked alongside people like Leo and his sister all the time. It felt like there were doors everywhere.

The short sword's handle stuck out of Abra's jeans, and she touched it. She wanted to stay, yes, but she was also a girl, a girl who very much wanted to go home and spend the rest of her summer in peace, and perhaps find a new litter of kittens, and fish in the river without anyone else around.

"I wrote this for your mother, in case she wonders where you've been," Mr. Henry said, and Abra took the letter he offered to her. She stared at the handwriting on the envelope, and it was the same handwriting as the letters her uncle sent her mother. She looked up at Mr. Henry with a question in her eyes. He gave a barely discernible shrug. She folded the letter and put it in her pocket.

"Will she remember me?" Abra asked.

"More than that, probably," Mr. Henry said with a twinkle in his eyes and a grin that scattered the small tattoos on his face. "You'll probably wish she's forgotten you, once you're back and you have to deal with a mother whose daughter has been missing."

Abra gave a tired smile. She was ready to see her mom, no matter what the reception was like.

"Good-bye, Abra," Ruby said.

"I'll come back to see you," Abra said. "I promise."

She stared at the girl, and though she was only a few years younger than Abra, she seemed so vulnerable, so unprotected. Abra glanced at Mr. Henry, and she knew he would watch over her.

"I'm sorry," she said to Ruby. "I'm sorry about what happened to Leo."

Ruby nodded in quick, jerking motions, and tears pooled in her eyes. "It's okay," she said. "Mr. Henry told me about what's on the other side of the water. It's . . . it's okay. I'm ready to meet my mother."

Abra took three quick steps and hugged Ruby one more time, the way a girl hugs a younger sister. She looked at Mr. Henry, and though she desperately wanted to hug him too, she only nodded, and he nodded back.

Abra lifted up the edge of the trapdoor and leaned it back against the closet wall. "I have to ask you something," she said without looking at Mr. Henry.

"Yes?"

"All those people."

He waited.

"All those people," Abra continued. "The people who died in the war in the Passageway. The people who ate from the Tree, people like Marie Laveau. What happens to all of them? What will happen?"

Mr. Henry sighed. "What do you mean?"

"Everyone goes over the water. I understand that. Everyone leaves. What happens next?"

Mr. Henry took a deep breath, then let it out in a long, gentle wave. In his eyes she could see the beginning of all things, but there was an openness there too, something that told her he did not know all ends.

"How it works depends on what's inside you—it depends on your heart and your soul. I cannot know this about you, just like I could not know it about Leo, or Beatrice, or even Koli Naal. Even Jinn! Even Jinn. We cannot see all ends. We can only see the path before us. The One who waits for us on the other side of the water will know just what to do with each of us."

Abra nodded solemnly and knew it was important. She wanted desperately to understand it, all of it, but she knew it might take some time.

"Okay," she said, and it was the closest thing to good-bye she could bring herself to say.

She stared at the ladder that led down into the darkness.

"Keep going down," Mr. Henry said. "And you'll find it leads you home."

Abra took one step down and stopped. "You're going to have to go first," she said. "I'd rather not leave with you two standing there staring at me."

Mr. Henry gave a small, gentle laugh. "Can you pull the trap-door down behind you when you go?" he asked. "We can't be leaving doors open. Goodness knows there are too many open doors as it is."

Abra nodded. Mr. Henry looked at her for a moment as if checking for something in her face, something that needed to be there. He seemed to find it because he smiled again.

"I'll see you soon," he said.

He turned away and walked out of the room, and Ruby followed, looking over her shoulder.

Then they were gone.

Abra's feet dangled down into the darkness, and it reminded her of the darkness in the forest that lined the dirt road that went into the city, or the darkness in the prison room when she had confronted Beatrice. She realized she wasn't afraid of the darkness anymore. She had been in it enough times to know that darkness is nothing but fear, and fear is nothing if you go straight through it.

Fear always comes with a door, a door that leads straight through.

A breeze blew through a window barely opened, and Abra could smell the sweet scent of azaleas and summer dirt and blue sky. She could smell the tall trees and the fallen needles and could hear insects chirping and squeaking and buzzing. She thought it was a good thing to be alive, to be there in that room, that city. She thought about the Edge of Over There, and the water, and what the telescope had shown her Over There, and she knew she would be ready to go when it was her time, but for now she was content to be Abra Miller, and to follow the path in front of her.

She stood up, not because she was scared but because she wanted to see something. The house was quiet and heavy, like the feeling that settles in after a sigh. She walked quickly to the front door and opened it and looked down the road, south, away from the graveyard. She found what she was looking for.

Mr. Henry and Ruby walked side by side down the sidewalk. He was large and imposing, scary with his shiny head and his tattoos. He had somehow pulled out a change of clothes, so he wasn't covered in blood anymore, but he was still rather scary.

Beside him, Ruby was tiny and fragile, like a flower that had recently blossomed. She looked up at him, but he didn't return her gaze. After she looked away from him, he looked down at her, and they walked on.

44

ABRA CLIMBED DOWN THE LADDER, and when she was all the way in the hole, she pulled the trapdoor down, closed it. It latched into place. There was no going back out. She took another step down, another rung, and found the darkness peaceful, almost comforting. She stopped for a moment and wondered where she was. She thought there were a lot of places on earth that weren't really on earth, a lot of passageways and corridors that could take us beyond what we know, into the margins. She took another step down, and another.

The rungs under her feet broke, and she dangled by her hands, grunting with the effort it took to hold on. The rungs her hands held splintered and she fell back, felt like she was spinning, and she still clung to a broken rung in her hand. Everything went black.

When she opened her eyes, she was on the floor of her bedroom, and instead of a ladder rung she was clutching her sword. In the other hand, she held tight to Mr. Henry's letter. In front of her was the atlas opened to the city of New Orleans, and the name of the city was circled in red.

Abra stood and took a deep breath. She hid the sword between her mattress and the box spring, and relief rose inside of her when she turned away from it. There was a weight to it that would not show up on any scale.

She walked down the stairs, holding her breath as she went, dreading her mother's response. She heard her little brother playing. It was a normal sound, an everyday sound—it was not the sound of buildings falling or angels crashing together. It wasn't the sound of the faraway water or the particular sound made when the leaves from the Tree of Life died and were swept away. No, it was an ordinary sound, and it was beautiful.

"Look at you! You're a mess!" Abra's mother said to him as Abra came around the corner, into the kitchen.

When her mother saw her, her eyes went wide, and the dishrag she held in her hands fell lifelessly to the floor. Her mother slowly raised her hands to her face and covered everything but her eyes, which were already welling with tears.

"Oh my," she said through her fingers, and everything was in those two words, everything in the world.

"Mom," Abra said, standing completely still. "I'm sorry."

Her mother walked quickly across the kitchen and hugged her and picked her up in the hug, and they wept and held each other. Her brother started laughing, so Abra went to him and pinched his cheeks and kissed his face through her own tears. She handed Mr. Henry's letter to her mother.

"Oh my," her mother said before she even opened it, and she had to sit in one of the kitchen chairs or she would have fallen over. And there was everything in those two words, everything all over again, except a different kind of everything, and Abra suddenly realized that her mother knew much more about all of this than she had ever let on.

"Abra," she said, pulling a chair over beside her. "We need to talk."

epilogue

"All shall be done, but it may
be harder than you think."

C. S. LEWIS, *THE LION, THE WITCH,*
AND THE WARDROBE

45

Samuel

WHEN IT SNOWS IN DEEN, when it really snows, and you're sitting beside a farmhouse window looking out over empty fields, the snow is everything. There is nothing else in the world but those swirling flakes, the tinny sound of them against the glass, the gusts that rattle the panes. When it snows in Deen, I can hardly imagine anything more beautiful.

I stare out the window as the weight of Mr. Henry's story sinks in. We sat there for days, never leaving, barely sleeping. He talked long into the night, and only occasionally did I interrupt him with a question or a comment.

Have you ever done that? Have you ever stepped out of your life for days at a time to listen to one single story? Maybe read a book without stopping? When you come back out of it, when you return to life from the midst of that story, you are a transformed being. You will never be quite the same again, no matter how hard you try to return to your old self. Stories will do that if we let them. They'll work their way inside, to the deepest parts, and they'll live there, and they'll change us.

Mr. Henry stares at me as he finishes his story.

"I'm not sure I understand," I say. "Why did Mrs. Miller have to talk to Abra?"

He holds up a finger, asking me to wait, searches through his pockets, and pulls out a small black book. He clears his throat and reads from it.

"When human beings began to increase in number on the earth and daughters were born to them, the sons of God saw that the daughters of humans were beautiful, and they married any of them they chose. Then the Lord said, 'My Spirit will not contend with humans forever, for they are mortal; their days will be a hundred and twenty years.' The Nephilim were on the earth in those days—and also afterward—when the sons of God went to the daughters of humans and had children by them. They were the heroes of old, men of renown."

"Angels married women?" I ask. "And had children?"

Mr. Henry sighs. "I still don't like it when you use that word. But yes, it's true. We're not all feathers and light, as you and your kind seem to think."

I clear my throat and stare down at the table. A realization enters my mind, something that makes everything else fit together. Yet I cannot say it out loud. I look up at Mr. Henry, and he nods.

"So you were the uncle in New Orleans?"

He nods.

"And if you and Mrs. Miller were brother and sister . . . " My voice trails off.

He nods, content to wait while I connect the dots.

SHAWN SMUCKER

"So . . . Mrs. Miller was one of you?"

"At least partially so." He stares at me as if I still haven't quite gotten all of it. "Many years ago," he says slowly, "two young girls wandered into the valley from the surrounding mountains. Their parents were never identified. They were adopted by a kind woman. They grew up in Deen."

In the silence I can hear the snow tinging against the windows.

"They raised families here in Deen," he says.

"And one of them was Abra's mother?" I ask.

He nods.

"And the other one was . . . " My words freeze in place because I know. A strange sense of urgency rises up inside of me, a combination of realization and denial.

"The other girl was my mother," I say.

He stares at me, waiting.

"So my mother . . ." I begin, then stop again. My words are coming in fits and starts, unable to keep up with the new information.

"Yes?"

"My mother was one of you too. That's why she was speaking with Tennin and Mrs. Miller about the Tree of Life."

Mr. Henry nods. "Your mother's mother was entirely human," he says. "But your mother's father . . . Well, he was not."

There is a moment in time when all the gears to a problem begin clicking together, when all the bolts slide the right way and the cogs begin to turn and it all ends in a realization too stunning for words. But I manage to speak again, even when I don't think I can.

"So, the pool Abra looked into was right. My mother knew the tree would be struck by lightning, didn't she?" Tears gather in the corners of my eyes. "And she took my place."

361

Mr. Henry sighs. "The vision I told you about, the one Abra saw in the clear pool on the plain of stone, was true. Tennin was here when you were a child. He warned your mother that you would die in a tree struck by lightning."

He pauses.

"But these are all other stories, ones we do not currently have the time to tell or explore further."

"We're out of time?" I ask, not sure how that could possibly be. "We've spent days on this story. What's a few more?"

"I haven't come here simply to tell you stories, Samuel," he says.

I look up at him, and because of how he said my name, I don't want to know why he's here anymore, because I can tell he's about to say something I don't want to hear. But he tells me anyway.

"You're dying, Samuel."

He lets the words sink in. I think of the Tree and the water and Over There. I think of the city and the door in the crypt and the shimmering fruit. I feel like I'm on the edge of the greatest adventure of all.

"But that's not everything, is it?" I ask. "You need me for something."

He smiles. "Yes, of course."

I wait for him to say what it is, what mission brought him into my kitchen. I wait in the silence of that snowy day, but when he doesn't say anything, I have to ask.

"What is it? What do you need me to do?"

He looks surprised that I don't already know, that I have not somehow deciphered my mission from his days-long story, and he chuckles to himself, whispering things that sound like words, exclamations. He shakes his head and laughs, and his laugh fills me with an anticipation I have never felt before. It's like the feeling you get on the last day of winter, or when you first wake up on your birthday.

Finally, he comes out and says it.

"The sword has come to you for a reason. We need your help to kill the Last Tree."

Read on for an excerpt of *The Day the Angels Fell*

Samuel

I WAS TWELVE YEARS OLD, and because I was crouched down in left field, picking at random blades of grass and not paying attention, I didn't notice the darkness gathering in the west. My father signed me up for baseball every year, even though I wasn't very interested in a game that seemed to be made up mostly of standing around and waiting, and on that particular day I was feeling happy the season was almost over. I stared at a small ant pile and poked at it, spreading panic. The ants dashed here and there, trying to rebuild what I had brushed away in an instant.

I heard the faint sound of distant thunder.

It would be remembered as the summer of storms. Nearly every week, massive dark clouds rumbled down over the western mountain range and drenched the valley. The fields outside of town were green from all the rain, and the creeks were muddy and full, bulging at the seams.

While I heard the distant thunder, it wasn't enough to get my attention, and I continued tormenting the ants. I glanced up at the parking lot and noticed that my mother wasn't there yet, which was unusual because she almost always came to pick me up well before practice was over. She normally parked up from third base and sat on the hood of the car, her feet on the bumper, until I saw her and waved. Then she'd get out a book and read until practice was over.

I had never had to wait for her before.

I heard a loud *ping* come from home plate, and I looked at the batter, maybe 150 feet away. It was Stony DeWitt, the biggest kid on the team, and he slammed a screamer that was rising, sailing over my head. I left the ants to recover what they had lost and started running back, back, back. The rest of the kids shouted at me to hurry. We grew tired of Stony hitting home runs every time he was up to bat, and we roared with delight whenever we could get him out.

The ball traced an arc over my head, bounced, and rolled to the short outfield fence. Beyond the fence was the town of Deen, Pennsylvania, which was nothing more than the intersection of two roads.

I reached for the ball, and the instant I touched it—the very instant, I tell you—lightning struck, and it was so close that the thunder clapped at the same time. It scared me and I dropped the ball. There are times in those kinds of storms when you begin to feel that there is no safe place, that the lightning will strike anywhere, that you have a target on your back and it's just a matter of time.

My breath caught in my throat and I scrambled after the ball, my insides jumping every which way. I turned to run toward the safety of the infield, but I realized the baseball diamond was empty. The lightning had scattered the kids to their parents' cars. Even Mr. Pelle, my baseball coach, who smoked the delicious-smelling pipe full of cherry tobacco, was running up the small hill to the parking lot, one hand holding a rubber home plate over his head, the other dragging a large red canvas equipment bag behind him. He stopped long enough to drop everything and cup his hands around his mouth.

"Go into the store!" he shouted, waving me off. "Get inside!"

My eyes scanned the parking lot again, the one that ran along the baseball field, but my mom still wasn't there. I turned and ran back to the chain-link fence, climbed over it, and raced toward the edge of town, only a few hundred yards away. Heavy drops hit the ground all around me. There were large amounts of time between the drops, and I could hear each individual one collide with the ground. When they hit my baseball cap or my arms they seemed far larger than normal, the size of marbles that exploded into patches of water wherever they landed.

I ran for Mr. Pelle's antique store, which was right at the intersection. I had made it into the parking lot by the time the next lightning missile struck, and this time I not only heard the crash but felt the sizzle in the air, the electric pulse spreading outward. The air woke up, like a viper sensing a small mouse dropped into its cage.

The rain turned into a constant sheet of water, and I felt like I was trying to breathe underwater. The air was lost, taken over by the downpour. There was no space between drops anymore. Everything, including me, was soaked in seconds. Water dripped from the brim of my ball cap, and my shirt clung to me, suddenly heavy, like a second skin.

On one side of Pelle's Antiques was Uncle Sal's pizza, and the smell of delicious cheese and pepperoni came at me through the rain. I ran into the small alley between Uncle Sal's and Pelle's, through the small waterfall tumbling out from the gutters where the rain already overflowed. I pushed open the heavy brown steel door and vanished into the stockroom of Pelle's Antiques.

The door slammed behind me, and I went from a white-gray day full of the sound of pounding rain and splitting thunder to shadows and quiet and the smells of old cedarwood, dust, and paint. I stopped inside the door as my eyes adjusted to the darkness. Outside, when the rain was coming down through that July day, the falling water had felt almost warm, but in the air-conditioned back room of the antique store, the water spread a chill over my body, and I crossed my arms, clutching my baseball glove as if it might bring me some warmth.

The rain made a distant rushing sound on the roof, and as I meandered through the irregular rows of furniture, I wondered again why my mother had been late, and where she was, and who would take me home. I passed high-backed armchairs standing upside down on barn-door tables, and under them were old windows without any glass panes. There were desks and side tables and large hutches. Wardrobes stood closed and ominous, daring me to open them. Lamps of every shape and size filled in the gaps: tall, skinny ones and short, fat ones, lamps with shades and lamps without shades, some with small white bulbs perched at the top like crystal balls, others with empty sockets.

I stopped in front of an old mirror framed in black, twisting metal, and I stared at my reflection in the peeling surface. I was a skinny kid and, being soaked through, looked even thinner than usual. I'm sure I didn't look as old as I wanted to look. My brown eyes were still the eyes of a child. I spent most of my childhood wanting to be bigger, stronger, older.

I heard voices in the prep room. It was the space between the large storage room and the sales floor, where Mr. Pelle stained and repaired and prepared one piece of furniture at a time before taking it to the store out front with the big glass windows that looked out onto Route 126. It was unusual for anyone besides Mr. Pelle or his family to be in that middle room.

I moved to the door. I could hear my own heart thumping in my ears, and my breath seemed suddenly loud. My sneakers, waterlogged, squeaked with each step.

But as I got to the swinging door, it was already leaning open a few inches. Outside, another lightning strike sent thunder through Deen. The sound of the rain was a constant hum, but the voices were loud. I peered through the crack in the door.

Three old women sat on one side of a large, square table. They were dressed like gypsies, with long, flowing robes that draped down from their shoulders. Scarves were wrapped around their heads, with gray and white hair peeking out from under the colorful fabric. Large golden earrings dragged their flabby earlobes toward their shoulders, and their arms were lined with bracelets that clinked when they moved. They sat so close together that their robes folded into each other, so close that they almost looked like one wide, colorful body with three heads.

They looked intently across the table, but I couldn't see that side of the room through the crack in the door. Someone was there, though. Their shadow, short and wide, draped itself across the table and toward the women. When the person spoke, it was a man's voice. At first he muttered and grunted to himself, the words all jumbled together. But I could only see the three old women, and they stared at him as if trying to decide if they should stay or go.

Out of nowhere, the three old women interrupted him, quietly at first and then louder. They chanted words, but not English words, not old, dead words that can barely stand on their own two feet. No, the words they chanted were alive, words I couldn't understand, words that had a fluttering, startling life of their own. Their words terrified me, but they also intrigued me. I was like a confused magnet, repelled and attracted all at once.

Part of me wanted to turn and run back out into the storm I had escaped from, back into the hair-trigger lightning and the thunder and the rain that had drenched me, but their words pulled me forward until I was braced against the frame, fighting to stay outside the room.

The lights in the building flickered, then went out.

Notes

1. "Marie Laveau Biography," Biography Base, accessed December 12, 2017, http://www.biographybase.com/biography/Laveau_Marie.html.

2. Bill Guion, "Etienne de Boré Oak (Tree of Life)," 100 Oaks Project, July 8, 2010, https://100oaks.wordpress.com/2010/07/08/etienne-de -bore-oak-tree-of-life.

Shawn Smucker lives with his wife and six children in Lancaster, Pennsylvania. He is the author of *The Day the Angels Fell* and *The Edge of Over There*, and you can find him online at www.shawnsmucker.com.

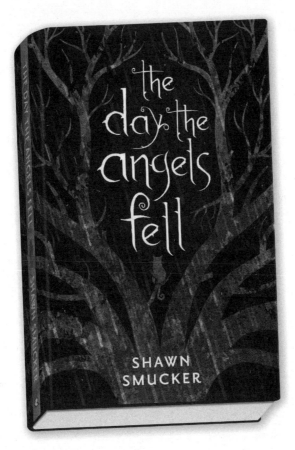